GOODBYE
CAUTION

The Lost & Found Series
Book One

JACQUELYN AYRES

Other Books

The Lost & Found Series
Goodbye Caution, Book 1
Goodbye Secrets, Book 2
Goodbye Uncertainty, Book 3

Coming Soon
Goodbye Reservations (Prequel to The Lost & Found Series)

The One

The GEG Series
Under Contract, Book 1
In the Mix, Book 2

Dedication

To Emmy,

I think you're *pretty awesome*, kid!

Prologue

December 26, 2012

Dear Journal,

    You were given to me today with an encouraging gesture to write my memories down. The task, though it needs to be done, is daunting. My head is spinning. Where do I start?

    You see, I've been "lost" for seven years. However, it only took three months and an extraordinary man to find me. I know . . . the math doesn't seem to add up. But it does—you'll see.

    I guess the best place for me to start is at the beginning (of the last three months, that is). Everything will fall into place for you from there, just as it did for me. I will write it as I remember it. I don't want to leave a single detail out.

    I must warn you (eye roll—only I would warn a journal!) that everything moves along rather quickly. I thought it was odd when it was happening—I couldn't slow things down, let alone stop them. Believe me—I tried! I know . . . I'm rambling. The point is, everything *does happen for a reason. They were right! Whomever "they" are. *Shrugs**

And now, without further ado, I give you the story of how this lost woman was found.

*Cue dramatic theatre music (I'm thinking Andrew Lloyd Webber–esque)!

Always,
Becca Campbell

Chapter One

Let's see . . . I have the Gustafson wedding and reception at three o'clock. Did they send me their seating chart? Shit . . . did they? Where did I put that? Oh, I'll look for it later. I need to reconfirm the caterer, the minister, the DJs, and the party rental store. I really should get my own stuff! Am I making the favors? No, no, that's the Millers' wedding next month. Let me jot that down so I don't forget. I have to place the order for the store on Monday before next crop weekend. Which theme am I doing for that weekend?

"Becca!"

"Huh . . . what?" I practically jump out of my seat to face Hazel.

"Becca, I have been calling your name for five minutes now! Where are you, honey?"

Oh no . . . here we go again. I love Hazel. She's a sweet, elderly woman with pure white hair and powder blue eyes, and she has been in my employ for four years. I think I pay her too much. She's an excellent employee; honestly, I don't know what I would do without her. Most of all, she's become a dear, dear trusted friend and a surrogate grandmother to my daughter, Morgan. Of course, being my daughter's surrogate grandmother leads to motherly tendencies toward me. This includes, of course, the *I'm concerned about you* lectures. I'm too busy today to endure one. Then again, I'm too busy most days—which is what causes most of these lectures. It's a double-edged sword. But really, today I just can't.

"Sorry, Hazel. What did you need?" I smile my brightest *I'm okay . . . I'm just daydreaming* (who's got time for that?) smile.

"Well, one of the girls in the crop wondered if we have any more 12-by-12 Cricut mats left. There's none out and they're not in their usual place in the stockroom." There's a sense of urgency in her voice. This is one of the things I love about Hazel and why she is such a great employee. Every customer is treated like the most important person in the world. I tell you, it's that kind of treatment that's really helped keep The Mad Scrapper in business.

"Oh, yeah!" I jump up quickly (again, to avoid a lecture). "I know just where they are. They came in yesterday." And I'm off to the stockroom. I grab several so that I can restock the display while I'm at it. "Here you go, Hazel." I smile and hand her one.

Oh no . . . her mouth is opening. She's going to say something! "Hey, have you seen Morgan?" Quick thinking, Becca!

"I think she went out to the stables to see what Charlie's up to." She rolls her eyes with a slight smile.

"Good. I'm gonna go see what they are both up to. Can you keep an eye out here?" I ask as I head out the door, not giving her a chance at that lecture. Phew—that was close! I head over to the stables to the left of the inn. Climbing up the small hill, I continue on with my mental list of things that need to be done.

I can hear Morgan's laughter coming from just inside the stables. Charlie must be telling her some new jokes. He's a great guy who knows his way around horses. His services come real cheap, too—free, in fact! He's been retired from the lumber mill for five years now. He grew up on a farm, and he practically begged me for the stable job I was offering. I do feed him, so I guess his labor isn't entirely free. He's such a great character to have around here, though; I'd feed him even if he didn't take care of the horses. Every Thanksgiving, I give him a hefty bonus so he doesn't think I'm paying him. It's hard to refuse the money around the holidays and, truth be told, I think he secretly depends on it. It was his idea in the first place to rent our stables out. When he first came on here, it was just Morgan's horse. He's really made this quite the profitable side business for me. He deserves that money. This has all become more than just a "hobby to keep an old man busy." Besides, it's very evident he's sweet on Hazel. Someday, she'll let her guard down and I'll be able to throw them a wedding here.

Between the stables, the scrapbooking store, and the B&B that hosts two scrapbooking weekends a month (or "crop" weekends, as we like to call them), I'm up to my eyebrows in work and up to my big toe in time. I'm always racing against the clock—hence Hazel's lectures.

In the midst of all of this, I'm trying to be a great mom and mold a very beautiful, outgoing, and wise-beyond-her-years ten-year-old. This is all for her. Everything I do is for her. She is the reason behind my drive. She is my world.

"Well howdy there, Mama!" Morgan tips her hat to me.

"That's an interesting accent for New England, honey." This kid cracks me up. This is her latest "thing"—trying on new accents.

"I reckon people from all walks of life move to New England . . . maybe that's why it's new!" I give her the chuckle and eye roll she deserves.

"Don't stay out here too long. C'mon in and get started on that diorama after you're done with Butterscotch."

"Ugh!" Morgan grunts. From the look on her face, I'll bet she's not happy she left it 'til the last weekend before it was due.

"Charlie, dinner's in an hour!" I shout down the corridor of the stable. "Don't let her keep you here any longer; it's getting cold out!"

"Okay, Becca. We'll be in soon." He comes out from Rocco's

stall and gives me a nod. I move Morgan's cowgirl hat and kiss her on the forehead. Back to the inn—and my to-do lists.

"Becca . . . do you have a minute?" Claudia asks as soon as I walk through the door.

Shit! Damn it . . . I was supposed to crunch numbers and see if I could give her a permanent forty-hour workweek.

"Hey, Claudia." I put my arm around her shoulders as we walk into my office.

"Becca, I know you probably haven't gotten the chance to see where you're at as far as offering me full time, but it's been two weeks and I've received another job offer," she starts.

"No! No, Claudia, please. You can't leave me!" I start to beg. Shit, why didn't I just take the time to figure this out?

"That's just it—I don't want to leave! I love this job. I love you and Morgan, Hazel, Charlie, and everyone! Do you think anyone else would let me come to work with rainbow-colored hair, facial piercings, and exaggerated makeup? No! I'd have to totally not be me and sell hardware like I know what the hell I'm talking about!"

Uh oh . . . her chin is quivering. She's right, though. Even I got a lot of flak for hiring her, but I just knew there was this wonderful, intelligent, and warm person underneath her costume. And oh, how everybody loves her now. She's become so great and knowledgeable at scrapbooking that she now teaches a few classes here. Why would I tell her to change her appearance when I'm in the business of pro-moting creativity? That would be very hypocritical.

"I guess there's only one thing I can do," I sigh. "I'm gonna need you to tell me when the extra twenty hours will work best for you." I'll figure it out. I always do.

"Becca, seriously?" Claudia screeches and hugs me like I gave her a million dollars.

Hazel opens the door.

"What's all the commotion in here?"

"Becca's putting me on full time—permanently!"

"Oh, it's about time! You should've done that months ago!" Hazel looks up as if some divine intervention took place here. Hey, maybe it has. No lecture from Hazel, and I do get to free up some time to spend with Morgan.

"You're right. Now, let's get back out there."

Mmm. I can smell dinner coming from the kitchen. I love crop weekends for many reasons, and the fact that Adam Stein, a local gourmet chef, is here for the dinner service those nights isn't the least of them. Luckily, trade works just as well—if not better—than the almighty dollar. Adam boards his daughter's horse, Princess, with me because he doesn't have the land, time, or know-how to do it himself. In exchange, he does the dinner service for my crop weekends. It's worked out beautifully!

It's a wonder how any of these scrappers will keep their eyes open tonight after Adam's dinner. Bleu-cheese-crusted filet mignon with port-wine sauce, rosemary-roasted potatoes, and glazed carrots. I'm not a big carrot fan, but the rest was just divine. Speaking of filet mignon—I really need to crunch our numbers.

Thankfully, Claudia has offered to stay tonight for the last crop night of the weekend. This gives me some time to finally look at the numbers and add sleep to my agenda for the evening. I head to the back of the store, which is adjacent to the inn, and through the French doors of my office.

"Hey, Morgy baby, glad to see I didn't have to drag you in here to work on that." I kiss the top of her head.

"Claudia gave me a great idea for my diorama, so I'm actually excited to get this done." She continues on with her "masterpiece" without even looking up at me.

"Well, I have some paperwork to do. If we finish up at the same time, we can snuggle up to a movie tonight. Your choice," I add.

"You don't have to do the crop, Mom?" She looks up, hopeful and excited. I feel a huge pang in my heart. Hazel is so right. I'm working hard to make sure Morgan has everything she needs—now and in the future. And the only thing she truly wants is me.

"Claudia is working it tonight. It's just you and me, kiddo."

She lets out a little excited screech and gets back to work.

I turn to my desk—*the war zone*. It's where I fight most of my daily battles. I'm always struggling to find something in the heaps of paperwork: a bill, a note, a seating chart. You name it; I'm trying to find it. It's chaos! To top it all off, I don't have a very good organizational program on the computer, either.

Focus, Becca. Focus. I sit down and open my calendar. Okay, I only have the Gustafson and the Miller weddings left for the fall. No others until spring. As much as I love doing the weddings, they're quite draining. However, the additional income is what enables me to make so many extra mortgage payments a year. I'm also able to build up our nest egg and give Charlie his yearly "bonus." My goal is to have the mortgage completely paid off within the next four years. I just wish I could add on more rooms right now. Next month starts ski season and we will be booked solidly until the end of March. *Oh well. Someday*.

Hmm . . . as long as we don't have anything major happen this season, and even with the added expense of Claudia's new hours, we should be in the black by two grand each month. Not bad. I glance over at Morgan to find her still working diligently. Eh, I guess I'll file this paperwork... .

Chapter Two

Ugh . . . six in the morning already? I distinctly remember throwing this alarm clock through the window yesterday! I must've been too tired to realize that my Jedi mind trick didn't work. I turn off my alarm, wishing I could afford the extra nine minutes the snooze button would allow. But, alas, I have about thirty people who will be looking for their breakfast soon.

I'm glad the alarm didn't wake Morgan up. We were up so late having our slumber party last night. Popcorn, cocoa, and *Ever After* with Drew Barrymore. I love that movie; it's my all-time favorite. Like most women, I'm perpetually a Disney princess at heart, waiting for my Prince Charming to come along. Well, now that I'm older, my idea of Prince Charming looks more like Christian Grey. Damn, that imaginary man is hot! Hmm. Where did I put those books? I think it's time for a reread of that trilogy. Ugh, my ADD is going to be the death of me. Focus, Becca. Thirty people. Breakfast. Now!

"Good morning, Hazel." She's already got my sausage bake in the oven, and the muffins are mixed and ready to go. "You got an early start today." Why is she already up?

"I couldn't sleep, so I thought I'd get a start on things here. I'm so excited!"

"Why's that?"

"My nephew called last night, and he's finally coming out. He's bringing a few friends to go skiing next month." She smiles and looks up at the ceiling, like another divine intervention has occurred. I am beginning to wonder if she does indeed have a direct line to the big guy.

"That's great. I know you've been trying to get him out here for a while. He's from California, right?" I pour the granola into a large crystal bowl and vanilla yogurt into its sister.

"Well, he lives there now, but he's from England. I can't wait for you to meet him! He's so handsome, smart, and confident."

"His name wouldn't happen to be Christian Grey, would it?" I sigh hopefully.

"No, it's Grayson, dear. Who's Christian Grey?" She looks at me quizzically. I'd introduce her, but she'd probably have a heart attack by chapter five.

"Oh . . . no one."

"Well, he'll be here in two weeks. He's not sure how long he's staying, but it sounds like at least three weeks. I hope you don't mind, but I've blocked your best room for him."

"Wow. Three weeks. He must have a great boss!"

"He works for himself," she offers.

"Hazel, I work for myself and I can't even take a day off."

"You *can* . . . you just choose not to, Becca."

"Hazel, c'mon. You know I don't have that much of a choice." I love her, but it's irritating when she acts like this. I work as hard as I do just to keep us afloat. I feel like if I relax for one second, then one may turn into two, and so on and so forth. I can't afford to let go of the reins, not until I have enough put away to carry us for a long time—God forbid.

"Becca, please don't overthink what I said."

Was I doing that? Of course I was. I overthink everything.

"I know what your goals are," she continues, "your worries and your struggles. But I also know Morgan is not going to stay this age forever. When things finally settle down to your standards and you start to catch up on your scrapping, well, honey, you're gonna have a whole lot of years of Morgan's life to fill those pages."

There it is. The arrow of truth—with a direct hit to my heart. Ooh, she plays dirty, this one! Seriously, I pay her way too much. I could easily hire somebody else for far less who wouldn't give me a reality slap upside my head every time she sees fit. I'd fire her, if I didn't love her so damn much . . . and need that slap on occasion. She helps me to stay on track with my number-one goal: to be a good mom.

Hazel was never able to have children. I know part of her "gentle" prodding is meant to help me not take for granted the precious gift God gave me.

"You know what, Hazel?" I can play dirty, too. "You're a great mom and grandmother, and we're so lucky to have you. I love you!" A hug and a kiss and I leave the room, knowing for once I've made Hazel speechless . . . and I meant every word of it.

I grab my iPhone and immediately set a reminder to go ahead and book the Disney Vacation for February break. I've been hemming and hawing over it like I do with everything. That's Morgan's birthday week, and I can't think of a better way to celebrate it. Put that in your hat, Hazel!

The next two weeks, with the exception of losing power during the Gustafson wedding, are pretty uneventful. Hazel's been laying the TLC on extra thick since that morning in the kitchen. There's a lot to be said about feeling appreciated. I think there's also a possibility she knows I pay her too much. Seriously, this inside joke of me overpaying her would have a lot more thunder if I could share it with somebody that knows her as well. Ah, someday—when Morgan gets older, I guess. For now, I laugh to myself like all the other crazy people in the world!

Speaking of crazy, Hazel has been a little cuckoo for Cocoa Puffs the past few days. I think if I get one more reminder that her nephew, Grayson, is coming tonight my head will surely explode. I know she hasn't seen him since her trip last year, but jeezum petes! Calm down, lady, it's not Elvis! Does she even like Elvis? Wow . . . my ADD? Off the charts. I can't even stay focused on my own conversations in my head. I actually distract myself from myself. Who am I, Sybil? Why is Hazel staring at me with a raised eyebrow?

"You're not going to be lost in your thoughts all day, are you?"

Oh, no she didn't. She totally gave me *the look*!

"You're just jealous." I smile.

"Of what?"

"That you can't hear what I'm saying and therefore cannot bestow your opinion upon me."

She offers a slight chuckle and shake of her head. Aha—I'm right!

Just then, Claudia rushes in all flustered.

"Becca! I'm so sorry!"

"For what?"

"I'm half an hour late and my cell died!" She quickly takes off her scarf and coat to hang them up. "Sorry," she says again and starts looking around, as if a magical agenda will fly to her out of nowhere. A total "deer in the headlights" reaction. I can relate . . . been there, done that, been there again—so on and so forth.

"Calm down, chicky! You're okay. Plug your phone in. Get some coffee and settle down. There's no fire!" *I am Becca: super boss!*

"Ugh, why are you so awesome?" She hugs me and runs off for her coffee.

"I ask myself that every day, but I just am. I am awesome." I shrug and turn just as I say the last part of my sentence.

"Hi, Awesome. I'm Grayson James."

I slowly look up as I take his hand to shake.

Now, at five foot six, I'm above average for a woman's height, but this guy towers over me. He's got to be around six foot four. He's breathtakingly gorgeous, with dark, chocolate-brown hair that is short and choppy. His matching eyes are delicious and rich in depth. Broad shoulders. He has to be the most beautiful man I've ever laid my eyes on, for sure. I feel Sybil in full force exploding in my head. *Princess Sybil is singing, "I know you; I walked with you once upon a dream." Submissive Sybil walks out in her panties and grey tie, asking to sign the fucking contract.*

Wait . . . did he just call me "awesome"? *Crap.*

"Hi, Grayson. I'm Becca Campbell. It's so nice to finally meet you." *Thespian Sybil saves the day!*

"Gracie!" Hazel practically screams as she rushes across the room to him.

"Gracie?" I ask, raising an eyebrow. *Sybil-Becca laces up her high-top Converse. She dribbles, shoots, and scores!* Becca is on the scoreboard. "Is that what you'd like to be called?" I add.

Grayson gives an embarrassed chuckle. "Oh, God, no! Bite your tongue, woman!" *You first! You first!* "Aunt Hazel, really, you mustn't call me that anymore." He holds Hazel at arm's length.

"Oh, I know, honey. I'm sorry."

The way she looks up at him, like he is the moon and the stars—it's so sweet.

"Becca, will you show Gracie . . . ahem, I mean *Grayson*, to his room? I'm just about to start teaching my class. I'm sorry, honey." She looks up at Grayson. "The class is only half an hour, though. That'll give you plenty of time to settle in."

My head snaps to Hazel and I mentally ask her if she is out of her damn mind. Oh, my God. I can't bring him to my room. Uh, his room. *I've got Sybil the horny teenager cracking her knuckles and shaking her ass in here!*

Feeling the heat rise to my cheeks, I glance back up at Grayson. He seems to be trying to bite back his amusement. His right eyebrow slowly stretches into a high arch.

"Hazel?" A small woman of about five foot nothing interrupts us.

"Oh. Hi, Terry," Hazel says with a smile.

"Can you show me which tool kit I need for your class? I'm so overwhelmed!" Terry's grip tightens around the straps of her craft bag.

"Sure, come with me." Hazel places a hand on her shoulder to lead her to our tool section. My eyes follow them for a moment.

"So, Becca," Grayson starts, and I bring my focus back to him. Jesus, he's so close. The butterflies that have lain dormant at the pit of my belly stretch their wings. "Ready to show me to my room?" His voice is soft, like a secret being whispered. I stare up into his eyes, feeling trapped by some sort of strange spell.

His index finger glides down my jawline and curls under my chin. He thumbs my bottom lip free from my teeth. I try to steady my breathing, but I feel that I am failing quite miserably. Grayson pulls his hand away as Hazel approaches.

"Becca, show him to his room for me, sweetie," she says, and rubs my back. Grayson's eyes scan me up and down. His expression is as if he's already "conquered" me. That arrogant son of a . . . *Thespian Sybil steps forward once again, in her best Shakespearian garb.*

"Actually, I'm sorry, Grayson. I'm in the middle of something right now. But Claudia or Morgan would be more than happy to show you up." Humph. I mentally flip my hair.

"What are you in the middle of?" Hazel asks, confused. *Really?*

I want to tell her I'm about to be in the middle of a panty check if I don't leave this room.

"I have a scheduled phone appointment with a certain somebody about a certain something," is what actually comes out of my mouth. Fortunately.

"Oh, okay, yes—you don't want to miss that!" Good, she knows I'm talking Disney. She just doesn't know I already had that appointment this morning. "I'll explain later," Hazel says to Grayson when she sees his look of confusion.

"Right. Well, Auntie, I surely can find my way." His smile to his aunt slowly turns into a mischievous smirk toward me.

"Bye, Gracie," I add, shooting him a "bring it" smile before walking away. *C'mon, Thespian Sybil . . . let me buy you a drink!* Oh, why does he have to be gorgeous *and* have an English accent? I seriously need to get my head on straight. How am I going to be around this guy for three weeks? *Oh, Thespian Sybil, we need to lock up the other girls!*

Since Mr. James's arrival three hours ago, I've locked myself (and the other girls) in what was once my office. It has now secretly become my panic room. I'd like to say I've gotten a lot done in here today, but all I've managed to do is move some papers around. I'm quite terrible at organizing. Mostly, though, I thought about my reaction today.

It was so unlike me. I never act that way around any man. Of course, he's probably the most beautiful man I've ever met—but I've been around other handsome men before. Okay, his accent doesn't help. To me, a man could be the roughest-looking bloke in the world, but an English accent will always soften him. *Did I just say bloke?* Jeez, Becca . . . whatever you do, do not imitate an English accent in front of him. That would be disastrous!

Oh, no! He has my best room. That's right next to my room. *Oh, Hazel, what are you playing at?* No—Hazel wouldn't have a hidden agenda. She knows, to a point, about my terrible marriage. How cruel George was to me (may he burn in hell). She knows this is why I don't get involved with anyone. Besides, she looks at "Gracie" like he's still five years old. Surely she's not trying to marry him off or anything.

How old is he, anyway? He must be in his thirties. I don't think he's younger than me. Then again, I never think anyone is younger than me. While the mirror and my birth certificate say thirty-five, my mind adamantly argues that I'm twenty-five. Christ, I need to pull myself together here. I have not put this much thought into one man since . . . since, well, Joe McIntyre! And you know what? When I met Joe McIntyre, I didn't act like some crazy schoolgirl—and I *was* a crazy schoolgirl! What is wrong with me?

Shit! It's two forty-five in the afternoon. I have to teach a distressing class in fifteen minutes. Oh, the irony! I'm distressed, and I'm teaching a class on how to distress . . . really? If he hadn't shown up here earlier than planned, I wouldn't be so distressed!

"Ugh . . . pull it together, Becca." I grab my instruction sheets to pass out to the croppers. I rush out quickly and look down, trying to catch some of the papers that spill from my arms. Rushing forward, I somehow manage to trip over my own feet (please, like that doesn't happen all the time!) and land against a hard, great-smelling, human wall. "Oh, I'm sorry," I start, as I look up to see whom I've just collided into. Of course. Just when I thought it was safe to come out of my "panic room." *This is exactly why I don't go swimming in the ocean!*

Occasionally, I feel the need to change the theme song to my life. And it's official. Today's theme song is "Ironic" by Alanis Morissette.

"Becca, are you okay?" Grayson shakes me lightly. I open my eyes.

Wait! I had my eyes closed while changing my theme song? Yes. Of course. I was being poisoned by the intoxicating smell that is Grayson James. British, beautiful, lovely scent . . . I'm doomed.

"Yes. Yes, sorry. I must've gotten up too quickly." *You believe me, right?*

"Well, are you okay now?" he asks. Concern has replaced his earlier arrogance. I find myself wanting to relax a bit, but his hands are squeezing my upper arms, his thumbs caressing my shoulders softly. The pack of baby butterflies in my stomach has morphed into a giant alien butterfly that is trying to break out. My heart pounds in my ears. Does he realize how hot that little beauty mark under his left eye is? I'm feeling the urge to kiss it.

"Becca?" he asks again. I can't speak. I just slowly glance in the direction of my shoulder. He follows my gaze, then stops his thumbs and pulls his hands away. "Right!" he says, with too much certainty as he runs his hand through his hair. "Well, I was wondering if I could, that is, if Morgan wouldn't mind, that I take her horse out for a ride. Uh . . . Aunt Hazel said there are some great trails around here." He blinks wildly. What is it with British men and the rapid blinking when they are nervous?

Wow, look at him go. I wish I knew Morse code. Beep, beep, beep, beep . . . beep, beep. It sounds—or looks, I should say—urgent.

"Is something funny, Ms. Campbell?" he asks with a hint of irritation. Apparently, I giggled out loud.

"No. No, I'm sorry." I touch his arm. "Yes, Mr. James, you may take Morgan's horse." I can be formal, too. "I'm sure Charlie would love to go riding with you. He'll show you some of the trails." He stares at me intently now that his eyelids have settled. I can see his eyes running side to side, like he's scanning my face. Did he go into Charlie Brown mode? "Mr. James? Grayson?"

Wait, when did he get this close to me? The muscle in his forearm slightly twitches under my touch. His breath is hot in my face. Again, when did he get this close? His eyes are still scanning my face as he gently grazes my cheek with the back of his hand. Oh jeez . . . he wants to kiss me! He's searching for my answer. Sybil? Any Sybil? I mentally beat on all of their doors. I'm alone; one crucial moment, and they've left me. My internal alarms all scream at once, and the girls fly into action out of nowhere and start the lockdown. Walls go up; extinguishers on the fire.

"Please don't." I grab his hand gently and look him straight in the eyes, giving him a look that says, *"I'm really, really sorry, but please back the fuck off."* I release his hand and arm. "Go see Charlie," I add, before I turn to walk away.

Before I walk too far, he takes my hand and turns me back toward him.

"You have a two-hour block of free time in your schedule tomorrow afternoon. Will you show me around your property?" He's blinking rapidly again.

Cautionary Sybil, director of all affairs of the heart, unrolls a rather long scroll of reasons I should say no.

"Yes. Now go see Charlie." I allow a small smile. I don't want to over-encourage him. I'm not exactly sure what just happened here. I've known him for about a New York minute, and he's managed to rattle my cage when other guys couldn't even get near it—no matter how long or hard they tried. "I have to go teach my class now." I look down at my hand. He's still holding it.

"What are you teaching?" There goes his thumb again.

"Distress." I can't help it; I release another giggle and shake my head, biting my lip to stifle any more that may come out. "Please, Grayson?"

"Yes?" His eyes search me again, thankfully at a further distance.

"My hand." I look to it.

"Right!" He releases it and runs his own through his hair again. "Charlie—horse," he states. "Well, not a charley horse. I'm going to see Charlie. About a horse," he corrects himself, flustered.

The lip biting is not effective, and I can't contain my giggle. He chuckles too, as if he can't help but laugh at himself. He runs his hands over his face. I think he's trying to pull himself together.

"Right!" he repeats, and heads for the door. But then he sighs and turns back to me. "I'm sorry, Becca," he says. "I'm a selfish man." He strides toward me with determination. Before I know it, he palms my face and pushes my back up against the wall. He searches again. This time he's not asking me—he's telling me.

My mental white flag goes up and I give him a slight nod. His lips slam against mine with such urgency I drop the stack of papers in my right arm. He deepens the kiss with a slip of his tongue and releases a soft groan when I run my hands up his back and pull him closer to me. His sense of urgency dissipates. I think he realizes he's won. His kiss is more playful as he explores my mouth and I, his. His lips trail across my jawline and down my neck. I turn my face into his palm and kiss the middle of it until he finds my lips again. Christ, I've got to be at least ten minutes late for my class and we're here in the middle of a full-blown make-out session, out in the open, where anybody could see us. Anybody. Morgan!

"Grayson, stop. Stop . . . please." I put a hand up between us.

"No. Don't . . . don't push me away." He breathes in between kisses.

"Morgan. Grayson. Please. I. Don't. Want her. To. Walk. In on us." My words escape each chance they get. "Please!" I say urgently as I turn my head to refuse his advances.

"Sorry." He tries to catch his breath as he leans his head up against mine. I move my face back to his and run my fingers along his jaw. I push up onto my toes to kiss the beauty mark under his left eye, then place a quick peck on his lips. He pulls me to him, hugging me and kissing the top of my head. I can't help but gasp when I feel his erection against my belly. He pulls back a little and looks down at me to see what caused my reaction.

"Don't worry," he chuckles. "He's a friendly bloke. He'll make you scream a little but, it won't be from horror."

"You're pretty damn sure of yourself, aren't you?" I snap. The cocky bastard! Just because I kissed him doesn't mean I'm going to sleep with him! I push him away and bend down to the floor to pick up the papers I dropped.

"Becca, darling ..." he bends down to help. "Where's your sense of humor? I didn't mean anything by it. I certainly never wished to offend you. C'mon, sweetheart." He tries to touch my cheek, but I smack his hand away.

"I am not your sweetheart! Will you go and see Charlie about the fucking horse and leave me the hell alone?" I grab the papers from him harshly, avoiding his eyes at all costs.

"Becca!" Hazel says in a shocked tone. I move my head to the right and find her standing a few feet behind Grayson. "How dare you talk to Grayson like that? He's my family! How could you be so disrespectful?"

Hazel has impeccable timing.

"Hazel ..." I start, my eyes welling up. I feel my chin quiver as the hurt blankets her face. I love this woman as if she were my own mother. I would never do anything to hurt her.

"No!" she snaps. "All I do is talk about how wonderful, smart, and beautiful you are, and how much I love you. I've been begging Grayson to come here for so long and the first day he arrives you show him nothing but ugliness! You were rude to him when he got here, then you ignored him all day. Now I find you yelling at him for no reason!" Her tears have made her powder-blue eyes more piercing. She's disappointed in me. I feel my heart breaking.

Like a five-year-old little girl wanting to make everything all better, I turn to Grayson. My tears pull away from their respective puddles in my eyes

"I'm sorry, Grayson." A little sob escapes my throat.

"Oh no, Becca, please. Aunt Hazel . . . really!" He looks at his aunt pleadingly. "You've walked in on the tail end of things. Becca had every right to lash out at me the way she did. I baited her," he argues as he walks over to her to grab her hand. "Auntie, I said something that was very inappropriate, and I probably deserved a good slap in the face for it."

"What did you say to her?"

She's not sure if she believes him. That sends another pang through my heart. It reminds me that he's her "real" family. Her loyalty is to him. Trying to avoid eye contact, I busy myself again with picking up papers.

"Really, Auntie, I'm already embarrassed. You would be ashamed of me and I couldn't bear that." He brings her over to me as I stand, having collected the last paper. "Really, you two love each other so much. I wouldn't be able to live with myself if I were the reason you had a falling out." He grabs my hand and squeezes it.

"You were still rude to him this morning. You ignored him all day. You never spend a full day in your office!" Hazel hates to be wrong.

"Yes, but Aunt Hazel, she's already made that up to me. You've should've seen how sweet she was to me a few moments ago." He smiles for our benefit, and I try to hold back my own. "I'm the one who caused all of this. Please, let's all kiss and make up." He keeps smiling, but raises an eyebrow at me. Cocky bastard!

"Oh, Grayson, you're right. I'm sorry, Becca." She hugs and kisses me.

"No, I'm sorry. I haven't been myself all day. I can't figure out the *devil* why." I shoot a look at Grayson as I accentuate the word "devil."

He gives me a shocked look and points his finger at himself. "Me?" he mouths, then shakes his head with a grin.

"I told him to ask you about the horse. I was hoping you had snapped out of it by now," Hazel says, and smiles up at me.

"Oh, I have. And I tried to be extra accommodating to Gracie! I really wanted him to know I'm sorry for my earlier behavior." I look past Hazel and catch Grayson's eyes. They look wild.

"Yes, Aunt Hazel, Becca was *very* accommodating. She's really sweet," he adds, licking his lips—and biting the bottom one.

Claudia steps into the room and clears her throat for attention. "Becca, you're twenty minutes late for the class. Did you forget?"

"Oh, God. Claudia, I'm sorry! Let's go." I release Hazel.

"I already taught the class, Bec. I just need the handouts."

"Oh, my awesomeness is rubbing off on you." I hug her and hand her the papers. "Where's Morgan?"

"She's 'teaching' the class with me." Claudia makes little air quotations.

"Do you need me?"

"No, no. We're good." She smiles, looking past me, and heads off.

"I need you," Grayson whispers in my ear as he wraps his arms around me from behind. I look around in a panic. "She went the back way to the kitchen." This answers my unasked question of where Hazel is. I relax a little and let the butterflies flutter around in my stomach as he kisses at my neck softly.

Cautionary Sybil blows her whistle and holds up a big sign that says: "NOTHING BUT TROUBLE!" She flips the sign. The other side says: "THREE WEEKS AND THEN WHAT?"

Yes, what the hell am I doing here?

"Grayson," I sigh, pulling myself out of his arms and turning to him. His hands immediately reach for my hips. "No. Stop, Grayson." I step back. "This ..." I wave my hand between him and me. "It's not a good thing. It can't happen." I shake my head.

"It's already happening, sweetheart. Don't fight it." He grabs my hand and pulls me to him.

"Stop!" I yank my hand away. "I love your aunt as if she were my own mother. I can't have anything come between us. I'm running a business here, *and*," I emphasize, "I have a very impressionable young daughter." I look down. "I'm sorry if I led you on. It was a very nice kiss, and I find you *very* attractive, but I just can't do this. It's a bad idea to begin with, and quite frankly, I don't want to be attached to anyone—whether it's three weeks or three days. I just can't. I'm sorry." I avoid his eyes to keep my strength. "I think it's probably best if we just avoid each other while you are here, in the most polite way we can." I take a deep breath. "Now, with that being said, I really should get to the kitchen to see if Adam needs help." I start to walk away.

"Adam? Who's Adam?" he asks. His long legs allow him to quickly catch up and pass me, and he takes my hand on the way by.

"By all means, why don't you come with me and find out?" No response. Not even a glance back as he leads me to the kitchen. "He's my chef for the crop weekends," I offer, and pull back a bit on his arm. "Hey, didn't you want to go horseback riding?"

"No, sweetheart, we'll go tomorrow. Right now I want to meet Adam."

"Why?"

"I'm hungry. I want to see what he's cooking for dinner." He looks at me like that should've been obvious.

As we head through the stockroom, I can't help wonder whether I actually spoke aloud when I said it couldn't work between us. He's acting as if I said nothing. As we walk past a few shelves with depleting merchandise, I pull my hand away to grab a pen and paper off one of the shelves.

"Becca, what are you doing?"

"I have to write this stuff down so I remember to order more." I quickly jot down the product numbers.

"Do you mean to tell that you do not have an inventory program?" he asks in disbelief.

"Yeah, I do. Right here." I wave the paper at him.

"While you're in the kitchen, I'm going to take a look in your office to see what you need. It already sounds like Aunt Hazel was not exaggerating." He rolls his eyes and pulls me along.

"Grayson, I'm not sure if I feel too comfortable with you going through my stuff." *Is there a better way to put that?*

"Sweetheart, I don't know if I feel too comfortable with *you* going through your stuff." He sighs. "I have an MBA and I'm pretty organized in every aspect of my life. Let me have a look. Then we'll go and get the programs you need." He brings my hand up to his lips and kisses my knuckles.

"Um . . . all right," I agree reluctantly. So much for politely avoiding each other. *Way to stand your ground, Becca!*

As we approach the door to the kitchen, he spins me around and pushes my back against the wall.

"Grayson!" I gasp with shock and look up into his eyes. His right hand palms my left cheek. His left secures a place at my waist.

"I'd like to kiss you again, sweetheart, before we go in there." His voice doesn't rise above a whisper as he leans in.

"Please. I just talked to you about this." I turn my face away.

"Oh, yes, I do recall your lovely speech." He smiles and cups my chin with his right hand to bring my face back to his. "Only trouble is, you've delivered it to the wrong guy. I'm a persistent," he nudges my lips with his, "and impatient bloke." Another nudge. "I'm afraid your words have fallen on deaf ears, sweetheart." He kisses the corner of my mouth.

"Persistent and impatient." I repeat the words breathlessly.

"Hmm . . . lethal combination, love." The words are barely out, and he attacks my lips. *Cautionary Sybil throws her note cards up in the air.*

Grayson takes my hands and presses them to the wall beside my ears. As his mouth travels down my neck, he slides them above my head and moves his left hand to grip both of my wrists. My core tightens as his free hand slides under my shirt, his fingers splaying over my skin. My breathing grows shallow. His circling thumb ignites a fire deep within the pit of my belly. His mouth teases mine, nudging my bottom lip 'til he finally pulls it between his teeth. I release a soft moan before he deepens the kiss again. *Good Lord, I don't think I've ever been kissed like this. Teenaged Sybil once again shakes her ass. I shouldn't be doing this. Dear God . . . I shouldn't be doing this.*

His hand travels higher and slides beneath my right cup.

"No," I gasp. My breast fills his hand generously and his mouth is on mine again, trying to quiet me while he rolls my nipple between his thumb and forefinger. "Get off of me!" I push him away, then adjust myself and move my shirt back in place.

"Becca." He tries to reach for my face.

"How dare you? You're nothing but trouble. And I don't need any more trouble in my life. I've had enough." I try to hold back my tears.

"Becca, I'm sorry. I don't know what else to say," he pleads.

The door to the stockroom opens, and Hazel pokes her head in.

"What is going on in here?" she snaps. Her gaze softens as she sees me crying and Grayson looking wide-eyed and guilty. "Becca, dear, what's the matter?"

Part of me wants to tell her what a cocky, arrogant son of a bitch her nephew is, but I can't bear to see her hurt.

"I'm fine. Can you and Claudia handle dinner? I'm not feeling so well." I look only at her.

"You haven't eaten all day. Can I bring your dinner up to you?" She glances from me to him.

"I don't have much of an appetite." I look down at my hands, allowing my tears to fall.

"Becca." Grayson tries again.

"Back off, Gracie!" Hazel snaps at him.

"Auntie!" he says in disbelief.

"Don't 'Auntie' me—I'm sure you are the culprit here! I suggest you leave Becca alone now!"

Damn, she's angry.

I go through the door, completely ignoring Adam in the kitchen, and walk into the dining area. I head around to the lounge—and the stairs. I just want to lie in my bed and try to comprehend everything that happened in the past hour.

"Becca. Becca, sweetheart, please." Grayson comes up behind me and turns me around. "I won't do that again." He hugs me tightly to him and kisses my hair. He smells so lovely. *No! No! No!*

"Grayson, please go downstairs. I need some space." I try to push him away.

"Let me bring dinner up for you," he says, keeping me at arm's length.

"Just leave me alone." I sigh and turn toward my door to unlock it.

"Let me." He grabs the key, then unlocks the door and opens it for me. "Can I draw you a bath?" *Really?*

"No, you can leave me the hell alone!" I pull the key out, slam the door in his face, and quickly lock it. *I'll draw my own damn bath!*

That's exactly what I do. I sink into my tub, my sanctuary—where I go to melt all problems away. *Damn it, I forgot wine.* I inhale the smell of my lavender and vanilla bath water as I close my eyes and listen to the fizzy sound of little bubbles fighting to stay intact.

What a day. What a crazy, confusing day. I don't even know where to begin to try and process everything. Did I overreact? Maybe it would all make sense . . . if we had been dating for like a week. I've only just met him. This has got to be the weirdest thing that's ever happened to me. What a strange man! Honestly, I can't even think of why he's so interested in me. I mean, he is gorgeous—and, well, I'm not. He should be with some runway model who would disappear if she turned sideways. I'm barely holding on to my size-twelve clothes with both hands. What does he want with me?

I press play on my remote and drown in the sounds of Bocelli. With my head back and eyes closed, it's easy to let the jets massage away my worries. I feel a breeze and open my eyes—only to find a glass of red wine on the step leading up to my tub.

The notecard attached to it reads, *"Forgive me, please."* I turn my head to the bedroom just in time to see Grayson shutting the door and locking it. He's left my dinner on a tray on my bed. I pull the notecard off and take a sip of the wine. It's sweet and bubbly. *Oh, hell.* I gulp it down. If he was smart, he would've brought me the damn bottle.

I climb out of the tub and put on my favorite comfy pajamas. My belly is grumbling, and that smells like—oh, yes—Adam's chicken cordon bleu. Steamed veggies and garlic mashed potatoes. There's peanut-butter pie for dessert and a diet ginger ale. I dive in.

I let out a disgusted groan over the amount of food I just ate and throw my napkin down on the tray. *Crap.* I haven't spent any time with Morgan today. I grab my tray and head downstairs to at least tuck her in.

Morgan's room is on the first floor with Hazel's. I felt it was safer for her to be away from the guests. When Hazel moved in two years ago, I gave her my room—adjacent to Morgan's—to spare her knees. She didn't mind being next to Morgan, and my daughter was thrilled.

I enter the kitchen, thankful to not run into Grayson, and begin washing my dishes.

"Mommy!" Morgan runs in.

"Hey, sweet pea." I hug her.

"Are you feeling better?" She leans up for a kiss.

"A little bit. I came down to see you for a little while and kiss you good night," I say as I finish up and dry my hands off. We walk into the dining room and head over to the store. "I just want to make sure the door is locked." I can hear the women in the crop room laughing and carrying on. I wave to them after locking the door.

As we turn to leave the store, I notice Grayson in my office—working. I'm a little irritated and at the same time glad he's doing something other than stalking me. He glances up as he walks across the office, then does a double take when he realizes it's me he's just seen. Suddenly, I don't like the French doors to my office anymore. He gives me a shy grin and a nod. I ignore him and let Morgan's overzealous wave be enough of a greeting. He turns his lovely smile to her.

"I like him a lot, Mama," she announces as we head to her room.

"Oh, really?"

"Yeah, and I have to tell you—I think he has a *huge* crush on you!" I turn the quilt down so she can climb under it, and she hops into bed.

"You don't say."

"Yes. He was asking me a bunch of questions about you."

"Such as?" *What the hell?*

She grins. "Oh, just your favorites. You know—movies, colors, books, flowers, perfume, things to do. You name it, he asked it! Then I asked him."

I'm almost too horrified to ask, but my curiosity gets the better of me. "About what?"

"If he has a crush on you. Well, actually, I asked him if he was cuckoo for Cocoa Puffs about you." She's giggling now, which always makes me laugh, too.

"And what did he say?"

"He laughed a big hearty laugh and then said, 'Morgy girl, I'm most certainly, without a doubt, cuckoo for Cocoa Puffs about your mother.' And I said, 'Well, get in line, buddy, because you're not the only one!' Mom, it's like I pulled the sunshine out of the sky. He was like this." She smiles and puts her hand across her eyes, then drops it fast, wiping away the smile.

"Morgan!" I laugh. I think I love her even more than a minute ago. "Then what happened?"

"He asked me who liked you and if you ever go out with them."

"What did you say?"

"I told him who has a crush on you, but that you never go on dates. He asked me why. I just shrugged and told him I don't know." She picks at her quilt. "Mama, why don't you go out with anyone?"

"Stop picking at that. I will when I'm ready—when the right guy comes along." I take her hand.

"Well, I think that guy is Grayson. Mom, he's in there organizing your *war zone*!" I laugh at her animation. "Do you like him,

Mom? Isn't he cute?" She entwines her hands in front of her heart and sighs dreamily.

"I was starting to. He is very handsome. I'm just not sure."

"Well, he has an English accent! I told him how much you love English accents, which would give him a better chance than the other guys."

"Oh, God." I sigh and shake my head.

"What?" she asks.

"Nothing. C'mon now, say your prayers."

She lies down and starts her prayers.

"God bless Mommy and Hazel and Charlie and Claudia and Butterscotch and Adam and Rocco and Grayson. And, God, please help Mommy see that Grayson is the right guy for her. I don't want her to be alone anymore and I'd really like to have a daddy I could bring to the father-daughter dance. Amen."

"Morgan, I'm not alone. I have you and Hazel. And Charlie always takes you to the dances." I try to console her. Well, maybe more me than her.

"Mommy, you need a guy around to tell you how beautiful you are. I also want a brother or a sister and you can't have one without being married. I love Charlie, but he's more like a grandpa." Someday this kid is going to be a great lawyer.

"Okay, sweetie, this sounds like a conversation for another night." I give her a kiss and pull her covers up. "Good night." I smile and turn off her light.

"Good night, Mama."

With that, I close her door—and turn right into Grayson's arms. "Ah!" I gasp, a bit alarmed. I steady my nerves and breathe him in. *Damn, he smells lovely.*

"Hi," he whispers, kissing my hair.

"Please let go of me." I just can't go through another round of this today.

His finger pushes my chin up so that he can look into my eyes.

"Okay. I just wanted to say good night." He runs his thumb across my bottom lip over and over again. I look to the side. "I'm a persistent man, Becca," he whispers.

Before I can say *I know*, his lips are on mine. He just gives me a few soft pecks before pulling away. He stands to the side to let me go. Wow, somebody has learned a bit about boundaries in the past few hours.

"Good night," I manage, and walk by him.

"'Night, sweetheart."

Chapter Three

Ugh . . . I really hate this alarm clock! I struggle to get out of bed. It's Sunday, so all of our weekend scrappers will be checking out later. It's going to be crazy busy! I stretch, make my bed, and go to retrieve a note I see at my door. Why is Morgan up so early? I open it. Oh. It's not from Morgan.

Becca,

Good morning, sweetheart. I hope you slept well. I finished your office, but please don't touch anything until I get up at ten. I have much to discuss with you about your business that I think will bring you great relief!

At ten-thirty, you have a two-hour break. Please do not reschedule this time. I want to go over everything with you, and you did promise me a tour! ☺ Maybe you could find it in your heart to forgive me and give me another chance.

Yours,

Grayson

PS. I had a tough time letting go of you last night.

PSS. And leaving you alone while you were in the bathtub.

PSSS. I think your kid is the only kid in the world I thoroughly enjoy the company of.

PSSSS. Probably because she's yours . . .

PSSSSS. Because, like you, I find even numbers unsettling.

I can't help but laugh at the fifth PS. He truly did ask Morgan about everything! It took me a long time to fall asleep last night. I know I overreacted. So he copped a feel? We're adults! I think I was just overwhelmed by the emotional, awkward day. I've never had a reaction to anyone like that.

I also feel like I can't trust myself. I haven't been with anyone since George—seven years ago. He was so cruel, so abusive. I know I'm afraid that's the only relationship that will come my way. Grayson's aggressiveness sent up red flags for me—but I realized he's confident, not cruel. He had no intention of hurting me, and he's been so remorseful over something so little. But it mattered to me and so it mattered to him. He has no knowledge of what happened to me. I think I need to try harder myself. Let go of things somehow. I have time; I'm going to write him back.

GRAYSON

I can't sleep. How could I sleep? I've been acting like a crazy, love-sick teenaged boy! Christ—what is wrong with me? Why does she affect me like this? I can't control myself, and she can turn off the heat at the drop of a dime. It's so . . . so infuriatingly hot!

I am one cocky bloke, though. I thought I had her in the bag yesterday when we met. Same flustered reaction I get from all of the girls. I was all set for a midafternoon shag, but she shot me down—just like that! And now I'm obsessed. I stole a glance over Auntie's shoulder at Becca's schedule. I spied on her in her office, for fuck's sake! Who does that? Not me! Well, until yesterday, that is. I couldn't keep my eyes off of her.

She's beautiful . . . long brown hair, big green eyes, and a woman! Not like the twiggies who always approach me. God, if I wanted to sleep with someone that looks like a ten year old boy, I would've been a gay pedophile. I love a woman with curves. A little extra healthy meat on the bones—something to grab on too. Becca's just perfect, right down to that fantastic arse of hers.

Quite the overreactor, though. Well, after talking to Aunt Hazel last night, it all makes sense. I think back to our conversation.

"Gracie," she knocked softly before pushing the office door open the rest of the way. I turned to her, happy for a little break from the train wreck that is Becca's office.

"Yes, Auntie?" I stood up and stretched.

"I need to talk to you about Becca." She gestured toward the other chair.

"Yes, please sit." I turned it around for her and resumed my seat. *"What is it?"*

"I saw you two kiss today." Her cheeks blushed at her confession. I didn't know what to say but I opened my mouth as if something brilliant was going to come out of it. Thankfully, she put her hand up to stop me. *"I would love nothing more than to see you and*

Becca together. However, there are some things you need to know."
She shook her finger at me. *"First, Becca is a good girl. She's not the type of girl you warm your bed with one night and kick to the curb the next."*

"Kick to the curb, Auntie?" I couldn't help my chuckle.

"Focus, Gracie!" She slapped my leg. *"Yes, I know all about your 'friends' back home. Don't think Susanna keeps me in the dark just because you do!"* Blimy! That's what happens when your staff becomes more like family than staff.

"I can assure you that I'm fully aware that Becca doesn't hold a candle to my other 'friends.'" I patted her hand, thinking this surely was the end to our conversation.

"We're not done here, Nephew," she stated with a bit of irritation. *"There is something else you need to know."* She took in a deep breath, looked up to the ceiling for strength (like she always does), and told me everything. I almost wish she didn't.

Fucking George, that abusive piece of shit! If he wasn't already dead, I'd have half the mind to kill him myself. Aunt Hazel showed me the pictures she came across, ones that Becca took after he'd beaten her to a pulp. Christ! How could he do that to her? I feel my stomach turning as a slideshow of those pictures flashes across my memory.

Aunt Hazel thinks that arsehole did far worse to her, too. Becca's never said much more, though. I can't even imagine. I don't *want* to imagine. All I want to do is pull her into my arms and tell her she's safe now. Not that she'd believe me.

After all that arsehole did to her, I can't believe she still tries to keep him in a good light for Morgan's sake. Auntie said Morgan doesn't have the heart to tell Becca that she remembers him as a bad person who hurt her mother.

I already love Morgan. She's the most incredible kid I've ever met! I actually caught myself off-guard last night when she asked me if I was cuckoo for Cocoa Puffs. I haven't laughed that hard in a long time and, at that moment, I wished I was her dad. Me . . . a father? That thought has never occurred to me! Then again, I haven't been quite myself since I stepped foot in this building. I feel as if I'm under some sort of spell. My eyes roll at the thought.

I was glad to see her again last night. Surprised at first, but then again, she is a great Mum. Of course she came down to say good night to Morgan. She wasn't too happy to see me in her office, though. Bloody hell, I wanted to shoot myself for offering! Spent the whole goddamn night straightening that mess out! But it was worth it. She let me hold her and kiss her. I think she was surprised that I held back. Aunt Hazel told me to slow down. That's what I'm doing . . . well, trying to.

Ugh, go to sleep, Gray! I roll over onto my side and see something on the floor. I get up and head over to it. Oh, dear . . . a note. I pick it up and am struck with Becca's lovely scent. Mmm. I can't stop breathing it in. I sit down, feeling a bit nervous to read it.

Dear Grayson,

Thank you for the lovely note this morning. And thank you so much for what you did in my office—or, as I like to call it, my war zone. That is until yesterday, when I secretly renamed it the "panic room."

I had a lot of time to think last night about everything that happened. I know I overreacted in the stockroom. I liked that you were touching me; I craved it. I was mad that I felt that way. Mad and scared.

I'd be very surprised if you didn't get your aunt to spill the beans on my past after the way you interrogated my daughter (which she loved, by the way). Just in case you didn't, though, I was married to a very cruel and abusive man named George. He did quite the number on me and that is all I'm going to say about it. After yesterday, I've realized that I've come a long way—and yet, have so far to go.

Listen, you're only here for three weeks. It might be in your best interest to walk away. I don't know what else to tell you. This is a crazy conversation to have when we haven't even known each other for a full twenty-four hours!

I'll see you at half past ten. Sleep well, Gracie!

Love,

Becca

PS. Thank you for the wine and dinner. My hunger won over my stubbornness.

PSS. I had a hard time dealing with the fact that you let me go last night, but it was a good choice.

PSSS. And the kisses . . . still thinking about them.

PSSSS. Thanks for thinking my kid is great!

PSSSSS. Because four just isn't right!

I'm so confused. How am I going to sleep now when I want to run downstairs, throw her over my shoulder, and bring her back up here . . . to my bed? I charge over to the dresser, throw the letter on top, and whip the drawers open like a madman 'til I find something to throw on. I can't believe she suggested I walk away—again! She craves my touch, tells me so, and then suggests I walk away? Ridiculous.

No. Nope, I can't sleep. I throw on my jeans and a polo shirt before heading downstairs. *Okay, sweetheart, let's see what it is you* really *want!*

I storm into the kitchen and find her at the sink washing her hands.

"Becca!" I snap. Shit, I didn't mean to do that. I've startled her. "Sorry, sweetheart. Can you come with me?" I soften my tone.

"Yes, Grayson." She dries her hands and follows me after a brief moment of hesitation. Shit, I've made her nervous. Not the start I was looking for. "You should be sleeping."

"I'll sleep later," I whisper, pushing her against the wall of the stockroom. Her breath comes out in erratic bursts. I was going to say something first, but bloody hell! I grasp her lips with my own. "You want me to walk away?" I ask, and pull back.

"No. No, I don't want that." She shakes her head and tugs me closer.

I pull away again. "You crave my touch?" I slip my hands under her shirt and hear her gasp. "Tell me when to stop."

She's searching my eyes. I attack her lips again and slowly unclasp her bra.

"Grayson, wait. Not here. Somebody could walk in." In a quick second, she's already redoing what I've undone. I plant my hands on her chest atop her shirt anyway and frown. She's smiling wickedly at me. Who is this girl, and where is Becca? She reaches up to touch my face, her fingers playing at my stubble. *Oh, God.* She kisses my beauty mark again, and I close my eyes and feel calm.

"Why do you kiss me there?" I open my eyes again to gaze into her emerald ones.

"I don't know. I just feel that I have to, like it was put there to be kissed. Does it bother you?" she asks, running her fingertips over it, her touch light as a feather.

"No. I love that you do that." *It reminds me of the love of my mother, who, incidentally, said the same thing about it.* "Why would you suggest I walk away, sweetheart? Honestly, have you met me yet? I can't walk away from you in this house."

"Grayson, you're here for three weeks. Then what?" She rests her head back against the wall.

"I have the means to be anywhere I want, when I want to be there. I'll have to leave to handle certain business obligations, but I can tell you right now—I'm not going anywhere. Not here," I touch my temple. "Or here," I put my hand over my heart. "I'm completely smitten with you. It's insane, I know. This is not a reaction I am familiar with. I'm in uncharted waters here, Becca. But I want to explore them with you." I strum her bottom lip with my thumb and keep my gaze soft on her face, hoping she can sense my sincerity. I see the struggle in her eyes, and I understand it. "Say something." I nudge her lips. *Let me fix you*, I silently beg.

"You need to go to bed. You've been up all night."

Don't shoo me away. "Come with me, Becca."

"I can't. I have forty-two people to feed."

"And you have a staff."

"No, Grayson. I'm sorry."

"I promise just to sleep. I won't do anything. Well, I would like to hold you." She doesn't believe me. I don't blame her. I haven't been able to keep my hands off of her. "Look, I made a promise to Aunt Hazel that I would take things slow."

"Your Aunt Hazel knows?" Her eyes widen with panic.

"Yes, sweetheart. She saw us yesterday having our first kiss. What a delicious kiss that was." I close my eyes to reminisce.

"What did she think? What did she say?" Did she just smack my chest? I open my eyes to find her five shades of red and worried.

Really, I'm hurt she's blushing about the fact that my aunt knows and not about the way my hands were just touching her or the way my mouth claimed hers.

"Well, she's very happy, but worried. This does pose an awkward situation for her."

"Sit-too-ation?" Becca giggles.

"Yes, sweetheart, I speak proper English." I smirk and continue. "It's awkward because we're the two people she loves most in the world. She would love for everything to work out for us. Nothing would make her happier. But she's worried that if things go wrong, she would be put in the middle. She loves her life here with you and Morgan."

"And Charlie," she adds.

"Charlie?" What does he have to do with this?

"Charlie is very sweet on your aunt. I think she secretly feels the same way about him. But, I think she's worried about betraying your uncle. I try to nudge her a little here and there, but she won't budge." She looks over at the door to make sure no one is there.

"Hmm . . . I'll have to meet this Charlie. It's absurd; Uncle Harold has been gone for ten years. He'd want her to be happy." ·

"That's what I thought from the way she talks about him. Listen, Grayson." Her tone changes. *Uh-oh.* "About us—I understand her concern. It wouldn't be fair to her if things didn't work out between us and she was put in that awkward position." She stops, and a cute little crease appears in her brow—she must be thinking really hard. I keep my mouth shut, but I'm feeling a little nervous about what she is planning to say. I don't want to keep dancing around the feelings we are having.

"I think we need to make a pact," she continues. "We need to agree now that we will not let our relationship have any negative effect on her—no matter what. We'll have to approach this *situation*," I chuckle as she emphasizes the American pronunciation, "as if she's our child. We can't let our relationship affect her."

My heart leaps at the words *our child*. I know she's talking about my aunt, but . . . oh God, I can't talk anymore. I grasp her face and kiss her with all the passion in my soul. I feel her weaken under my spell and give in. This kiss is even more delicious than yesterday's.

"Becca, let's go upstairs. Now." She needs to say no. I won't be able to control myself.

BECCA

"Grayson, no." I can barely catch my breath. I *want* to go upstairs with him. But we are moving way too fast. I'm not sure I'm ready for this. I'm positive I don't want everyone knowing, which is what will happen if I do this now. I'm too busy doing the walk of confusion; I don't need to add the walk of shame to my résumé. I feel him pull my hair tie out. As soon as my hair falls, he wraps his hands in it and pulls me back to his lips. I can feel his urgency growing against my belly.

"Gray. Gray. Stop. Please, I can't." I try to push him away, but he's too strong. I suddenly don't feel so well. I stop returning his kisses. *The room is spinning.*

"Becca? Sweetheart? Becca, wake up—please!" I hear Grayson yelling and feel the cold floor underneath me. "Becca. Aunt Hazel!"

"Shh ..." I whisper.

"Becca? Sweetheart, open your eyes." I do so as he lifts me from the floor. I wrap my arms around his neck.

"What happened?" I ask. I feel so confused.

"I was acting like a fucking animal and you passed out!" he says through his teeth. I know he's mad at himself.

"So this is what the world looks like from up here?" I say, and kiss his mark to lighten his mood. It works. He closes his eyes and takes a deep breath as he leans his forehead against mine.

"I'm a selfish man," he whispers.

"I know, baby."

His eyes flicker open at my endearment just as Hazel hurries into the storeroom.

"What happened?" Hazel cries. She holds the door open for us.

"She passed out, Auntie." The words are barely audible, like he knows he's going to be grounded. I smile at him. She has that same effect on me.

"Why did you pass out, Becca?" She looks from me to Grayson, and he opens his mouth to confess—but I beat him to it.

"I haven't eaten much in the past two days. I've hardly slept all week. I think I've done a number on myself, but I'm okay now. Good thing Grayson was with me, or I'd still be on the floor." He gives me a shy smile. His eyes warm, secretly thanking me.

"What were you both doing out there? Especially you, Gracie, you went upstairs to bed."

Oh you smart, suspicious woman! Again, I talk for him.

"He was heading upstairs. We ran into each other in the hall and he wanted to show me something that he forgot to write down." I'm actually uncomfortable with this new, amazing ability I've acquired—lying to this powder-blue-eyed woman, when I've never been able to before.

"Aunt Hazel, I'm going to bring Becca upstairs. I don't think she should work this morning."

"Yes, you're right. I just have one more question." She places her index finger up to her lips, her eyes staring with thoughtful suspicion.

"Yes, Auntie?"

"Becca, why is your hair down? You always have it up."

"It was falling out. I must've passed out while I was retying it." Boy, I'm quick!

"Can I take her now . . . err, upstairs?" Grayson stumbles. I have to stifle my giggle. It's been a long time since I've felt like a teenager trying to avoid getting in trouble.

"Go ahead. We'll be fine down here." She sighs, defeated. Grayson turns and we head out of the kitchen, toward the lounge, and then up the stairs.

"Who is she—Nancy Drew?" I ask, a little exasperated.

"I just can't get over the remarkable way you lied to her . . . again, I might add. That does make me rather nervous." He chuckles, but his face looks half-serious.

"I can't either. I'm usually not very good at it unless I'm protecting somebody I care about. Otherwise, I don't do it." Grayson comes to an abrupt stop mid-climb. "Why did you stop? Do you want me to walk up the rest of the way?" I can tell he works out but, I'm no supermodel. I'm sure he's getting tired of carrying me. He just stares. His eyes are like chocolate Kisses . . . no, more like Dove dark chocolate. Great. Now I'm thinking about chocolate! I kiss his lips. "I'll get down now."

He continues to carry me up the stairs without saying a word or even shifting me to make himself more comfortable. *That was weird.* I hand him my room key. He opens the door and places me on my bed.

"Where are your pajamas, sweetheart?" he asks, walking over to the built-in drawers.

"Um, bottom drawer." He pulls a pair out and walks back to me. He reaches for my shirt, and my nerves go through the roof. I stand up. "I'll just go change in the bathroom." There are too many reasons I don't want him to see me naked.

"Becca, not to sound like an arrogant arsehole, but I will see you without clothes at some point. Soon. For a very different reason. Right now, I want to get you dressed for bed. If you go into the bathroom, you may pass out again and hit your head. Lift your arms." He grabs ahold of the hem of my shirt.

Does he even realize he's part of the reason I passed out? I definitely can't tell him. I lift my arms and feel my face begin to flush. He pulls my shirt off and lays it on the cushioned hope chest at the foot of my bed. His eyes come back to mine, but they slowly travel down. His fingers reach up and trace the skin above the top of my bra. They trail down to my stomach and unbutton and unzip my jeans.

"Grayson, shirt first, please." I'm barely audible, so I clear my throat.

"Right." He pulls my PJ top down over my head. As I put my arms through, he kneels on the floor and softly covers my stomach with kisses. I try to keep my breathing steady, but I think I may be heading into sensory overload here. He kisses my scar and I let out a little gasp. "What's this from, sweetheart? Did you have your appendix out?" He continues to kiss me there.

"No." I try to pull my shirt down.

"What's it from?" He looks up at me.

"It was proof," I state flatly.

"Proof of what?"

"That he would kill me if I left."

His eyes show horror, than anger. His jaw twitches and his hands close into fists. He looks down. I'm not quite sure what I should do.

"Right. Let's carry on here, shall we?" He pulls my jeans down a little harsher than I think he means to. I know his anger is not toward me. I step out of them, and he reaches for my panties. I stop him.

"What are you doing?"

"Morgan told me you don't wear panties with your pajamas." He looks at me like I have five heads.

"She told you that?" I need to have a *very* serious discussion with my daughter about offering up personal information. I mean, this is way beyond my favorite color!

"Yes, I have to say . . . it was by far the best piece of information I've received." He chuckles.

"Well, I can wear them now." He doesn't argue. I think it's obvious I'm pissed. He helps me into my bottoms and gives my belly one last kiss before pulling down the bed covers for me.

"In you go, sweetheart." he pats my bum and I climb in. I pull my hair to the side and lay down only to find him pulling off his shirt.

"What are you doing?" I gasp, possibly because he is quite the vision. Broad, muscular shoulders. Perfectly ripped, all the way down.

"I'm going to bed. I have been up for over twenty-four hours now." He smirks and pulls his jeans off. Boxer briefs are very complementary to his physique.

"Don't you think you should sleep in your . . . wait, what are you doing?" I sit up in bed as he goes to take his boxers off.

"Just kidding, sweetheart." He laughs at my reaction and jumps into bed next to me. "No, Becca—I want to be here with you to make sure you're okay." He pulls me into his arms. His scent is so lovely. I lean up, undo my bra, and slip it off underneath my shirt. He encircles me in his left arm and places his right hand on my bum, hoisting me up closer to him. I place my leg halfway onto his body and allow him to continue caressing my bottom. Of course, the pack of butterflies in my belly goes wild. I can feel him grow beneath my leg.

I don't know what is coming over me. It must be Sybil the horny teenager. I ignore Cautionary Sybil and climb on top of him, kneeling on either side of his body. He looks bewildered. I bite my lip. I may be getting myself into a situation I won't be able to get out of. Grayson traces the skin across the top of my PJ pants and licks his lips. He tugs lightly at the hem of my shirt, pulling his bottom lip in with his teeth. He wants me to take it off? Uh . . . I can't do that. Oh God, what am I doing? I'm teasing him. Why did I do this?

I shake my head and grab his hands, placing them on either side of his head. Okay, I like this. I'm in control. I lean down. My teeth have a turn pulling at his bottom lip and a little groan escapes his throat. His pelvis rises up against me. *Teenage Sybil does the fist pump as she takes the wheel.* I respond by meeting his next thrust and the next.

"Becca, please . . . let go of my arms now," he musters against my lips. I do so and he grasps my hips, helping me push against him as hard as I can. Our mouths are wild as we try to savor each other.

And then it happens.

All of the Sybils gather together in white robes and sing in unison. I bury my face into his neck to muffle the unfamiliar sounds coming from my mouth. I exhale, a blanket of calm enveloping every neuron in my body.

"Becca." He's breathless. "Climb off, love." He pats my bum lightly.

"Oh, okay." I do so, and he heads to the bathroom. I lay back and throw my arm over my eyes. Wow. That was so intense . . . with our clothes on! I may go into cardiac arrest when we actually have sex.

"Hey, where are you, darling?" He moves my arm and smiles down at me. His face is red.

"Sorry." I half smile and glance toward the bathroom.

"It's okay, sweetheart. How do you feel?" He runs his finger across my cheek and over my lips. I kiss his finger.

"Like I need to go take my panties off."

He chuckles and lets me out of bed.

Sans panties, my breath back to normal, I return to the bedroom. Grayson is half asleep but manages to lift his arms a little. I climb in and let them blanket me.

Chapter Four

"Becca—*psst*—Becca."

I open my eyes to find Hazel standing over us, hands on her hips. *Oh, shit!* I untangle myself slowly from Grayson and climb out of bed.

"What time is it?" I go for my usual tactic of distracting her with questions. However, there's a six-foot-four white elephant in the room. Somehow, I don't think I'll be able to avoid the lecture.

"It's almost noon and you are teaching at twelve-thirty. Can you still do it?" She keeps looking from me to him. Luckily, he's her nephew, so she's whispering as to not wake him up. If it was someone else, I don't think she would be this thoughtful.

"Yes. I'll teach. Let me get dressed and I'll be right down." I pick up my clothes and try to head to the bathroom. She grabs my arm. *Shit!* I take in a deep breath and turn around.

"Why is Grayson in here?" *And so it begins.*

"He was worried. He didn't want me to be alone in case I passed out again." It is true, so I'm not lying. "We didn't do anything. You can see I'm fully dressed." Then again, a little white lie never hurt anyone.

"Why is he not dressed, or on the couch there?" Her eyebrows go up. She's waiting to catch me in a lie. I am going to start calling her Nancy Drew—it's a done deal!

"He wouldn't fit on the couch. His feet are hanging over the edge of the bed as it is!" *Yes, go with the couch question.*

"Why is he naked?" Ooh, she's getting impatient with me. I hold back my nervous giggle.

"He's not naked, he's in his underwear. That's how he sleeps, I guess." Well done, Becca. Act like it's not a big deal.

"Why didn't you tell him to get a pair of pajamas? I know he has some because I unpacked them." I can see she thinks she's had her *ah-ha!* moment. Suddenly, I feel myself grow a pair.

"Hazel, I am thirty-five years old. If you were thirty-five years old and a gorgeous man with an amazing body wanted to sleep next to you in nothing but his underwear, would you argue with him? I mean, Christ, forget that he's your nephew for one moment and look at him! Would you say no to that?" I point, directing her eyes to the fine specimen of a man sprawled out in my bed. Hazel takes a moment and stares at her nephew. Wow, she's really thinking about this. Her eyes wrinkle at the corners and she puts her hand over her mouth to stifle a giggle while she shakes her head.

She grabs my face and kisses my left cheek.

"Oh Becca . . . I just love you!" She smiles. "Hurry and get dressed, honey. I have lunch made for you." She kisses me again.

"I love you too, Mom. Thanks for not grounding me," I tease, and she lets that giggle escape before she leaves.

"Well played, darling." Grayson smiles, his eyes still closed. "Now, why don't you give this gorgeous man with an amazing body a kiss before you leave him?" He stretches out his arms.

"You were awake the entire time? You know, I'm beginning to think you're a real wuss when it comes to your aunt." I smack his hand playfully, but climb back in and kiss him.

"I wasn't awake until she started with the '*psst . . . psst.*' Christ, for a moment I thought I was twelve again. That's how she's always awoken me. I love her but, it's the most irritating sound in the world." He traces my lips and kisses them again.

"I think it's just the way she does it." I laugh. "That's how she wakes me, too, and I feel the same way."

"But you don't have the heart to tell her, right?"

"Right," I agree.

"Becca . . . I love this."

"Love what?"

"That we both know Aunt Hazel so well and that we both love her so much. She's the only family I have. Your relationship with her takes that pressure off of us as a couple. Do you know what I mean?" There is so much warmth and sincerity in his words, it's hard to believe I thought him arrogant at all. *So . . . couple?* I stare into his dark-chocolate eyes. Yeah, I'm good with that. *Cautionary Sybil shakes her head in disbelief.*

"I do, baby." I sweep his lips again with mine.

"I love hearing you call me that. Which is interesting."

"Why?" I prop my head up with my elbow.

"I've always disliked it. But for some reason, it sounds different coming from you." He squints, looking puzzled.

"Well, this bit of information should intrigue you even more: I have never called another man that, only Morgan."

"Not a boyfriend in high school? I thought calling your sweetheart 'baby' was part of the American high-school curriculum." He laughs.

"Nope, but I think you're right—which is why I didn't do it. My aunt and uncle have always called each other 'baby.' They're the love of each other's lives, so it always seemed sacred to me. That's probably why I didn't ever call my boyfriends that. I guess it's more of a family thing for me," I ramble.

"What about your husband?"

"No, Grayson, I told you. You're the only man I've ever called 'baby.'" He needs more sleep.

"But he was family."

"Yes, but it never felt right. It was too sacred. I guess I didn't lo ..." I trail off. *Becca, really, don't hold back now! What are you doing?*

"You didn't what, Becca?" He moves his face closer to mine and searches my eyes.

"Um . . . understand why I didn't, I just didn't. I didn't think about it." That's a half-truth.

"That's a half-truth, Becca."

"I just said that in my head!" *Really?* Mental face-palm—make that two. Think quickly. Think quickly.

"Sweetheart, what is the other half? The half you were going to say before you caught yourself." He's smiling, but I can see he's getting impatient.

"Happy anniversary!" I kiss him.

"What are you talking about?" He shakes his head as I climb out of bed.

"We've known each other for a full *twenty-four hours*!" I emphasize, and head to the bathroom to change.

"This conversation is not over, sweetheart," he states loudly.

Oh God . . . what am I doing? What is wrong with me? This is not me. Not ever—not before George—not ever! I know they say that when you know, you know. But do I know? I need to make a list, to find a quiet place today and write out the pros and cons. I can't think of anywhere I can go that he won't want to come with me. Maybe tonight, when he's in his room. Wait, what am I thinking? He's not going to sleep in his room. I wouldn't be surprised to find all of his stuff in my room after I'm done teaching the class. No, no . . . he can't do that. It would completely freak Morgan out because sometimes she wakes up in the middle of the night and climbs into bed with me. Yes—thank you, Morgan! Well, until my list is done and I've sorted out my feelings, anyway.

I hear a knock on the door.

"Uh . . . sweetheart? I know you're busy in there coming up with ways to avoid my question, but you're running out of time to eat lunch before your class."

"All done." I open the door and come out. He's laughing. What's so funny? I look down. Right! I march back into the bathroom and this time I remember to get out of my PJs and into my clothes. *Damn him.* I tie my hair up and head out only to walk right into him. I close my eyes and change my theme song to "He Drives me Crazy" (replacing *she* with *he*, of course) by the Fine Young Cannibals. Does this man ever not smell incredible? I open my eyes and look up. He's biting his lip, trying not to laugh.

"I hate you." I sigh, defeated. I don't know why.

"That's a strong, very negative word." He frowns.

"Sorry ..."

"Well, I opposite-of-the-word-you-said . . . you." The back of his hand caresses my cheek. He kisses my forehead. *Cautionary Sybil taps her notepad with her pen and stares down over the brim of her glasses.* I lightly push by him and toward the door, but I only make it halfway across the bedroom before I stop. *Cautionary Sybil waves her hands and shakes the pad.* I turn back to Grayson. He's leaning against the bathroom door, looking down at his foot as he kicks the frame. I've hurt him—I think. I don't even realize my feet are moving. *Cautionary Sybil throws the pad and pen up in the air as she turns around and walks away, shaking her hands at the sky.* I reach Grayson and palm his face, startling him.

"I didn't really love him." That's all I can offer at the moment. He lifts me up to hug me and I wrap my legs around his waist. I kiss him with his back up against the doorframe. I kiss him with my back pressed against the bedroom wall. I kiss him with my back flat on the bed.

"Gray. Gray. Grayson . . . I . . . you . . . class . . . stop." I'm trying to gain some control over myself. I do have a class to teach in fifteen minutes. He carries on, ignoring my pleas. *Calm down.* I'm just going to stop reciprocating. I lay still, eyes closed, waiting for him to comprehend that he needs to stop. Breathe. Breathe . . . he's not George. He's not going to hurt you. His mouth travels down to my breast. Breathe. Breathe. *Sweet Jesus.* The most delicious electric current hits my groin when he pulls my nipple between his teeth. I fight the urge to move my hips for encouragement. *Here comes Sybil the horny teenager, and she's shaking her ass like there's no tomorrow.* Huh? Why did she stop? Wait, why did he stop?

"Becca?" He sounds nervous. I open my eyes. "Oh, thank God, sweetheart." He kisses me. "I thought you'd passed out again. Why were you just lying there?"

"I couldn't get you to stop so I could go to my class. So I just concentrated on my breathing and waited for you to notice." I almost hate to tell him this, and that twitch of his jawline is just the reason why. He's mad at himself. "It's okay. I'm okay. I just need to get to class, baby." I brush his lips with mine.

"Is that what happened this morning? Did I give you a flashback or something?"

Oh man, this is so not something I have time to discuss right now.

"Be patient with me, please . . . I'm trying," I almost whisper.

"Bloody hell, Becca! Be patient with *you*? I'm the one over here behaving like a fucking animal! I should be the one begging for patience!" He stands up and paces, running his hands through his hair. "Shit!" he yells. "Shit! Fuck! *Shit! Shit!*" He punches an imaginary person.

"Mr. James!" I snap with a slight giggle as I stand up on the bed. "This is a family establishment. Please refrain from using foul language in the earshot of one child and several elderly scrapbooking women who would certainly gasp in shock. Now, come here, give your sweetheart a kiss, and wish her a good class." I point my finger down in front of me. He gives me a wickedly brilliant smile and obeys my orders. "I'll see you in a little over an hour." I break from his lips.

"Don't forget to put the girls back in, sweetheart." His eyes drift downward.

Huh? Oh . . . oh, right. I smile and fix myself.

I enter the hallway and Hazel's right there, catching her breath.

"Why was Grayson yelling like that?" The question is out of her mouth before I can even close the door behind me. I hesitate—since we weren't having sex, I don't want to lie. Grayson pops his head out.

"Sorry, Auntie. I smacked my foot right into the hope chest at the end of Becca's bed."

"Well, try to control yourself. And, Becca, you need to eat your lunch," she adds as she turns back toward the stairs.

"See, I'm not such a wuss after all. By the way, which class are you teaching today?" He reaches for my hand. I give it to him and he kisses my knuckles as I think about the class.

"It's three different page layouts I've created." I let out a burst of laughter. He looks at me strangely. "Would you like to know the titles of these layouts? I'm sure you will find them amusing and iron- ic."

"What are they?"

I hold my breath, trying to stop laughing, which just makes him laugh at me.

"Okay. Okay . . . phew." I start giggling again. "Okay, the first layout is 'Watching You Grow,' the second is 'Big Boy,' and for the grand finale . . . wait." I start laughing again. "Okay, ready? Third is 'Wild About Animals.'" And now we're both in stitches. "Oh my God. How am I going to do this without laughing?"

"You'll do fine, sweetheart." He chuckles and pulls me to the door for a kiss.

"Bye, Gracie!" I wink.

"Bite your tongue, woman!"

"You first."

"Don't tempt me." He smacks me on the ass as I walk away. "Becca?"

"Yes?" I look back.

"Is it all right that I did that just now?" He furrows his brow.

"Yes, baby." I blow him a kiss and head down the stairs.

This class is pretty easy since I have everything precut and ready to go. It's mainly about teaching the scrappers how to make my layouts their own. I show them my "Big Boy" page, about Rocco, my horse. I used Morgan for the "Watching You Grow" page, obviously, but Hazel did her garden. "Wild About Animals" could be about pets, zoo animals, or children. I like these types of classes because they get people out of their one-dimensional thinking. You can really get stuck, laying out each page in the same style, especially when you rush through to catch up. Then it doesn't seem so special anymore. Sometimes just popping the title or the pictures adds so much. Throw some ribbon on there. *Take time to remember the time.*

"Don't just slap a few pictures on there with stickers. You're scrapping these pictures because this moment in time was important. Honor that on your page!" I watch as some of the ladies nod at me while, others seem to get excited over sudden ideas. "I'll leave you to finish. Hazel has brought some pastries for you to enjoy." I point to the buffet table against the wall. "There's fresh coffee and hot water for tea as well. Thank you, ladies, and I hope you've enjoyed your weekend. Please feel free to ask for help with anything." I see Shelley—I think that's her name—raise her hand. "Yes . . . Shelley?" I wince, unsure.

"I'd like to know who the hottie staying here is. I'd lay *him* out, if you know what I mean." She pulls her mouth to the side when she says the last part. I giggle. I know exactly what she means.

"That would be Grayson, Hazel's very handsome nephew."

"Well, is he taken? 'Cause I'd like to take him . . . if you know what I mean." Side-mouthed again. *God, she's annoying.*

"Well, I was about to say that he's also my boyfriend." *Wow. Did I just say that?*

"Oh, Becca, that's wonderful!" Susan, a frequent, longtime guest, clasps her hands.

"Yeah. I think so." I can't stop grinning.

"Look at her! She's glowing!" adds Denise, another longtimer and Susan's best friend.

"Shit, I'd be glowing too and walking around like I'd been on a goddamn horse for a week—if you know what I mean." Side-mouthed Shelley strikes again.

Her friend Cathy gasps and smacks her arm. "Shelley!"

"That's okay, Cathy. Really," I say with a laugh. And the inquisition begins.

"How long?"

I tell them we're pretty new.

"Is he the one?"

I'm having fun finding out, I say.

"How often are you having fun finding out?" Shelley asks. "And how long does it last?" Cathy smacks her again. I bite my smile back and wave the words away.

"The details might be more than your imagination can take, Shelley."

"I wouldn't say that. My imagination can take a lot. So if you're ever in the market for a new best friend to talk to about all your sexcapades with him—" she puts her hand up to her ear like it's a phone and mouths *call me.*

"Shelley! How does your husband handle you?" I grin.

"He doesn't. That's why I was interested in your boyfriend handling me . . . well, I'm still interested." Side-mouthed. She whistles and starts fanning herself as Grayson strolls into the room, winks at me, and gives me a kiss.

"Hello, darling. Are you hens still at it in here?"

"Grayson, you can't call my guests hens," I hiss through my teeth.

"Sorry, I'm British," he says to the ladies. "That usually works for an excuse," he whispers against my ear.

"Oh my God! He's fucking *British*, too? Girl, you hit the jackpot," Shelley says.

"Honestly, Shelley!" Cathy sounds pissed now.

"Ka-ching!" I say loudly and smile up at Grayson. He laughs and kisses me again. "You know, if things don't work out between us—" his smile disappears at my quiet words. "Shelley over there just might be the woman for you."

"Really?" His eyebrows shoot up.

"Yes. She would love to be handled by you. She'd love to lay you out and, if she had you, she would be glowing and walking around like she's been on a horse for an entire week!" I say with a matter-of-fact look.

"What are you two talking about over there?" Shelley asks impatiently.

"Hold on there, doll!" Grayson smiles as he looks over at her. "She's telling me what she has planned for me tonight. I, in return, am going to explain to her all the many different ways I plan on shagging her." He winks. "Give us a moment, love, and I'll be over there to see who the 'Big Boy' in your life is!" I look away, tears in my eyes from trying the hardest I've ever tried not to laugh.

"You know, sweetheart, I think I was wrong. Shelley is definitely the one for me. I'm sorry. Really, I am. She's just what I've been looking for. Hair dyed Raggedy-Ann red, kept short and tightly curled . . . bedazzled blue track suit . . . and, are those? Oh, yes! Orthopedic shoes! She must keep nothing on but those and the glasses hanging from the chain around her neck while I'm shagging her! She'll have to be on top . . . yes . . . what a glorious sight to behold— her glasses slapping her liver-spotted titties as she rides me into the sunset." That's it. I can't hold back anymore. The laughter explodes out and I can't even breathe. *Oh no! I'm going to pee myself!*

"Excuse me!" I shout, and run to the ladies' room.

"That's what happens, ladies, when I talk to her about shagging—it sends her right into nervous giggles. Now, who is your "Big Boy," Shelley?" I hear Grayson from the bathroom. I absolutely cannot remember the last time I've laughed this hard. Seriously, two seconds from wetting myself!

I hear the door open.

"Mom, are you okay?" Morgan asks.

"Yes, sweetie. How was your riding lesson?"

"Fine. What's so funny?"

"Oh, Grayson made me laugh . . . it was big-people stuff, so ask me again in eight years," I add quickly.

"Oh, well, it's good to hear you laugh like that, Mommy. I like Grayson. Can he be your boyfriend?" She sounds hopeful.

"Yes." I flush and open the stall door. "He can and he is and I'm so glad you approve. You know, you helped me make that decision." I wash my hands and hug her.

"Yay! When are you getting married?"

At the pace we're going, probably tomorrow.

"Oh, honey, that's not something to rush into." I kiss her head. "C'mon, let's go rescue Grayson from all of those ladies out there." I grab her hand and open the door.

"Yeah, especially Shelley. She's got the hots for him." She sighs and rolls her eyes.

"Ah—there are my girls!" Grayson announces as we walk into the lounge. "Enjoy the rest of your stay, ladies." He waves goodbye to them before stepping between us and grabbing both of our hands. My heart swells. "What would you like to do, Morgy girl?" He swings her arm wildly, making her laugh.

"There's a new Disney movie I want to see." She looks unsure. He lets go of my hand and pulls out his iPhone.

"What's the name of the theater, sweetheart?" he asks, and she tells him.

Just as we cross the threshold to the store, Hazel hangs up the phone and looks up from the counter. "Becca, Claudia can't come in today. She's not feeling well," she says.

"Oh, that figures!" Morgan pouts.

"What figures?" Grayson squats down as he continues to search.

"We can't go now."

"No, that's not what I heard. I don't work here. Do you work here, Morgy? Are you on the schedule?" He raises an eyebrow. "Ha! Look at that! Is this the movie?" She nods. "Good, say bye to Mum and Aunt Hazel." He chucks her under her chin.

"Really?" Her eyes are wide with excitement.

"Mum?" He looks up at me with raised brows.

"Yes. Get your coat and go to the bathroom!" I have to yell because she's taken off already. I turn to Grayson and wrap my arms around his neck. "Thank you," I say, and give him a soft peck on the lips.

Morgan comes running back, clutching her coat, and pulls at Grayson's sweater. He looks down at her, and she starts to hand him the keys to my truck—but then pulls her hand away.

"Actually, I'll go wait in the truck while you smooch with my mother." And with that, she runs out, leaving us to our laughter.

"I think I'm just as crazy about that kid as I am her mother," Grayson says. He pulls me close.

"She's crazy about you, too. Completely thrilled that we're together. This is really nice of you to do. Thank you."

"No 'baby' at the end of that?"

"Oh, I think I'll be saying that word a lot tonight while I'm praying." I smile mischievously.

"Huh?"

I pull his head down. "Oh God, baby," I whisper in his ear. I wink and turn to walk away. "Shag you later, Gracie!" His eyelids were doing Morse code again.

The next three hours are typical of those at the end of a crop weekend: last-minute purchases, helping croppers pack, and loading cars. The rooms are already filled with skiers and foliage hunters. The fireplace crackles in the main hall, and we have cookies and fresh coffee and tea ready for the newbies. Dishes from lunch are done and put away, and the store is closed. Charlie should be coming in at any moment to see what I've cooked for dinner, and I know he'll be happy to see his favorite: German meatballs, mashed potatoes, and creamed corn. It's a nice, comforting Sunday supper for fall.

I'm just waiting for Grayson and Morgan to get home. Wow . . . I love that, Grayson and Morgan coming home from being out together because they both wanted to be with each other. They texted earlier and said they were having a great time.

I feel like I've had a week to think about everything, which I guess makes sense, since Grayson and I seem to operate on dog years. Three hours *is* like a week to us! I really hope he knows that I meant what I said before he left. I did say it playfully, but I wouldn't have said it if I didn't mean it.

George was the last man I was intimate with. And most of the time, it was forced and painful. *Becca, shut up! Stop thinking about that asshole!* Think about Grayson—lovely Grayson. Yes, it felt amazing today . . . everything, even when he had trouble stopping. I want my body to remember intimacy like that. I want to free myself from George once and for all.

"Honey—we're home!" Grayson and Morgan shout at the same time.

"In the kitchen!" I yell back.

"Mommy!" Morgan comes running in, her arms loaded with bags.

"Morgan, what is all of this?" I'm floored at the sight of it all.

"Hi, sweetheart." Gray follows her in and wraps me in a hug. "Don't be mad," he begs.

"Look, Mom!" Morgan demands my attention. I watch as she shows me a total of fifteen—I think—outfits: two dresses, hair stuff, a cowgirl hat, cowboy boots, a riding hat, riding pants, riding boots, and a charm bracelet with a heart and her birthstone (amethyst), my birthstone (aquamarine), and a garnet.

"Yours, I presume?" I arch my brow at Grayson. He looks at me sheepishly. "I just took her shopping a few weeks ago. Morgan, you shouldn't have done this."

"In her defense, we ran into her nemesis, Ashley," he says, and points his nose up in the air. "She's a terrible little brat!"

"Grayson!"

"Sorry, love, but it's true. We went into the specialty shop for me to get a pair of riding boots and there she was, little Miss Snobby Snobbikins. She saw Morgan and baited her. 'Oh, Daddy, you're the best daddy in the world! Thank you for my boots, Daddy! Maybe I should give my old boots to a girl who doesn't have a daddy. Morgan, my daddy has bought me these new boots, so I'd like to give you my old ones.'" I'm trying to hold my composure, but he's imitating a little girl's voice—in his British accent. "So I grabbed the clerk and brought him to Morgan and asked him to please measure my daughter's feet for a pair of Richmond Ladies' Field Boots. Well, Ashley's jaw was on the floor!" He smirks.

"My boots cost a hundred dollars more than hers!" Morgan jumps up and down excitedly. *Christ, those boots cost a car payment . . . a three-hundred-and-fifty-dollar car payment!*

"Grayson, this is not the kind of behavior I want to teach my daughter!" I snap.

"And then once we got started . . . we couldn't stop," he adds, this time with less excitement.

"Sounds like very familiar behavior to me!"

"Mom, please don't be mad at Daddy."

"What?"

"Sorry. I've been calling him that for the past hour at the mall. I meant Grayson." She looks down and plays with her charm bracelet.

"I just need a moment." I head out of the kitchen and up to my room. I've barely sat down on my bed when Grayson walks in.

"Grayson, this is not just about you and me. Morgan's been saying she wants you to be her father since last night. Then today you go and announce to the world that you *are*." I start to cry.

"Well . . . really . . . only to a shop in a small New Hampshire town, not the whole world, darling." He sits next to me and rubs my back.

"And you've met the biggest small mouth in this small town. Everyone will know tomorrow that Morgan has a British daddy, and when somebody calls her out on it, she's going to feel like absolute shit!" I'm sobbing now. "What if we don't work out? It would shatter her world, Gray."

"We are going to work out, sweetheart. I love you. I love her, too. I've never felt anything like it. I took great pride in calling her my daughter today, and I loved hearing her call me 'daddy.' It was the most beautiful sound I've ever heard—though I may change my mind when I hear your 'oh God, baby' later." And there it is . . . I'm laughing again. "C'mon, sweetheart, don't do this. Morgan was so excited! And she made me do something I've never done before."

"What's that—go broke?" I smirk.

"Oh, no, long time before that happens. No, I was taking a sip of my bevvie, not hurting a fly, and she asks me when we're gonna get crackin' on a sibling for her. Well, down the wrong pipe it went, then back up and out my nostrils—I about choked to death. I was a complete mess! And you know what she did?" I shake my head. "Exactly what you're doing right now. She had herself a good laugh!"

I stop to lean in and kiss him.

"C'mon, let's go help her unload her stuff in her room." I pat him on the knee and get up. "How much do I owe you for it?" *Good-*

bye, college fund.

"At least ten 'oh God, baby's. By the way, what time does Morgan go to bed?" He pulls me to him.

"Eight." The butterflies in my belly burst into their contemporary dance piece.

"Hmm. Eight it is." He kisses me before we head out the door.

I can hear Morgan crying to Hazel as we approach her room at the bottom of the stairs. I open her door.

"Please don't break up with Grayson, Mommy. I'll take everything back." She runs to me and gives me a hug. Hazel shakes her finger at Grayson.

"I'm not breaking up with him and you don't have to return your gifts." I kiss her head.

"Really?"

"Really." I wipe her tears away. "C'mon, let's go have dinner."

Charlie and Grayson get on great at dinner, which I can tell pleases Hazel. Afterward, I go to Morgan's room to help her pick out a new outfit for tomorrow. The prices appall me! I scold Morgan for letting him spend so much. She gets ready for bed and says her prayers, reminding me that I will be saying my "prayers" very soon as well.

"Good night, baby. I love you." I turn her light off.

"Wait," Grayson says as he enters her room and turns the light back on. He gives Morgan a kiss. "Good night, little sweetheart."

"Good night." Pause. "Daddy," she whispers. He kisses her again and meets me at the doorway. I turn off the light and shut her door. Grayson grabs my hand and leads me up the stairs. My knees feel like Jell-O. I'm so nervous. *I'm okay. I'm okay.*

"I ran your bath and brought you up a glass of wine, sweetheart." He kisses my hand. Again, he should've brought me the bottle.

"Thank you." We get into my room and Bocelli is already on. How sweet. He shows me to the bathroom, which is full of lit candles. It smells like vanilla and lavender.

"I'd like to bathe with you." He pulls his shirt off.

"Um . . . okay." I'm so wracked with nerves. He hands me my wine, but I barely get a sip before he takes it from me and turns me around. I feel my hair fall around my face.

"Arms up," he says into my ear, then kisses it. Up they go, along with my shirt. He rubs my shoulders and plants soft kisses on my neck. I feel my bra unclasp. His hands slip under the straps and he guides it down 'til it falls to the floor. A jolt of electricity shoots to my groin as he runs his fingers up my forearms and shoulders, down my back, around to my stomach, and then up again to cup my breasts. His thumbs tease my nipples until they peak. I moan lightly and rest my body back against his chest. I can feel him growing behind me.

"You okay?" He sounds breathy, like he's trying to keep his voice steady.

"Uh-huh." That's all I can manage. He lowers his hands to my jeans. I hear them unzip. He squats and tugs at them, and I step out. He bites lovingly at my bum before he pulls my panties down and bites me again. *All Sybils are on deck, pole dancing in slutty lingerie.* He stands up and turns me around.

"God, you're beautiful," he gasps. I bite my bottom lip and reach for his jeans. He takes a sharp breath in through his teeth as I trace my finger across the hem, then unzip and pull them down. I kiss him across his chest and tease his nipples the way he teased mine. I can hear the air rush in and out of his nose, the soft sounds escaping his throat, and feel the rapid rise and fall of his ribs. I travel down his chest and stomach with my mouth, playfully biting him along the way. "Becca." He pulls me away from his happy trail, then grabs my hand and guides me into the tub. I submerge fully into the hot, scented water, never breaking eye contact. My eyes finally wander away from his as he unveils his manhood.

Apparently Rocco should no longer be the focus of my "Big Boy" page.

Grayson climbs in behind me. He moves my hair to one side, allowing his mouth access to my neck. I reach for my hair tie and pull my hair back up in a messy bun.

"I like it down," he protests weakly.

"I'll let it down when we get out. It'll be too much to dry." I look over my shoulder at him. He nods and offers me a shy half smile, then grabs a washcloth and soaks it. He brings it above my shoulders and wrings it out over them. I squirt some body wash on the cloth when he offers it to me, and he lathers it up and softly massages my shoulders. I close my eyes and relish in his touch, the hot bath, the candles, and the soft music in the background. Gray pulls me back to rest against his chest. He holds my right arm out, running the washcloth down the length of it. Then the left arm. He continues with my breasts and my stomach, and then he lifts my right leg up to run the cloth down it. He places my leg over his before he moves on to the left. I turn my face into his neck as he descends between my legs with it, meticulously washing—driving me mad. He ditches the cloth as he raises his right knee to part my legs more. His mouth covers mine, his tongue sliding across the slit of my lips, willing them to part. My right hand reaches up and I grab a fistful of his hair, pulling him harder to me as I allow his tongue's intrusion. His fingers tickle the skin of my inner right thigh as they glide down it, into the water and over my sex.

"Stop," he mutters against my mouth. His left hand grasps the inside of my left thigh to prevent my wriggling as he circles my clitoris, his fingers dancing against me. I turn my face into his neck again and bite gently, trying to keep my breath steady as his finger slides down toward my entrance. The anticipation is making me dizzy with want. I bite at his neck again and push my hips up slightly to encourage him.

"Ahh!" I gasp as two of his very long fingers enter me. He palms my clitoris, giving me the complete workout.

"Don't fight it, sweetheart," he says breathlessly in my ear, his fingers gripping my left leg to keep me open. I'm lost. I feel out of control. "C'mon, Becca . . . c'mon, sweetheart." His voice coaxes me, my rise. "Pray for me, darling."

"Oh God, baby . . . oh God!" I cry from the pleasure that washes over my body. His mouth covers mine again, helping me through the intensity of my last quakes. He slowly pulls his fingers out and concentrates solely on kissing me. Our tongues caress each other through a cycle of playfulness, urgency, and reluctance. *Oh God, I want him.* The nerves are gone and I'm running on pure adrenaline. A soft giggle escapes me. Funny—just twenty-four hours ago, I was in this tub working over my grief at him doing something far less offensive.

"Here, sweetheart," he says against my lips, handing me my wine. I take in a long sip and place it back down. He pulls me to him. "Five more minutes and then we'll get into bed." He kisses my shoulder.

"I'm ready to go now," I say, a little embarrassed.

"Five seconds it is." He hits the drain and stands up, pulling me with him. I grab a towel and dry his chest as he wraps me in one. We step out and I continue to dry him off. He grabs the towel from me, then pushes me out in front of him and smacks my bum. I pull my hair tie out—as promised—and dim the lights. Grayson pulls me to him and we stare at each other intently, our feet gliding toward the bed like we're dancing a slow waltz.

Feeling the edge of the bed at the back of my legs, I sit and begin to crawl back on my elbows. When I can reach the stereo remote, I grab it and set "Lullaby" by The Cure on loop.

"You like The Cure, sweetheart?" he asks, climbing on top of me.

"Yes." It comes out as a whisper—I'm intoxicated by his scent and the music.

"Why this song?" He searches my body with his hands and follows with his mouth.

"Um . . . I'll tell you later." I run my fingers through his hair, encouraging him as he travels down.

"Interesting choice, love." He bites at my inner right thigh. What's with all the biting? Actually, I kind of like it.

"Oh . . . um." I clutch the sheets as his tongue caresses the most sensitive part of my body. He begins a wicked cycle of teasing, biting and licking. My body goes wild. He holds my hips to try and control their movement.

"Becca, darling, you taste wonderful." He groans and places two fingers inside of me again, caressing my sweet spot. "You are so ready for me." *Yeah—no kidding!*

"Oh, no. Oh God, Gray—oh God, baby!" I muffle my scream with a pillow.

"What did you say, sweetheart?" He pulls the pillow away. I can sense his grin. He's so proud of himself.

"I said, 'oh God, baby.'" I kiss him as he lays his full weight on top of me and wedges himself in between my legs.

"I'm going to make love to you now, sweetheart." And before I can say a word, he thrusts inside me. I grab his shoulders and wait for my lungs to exhale. He pushes further and I whimper. "Christ, Becca!" He grits his teeth. What did he expect? It's been a long time. "Are you all right?" he asks, and touches my face.

"Yes." I lower my hands to the small of his back and kiss his beauty mark. He glides out and pushes back in. We find our groove together and I feel as if I've been transported to another dimension. *He feels so good . . . so right.* I'm lost in his kiss, the touch of his hands, the feeling my body is experiencing. "Oh God, baby . . . I love you." The words, foreign to me, ignite a fire in him. His thrusts become more powerful. He holds my right leg up and buries himself deeper inside me. I muffle my cries in his neck and meet his thrusts. "Please, Gray . . . please, baby," I beg.

"C'mon, sweetheart, say your prayers." In response, I grab his ass, helping to deepen the thrusts, and squeeze myself around him every time he pulls out. "Bec . . . oh . . . what ..."

"Shh . . . let's pray together, baby." I bite his lip and squeeze again. Within moments, we're stifling each other's moans with our mouths and I feel him spill inside me. The weight of his body crashes down on mine. "Oh God, baby," I whisper in his ear.

"Becca, you take my breath away." He pushes my hair out of my face, then pulls out and tugs me onto his chest. *All the Sybils are smoking a cig. But Cautionary Sybil jumps up in a panic and looks down.*

"Gray." I try to remain calm.

"Yes?" He kisses my forehead.

"Um, where's . . . did you . . . please tell me you used protection." There—I spit it out!

"Let's get some sleep, sweetheart." He squeezes me.

"You are, indeed, a very selfish man!" I can feel tears filling my eyes.

"I know, sweetheart. Forgive me." He lifts my chin and pecks at my lips softly, again and again. The tip of his tongue begs for them to part, and they do. He deepens the kiss and holds me tightly to him. I'm like putty in his hands. He takes me again and manages to get those last "Oh God, baby"s out of me, and I go to sleep thoroughly shagged, exhausted, and defeated.

Chapter Five

"Ugh . . . bloody hell." Grayson grumbles at the sound of the alarm.

"My sentiments exactly." I yawn and sit at the edge of the bed. *Jesus, I'm sore.* I turn off the alarm on my way to the shower.

"When can you come back to bed, sweetheart?" I hear him ask as I start the water. I just ignore him. What is he playing at, anyway? Does he want to get me pregnant? I need to get away today to think. Maybe I'll take Rocco out. I haven't ridden him in two weeks. The glass door to the shower opens. *Really? C'mon!* "Becca, are you okay?" He pulls me against him.

"Grayson, I'd really appreciate the chance to shower by myself, please," I try to say as calmly as I can.

"Sorry, sweetheart, but I believe in the conservation of water," he states cheerfully and grabs some body wash. I know he's trying to get me out of my foul mood, but it's just not going to happen.

"What about the conservation of our relationship?" I ask. He nudges me over to get under the water and rinse off, then walks out of the shower and the bathroom. All righty, then! I reward myself with a long, hot shower. I step out of the bathroom wrapped up in my towel, only to find the bedroom empty and a note on the bed.

Dear Ice Queen Becca,

I do hope your shower alone was a hot one so you can

melt back into the warm, beautiful woman I bedded last night!

Grayson

Bedded? Who the hell uses that term these days? And ice queen, huh? Wow. I get dressed in chocolate-brown jeans and throw on a rust-orange cotton V-neck with long sleeves, then blow-dry my wavy hair. I throw on some makeup and put my riding boots on. I should have enough time to put the quiches in the oven before waking Morgan up.

"Morning, Hazel." I sigh as I walk into the kitchen. I quickly glance over at Grayson. He's leaning up against the counter by the sink and finishing a glass of OJ, staring at me over the brim of the glass.

"Becca! Oh, good! I couldn't remember how many quiches we were making this morning." Hazel holds her hands out to show me how many pie shells I've already baked.

"Yes. I'm making all of these because I'm going to town and I want to give Henry one. Tommy, too." I pull out the eggs and the other ingredients. After tying my hair up, I make four Lorraines, four Mad Scrappers, and four Meat Lovers. Grayson sits at the kitchen table watching me. Neither of us says a word. Hazel sets up the granola, yogurt, and cereals. I get the bowl of fresh fruit.

"Can I help you, Aunt Hazel?" Grayson walks over to her just as she manages to open the bag of mini bagels.

"I'm good, dear, but why don't you ask Becca what she wants."

"I would, but I don't think Becca knows what she wants," he snaps, the words directed more toward me. I give him no reaction whatsoever as I grab the dishes to bring out to the buffet.

"Gracie, get the silverware caddy," Hazel suggests. I set the dishes down, take the caddy from him so I can restock it, then grab the linens and begin to cover the tables. *Let's see . . . that's forty-two people minus the six of us . . . that makes thirty-six.* Okay, six tables. The napkins are next. *I wish he would stop watching me!* I head back into the kitchen to start bringing trays out. Grayson goes and gets a tray as well.

"Where would you like me to put these, Becca? Besides up my arse?" He smirks.

Damn it! I bite my lip to hold off a smile and point to the tray's home. He places it and grabs my arm, turning me to him. He chucks my chin and bends down to kiss me. I turn away.

"Do you regret last night?" He's barely audible.

"No," I say quickly. A look of relief comes over his face.

"Then what is it, Becca? It can't possibly be what I did last night because you let me do it twice thereafter." He has a point, but the damage had been done. What would stopping have accomplished?

"I can't talk about it right now. People are going to be coming down for breakfast." I try to pull away.

"Becca. Becca!" he calls after me.

"Everything all right?" Hazel seems cautious, which is unlike her.

"Yes, it's fine."

"Grayson was very upset this morning. He said he was very confused. Does that make sense to you?" There she is . . . good ole Nancy Drew.

"Yes, because I feel the same way."

"Becca, he's head over heels. I know it. He's never felt like this. But he, like you, is used to the way his life normally is." *Oh, Dear Abby ...*

"Well, there's a bit of difference, Hazel. If I was out in California, I would not be at his job all day causing distractions. I can't get away from him to think things through." My voice is barely above a whisper.

"You two are moving too fast. That's your problem. Slow down," she warns.

"Have you met your nephew?" *Did I just say that out loud? And with so much snark?*

"Becca, you've said no to all the other guys that come through here. You can say no to my nephew." Again, has she even met him?

"What other guys?" Grayson speaks up.

"Oh, Grayson, she's got every guy in town hot for her. Don't be so silly—she's a beautiful girl!" she says.

"Hazel, you're exaggerating. Honestly!" I say.

"What guys?" he repeats.

"Grayson Michael James! You watch your tone with me!" she yells at him. *Holy shit!* I try to pick my jaw up off the floor. I have never heard Hazel, sweet, grandmotherly Hazel, yell like that.

"Sorry, Auntie. What guys?" he asks again. I mouth "wuss" at him.

"Oh, Grayson, knock it off. Green is not your color." And with that, she storms out of the kitchen.

"What guys, Becca?'

"Oh, grow up, Grayson!" I storm out.

GRAYSON

Is there something in the fucking water this morning? I went to sleep one happy bloke and woke up to this nonsense! Did I go around killing puppies in my sleep? They win! I'm getting out of here for the day. Let 'em sort themselves out. *Christ!*

I sit in the lounge area and call my personal assistant, Carol, to find a car service for me. I apologize profusely for waking her as is it four in the morning on the West Coast. I must remember to bring her back a nice gift.

I have half an hour to pack my duffel bag for the gym and surf the web for some ideas to keep me out of the house . . . inn . . . whatever. I wish my mates were here now. They're going to think I've gone mad. I may have to agree with them.

"Grayson." My aunt interrupts my thoughts.

"Yes, Auntie?"

"Becca needs to see you in her office." My aunt is looking at me lovingly again. They're crazy, the pair of 'em! I head over to the store. I hope she doesn't expect me to go over everything with her now—Christ! When I reach her office, I see she's got her head in her hands.

"Becca?"

"Hi." She looks up. "I need to place an order today. Actually, a few orders to different places. You told me not to touch anything."

"Place the orders tomorrow." *Really?*

"I can't do that. The shipping will be higher," she argues.

"Bloody hell, Becca, order it tomorrow. I'll pay the shipping, for fuck's sake!"

"What's that about?" She jerks her head back defensively.

"Oh, the pair a ya are driving me crazy! I don't have time to go over everything right now. I have to go pack." I turn and leave the office.

"Pack?" She runs out and grabs my arm to stop me. I look down and see panic on her face.

"For the gym, sweetheart, but it's nice to see you would be upset if I left." I touch her cheek with the back of my hand.

"Of course I would be, baby." Ah. There she is. And this time she doesn't turn away from my kiss. She asks me how long I'll be. I tell her a few hours. I can't stay the whole day away from her. She hugs me tightly and I breathe in the scent of her hair.

"Becca, sweetheart." I kiss her hair. "You are going to have to learn to tell me what you are feeling and thinking. You can't just push me away to figure it out or until you are over it."

"I tried to tell you this morning that I wanted time to myself. I have to think things through, sort everything out and make sense of it, before I go blurting out my confusion." It's hard to stay focused on what she is saying when she's looking up at me with those gorgeous green eyes.

"I gave you the time, Becca, if you recall correctly." God, I just want to take her upstairs and hear her pray again. Incidentally, I was right. Becca's "oh God, baby" is now the most beautiful sound I've ever heard. Sorry, Morgy girl.

"Grayson, are you listening to me?" Becca slaps my chest. I close my eyes, trying to fight off my arousal. It's not easy, between her slap and the memory of sweet prayers last night. It would not be good to show up at the gym with "things" poking about!

"I'm sorry, darling. What?" I ask, finally opening my eyes.

"I said . . . yes, you gave me time to think, but then you left me an insulting note."

"Insulting? It wasn't meant to insult you. I was just calling you out on your behavior. Listen, sweetheart, I know America is the land of sugarcoating, but England produces blunt chaps. I won't sugarcoat anything for you. It's not in my nature. If you feel insulted because somebody called you out on your behavior, then I suggest you don't behave that way anymore."

Bloody hell, there she goes, storming off again! Well, I'm not chasing her. The car is here. Ten minutes early. *Shit.*

I go and grab my gym bag from my room and head back down to find Morgan on her way to the kitchen.

"Good morning, little sweetheart. You look lovely." I give her a great big hug and a kiss on the head. She waves me down to her level. I oblige.

"My daddy bought me this outfit," she whispers in my ear. My heart does a backflip. I love this girl. I want to be her father so badly. It is the most unique and unexpected feeling I've ever had. She even looks like she could be mine. Like me, she has dark brown hair and dark brown eyes. She looks just like Becca . . . thankfully. Someday she will be my daughter and I will never tell a soul that she is not my blood.

"Your father must love you very much," I whisper back and hug her tightly. I release her to find tears in her eyes. I've upset her. Did I go too far? "Morgy girl, what's the matter?"

"I'm just happy. My dreams are coming true. I mean, you're right up there with Disney World." She smiles.

"You want to go to Disney World?" I palm her face.

"Oh, yes!"

"I'll talk to Mummy then." I kiss her forehead. I know Becca has already set a trip for February. I've seen the plans and itinerary she booked. Pretty modest—she actually can afford more—but I'd like to upgrade everything for them. I wipe Morgan's tears away and shoo her off to breakfast.

"Morning, baby." I turn back, thinking Becca is calling to me, but she's greeting Morgan. *Baby* is for family only—it's sacred. Her feelings for me are sacred. Ugh, I can be such an arse! I head over to Becca and Morgan, secretly begging her not to brush me off or ignore me.

"I'm off to the gym then, sweetheart. I'll go over everything with you when I come back if you have the time. I love you, baby." And she bites her lovely lip to hold back a smile. "Sound weird coming from me?" I ask. It felt foreign.

"Yes, but I know what you're trying to say." She grins and reaches up on her tippy toes to kiss me.

"Is that how you're going to kiss on your wedding day when the guy says *you may kiss the bride*?" Morgan asks, as if she wants us to pass the butter or know what time it is. Becca pulls away, her cheeks pink with embarrassment.

"No, Morgy girl, I'm going to kiss her like this." And I dip Becca back and kiss her dramatically. Morgan laughs. Becca does, too. It's clear . . . I'm off, as the Americans say, *the shit list*. "I've got to go, darling—the car's here." I pull her upright and give her another quick kiss.

"Don't tire yourself out." She grins mischievously.

"I won't. I've got you for that, sweetheart." I whisper in her ear and kiss her again.

I'm leaving a very happy man. Not only am I off the shit list, but I find myself back on the shag list. I like that list much better! Speaking of shagging, I must order a king-sized bed for Becca's room. I hate having my feet hang over. I'll do that today after my workout. Actually, come to think of it, I've got several things to do today. I'm going to need a couple of hours in my room to work on what I have planned for Becca.

It's a chilly morning, but I love the crisp fall air. I wouldn't mind living here, especially with my three favorite girls. I'll have to travel to the West Coast a lot. I can't very well move my headquarters. But, I will build a satellite office. That would bring many jobs here. I'm sure there are many new business prospects in New England that I haven't even uncovered yet. Of course, I can write songs no matter where I am. I'm even feeling more inspired to write—a song hit me in the middle of the night last night. I had to go into the bathroom to jot down the music and lyrics. Yes, I must order a grand piano today as well. Lots to do! Lots to plan! I think Becca will be thrilled when she sees what I have planned. She's a very bright businesswoman. She's just a little misguided and inexperienced. I'm looking forward to going over everything. But first, I must kick my arse in the gym!

"Hi, Aunt Hazel. Are we feeling more cheerful this late morn?" I give her my biggest smile and close the door behind me.

"Oh, stop it." She smacks my arm playfully and hugs me. "How are you and Becca now?"

"Fantastic! Where is my beautiful girl?" I wish she had greeted me at the door.

"She went out with Rocco . . . her horse, Grayson, before you turn green again."

My surge of anger must've come across my face. Honestly, I have never been the jealous type. I think I've gone mad!

"When did she leave?"

"About half an hour ago. She usually goes for two hours, but she said she might not last that long today because she's sore. I guess she slept funny." My aunt is completely oblivious to our shenanigans. I grin obnoxiously. "What's that look for?" she asks.

"What? Oh, sorry."

"Well, I have to go make Charlie the special tuna salad he likes." She glances at her watch before she turns to leave.

"Special tuna, just for Charlie? What about the rest of us?" I bait her.

"You can have some, too. He likes it a special way: celery, onions, romaine lettuce, salt and pepper, on a croissant, and Bob's your uncle!" She smiles.

"Oh Auntie, it's been a long time since someone's finished with 'and Bob's your uncle'!" I laugh. "It's good to be around family. And speaking of uncles, I had a dream about Uncle Harold last night." I lie because my aunt believes in this rubbish.

"Oh?" Her eyes are wide, waiting for a message from the other side.

"Yes. We were, as a matter of fact, standing right here. Odd. He said to me that he's okay and my parents send their love. Then he told me to tell you that he loves you and to 'stop being a silly old woman. He's a good ole chap!' Auntie, he was pointing in this direction when he said to stop being silly." I point in the direction of the stable. "Do you know what this all means? I tell you, I haven't dreamt about Uncle Harold in years!" I can't believe I just came up with all of that.

"Yes, it makes perfectly wonderful sense. Thank you, Gracie!" She smiles through her tears, hugs me, and runs off like she'd just dropped twenty years. If my calculations are correct, that ought to keep me on Becca's shag list for a while.

Humph . . . off to work. Carol should be calling me soon with the availability of the best architects in New England. My financial advisor is coming in two days. My mortgage guy will call in an hour to crunch all the numbers. Hopefully Becca doesn't check on me. I need everything set in place before I talk to her.

BECCA

"Sorry, Rocco." I kiss face and pat his shoulder. "I'll make sure Charlie takes you out tomorrow." I give him an apple. "I did last an hour and a half out of the two hours I usually ride." He walks away. I think he knows he's not the only man in my life anymore. Oh well, he'll get over it. I better head in. Poor Hazel and Claudia have been picking up my very unusual slack the past few days. At this rate, I'll be paying Claudia overtime. Probably the next three weeks. I'm going to run that girl ragged! I'm sure she'd be happy with the extra cash and, of course, I'm happy for the extra time with my family. *My family.* That sounds so nice.

Cautionary Sybil shakes her head at me and points to her ring finger. I tell her to fuck off. *She shows me her letter of resignation.* I accept. Good riddance!

Let's see where that handsome non-husband of mine is.

"Hey, Hazel, I'll be down in a minute to help set up lunch. I just need to change. Have you seen Grayson?" Wow, she looks very chipper! I can't remember the last time I saw her humming about, and with a smile, no less!

"He's upstairs in his room, dear. I'm just about done with the setup, so take your time." She hums along back to the kitchen. Wow. Um, okay. I think I'll just pop in by Grayson to tell him I'm back. I should change first though.

I put on my black yoga pants with a pink sports tank top. I have my ballroom-dance lesson with Will at one this afternoon. Thank God he comes to me! Although I know it's because he likes to use my wedding hall, which is an oversized barn I converted a few years back. He's always trying to convince me to add ballroom-dancing weekends—with him handling the ballroom part. As it is, he teaches a lot of beginner classes here for my guests who request it. There is a ton of interest in it because of *Dancing With the Stars*, but I just can't add one more thing to schedule. I don't spend enough time with Morgan as it is. I love our crop weekends, but when you have a whole weekend dedicated to an event, so much goes into it. We'd have to offer dinner, which raises the food expense, and I'd need to hire another chef—Adam can only do the two weekends a month. I book weddings on non-crop weekends, so it would be more of a hassle than it would be a help. Besides, financially, it would be point-less, as I'd have to pay Will.

Despite hearing the irritated tone in Grayson's voice on the other side of the door, I decide to knock. He opens it abruptly.

"Carol, hang on," he says into his phone, then takes a deep breath and smiles my way. "Hello, sweetheart. Did you have a good ride?" His smile becomes ginormous, as if he's remembering something. *Oh, you cocky bastard! I know what you're playing at!*

"Yes. I had a wonderful ride. Although I think I've left Rocco terribly confused." I bait him.

"Why's that, darling?"

"Well, usually when we do the small jumps over fallen tree limbs on our favorite trail, I say 'Good boy, Rocco!' but today ..." I leave him hanging.

"Today what?"

"Today I said," I pull him down to whisper in his ear, "oh God, baby."

"Carol, I'll have to call you back in twenty minutes or so. Work on what we talked about. Bye." He hits "end" on the phone and locks the door in one motion. He pulls me to him, knocking the breath out of my lungs with his kiss. He picks me up and throws me onto the bed. Before I can say *boo*, he's pulled my pants off.

"Grayson, wait! We can't . . . I—" I can't get a word in. "Condom!" I pull away from his mouth. "Grayson!" I gasp as he thrusts himself inside of me. I can barely catch my breath; his thrusts are so powerful and fast. I can't even keep up. I resolve to just hold on for the ride. I don't know how much time goes by, but Grayson's pace eventually slows. He's clenching his teeth. I know this look and I feel the reason for it. He slams his now sweaty head onto my chest. I'd yell at him and push him off if I had any strength or could catch my breath. It's clear to me that he has an agenda. The butterflies' contemporary dance dramatically ends with a *thump* at the bottom of my belly. My heartbeat switches from an erratic tempo to a nervous one.

"Gray, get off of me. I'm going to be sick!"

He rolls to the side and I jump off the bed, grabbing my pants on the way to the bathroom. I make it just in time. If this were pea soup, I would need an exorcism right now.

"I'd come in there, sweetheart, but I'd be of no use. I have a weak stomach. Do you want me to get Aunt Hazel for you?" *Is he for real?* Oh, yes, please send Aunt Hazel in. I'm sure the sight of my bare bum leaping in the air with every heave will be quite the sight for her! Let's not mention your potential offspring running down my legs! Yeah, that'll help maintain the "good girl next door" image she's always had of me. Right.

"No," is what I manage to say. It seems to me that I'm finished here. I clean up "everywhere." *Did I just use quotation marks in my own head? God, I'm losing my mind.*

"Sweetheart, are you okay now? Listen, that's work on the phone. I've got to take it. I'll come down and show you the office in an hour or two." I know I just heard the words, but I can't believe my ears. *Is he fucking kicking me out?*

Oh, hell no! *Ghetto Sybil has her knuckle rings on and she's pounding her fist into her hand.* I open the door and hear Grayson tell Carol to hold on as he walks toward me. As soon as he's close enough, I jump and punch him in the face. Then I continue to the door, leaving him shell-shocked.

"You know, a real lady would have been satisfied with giving an open-handed slap!" he snaps

"Well, a real lady's never had to fight like I've had to!" I snap back and slam the door. *Ghetto Sybil yells, "I'm from Jersey, bitch—that's how we slap a fool!"* Damn straight, Ghetto "S"! *Country Sybil holds up a box of tissues and nods toward my room.* I close and lock the door behind me, and head into the shower to wash and let the sound muffle my crying.

I think about calling Will to cancel, but decide against it. I'm not going to spend the day cooped up in my room because Grayson's being an asshole. He is the most impetuous man I've ever met in my life! He clearly does not think or reflect on things that have caused several of our issues. I take this time to make him a list.

> Grayson,
> Here are the reasons why you are pissing me off! Please take them all into serious consideration.
>
> Thank you, Becca

1. Women have the right to choose. I do not choose to be pregnant at this time or anytime soon. I do not believe in abortions for myself unless in an extreme circumstance. Therefore, you are forcing me to possibly carry your child—unacceptable!
2. You can be blunt without being stupid about it! Blunt enough for you?

3. In two days, you've managed to make my daughter believe her dreams of a father are coming true. You can take my heart and shatter it into a million pieces, but don't fuck with hers! If you do, I will show you just how unladylike I can be!

4. Speaking of being a "lady." You don't put a woman you "love" in a "wham bam, thank you ma'am" situation, then tell her she's not a real lady because she gives you the wallop you deserve, you asshole! Let's not forget the shooing me out after said tryst!

5. Why don't you take the time to look up PTSD? I can guarantee you'll have the whole night to do it!

6. ~~I wish I never called you "baby"!~~

There! I'll put it under his door and head to the barn to meet Will.

Will always makes me laugh. I could definitely use some cheering up. The only problem with my weekly lesson is it's always accompanied by a request for a date. I was excited this morning to report to him that I'm off the market so he could finally pursue other options, but now, I don't even know if I can say that. I guess I won't. I'll just reply with something sweet, like "I wouldn't want to break all of the other girls' hearts. It's too much of a burden to bear." Yeah, that's a new one. I'll go with that. Truth is, from what I've heard, he could care less about the other women in town. He's made it very well known that he only has eyes for me. I've also heard that I'm the only one he does Latin dances with because it allows us to get "hot and sexy" and he loves to watch my ass. Mental eye roll! Whatever. Those are my favorite anyway—they're fun.

"See you later, Hazel." I wave with my dance shoes in my hand and run outside to meet Will. He gives me a big "I don't want to let go of you" hug, kisses me on the cheek, and grabs my hand to head over to the hall. He actually is a great-looking guy. Wavy, light brown hair, blue eyes, full lips, and fair skin—plus, he's funny as well. He would be a great catch. If only he were a complete asshole, because apparently, that's what I'm attracted to.

"Hey, so, I want to rehearse the rumba routine again for this weekend's showcase. You're still on board, right?" Will places a piece of my fallen hair behind my ear. If Grayson saw that, he would have a fit!

"Of course I am. Don't forget: I'm promoting my business, too." I smile and go over to the stereo to put in our CD in for the rumba, then put my dance shoes on and hit "play." "L'Amour Toujours" by Gigi D'Agostino blasts through the sound system and we begin our very sexy, sultry rumba.

Chapter Six

GRAYSON

"What . . . the . . . *fuck*? Carol, I have to go. I'll call you later. Yes, everything is all right. I don't know. Let me go. Bye."

I can't believe Becca punched me in the face. She's mad! She's absobloodylutely mad! I can't believe she said that—I'm not George! I would never hurt her intentionally and certainly not the way he hurt her!

I walk over to the mirror. Damn, she got me good. My cheek is bright red. Had I'd been an inch shorter, she would've given me a nice shiner.

And why did she get sick like that? That was so weird. Listening to it from outside the door, I thought I was going to follow suit. I can't stand vomit. Doing it, hearing it, or seeing it.

Should I cancel the architect for tomorrow? No. No, I can't. I'll just get her out of the house somehow if she's still mad. I don't even know how to fix this. Again, she doesn't tell me what she's thinking! Christ, I know she's mad, but why? Ah, I suppose I do know why.

But to react that way? Ugh . . . bloody hell! I grab my convulsing phone off the bed before it self-destructs.

"Yes!" I answer it. "Right! Yes. That's the best you can do? She doesn't have that much left. Her credit is impeccable! What's that you say? All right then. Yes, I'll do that. Okay, draw up the papers. Very good then. Ugh . . . Peter, be a good chap and draw up both offers. Thanks, mate! You, too."

For the first time since ever, I feel very unsure. I want to give her the world. But she's so stubborn and independent; I may be doing all of this for nothing and just gaining another argument. Well, it's not like I'm forcing her hand in anything. Okay . . . maybe one thing. Which is partly or solely why she's pissed. Why am I doing this? It's completely out of character for me. This week I found love. Next week, I think I'll find a therapist. If I actually said that to someone, they would laugh and probably say, "I know what you mean, mate!" But I'm serious. She's got me mad! I need to clear my head. I head to the door; a walk will do me good.

I see a square envelope on the carpet as I approach the door. Bloody hell! Why does she slip notes under my door instead of just talking to me? I pick it up. Still mad . . . not scented with her perfume. I don't want to open it. What if she's calling it off? *Be a man, Grayson!* Right! Opening an unscented note from the woman I love who's possibly about to crush me. Here we go. It's a list. Okay.

1. She's right, but I have this incredible and absolutely insane need for her to have my child. I don't know what to do here. Well, I know what to do, I just can't. Maybe I'll work on persuading her; then I'm not taking her decision away. I think I'm off my rocker! What the hell is wrong with me?
2. Hmm . . . I have to think about this.
3. I love Morgan! I would never do anything to hurt her. I certainly don't want to hurt Becca. I should've never said what I did. I was stunned and pissed.
4. Oh. I didn't think about that. If she only knew I was sending

her away to work on my surprise for her.

5. Um. Okay. Oh . . . off the shag list and definitely back on the shit list!

6. Oh no. No! Please tell me she crossed that out because she didn't mean it, and not because she had no number seven.

I actually feel my heart breaking. This is it. This is what they mean by "heartbreak." I feel as if I'm going to be sick. No. She crossed it out! She didn't cross it out well enough for me not to see it, though. Is this a game? "I want to hurt you but I really don't mean it"? I'm so confused. I need to go for a drive.

I head over to the table by the window to shut my laptop down. I glance out quickly and see Becca walking out of the store. Where is she going?

"Who the fuck is *that*, and why is she in his arms?" I ask aloud. Look at him, smelling her fucking hair and savoring it! She's holding his bloody hand and going for a walk? Look at her fucking laughing with him. She just shattered me and she's off laughing with another bloke? I rush out of my room and down the stairs. I'll rip his fucking head off!

"Aunt Hazel!" I snap. "Sorry," I say quickly. "Who's that bloke Becca's with?"

"Grayson, honey, what happened to your face?" She tries to touch it, but I pull away.

"Auntie, please—who is that?" My fists close tightly as I wait for her answer.

"Gracie, calm down. It's just Will. He's her friend and dance instructor. They're going to the hall out back for her lesson." She's looking at me like I've gone mad. Well, in all fairness, I have.

"Will? Is that the bloke who's telling the whole town that Becca's his girl and eventually she will give in to his charms?" My face is hot with rage.

"Um . . . yes, but Grayson, she has no interest in him. She loves you," she tries to reassure me. It doesn't help.

I run out and head to the hall. Inside, they're dancing—it looks like the rumba. A very sexy, over-the-top rumba. Oh, yes. I remember Morgan saying he loves Latin dances with Becca because he enjoys watching her bum. I can see his point. God, look at her go—she's fantastic! I decide to wait out the dance instead of barging in like a raving lunatic.

I can feel my fists pumping open and shut whenever he touches her body. Their hips gyrating. His hands on her bum. I am moments away from losing it. She runs her hands through his hair, bringing his face close to hers. Then the song's done. Torture's over. What the bloody hell? I watch as Will rests his forehead against hers. She shakes her head slightly as he pulls her closer. I can't make out it his words. She's trying to pull away. Good girl. Will leans in to kiss her. I'm off like somebody's shot the gun at a race.

"Keep your bloody fucking hands off of her!" I yell as I push him so hard he flies down to the ground.

"Grayson!" Becca gasps. I ignore her.

"Who the hell are you?" Will asks, shocked as hell.

"I'm her boyfriend, you arsehole!"

"Becca, I just said all of that stuff to you. Why didn't you tell me you have a boyfriend?"

"You didn't tell him?" I feel my heart drop again as I stare at her in disbelief. Her silence is deafening. "Right!" I say through clenched teeth and turn on my heel to walk away. I think I've made a big enough arse out of myself.

"Grayson, what's wrong?" Aunt Hazel asks as I walk through the door.

"I'm going home tomorrow, Auntie. I'm sorry. I can't stay." I hug her and, because she's raised me since I was fifteen, allow myself to cry a little into her neck. "Sorry." I wipe snot on my sleeve. *Christ, Grayson, pull yourself together! What is the matter with you?* "I'll be up in my room. " I head up. I feel destroyed. Several minutes pass and there is a knock at my door. I ignore it, but it opens anyhow.

Becca stands there, dangling her master key like she's revealing the secret to a magic trick.

"Go away!" I snap.

"Um, Hazel just gave me a 'what for,' and . . . um, she quit on me. Gray, I thought we made a pact." Her chin quivers. "I thought we said that we would not put her in a position to choose sides."

"No, you said that. Besides, she'll always choose me because I'm her real family, not you." Take that, Becca Campbell!

"Oh." She sits on the bed next to me. "She said you were leaving tomorrow. Grayson, first of all, I didn't tell him because he wouldn't let me get a word in edgewise, and second, I wasn't sure if you still wanted me." Her voice cracks. "He commented on how loose my movements were and how much more sensual I am today. He was right. It was because I could still feel you inside of me and I was moving my body to the way you make me feel when you are touching me. I was able to let go more. He took it the wrong way and thought I was finally giving in to him. I wasn't, Gray. I wasn't trying to lead him on."

I close my eyes as Becca softly covers the side of my face and neck with sweet little kisses. She's crushed me over and over again in one hour's time. She compared me to George. She punched me. She said she wished she never called me "baby." I'm so mad and so hard for her all at the same time! Talking about still feeling me inside of her did it. I'm all over the place. Here I am, moving heaven and earth for her, and she's treating me like this? No. I'm furious and she's going to know it! She leans over my face to find my beauty mark. I grab her under her chin and squeeze her cheeks as I lift her off of me.

"Don't you ever fucking touch me there again! That is sacred to me, and I take it back!" I yell.

A look of fear comes over her face.

"I'm sorry. I'm sorry, Grayson . . . please." I let go of her face and push her down onto the bed. I pull her pants off and kneel above her, between her legs. She watches me as I slowly unbuckle my belt.

"Take your top off, Becca," I demand flatly. She takes it off without the slightest hesitation. "Bra, too." I pull my pants off and stare down at her. *God, she's so beautiful.* "You like feeling me inside of you?" I ask as I start to flick lightly at her clitoris.

"Yes." I hear her breath catch.

"Do you like this?" I tease her more.

"Yes."

"How about this?" I insert two fingers inside of her. She's already wet.

"Yes," she practically cries.

"Is this from dancing with Will?" I pull out my fingers to show her.

"No, it's from you."

"Do you want me?"

"Yes." I reinsert my fingers and find her sweet spot. I work her through three orgasms. "Please, Gray," she pants, her hips rolling uncontrollably. "I need you."

"I'm going to come inside of you," I inform her.

"I know. I want you to."

"Why?"

"Because I love you, Grayson. I want all of you and whatever comes from that. Because I want you to trust me again, enough to kiss you there." She points to my mark.

I just gave her three orgasms. She didn't say "baby" at all, and I need her to. I never thought so much could ride on one silly word. That it could have such significance. But it does. I need to know her feelings for me are sacred.

I work her into another frenzy and, just as she's about to climax, I pull my fingers out and bury myself inside her as hard as I can. I want her to feel the pain she caused me. I pull her left leg up and over me to flip her. "Good girl," I say when she gets her knees under herself. I slow my pace and listen to the beautiful sounds coming from her as she pushes back against me. I slow it down more as I grab her bum cheeks and squeeze, release, and smack them. Oh God, the way she moans over it.

"Do you trust me?" I ask.

"Yes." Her voice is barely above a whisper. Humph . . . no "baby." I pull out of her and insert my fingers again to pull some of her natural lubrication, then run them up to her bum and massage around her opening. I thrust inside of her again, my fingers continuing their massage, then insert my finger at the same time as my next hard thrust. She goes wild, burying her face into the pillow.

"Come on, sweetheart, don't you have something to say?" I quicken my pace and find her clit with my free hand. She meets my thrusts. She's getting there. "Tell me, sweetheart—say it!" I yell through my teeth. Here it is; I can feel her tensing up. I work her slowly and listen closely, wanting her to say it.

"Oh . . . oh God. Oh God, baby!" she cries. I pull myself and my finger out of her, then flip her back over. She looks exhausted. I bury myself inside of her again. She welcomes me into her arms and meets me. She squeezes around me, the intensity driving me mad.

I close my eyes. "Oh God . . . bloody hell!" I attack her mouth to muffle our sounds as I spill inside of her.

"I love you, Gray. That's it, baby . . . c'mon," she whispers in my ear as I have my last surge of pure pleasure. I fall completely onto her. She holds me and softly rubs my back. She kisses my face everywhere but there. "Can I?"

"No." I turn my head.

"Can I stay here with you until Morgan gets home?"

"No." Why did I just say that? I want her here.

"Please, baby." I can hear her tears forming.

"No. I want to go to sleep now. Please leave," I say, and climb off of her. She sits up and grabs her stuff. Her shoulders are shaking. I can't do this. "Becca, sweetheart, come here. I'm sorry. I don't really want you to leave. You've just got me so confused." I pull her against my chest and grab my phone off the nightstand. "What time does Morgan get home?"

"Four." I set the alarm for a quarter to.

"Go to sleep, sweetheart."

"I love you."

"I love you too, darling. Now get some sleep." I don't have to say it again—she's out.

I'm awakened by Becca's thrashing.

"No! No, George . . . please! I'm sorry! I'll do better! Please . . . please stop! No! No, not Morgan!" she screams, tears running down her face.

"Becca! Becca, sweetheart! You're safe! Wake up!" I hold her and shake her a bit.

"No, George!" she screams again before she awakens. She tries to shake me off, fighting me.

"Becca, it's me. It's Grayson." I try to reassure her.

Aunt Hazel barges in.

"Becca . . . Becca, you're safe. Let her go, Grayson!" She sits on the bed. "Becca, c'mere, sweetie. You're safe. It's Hazel." Becca climbs into her arms. "Shh, shh. You're okay." Auntie rocks her and rubs her head. "Grayson, why is she naked?" She shoots me a look of disapproval.

"Oh, Auntie, this is embarrassing enough. Please don't make me spell it out for you!" This has got to be one of the most awkward, most uncomfortable moments I've ever had in my life.

"What did you do to her? She hasn't had a nightmare like this in a long time." Auntie's on the verge of crying.

"Auntie, I made love to her. It's not the first time, but it *is* the first time she's had a nightmare with me." I can't believe I have to state the obvious.

"Don't be a daft arse! I know what the pair of you did! Did

you do anything that would trigger her PTSD? Did you hurt her, hit her, threaten her, or make her fear that you would do any of those things?" *Um . . . yes, no, no, probably. Oh God.*

"I grabbed her face and screamed at her," I say quietly.

"Will you two stop talking about me like I'm not in the room?" Becca sits up and wipes away the tears.

"That was a bad one, honey. I heard you all the way downstairs. I'm sorry this happened." Auntie is crying and kissing Becca's face.

"I'm okay. It's been a stressful day for me. That may be what triggered it," she offers. "Hazel, please don't leave me. I'd die if I lost you. You're my best friend and mother all wrapped up in one." Becca sobs.

"I'm sorry, Becca. I didn't mean what I said. I couldn't leave you and Morgan. I was just so upset. I've never seen Grayson cry like that, not since he was a little boy." Auntie hugs her. I feel humiliated.

"I'm sorry I hurt him. I am, Grayson—I'm so sorry." She grabs my hand and squeezes it.

"Auntie, would you mind giving us a few moments so we can get dressed?" I've had enough of this awkwardness.

"Oh. Oh, yes. Sorry. You *are* staying now, right?" she asks as she stands.

"Auntie, please." I put my hands over my face. She shakes her head and leaves.

"You *are* staying, right?" Becca repeats, then climbs on me and starts kissing my neck. She did call me "baby." But is it because I coaxed her?

"Becca, why did you say you wished you never called me "baby," then cross it off?" I lift her chin to look into her eyes.

"I was mad. I wrote it to hurt you, but then realized it was going too far. So I crossed it off."

"Why didn't you rewrite the note or cross if off to the point where I couldn't see it? Do you have any idea how much that hurt me, or the thoughts that went through my head? I actually felt my heart break. You crushed me." I turn my face away from her.

"I was stupid. I'm so sorry. Please, please forgive me. I was in a rush. I thought you would know I was being silly." She tries to kiss me. "Grayson, please." I bring my face back to hers and study her. I pull her right leg over so she sits astride me. She yelps in surprise as I quickly sit up with her so we are face to face.

"I rushed you out today because I've been working on a surprise for you. I didn't mean to make you feel bad. I like making you feel good," I add with a mischievous grin as I lift her a little so I can enter her. She places her head between my shoulder and neck and lets out a small whimper.

"Please go easy, baby. I'm so sore," she begs in my ear. I bring her hips all the way down so I can finish filling her. She wraps her arms around my neck tightly.

"Show me, sweetheart. Show me how you want it," I whisper. She brings her face to mine, forehead to forehead, and moves her hips slowly, squeezing me with every rise.

"You really want a baby, Gray?"

"I need to have a baby with you."

"Why? Why now?"

"I don't know. Please, let's stop talking." Her hips pick up the pace as I roll and pull at her nipples. She attacks my mouth with her own, and I know she's getting ready to pray.

"Oh God, baby . . . ah . . . God." Her cries are my undoing, and I join her. My last thrust causes me to shudder. I lay my head on her shoulder. She holds me and rubs my head, and I feel like I am home. *She is my home. I love her.* I lift my head to look at her. Her green eyes search my brown ones. I know what she is asking. I nod and a small sob escapes her throat. I feel her sweet, comforting kiss on my mark. It brings me the calm I so desperately need. My alarm goes off. "Let's take a shower, Gray." With that, she lifts off of me, and we head to wash away the day's worries.

BECCA

Grayson is back to his playful self in the shower. I feel like I've been on the biggest roller coaster ever built. We both agreed to communicate our feelings right away, and I plan on sticking to that.

"C'mon, sweetheart. Rinse off. Our da . . . girl will be home any minute."

My heart pangs. He so badly wants to call her his. I love that he's fallen in love with her as quickly as he's fallen for me. We are a package deal.

"Okay, baby." I turn the water off and grab a towel. Yeah, I don't remember the last time I've showered three times in one day. We dress quickly and run down the stairs hand in hand. We grab our coats and head out the door for the long walk down the driveway to the bus stop.

It's a brisk fall day. The leaves are turning bright red, yellow, and orange. This is my favorite time of the year, and I am in the most beautiful place to experience it. *Oh, shit!* I didn't cook anything for dinner.

"What is it, sweetheart?" He chucks me under my chin.

"I forgot about dinner."

"Don't be silly, sweetheart. We'll just order in, or go out." He seems relieved that my concern was only dinner.

"Here she comes." I smile as I see the bus's yellow lights flash, warning people of an impending stop. As it pulls up, I see Morgan by a window, her eyes downcast. When she looks up and sees us waiting at the stop, her face lights up like a Christmas tree. The doors open and she rushes down the steps.

"Hi, Daddy!" she yells, and leaps into Grayson's arms. I know why she did that. I see all the kids' faces watching from the windows. She must've been teased and called out today. Grayson swings her legs over his arm and carries her like a damsel in distress.

"God, I love you, Morgy girl," he says, nuzzling and kissing her nose. We head back up to the house. Grayson carries her the whole way, like she's light as a feather. I think I've just fallen more in love with him.

"How was school, sweetie?" Do I dare ask?

"Awful, but tomorrow will be better!" She smiles and hugs Grayson's neck. I think she loves him even more today as well. We head into the inn. Charlie is on his way out with a bewildered look on his face.

"What's the matter, Charlie?' I've never seen him like this.

"Um . . . Becca, I won't be here for dinner. I'm going home to freshen up. I have a date tonight." So, he's in shock. I giggle.

"With who, Charlie ole chap?" Grayson says cheerfully.

"With your Aunt Hazel. She finally said yes. Then she laid one right on me!'

"Charlie, that's fantastic!" I hug him. "Wait right here!" I run into my office and pull two hundred dollars from my petty-cash box, then hurry back out. "Charlie, don't get mad at me and don't be stubborn! I want you to have this. Take her someplace real nice. Please, Charlie. I love you both so much." I'm so happy, tears have sprung in my eyes.

"Oh, Becca. That's nice, honey, but I've got it." He pushes my hand away. I know he doesn't have much to spare.

"I'll deduct it from your bonus," I offer.

"You will?" I got him!

"Yes." I hand him the money.

"Well, okay then. Thanks, Becca." He hugs me and heads out the door.

"I think you are the loveliest person I've ever met, sweetheart." Grayson pulls me into his arms.

"I can't believe she said yes!" Now I'm bewildered.

"I knew she would. I'll explain over dinner." He kisses the top of my head.

"You know, baby, you've got quite the talent for making people do what they normally would never do." I give him a crooked smile.

"Don't I know it, love?" He laughs as he hangs up all of our coats.

"Well, we can't go out for dinner, so what are going to have, Mommy?" Morgan sighs. "I'm hungry."

"You know, I could go for some Chinese. What about you, Gray?"

"Ugh . . . no, darling. I want steak and potatoes." Grayson places another log on the fire. I take a seat on the sofa in the lounge and watch him poke the embers around. "You know, sweetheart," he starts, glancing back over his shoulder at me. "I've noticed that you are quite the prisoner to your business. You should be able to go out for dinner." The complaint is very familiar to my ears.

"That's what I always tell her," Morgan adds.

"Well, that's going to change, Morgy girl." He stands up and pulls her to him, patting her shoulder. What's he getting at?

"Why don't we place an order at Adam's restaurant and you and Morgan can pick it up?" I suggest, and get up to get the menu.

"Morgan," I hear him say. "There are going to be a lot of great changes around here. Just you wait and see, little sweetheart. We're going to have plenty of family time from now on."

"Yay!" Morgan cheers with excitement. I don't know what he has planned, but if he found a way we can all have more time together, then I'm all ears.

Hazel walks into the main area just as I finish ordering dinner and hang up the phone. She's quite the sight.

"Oh, Hazel." I smile and run up to hug her. "You look beautiful! Charlie's eyes are going to pop right out of his head!"

"Auntie, you really do know how to light up a room!"

"Oh, stop it, you two." She waves her hand, her cheeks pink. "Do you think I'm overdressed? I'm not sure where he's taking me." She turns in a circle. She's wearing the black-lined mauve skirt suit I bought her last year, along with pearl drop earrings, a matching necklace, and black heels.

"No, you're not overdressed. You look wonderful." I hug her again and take in the scent of her classic Chanel No. 5.

"If you weren't my aunt, I'd be pushing Becca aside!" Grayson adds.

"Ready, Daddy?" Morgan comes back from dropping her school bag off in her room. Um, yeah, I think she's got her mind set and I don't know if I'll be able to break her of calling him that. He's not much help—he glows every time she says it, and never corrects her. "Grammy Hazel, you look beautiful!" Morgan started calling her that three years ago, and I love it. Hazel absolutely adores it, too. She tells everyone Morgan is her granddaughter.

"C'mon, little sweetheart." Grayson grabs her hand and gives me and his aunt each a quick kiss as they head out.

"Becca, it's been over fifty years since I've been on a first date. What do I do?" she asks as we sit on the sofa.

"Well, it's been about twelve years for me, so I'm not much help!" I laugh. "But look at it this way. It's Charlie. You two know everything there is to know already. You're over that awkward hump. You get to go to dinner and just talk about everyday things."

"I kissed him today. I don't know what came over me!" Her eyes widen.

"I know." I laugh. "I think you knocked his socks off. He came out here in a daze!" She giggles with me. "Is he a good kisser?" I ask like any old girlfriend would.

"Oh, Becca. Really!" She slaps my leg, but then giggles and nods her head yes. I'm feeling so inspired. Seventy years old and falling in love. How wonderful!

"How are you and Grayson, dear? You two seem much better."

"Hazel, he's the most amazingly frustrating man—and I'm head over heels! I think we've had more bumps in the road in a few days than most people have in six months. How can this all be happening so fast like this? It's all surreal. You know me, Hazel. This is *so* out of character for me." I'm taken aback as I talk about it for the first time. She knows how fast we've moved.

"Becca, it was just meant to be. When you find *that person*, all caution goes out the window. When I met Harold, we fell fast as well. We were secretly engaged a week later. A week after that, we were married and living together. My parents didn't know because I was away at college. We took precautions so I wouldn't get pregnant, not knowing we didn't have to bother." She looks down and a sad expression blankets her face. I'm mesmerized by this story. I've never heard it. "We told my parents a year later of our engagement, and had a proper wedding six months after. We were happily married for forty years." Her eyes fill up.

"Has Grayson ever heard this story?" I ask through my tears.

"No, dear." She blows her nose into her kerchief. "You are the only one who knows."

"Look at you—lucky at love twice! You're a pretty special lady, Mom." I add the last word because, quite frankly, that's how I feel.

"I wish I was your mother." She smiles, her powder-blue eyes even more brilliant from her tears.

"You are in every way that matters." I hug her.

"You know, you and Grayson have that in common."

"What's that?"

"You both lost your parents at a young age. Grayson was thirteen when my sister died of ovarian cancer. He was devastated. She was his world, much like you are to Morgan." She tears up again.

"What about his dad?" I ask.

"Car accident two years later. Harold and I moved to England to finish his raising. We didn't want him to lose his home, too."

"That was very good of you both." I grab her hand.

"Oh, we've always cherished him as if he was our own." She tries to hold back a sob and looks off in the distance.

"Well, he thinks the world of you. He loves being here with his family." I try to cheer her up.

"Yes, well, he's a good boy, Becca. Just give him time to sort his feelings out. He's all over the place, just as you are." She dabs at her eyes.

"There's my girl!" Charlie speaks up as he enters the room. "Hazel, dear, what's the matter?" A concerned look comes across his face.

"I'm okay, Charlie. I was just reminiscing with Becca. I'm a sap, what can I say?" She stands up to greet him. He presents her with a corsage. Oh, how sweet and romantic. So old-fashioned. I could just squeeze the pair of 'em!

"Becca, honey, can you help me pin this on my sweetheart here? I don't want to stick her." Charlie holds up the corsage. I get up and pin it on for them. It's pink roses—Hazel's favorite.

"Wait, let me get my camera! This is one for the books," I say, and run out to get it from my office. They're ready and posing when I return. "Okay, now . . . smile!" I snap a few shots.

"Mummy, we're home!" Grayson and Morgan shout. Shoot, I didn't even set the table. They walk in, followed by a couple who are dressed to go out for dinner as well. They ask me to take a picture of them in front of the fireplace and they are on their way.

"Grayson, you have one beautiful aunt here." Charlie stretches his hand out for a shake.

"Don't keep her out too late, Charlie ole boy!" Gray teases him as he shakes his hand and pats him on the back. Charlie takes Hazel's arm and they head out for their very first date.

The rest of the evening is uneventful, with the exception of a few guests asking for directions. We both tuck Morgan into bed at eight, and she loves every minute of it. She's continued to call Grayson "Daddy," and I've stopped correcting her. What's the point? He won't stop her from doing it behind my back.

During dinner, Morgan informed us that it's Bring a Parent to School Day next week, where all the parents attend class and talk about what they do for a living. Morgan asked Gray to go because I go every year and everybody already knows what I do. It's getting boring, she said. I'm hurt, but she is right—and Grayson's over the moon about it. I just sat back and watched the pair of them at dinner, laughing and carrying on. So natural, like it's been this way her whole life. I realized at that moment that I do indeed want to have his baby. I'm in love with him. I'm in love with him and Morgan together. I'm in love with our out-of-the-ordinary, out-of-the-blue family. I feel like for the first time in twelve years, I can relax and take life in. I am content. I never knew what that meant until now.

I'm just finishing up dishes when Grayson pops his head into the kitchen.

"Sweetheart, come to the office when you're done in here so I can go over everything with you," he says.

"Yep. I'm coming." I dry my hands on the dish towel. Before I head into the store, I leave a sign out telling guests to press *5 if they need anything. That will buzz my phone in the office. I head in and sit next to him as he starts pulling up different programs.

"Okay, sweetheart." Grayson puts a pair of black-framed glasses on before looking at the monitor. "This is your POS—point of sales. When you ring something up at the register, the stock amount will decrease here so you know how many of that item you have left. Honestly, I can't believe you were still doing this manually." He shakes his head.

"You entered all of my products into this system the other night?" I can't believe he did that. What a pain in the ass it must've been!

"Yes, it was painful," he states. It's eerie how he does that; it's like he knows what I'm thinking.

After he shows me everything I need to know about the inventory system, he moves on to scheduling. Staff hours, crop weekends, weddings, miscellaneous functions, and every night's guests, all organized under one system. Then there is another program that has all of the weddings I've done this past year. It shows everything I had in my files. Who the vendors were, what the dinner was, everything—along with cost and profit. He even did the same thing for my crop weekends and other functions. He shows me where I was wasting money and where I could gain more. We move onto the finance program, which he's separated into two main categories: business and personal.

"Okay, sweetheart, I really need your undivided attention now."

What's he talking about? I've paid attention the whole time. I'm fascinated that my life was made so much simpler. But I fix my eyes on his just the same.

"Sweetheart, before I say anything else, I want to tell you how proud I am of you. You are completely disorganized, but from a business perspective, you hit the nail on the head here! You are doing fantastic in the shittiest of economies! Did you know you would do so well? I'd love to hear how you came up with all of this." He leans back in his chair to listen.

"Right now?" I ask, surprised.

"Yes, please. I've been dying to hear about it ever since I buried myself in this the other night."

"Oh, well, um . . . about six months before George's last deployment, we went to another couple's house for dinner. Mike, the husband, was in George's company in the army. They both knew all about him, how he was reckless and thought he was indestructible. He was very alpha-male-on-steroids. Basically, his life's mission was to be looked at as the 'biggest man on campus,' for a lack of a better analogy. They even knew he beat me all the time." I pause when Grayson winces. "I never admitted to it, but you'd have to be an idiot not to see it. Anyway . . . Claire, Mike's wife, had said a few days earlier that her husband was pretty sure George would get himself killed in the field one of these days. Apparently, it almost happened on two different tours. They wanted to make sure Morgan and I were taken care of. So they formulated a very simple plan that George would easily fall for." I take a sip of my water. Grayson is watching me intently.

"Over dinner, Mike started talking about raising his life-insurance policy amount. He said that all of the guys were doing it, that it's what *real* men who are fighting for our country do. He mentioned how shameful it would be if he didn't take care of Claire in his death. 'We take care of our families no matter how many bullets we catch,' he said. Ugh. It went on for an hour. George said nothing. What could he say? We had nothing besides what the military offered. No extra. Since he didn't say anything, Claire piped up and said, 'Honestly, Mike, you really think I'd need five hundred thousand? That's a lot.' Mike said he wished he could raise it higher. And that was that. We went home.

"The next day, George told me we had an appointment to go to. I never asked what for, I just went. It was at an insurance agency, and he took a million-dollar policy out. Not because he was concerned about our well-being, of course—he just wanted to be able to brag about it!" I start to giggle because, to this day, I find it remarkable how someone could be so stupid and narrow-minded.

"And why, again, was he such a great catch?" Grayson asks, furrowing his brow.

"Oh. Well, he wasn't like that in the beginning. He was sweet to me. Always jealous, though. He kept pressuring me to marry him, but I wasn't ready, so I wouldn't budge. He told me I'd be his wife one way or another, and two months later, I was pregnant." I take in a deep breath. "After I married him, I found out that he had replaced all of my birth-control pills with just the sugar-pill part."

"How did he do that?"

"A friend of his was a drug rep. He gave him tons of samples, not knowing he was taking all the blanks out and switching them. I didn't even know about the samples until the friend said to me one day, 'Guess all the samples I gave you were a waste!' Something like that. I thought that was odd, so later when George went out, I went through his stuff. I didn't even know what I was looking for, really. Then, when I was flipping through his calendar book, I noticed he was keeping track of something. When I looked a bit closer, I realized it was my cycle—that whenever a condom would magically break or he'd go ahead without a condom, saying 'at least you're on the pill,' he knew I was ovulating. I was so engrossed in the calendar I didn't notice he'd come back, and he caught me. That's the first time he hit me." I stop and look up at Grayson. He has a wan look about him, and he's blinking rapidly. I know what he's thinking.

"You're a blunt Brit, Grayson. You haven't been sneaking around. You've made your agenda very clear from our first time, in not so many words. It's different. I know that it is. Grayson, I want to have your baby. I want this with you." I sit on his lap and bring his face to mine.

"Becca, darling, I'm sorry. I can't believe I grabbed your face like that today. Oh God. What you must think of me? Your fear; it scared me. Now I know what that fear was." He's getting choked up.

"That fear is what George lived for. He would start with me just to get that reaction. He never hurt Morgan, but he would threaten her just to get a rise out of me. It turned him on. He'd make me do things and told me if I was good he wouldn't hurt her." Oh my God, I've never told anyone but my therapist this. "I can't say any more, Gray."

"Shh, shh . . . no, no, sweetheart. Don't push yourself. I don't need to know until you need to tell me." He wraps his arms around me tightly. "Becca, I can be an aggressive lover, you know that. I'm afraid I've triggered some things for you." Oh, he's beside himself now.

"Yes, you're very aggressive." I smirk. "It's different. You devour me. I know you can't get close enough. I know you're just craving more. He was such a vicious animal who wanted to hurt me because it made him feel powerful. It's not the same." I kiss his lips.

"I do love you, Becca. I don't ever want to hurt you. Please tell me you are certain of that." He leans his forehead to mine.

"I am most certain of that. Now, shall I carry on with my story involving my brilliant business mind?"

"Most certainly!" He grins.

"So, six months later, the fucking 'roid droid headed off for another tour."

"Was he on steroids?"

"No, but you'd certainly think so. He pumped iron so much, he had no neck left. It was gross. Incidentally, I absolutely love your body. You're ripped just right." I run my hands across his chest and over his shoulder.

"Becca, darling, the sooner we get through all of this, the sooner we can move on to that." He kisses me as he grabs my hand.

"Okay." I give him a playful pout. "Less than a year after he left, they told me he was missing in action, but presumed dead. It took another year to get him declared because there was no body, just documentation to support his whereabouts. It stated that he was in the same location where an explosion went off, killing several men. I was finally able to collect the insurance money. After having that long to think about what to do with the money, I knew I didn't want to just live off of it. One million seems like a lot, and it is to a point, but unless you're smart with it, it won't carry you that far."

"It was very smart of you to realize that. A lot of people wouldn't."

"I know." I pause before continuing. "During that year of waiting, I started scrapping and got hooked. My best friend took Morgan for the weekend and I went away with other scrap friends to a weekend crop. I loved it. I knew it was what I wanted to do. I also knew it was going to be a lot of work, but I was excited. And it would work, too—I listened to the women around me talking about the economy and they all said the same thing. They were going out less, buying less, traveling less, and spending more time at home with their families and doing hobbies like scrapping. Some of them saved leftover grocery money each week to get away for the weekend once or twice a year. This was all before the economy got really bad, too.

"A few months later, my favorite scrapbook store closed. It made me so sad to lose one of my favorite hangouts. And it got me thinking. Sure, the chain stores are cheaper, but you don't always get the specialty things—the unique stuff that only scrapbooking stores have. So I said, 'Self, you should have a scrapbook store attached to your B&B!' That way, the locals would have a place to come to, and the crop weekends would more than help support the store's overhead. But it has done way better, because I chose a location that has tourism all year and people are more inclined to check out specialty stores when they are away. Plus, my everyday guests buy stuff because they either scrap or know someone who does." I take a deep breath and another sip of water, and notice Grayson grinning at me. "What?"

"I could listen to you all night."

"Oh God, baby . . . that's nice." I tease him—or am I baiting him? He mouths "stop" to me, and it makes me smile. "I came up here to look for the right property, and this place popped up. I paid a very hefty down payment, built the store, hired your aunt, and Bob's your uncle!"

Grayson laughs heartily.

"Let me guess . . . Aunt Hazel taught you that line."

"Yes, why?"

"It's an English saying. Nobody really says it over here. It sounded cute coming from you. What about the weddings and the stables?"

"People kept asking me about hosting small weddings, and when I agreed, I found them to be a lot of fun. It just escalated from there—I remodeled the barn out back to accommodate the larger weddings and functions. It is getting to be a bit much, though. I'm hoping I won't have to do it in a few years." As soon as I say it, Gray is punching something into the computer.

"Go ahead. The stables?"

"I brought Charlie on to take care of Butterscotch, and then Rocco. He brought up the idea of boarding other horses."

"You only pay him once a year. Why is that?" he asks as he studies the screen.

"Do you want me to get off of your lap?" He shakes his head. "Okay. Well. I was trying to hire someone. I knew Charlie from around town and he offered to do it for free. Said he grew up around horses his whole life, and he needed something to keep him occupied in retirement. I told him I'd feed him three square meals a day. He thought he'd hit the jackpot." I laugh. "He mentioned boarding almost as soon as he got here. He takes care of all the horses, so I give him a 'bonus' in November."

"And the 'bonus' basically covers a year's salary."

"Well, I try my best." I play with my hands.

"I can see that, sweetheart. I also bet you do it in November so he won't refuse it with Christmas around the corner." He rubs my leg.

"What are you looking at, baby?"

"Your wedding schedule. You have one coming up, and another next April." It looks like he's blocking the rest of the next year off.

"What are you doing?" I sit up.

"I'm blocking the schedule. You want to be done with weddings. You're done."

"No. I can't do that yet." I try to grab the mouse from him.

"Stop it, Becca," he says. I stop. "First of all, sweetheart, by this time next year, you will likely be married to me, and you will not have to worry about a single penny. It would actually work better for my plans if these people cancel. Sweetheart, I do need you to get off of my lap now." He pats my leg. I get off and sit in the chair next to him. I watch as he clicks into the Johnson wedding file. He attaches it to an email. I lean forward to see what he's doing.

Carol,

See attached file. Please contact Mr. Johnson and Miss Plutes and ask them if they'd be willing to change wedding venues if we cover the costs up to twenty thousand. Please explain to them that The Morgan Inn is looking to renovate, and their wedding would delay the process. Call ASAP with answer!

Grayson

"Are you out of your mind?" I smack his arm. "Don't hit send!" He does. "Grayson, these people are supposed to pay me twenty thousand, not the other way around! What are you doing?"

"Now, I want to talk to you about your finances." He pulls off his black reading glasses, which, incidentally, make him look even hotter. *How is that possible?*

"Oh, yeah. I should mention that my boyfriend likes to piss money away," I snap sarcastically. His smile is huge but thoughtful.

"I think if it was anyone else, I would be insulted that you don't know who I am and how much I'm worth. Clearly Aunt Hazel has respected my wishes. You haven't even bothered to Google me, have you?" He pulls my feet up onto his lap.

"No. Should I? I know that you have your own business and an MBA. Why would I Google you? Besides, I know what you are worth," I add nonchalantly.

"You do?" His brow arches.

"Yes. Everything." I smile softly at him.

"You have a dimple." Wow, he must have ADD like me.

"So do you. Just a little one." I place my finger on his chin. It is very slight and could easily be missed, but he is my favorite subject and I love to study him. Well, except on Google, apparently. "C'mon, my MBA, it's getting late." I nudge.

"Right, Dimples ..."

"I have *one* dimple. Therefore you cannot use that nickname. Now carry on, Mr. James." I nudge him with my foot to stop his goofy grin.

"Okay. We have a big day tomorrow. I have a banker coming here at ten to show you two refinance options." I open my mouth to oppose. "Uh-uh, wait . . . before you say anything," he continues, "I know what you are trying to do, Becca. You want to pay off your mortgage. Sweetheart, you're so worked up about having enough money for this and that and you're giving the bank an average of ..." He looks over his notes. "Six to ten thousand a month. Sweetheart, you don't have much to go. If you refinance, you'll have a much, much lower interest rate and your payments will drop down to around three hundred a month. Becca, you should be putting that money away or investing it, not throwing it away. Wouldn't you rather put it into expanding your buildings here?" He raises both eyebrows at me. I open my mouth again, but decide against arguing. "Because of the economy, if you sold this place tomorrow, you would lose a hundred and fifty thousand dollars of the money you already put into it. Even if you had a rough month or two, a three-hundred-dollar mortgage won't break you." He sits back and lets me soak this all in. I had thought about refinancing before, but I was doing so well—I just wanted to get rid of the mortgage so I'd never have to worry about us losing our home.

"How do you know what my payments will be?"

"Well, the banker will come with two options. The first one is by yourself; that payment will be somewhere around six hundred. The other option is if I cosign. That lowers you down to roughly three hundred." He's searching my face. I think he's trying to gauge what I'm feeling.

"Okay. What I asked, though, is how do you know what my payments would be? You would need all of my info, including my social security number, for a credit check," I ask again.

"Carol handled all of that. Now, at noon, I have an architect coming to look at the place and draw up some plans."

"Grayson?"

"Yes, love?"

"How was Carol able to handle all of that?" I feel my blood boiling just a bit. I am trying my hardest to remain calm.

"I gave her the information. So I was thinking that we could —"

"Grayson!" I cut him off again.

"I gathered the information, Becca! That's all! Let's move on!" He blinks rapidly, his tone short and irritated.

"Okay." What's the point? It's already done. It was for good, not evil. I don't want to fight.

"Okay? Okay. Right. I was thinking we could build our house in the back. We shouldn't be on top of our guests."

"Especially with the baby coming." I giggle.

"And I don't want Morgan living like this anymore. She should have her own house. I think we can hire more staff here for the inn, store, and stables. We have seven empty horse stalls that could be filled. We can convert the barn into crop-weekend quarters. Everything should be in there, and then it can be used for any overflow of guests as well."

"I had thought of that, Gray but it will be very expensive."

I get an eye roll from him.

"And that covers just about everything but the Disney trip."

"What about the Disney trip?" What does that have to do with any of this?

"Well, I added myself on and upgraded everything. You're still paying, of course," he adds before I argue. I laugh. "My finance guy is coming in two days. He will go over your numbers with you and help you decide where you want to invest everything. I say put it all in a trust fund for Morgan. You won't need any of it," he says, shrugging his shoulders.

"Why is that?"

"Because you'll be married to me and want for nothing." Now

I'm the one rolling my eyes.

"Well, what do you think, love?" He glances over to the computer, then back to me.

"I am impressed, Mr. James . . . with everything. Thank you, baby." I bite my bottom lip. *God, I love it when he puts those glasses on.*

"Well, tell me. Yes to what and no to what?" He scrunches his face when he sees how I'm looking at him. "What?"

"You are fucking hot in those glasses! And yes."

"Really . . . ? Yes to what?" His hands move from my feet and slowly up my legs.

"Yes to everything. Yes to you." I lean forward for a kiss.

"Really, sweetheart?" His smile goes to full wattage. "Will you let me cosign?" He tilts his head.

"I'm guessing I don't have a real choice. What would happen if I choose the loan with just me?" I challenge.

"Honestly?"

"Honestly."

"I'll pay the balance in full next month." He looks down.

"You had that planned out already, didn't you?"

"Yes?" He looks up, his eyelids again blinking madly.

"You won't do that now that I've agreed to you cosigning, right?"

"Right!"

"Grayson?"

"I swear! I won't."

"Okay. Let's lock up and go to bed." I kiss him once . . . twice . . . mmm, God, he's delicious.

We head out of the office and stop short when we see Hazel and Charlie kissing good night. We hang back. Five minutes pass, then ten.

"Good Lord! How long is he going to snog her for?" Grayson's getting impatient. Quite frankly, so am I.

"C'mon. If she can walk in on us naked in bed, we can walk in on her kissing." I grab his hand and lead him in.

"Good call, love!" He smacks my ass, then goes around turning off most of the lights. I go to the front desk to check messages and set up any wake-up calls.

"Sweetheart, can you give these two a room?" Grayson hits the front desk with his hand, and Hazel and Charlie jump ten feet in the air.

"Oh! Oh my." Hazel looks very flustered. I slap Grayson's arm and he smiles wickedly at me.

"Hazel, I'm going to go check on Morgan, and then we're heading up. Just lock the front door." I yank Grayson away. "Come, dear, leave your aunt alone. Let's go check on our daughter." I drag him away.

We walk to the suite where Hazel and Morgan sleep. Grayson pulls me to him, then forces me to back up against the wall.

"I love that you just said that." His breath is hot in my face.

"Said what?" Huh? Between his close proximity and the ten million butterflies that just took flight in my stomach, concentration is a concept lost on me.

"*Our* daughter."

"Oh."

"I love you, Becca. Thank you for not fighting me tonight about . . . well, anything." He leans down and lets his lips run across mine in a barely there touch before he continues onto Morgan's room. What was that?

Horny teenaged Sybil, who incidentally now prefers just Horny Sybil since her graduation to womanhood yesterday, holds her hand up to catch a new pair of panties. She changes quickly.

I follow Grayson as he opens the door. He pulls her covers up and kisses her head. "I love you, Morgy girl. I'm going to give you the world," he whispers to her.

"I love you too, Daddy," she says in her sleep. I go and give her a kiss as well. We leave the room and head upstairs.

While Grayson grabs a few things from his room, I unlock my door and flip on the lights.

"Wait! What the ...?" I know I haven't been in my room since this afternoon, but my bed was definitely not this big.

"Ah, good! It's arrived! Come, darling, and see if it's comfortable for you." He jumps on the new king-sized bed. I sit down with him and bounce a little. Why do people do that—bounce on our bums to see if a mattress is comfortable? We both lay back. "Is it all right?"

"Yes, it's great." He does the strangest things, this guy! I yawn. "I'm going to get dressed for bed."

"You mean undressed, right, darling?" He leans over and places his hand on my belly, beneath my shirt.

"Grayson, as much as I would love to, I am so tired. And extremely sore. Can you give me the night off?" I reach up and play with the stubble on his jaw.

"I'll try, love, but I won't promise." He gets up, walks over to my drawers, and rummages through them. "Tomorrow, we are going lingerie shopping for you."

"Check the next drawer down." I remember a few things my best friend Stacey bought me.

"This is much better." He pulls out a red satin nightgown. "But who were you wearing these for?" He pulls my shirt off.

"No one. They've been in that drawer for two years. My best friend bought them for me to encourage me to date. I'll have to call her tomorrow to let her know I've finally worn one." I close my eyes as Grayson works at my bra. The air greets my breast. I jump slightly at the touch of his tongue gliding across my right nipple before his teeth nip at it. "Baby, stop!" I slap his arm. He pulls his mouth away from my breast with a groan of disapproval and tugs the nightgown down over my head. I pull my pants off. He follows suit with my panties.

"Do I have to remind you that you don't like to wear these to bed?" There's that mischievous grin. He's guaranteeing himself easy access in case an emergency situation should arise. I leave him to undress and go into the bathroom to brush my teeth, but he follows me. He's buck—of course.

"Are you following my rule?" I smirk.

"I like your rule, sweetheart." He stands right up against me on purpose and reaches around for the toothpaste. The feel of him ignites wicked little fires in my body. I wait for him to finish.

The bed feels so good. I feel like I haven't slept in a hundred years. Grayson climbs in after me and runs his hand up my backside.

"Is it all right if I caress you for a little bit, love?" He kisses my back.

"Sure. It feels nice." His left hand glides up my right side, across my shoulders, and down to the small of my back. He caresses my left bum cheek softly, palming and squeezing it a little as he caresses me with his thumb. He does the same to my right side. It's hypnotic and comforting. I can feel myself almost drifting off. "Oh!" I moan when he smacks my left cheek.

"Is it okay that I did that, Becca?" He nervously rubs where he just spanked me.

"Yes, Grayson, but please, don't get yourself worked up. I can't tonight. Please," I beg, feeling half asleep and half aroused.

"Right, darling. You just have a fantastic bum." I can hear the longing in his voice. "Sweetheart, really, it's too late. I'm worked up." I'm not looking at him, but I sense his urgency. He spanks me again. *Submissive Sybil has her flogger in her hand.* His hand comes down on me again. My whimperish moans drive him wild. "Sweetheart, please? This is an emergency! Turn to me, Becca. I need you."

I turn over. He hikes my nightie up more and pulls my legs apart.

"Are you okay? Have I upset you or made you nervous?"

I know what he's thinking. He's not George, but he'll be worried for a long time that I'll think he is.

"Grayson, I am not upset or nervous, but I am thoroughly turned on. So thoroughly, in fact, that I have quite the unusual desire." I push him onto his back.

"What's that, Becca?"

"Close your eyes, baby."

"You're not going to sock me in the face again, are you?" He's blinking like mad.

"No." I drag my lips against his to return his earlier tease. "Close your eyes." He closes them and takes in a deep breath. I trail wet kisses across his chest, down to his six-pack, and across his lower abdomen. I let my hair tickle him.

"Becca. Becca, sweetheart." He has such a yearning in his voice. I massage his inner thighs.

"I definitely need to redo my 'Big Boy' page." I smile as I admire the magnificence of him. I don't normally find penises interesting to look at, but he's even beautiful there! I wrap my hands around him. "You can open your eyes now." He opens them and props himself on his elbows, looking at me anxiously. I give him wicked smile then proceed to make love to him with my mouth.

He is wild under me. For the first time in my life, I'm actually enjoying this. Several minutes go by and I've got quite the groove going.

"Becca! Becca, stop!" He panics and grabs me by my underarms to pull me up. I sit astride him, allowing him to enter me, and whimper lightly into his shoulder. Christ, I'm so sore. He grits his teeth. I can feel him tense up as he pushes me down harder, trying to fill me as much as he can. I throw my head back and arch my body to help him. "Becca . . . God . . . Christ!" he yells as he finishes. I lift myself off of him and immediately lie down to avoid the mess of gravity.

"Sorry, baby." I smile and pat the bed, inviting him to stretch out beside me.

"You okay, sweetheart? Are you mad at me?" He searches my face.

"No." I kiss him.

"I just wanted to make my deposit in the right bank account . . . if you know what I mean." He imitates Shelley, putting me into stiches.

"Okay. Deposit is received. Can I go to sleep now? I've had an exhausting day, and I have to get up in five hours." I kiss his lips again, then his mark.

"I want to marry you." He rests his head on my chest.

"I know you do." I play with his hair and kiss it before I drift off.

Chapter Seven

"Mmm ..." I stretch. Oh, this bed is so silky and comfy. I turn over and open my eyes to brightness, then look at the clock. *Nine!* "Oh my God!" I jump up. *Where is Grayson?* I head into the bathroom to get ready and find a note on the mirror.

> Becca,
>
> I trust you slept well this morning. I couldn't sleep, so I went downstairs and took care of breakfast with Claudia. I'll be up by 9:15 if you're not down here by then. I love you and your fantastic bum!
>
> Love,
>
> Grayson

God, that was sweet of him. It was so nice to sleep in. I jump in the shower and start running through my to-do list for today. The banker and architect are coming today—that's exciting! I rush through drying and head out to the bedroom. Grayson's placing a tray down. He looks up and flashes me a fabulous grin.

"Good morning." I walk up to him and kiss him once . . . twice . . . ugh, he's always delicious.

"How are you feeling, darling?" He looks down at me.

"Blissful. I can't believe you worked breakfast for me."

"Sweetheart, I just put the baked French toast you made last night into the oven. It's not like I whipped anything up. Come now, eat and get dressed. We have an appointment in an hour." He grabs the lapels of my robe and pulls me in for another kiss.

Breakfast is delicious. I need to give myself a raise! I throw on a pair of jeans and a long-sleeve purple V-neck—and notice that Grayson has been watching my every move. "What?" I snap.

"Sorry, love. I'm just admiring the view that is my future wife. Let's pick a date today, shall we?" He pulls out his phone.

"Oh," is all I can say. No on-bended-knee, I-can't-live-my-life-without-you proposal?

"Oh? What's the matter, sweetheart?" He chucks me under my chin.

"Nothing. Let's look." I say flatly. He squints, trying to figure me out.

"We can do it later. Actually, we should wait until the lawyer gets here at two." He closes the calendar.

"Oh, for the prenup?" Wow. He moves so fast.

"No, darling. You said George's body was never found. I want to make sure you are no longer tied to him in case he miraculously appears."

"That's why I've saved all of my documentation. That's my worst fear." I look away.

"Well, we'll fix that today, sweetheart." He hugs me and, with that, we head out and down the stairs. "I've talked to Claudia about some of our plans and asked her what kind of role she would like here."

"That was good of you, since we're hiring. I want her to be high on the pyramid." I suddenly feel overwhelmed by the amount of change that is going to happen. The room spins. "Grayson!"

"Sweetheart." He grabs me. "What's the matter?"

"I just got dizzy. I'm . . . I'm okay." I push him away.

"Sure?"

"Yes." I take a deep breath.

"Becca, don't lie."

"I'm not. There's a lot of change happening. It's good—just overwhelming." I promised to communicate.

"Change is hard, sweetheart, even when it's good. We're both going through a lot and changing a lot to be together. I love you. You're worth it." He kisses the back of my hand.

"You're worth it, too. I love you."

"I love you ...?" he teases.

"Baby, baby, baby," I add.

"C'mon, sweetheart, there's the banker now." Grayson drags me to shake Mr. Williams's hand.

We head into my office. "Ms. Campbell and I will sign together."

"Oh. Very good, then." He pulls out the correct paperwork and sets it in front of us. I read over Grayson's shoulder to make sure there isn't anything weird in there. My untrained eyes find nothing out of the ordinary. *Shocker!*

"Here you go, Becca." He hands me his pen. I sign. He signs. Done! I've gone from paying three thousand a month to three hundred, and I can save the rest. Mr. Williams bids us a good day, then lets himself out.

"So, do we refinance again to the build the house?" It's an innocent question. I hardly think it deserves the scoff and eye roll I get.

"We're paying cash, sweetheart. Honestly, that's a silly question."

"It's not, Gray. It's our home; we should pay for it together," I say quietly.

"Becca, you are going to be my wife. You must understand that I will be taking care of most things. I know you're independent—I love that about you, and I certainly don't want to it change. The bed-and-breakfast is your ship, your bread and butter to go toward whatever you want. The rest, I will take care of. Understand?" He's blinking in Morse code again. Jeez. Do I fight that much?

"Okay, Grayson. What's the budget for the house? What about the renovations for my 'bread and butter'?"

"There's no budget for our home and I will pay for all renovations. We can work out a monetary payment plan for them." He sits back, hands behind his head.

"Monetary . . . not sexual?" I smirk, and he laughs.

"I'd love sexual payment, but I didn't want to insult you." He glances out into the hall and stands. "I think he's here. He was able to push our appointment up." I look through the glass door to see who he's talking about.

"Oh!" It's Ray.

GRAYSON

"Mr. McNeil! Please come in." I wave him into the office.

"Becs—there you are!" He bypasses me, heading right toward Becca and giving her a hug. *Becs?* I'm pretty sure I'm going to fire him already.

"Gray, this is my friend, Ray. Oh, I rhymed." Becca giggles and hugs him again. *Is she for real?* I shake his hand. "We go back a long time."

"Oh, did you two date?" Ugh, mental head slap. Why did I ask that?

"Oh, no. This one wouldn't give me the time of day." Ray chuckles, his arm around her shoulder.

"Oh, stop." Becca laughs and slaps his shoulder playfully, then glances at me. She stops laughing and gives me the full eye roll I probably deserve. "Our girls are best friends and in the Girl Scouts together," she says, mouthing "stop it" as Ray reaches for his bag and pulls out the map of the property. I didn't know Morgan was a Girl Scout. *I still have so much to learn about my girls.*

"So what's going on, Becs? Are you selling to Mr. James?" He sits halfway on the table, his left leg dangling over the edge. He's a clean, rugged-looking bloke with wavy brown hair. He's dressed casually—jeans and blue shirt with the top unbuttoned—and he looks confident and laid-back. I can see he's a man's man and, for the women around here, probably a good piece of eye candy. I look at Becca and study her body language. Is he eye candy to her?

"No, Ray, I'm not selling. We're building on." Becca smiles over at me reaches for my hand. I oblige and look down at the map with her.

"I was going to ask if you two were partnering up, and I can see that you are . . . just not in the way I thought." Ray slaps me on the back. Man's-man code for "job well done, mate!"

I like Ray. I don't want to but, I do. Becca's definitely not interested in him. I'm being silly. I'm Becca's eye candy. Why do I doubt myself?

"So, Ray, let's see what we're looking at here!" I say cheerfully. This earns me a warm and loving glance from Becca. I hug her close with my left arm.

"Well, here's the layout. This is where the property ends." He points to the edge. "You wanted a secluded area, so we can go up this way." He drags his finger along the mountains. "My guys are headed up there now to see how much blasting we'll have to do."

"Blasting?" Becca asks.

"Yeah, Becs. We'll have to blast through the granite to flatten out an area for your home."

"Why do we have to live so high up on the mountain? Christ,

it'll take us ten minutes to get Morgan to her bus stop. At that point, we may as well drive her to school!"

"Becca, we can't have our house right in back. We have to be secluded." I close my eyes. I probably should have told her last night who I am and what I do for a living.

"Grayson, that's absurd! Why do we need to be away from the public? Honestly!" I don't think she would behave this way toward me if we weren't in front of a friend. A friend who is laughing his arse off.

"Dude, she has no clue, does she? Oh, Becca ..." It seems Ray can't stop laughing. "I'll meet you two in the hall. That ought to give you some time to explain to our girl here why a security gate will be at the front of the driveway to your secluded home. Good luck, man!" He slaps me on the back again and heads out. I can see us being good mates. I feel as if I went to university with him!

"Grayson, why is Ray laughing at me?" Right . . . Becca.

"Uh, well . . . Becca, sweetheart, I'm pretty well-known. With the exception of you, of course. Why is it that you seem to be the only person who doesn't know who I am?" I do feel the tiniest bit insulted. I mean, Christ, I was on the cover of *People* this year as the "Sexiest Man Alive"!

"I'm sorry, Grayson." She touches my arm.

"I've written a slew of number-one hit songs for people. This has earned me a reputation and a good amount in the bank. I bought my own record company almost four years ago. I also have some other businesses I'm vested in, but music is the main one. Ask Aunt Hazel to see her copy of *People*'s 'Sexiest Alive' issue."

"Why, are you on the cover?"

"Yes, but it also gives a good summary of my fortune and fame." I roll my hand in the air to make her laugh. It works. She stands there, a look of contemplation on her face. "Becca, what are you thinking about?" I feel a bit nervous. My eyelids prove it. *Damn eyelids!*

"I knew you were the sexiest man alive, but I guess the whole world knows it, too." She palms my face and kisses me. "I was going to ask you why you ordered a grand piano. No need now."

"That's it? No twenty questions? No singing my resume?" I'm . . . I don't know what I am. This is very odd. Not that the past several days have been typical for me.

"Grayson, why would I ask you to sing your resume? Oh, unless you want to, of course." She's looking at me with complete and utter confusion.

I try to explain. "Sweetheart, people often ask which songs I've written. Sometimes they request I sing a little 'til they recognize them."

"Well, that sounds annoying." Her nostrils flare for emphasis.

"It's terribly annoying, darling!"

"Well, let's avoid that. How about when a song of yours comes on, you say, 'That's one of my songs, love,' and I'll tell you I love it. Unless, of course, I don't, and even then, I'm still proud of you!"

"Did you just attempt to imitate my accent?" I almost can't contain my impending laughter. She's so cute!

"Yeah, why? It didn't sound like you?" She bites her lip.

"Oh, it absolutely did . . . if I was a chimney sweep in *Mary Poppins*!" And there it is, that school-girl giggle. God, I'm crazy about her! I pull her to me and help her stifle her laughter.

A loud knock sounds at the door.

"Hey, you two!" Ray comes in. "I believe they have rooms here. Look, I know you're my richest client, but dude, you're certainly not my only one. Let's get crackin'!"

"You've certainly got a pair there, don't ya, mate?"

"And the backbone to carry them, man!" he says before heading out.

"Holy shit! I love this guy! He's fantastic! Look at him walking out of here like he owns the place!" I can't get over the bullocks on this guy.

"Uh-oh. Do I detect a bromance brewing?" Becca asks.

"You know what, sweetheart, you just might be." I'm laughing, but I'm actually very serious. If I'm going to be living out here in the sticks most of the year, I need a good mate I can throw a few back and laugh my arse off with.

"So, what do you kids want to see here?" Ray walks through the hall with us.

"We want twenty rooms, all doubles, with the exception of five. We'll need a state of the art—"

"Gray." Becca interjects.

"—kitchen. We'll want a dining area."

"Grayson."

"Then, we need the hall to be able to—"

"Hey, Ray." She grabs his arm to turn him to her. "When he's finished telling you what I want, please come and see me so I can tell you what really needs to be done in here. I'm going to go start on the *bread and butter* for lunch! See you both back at the inn." And there she goes, my hot-headed beauty.

"Dude . . . she's pissed!" Ray offers.

"Ray, who does your marketing?"

"Amy, my office manager. Why?"

"You better call her up and tell her to add 'impeccable talent for stating the obvious' to your website!" I state flippantly as I watch Becca round the corner and head out of sight. I pull out my phone and call the store.

"Mad Scrapper, this is Becca speaking."

"I'm trying to decide if it's more interesting or more ironic that the name of your store is 'Mad Scrapper,' since you are indeed a scrapper who is mad!" I went for a laugh. I got a dial tone. I should be infuriated, but it actually turns me on.

"Yes, Amy, please put 'impeccable talent for stating the obvious' on my site. Dude, should that be in all caps?" I stare at Ray. Have all the people up here lost their bloody minds? "Ha—gotcha, man!" He hangs up the phone with a laugh. I join in.

"Ray, go ahead and ask Becca about this, but don't let her skimp on things. Let's go see what your boys have for us." I slap him on the back and we head up.

"Now, if we are unable to get a house up there for you, we could head back this way." He extends his arm out to the right. "The only problem is that we would be cutting into a couple of the trails, and Becca loves her trails." Just as he says it, his guy comes down the mountain, shaking his head and waving his arms. "Well, there's your answer, Gray. I can bet I know the one you'll get from Becca about the trails."

"*Shit! Shit! Fuck! Shit!*" I grab at my hair as the profanities fly out of my mouth.

"Fuckity fuck . . . shiiiitty shit!" Ray adds. After a moment of silence, we're laughing again.

"Ugh! What am I going to do, mate? This is Becca we're talking about. I can't just tell her we're moving away!" I release my hair.

"Listen, Gray, I know the neighbors. I'll feel around and see if anyone is interested in selling to you guys. Times are hard; it might just work to your benefit." He shrugs.

"You're a brilliant man, Ray! Tell them I'll offer them more than what they paid."

"Dude, you're crazy!"

"Yes I am, Ray. Yes I am. Now, when are you taking me out for a pint? I'm surrounded by women 24-7 'til my mates fly in this weekend."

My phone rings while Ray checks his.

"Tomorrow night. I can break free around nine."

"Sounds good." I answer on the last ring. "What? Oh, bloody hell! Okay, I'm coming now." I hang up.

"What's the matter?" Ray rushes with me.

"Becca's passed out again."

"Again?"

"Yeah, this happened a couple of days ago."

"She pregnant?" Normal question, but I stop dead in my tracks.

"No. No, she couldn't be." I run up the steps of the Mad Scrapper. "Aunt Hazel, what happened?" I get down on the floor next to her. "Becca. Becca, sweetheart?"

"Nobody knows, Grayson. We just found her like this," Claudia says. Becca's eyes start fluttering.

"Sweetheart. Sweetheart, are you okay?" I pick her up.

"Grayson, you're going to hurt yourself."

"Nonsense. What happened?"

"I'm overwhelmed, I think."

"We're calling a doctor."

"Okay." Good, she knows not to argue. I carry her up the stairs to her room and lay her down on our bed.

BECCA

Honestly, I don't know what's wrong with me. One minute I'm hanging the phone up on Grayson, and the next I'm waking up on the floor.

"Becca, how many goddamn doctors do you need?" He's pacing as he goes through my phone. He's worried. I hate that he's worried. I love that he's worried.

"Dr. Peto, babe. Let me call. I'm fine." I reach out for the phone.

Grayson raises his hand to stop me. "Yes. I'd like to make an appointment with Dr. Peto. For my fiancée, Becca Campbell. March fifth, nineteen seventy-seven." How does he know my birthday? Morgan, probably. His fiancée, huh? I wish he would ask me properly. I don't even have a ring. I'm not one that requires much jewelry, but I would like an engagement ring. God, this is the most untraditional relationship in every sense. We've barely been together four days and *poof*—it's a sealed deal! He hasn't even taken me on an official date. What are we doing? What am I doing? This is crazy!

Is this what happened with Hazel and Harold? At least they were together a whole week before they were engaged. I need to talk to her. I need to know if she and Harold were this crazy. They did last forty years. She was only twenty. That's a good sign.

"Becca!" Grayson snaps.

"Sorry."

"Are these the only two times you've passed out recently?"

"Yes," I answer.

"Yes. Just recently," he says into the phone as he stares out the window. I know he's blaming himself.

"Okay. Tomorrow at nine. Very good, then. Thank you." He hangs up.

"Grayson, can you come over here?" I pat the bed.

"I think I should leave you alone to rest, sweetheart." He turns to head out the door.

"It's not your fault." I sit up.

"It bloody well is my fault! Now lie down!" he snaps, and swings my legs back into the bed.

"No it's not, and I'm not tired, damn it! Now stop!" I push his hands away. "I passed out the other day because I had a flashback of Geor . . . oh my God! Grayson! That's what happened today. I was hanging up on you and looking out the store window and I could've sworn I saw George in the parking lot, in a construction hat!" I remember the room spinning now. "Was I hallucinating?"

"Stay here!" Grayson barks and opens the door. I hear him shouting for Ray as he heads downstairs. Several minutes pass and Hazel comes in.

"Oh, Hazel, I must be losing my mind." I start crying.

"Shh, shh." She wraps her arms around me.

"What's going on down there?"

"Grayson and Ray are rounding up all of the men and questioning them to see if they saw somebody they didn't know."

"Hazel, what if I was hallucinating? I'm so stressed out. Grayson is my first relationship since George. We're moving crazy fast. He's turning my world upside down with renovations, a home, and a wedding. I'm so overwhelmed. Maybe I'm losing my mind."

"A wedding?" Her eyes light up. *Really—that's what she got from all of that?* "When?" she asks.

"Oh, who knows with Grayson? Maybe tomorrow! Maybe our first date will be on our honeymoon!"

"Where's your ring?" She grabs my hand.

"Who knows, probably hidden away with a real proposal?" I throw my hands up in the air.

"What are you talking about, dear?"

"He hasn't properly asked me. He just said, 'I want to marry you, let's pick a date.'" So I am mad about it. I was trying not to be, but it really sucks. If I were with Ray, he would've done something sweet and romantic. Ray, oh man . . . I know he likes Grayson, but I could see he was a little crushed. He tried to cover it up, so I ignored it.

"Becca, I'm sorry. I'll talk to him."

"Yeah, you should. I don't mean it like it's your responsibility. I just don't want to get into an argument with him. Hazel, can I ask you some personal questions?"

"Some?" She giggles.

"Well, yeah. One may lead into another." I play with the hem of my pillowcase.

"Okay."

"Did you and Harold . . . uh, well ..."

"Did we have sex that first week?" she finishes for me.

"Yes." I look at her shyly. She chuckles, her face bright red.

"Becca, we were like jackrabbits! We couldn't get enough of each other!"

"I keep worrying that Grayson and I are a fluke, or that we're just being blinded by our lust. I think I worry even more because of Morgan."

"Do you have butterflies every time he touches you?"

"Yes."

"When you're with him, do you feel as if life didn't exist before him?"

"Yes." I sit up straight.

"Throw caution to the wind, darling, because this is the real thing. It's love at first sight. It does exist. She's a rare gem and doesn't show herself to many, but boy—she's a beaut! Honey, I love you and him both. If I thought this was all wrong, I'd tell you." Just as she finishes her sentence, Grayson walks in.

"Well? Am I crazy?" I ask, but I can see from his face that something's not right. He's worried.

"I've got a security team coming up here in one hour. It's a precaution, but the four of us are going to be protected 24-7 until we are certain. Becca, let's go get Morgan from school now." He offers me his hand. "Aunt Hazel, Ray is staying behind with you while we're gone."

"Gray?" I look up at him.

"It'll be okay, sweetheart. I promise." He kisses my hair and we're off.

"What did you find out?" I finally ask as we head down the street to Morgan's school.

"One of the men saw a guy he had never seen before. He asked him to grab something. The guy never came back." His eyes stay focused on the road ahead. I feel like I'm going to vomit.

"Should I contact the service to see if there is any updated information on him?"

"I have my men working on that." He hits the blinker and turns into the school's parking lot.

"You have men, baby?" I smirk.

"I have men, sweetheart." His voice is flat.

"Will you come inside with me?" I ask as I unbuckle my belt.

"Yes. Stay in your seat. I'll come to you." Not a flicker of emotion has crossed his face. He is ultra-focused. I sigh when he walks around the car and opens the door for me.

"Grayson, maybe it's all coincidence."

"Sweetheart, I'm not taking a chance. Not a single one. I'm going to protect my family." He searches my eyes.

"I know you are. I love you, baby." I pull his face down to mine and brush his lips with my own. It's quick—no lingering or letting his guard down. Wow. So much focus. I grab his hand and we go to collect our daughter.

"Morgy girl, I've got a game for you. A guessing game," Grayson says cheerfully as he pulls her hoodie up to cover her head.

"What's that?" She's so excited that we came to get her early.

"I want you to look down and count how many footsteps it is until our car. See if you get the same number as me."

"But your feet are bigger!"

"Yes, but I've multiplied mine by two. Come on, I'll give you five dollars if you guess my number within ten. Do you think you can do it?" He holds up a five dollar bill.

"Of course I can." She grins.

"Okay. Here we go. Head down." Morgan complies.

"Forty-six!" she yells as he opens the car door for her.

"No, it can't be!" he says as she climbs in. "You are two off from me! I came up with forty-four. Here's your five. Fair is fair." We get in and drive home, listening to Morgan talk about her short day at school.

"Gray." I nudge him. He looks over at me. "We need to tell her about the security."

He nods. "Hey there, Morgy girl. Listen up for a minute."

"Yes, Daddy." A small smile finally appears on Grayson's lips.

"I have a fan acting very silly, so there are a bunch of men and women around the inn to keep us all safe."

"Like Secret Service agents?" she asks, her eyes wide.

"Yes. Just like Secret Service." A full-blown smile appears now. God, he loves her. I find it absolutely amazing that he's fallen this deeply in love with her as well. It's a good thing I'm not the jealous type.

"So we get the Secret Service because you are the president of your company?" Morgan leans her head forward in between us.

"Morgan, sit back! That's not safe!" Gray snaps. Morgan obeys and stares out the window. Her chin quivers—his tone has hurt her feelings. Gray glances in the rearview at her. "Sorry, Morgy. Uh . . . yes, I'm the president of my company, but these aren't the real Secret Service agents. They are just similar to them."

"Did a fan threaten your life?" It sounds like she's trying to be brave, but her voice shakes. I can tell she's worried. She's just acquired a father that she loves very much, and she's scared he'll be taken away from her.

"No, little sweetheart. She's just a little . . . delusional. Do you know what I mean?"

"I think so. They think if they get to you, you will fall in love with them?"

"Yes. That's it, Morgan!" He flashes her a smile in the rearview. I think we could both agree that this kid is brilliant.

"A lot of girls feel that way about Justin Bieber." Morgan rolls her eyes. "They are so stupid."

"Morgan, that's an ugly word! Please do not use it!" It's my turn to snap at her.

"Sorry, Mama." Ugh, brilliant girl. Whenever she wants forgiveness, she uses her secret weapon: "Mama." It's a reminder of when she was very little and it always makes me melt, like I'm butter in her hands.

"Okay, then. We're home. Let's find out who's assigned to you," Grayson says, and we all climb out.

"To do my bidding?" She gives a toothy, mischievous smile.

"No, to protect you. Don't give this person any reason to not want to do their job well!" I turn her around and tap her butt.

"Hey!" She laughs and we head up to the store entrance.

"They should be here by now. I told Claudia to send them into the crop room for a debriefing," Grayson says as he opens the door. A very serious-looking man approaches us as we enter.

"Mr. James, I'm Gregory Thomas. I'll be leading the team here." They shake hands. Mr. Thomas has crew-cut blond hair that is graying slightly at his temples. His eyes are bright blue, his face ruddy. He's tall, but like most people, Grayson towers over him. There is a team of about twenty-five people in the room. *Holy shit.*

"I have two questions before we get into everything here," I pipe up.

"Yes, Mrs. James." Thomas gives me his full attention.

"It's *Ms. Campbell.*" I correct him and watch Gray frown slightly.

"Sorry. Ms. Campbell."

"Oh, that's okay. First, who will be assigned to my ... our ... daughter?" I correct myself quickly and feel Gray's squeeze my shoulder in thanks.

"This is Tanya Smith. She will be with your daughter, ma'am." He points to a light-skinned woman of African descent. She steps forward, extends her hand to me, and nods when I shake it.

"Tanya, what are your credentials? How can you protect my daughter from the subject in question?" It's a legit question, I think. I know how strong George was—or is. I know all about his training.

"I'm an ex-Marine with a black belt in MMA."

"MMA?" I ask.

"Mixed martial arts," she says. I nod. "I've also been trained at Crucible, just like everyone else here. I can assure you that your daughter is safe in my hands."

"Do you have children?"

Her eyes soften, and I know the answer.

"She'll be safe, Ms. Campbell."

"Becca," I offer.

"Becca." She nods.

"Okay. Next—how do we keep my guests oblivious to your presence?" I look around at the team dressed in black uniforms.

"Ms. Campbell?" Thomas asks, tilting his head to the side.

"My guests are on vacation. They don't need to feel that they are not safe here. Please tell me you will dress to blend in."

"Yes, Ms. Campbell, we will do our best." Thomas jots something on his notepad.

"Tanya, would you mind going with Morgan so we can continue in here?" I kiss Morgan's hair.

"But, Mom, I want to stay and hear everything," she complains.

"Come on, Morgan, can you show me which horse is yours?" Tanya asks. Morgan's face lights up. She's very proud of Butterscotch. They leave and the debriefing begins.

I tell them what I think I saw. I give them a brief history of my relationship with George. Finally, I give them the best profile I can of George from seven years ago. Obviously, if he's alive, I don't know of any new training he's acquired. As they put together his profile, I feel as if I'm on an episode of *Criminal Minds*. I look around to see if there's anyone like my favorite character, Spence, played by Matthew Gray Gubler. Just love him on the show—he's so brilliant, and it's very attractive. But I don't see anyone that seems remotely like him. Bummer.

Melissa is assigned to me. I think it's because she looks the most like me—minus fifty pounds. I look over at Gray to see if he's attracted to her at all. She seems to have a hard time peeling her eyes away from him. I suppose I'll have to get used to that. Is it bad that I'm not a jealous person? Will it make me oblivious? Hmm, that's a tough one. I don't want to look like an asshole by acting jealous, and yet, I don't want to look like an asshole by being oblivious. You know what? I'll just stick with my gut. It's never steered me wrong before! *Ahem.*

"Becca, snap out of it and focus!" Grayson taps my arm.

Huh? Oh.

"Sorry." I smile sheepishly.

"C'mon, sweetheart, you need to rest." He reaches for me.

"I'm not tired," I complain quietly, but take his hand.

"I can help you with that." He smirks and raises an eyebrow.

"I'd love that." I allow him to lead me upstairs. Our detail follows us. I turn to them. "Will you two be outside our room?"

"Yes, ma'am," Derek answers. I see a slight flicker of embarrassment cross his face. Melissa blushes enough for them both. Derek may be flushed too, but his African ethnicity makes it difficult to tell. He's the biggest guy they have here. He almost matches Grayson's height, but is double his size. Something tells me he's just a big teddy bear on the inside, though. I like him. I can sense a family man in him.

"C'mon, love." Grayson pulls me into the room. I close the door and see the envy on Melissa's face. I know she'd like to be the one in here with Grayson. I have this strong urge to be extremely loud. Hmm . . . I'm not jealous of her, but I'm totally eating up her jealousy of me. That's not good. Besides, I don't want Derek to feel uncomfortable. And these people should not know what I sound like in bed! Ugh. This is so weird! We've tried to be quiet so other guests wouldn't hear us, but they were never standing outside our door. I quickly turn on my iPod and play Jordan Knight's "Unfinished" album.

"Looking to drown out our sounds, sweetheart?" Gray wraps his arms around me from behind. I'm immediately intoxicated by his lovely scent. His shirt is already off. I turn around and place my hands on his chest. God, he is a beautiful specimen. I feel my insecurities rise. *Why does he want me?* I have to work so hard to stay in a size twelve, and Melissa outside there is easily a size six—if not a four. "What is it, sweetheart? Why are you frowning?" He chucks my chin. I know for a fact that men find insecure women unattractive. I don't want to say anything negative about myself.

"Melissa's attractive. She's got a great figure. I wonder what her exercise regimen is." I'm so sly.

He crooks his head sideways. "I'm not attracted to her, if that's what you're trying to get at."

"No. I know that. Hey, I wonder if she's single. If I like her, I could introduce her to Ray." I suddenly feel brilliant.

"No, sweetheart, Ray won't go for her." His smile is slight as he pulls my shirt off.

"Why? How do you know?"

"Because Ray, like me, only has eyes for you."

I gasp lightly. How does he know? Did Ray tell him?

"I saw the way he looked at you this morning," Grayson continues. "I saw his face when he realized that we are together. He's a great fellow. If he looked at my car like that, I'd give it to him. But I can't give him you. I think he and I will become great friends, but you will always be the elephant in the room of the friendship. I find it comforting and disturbing all at once." He seems very puzzled by his feelings. I can't get past him referring to me as the "elephant."

"Why is it comforting and disturbing?" I lean into him as he unhooks my bra.

"Because I know he feels the same way about you that I do. That's the disturbing part. But because he feels that way, I know he will look after you if, for some reason, I'm unable to. I trust him with you. He's a gentleman through and through. It's hard to find a guy like that. Becca, why aren't you with Ray?" He palms my face, drawing my gaze up to his.

"I . . . I wasn't ready. I didn't feel the way I feel with you. I was able to shut him down."

"Why do you speak in past tense?" He's searching.

"Last year, he and I had a moment. We were caught in a downpour. It was so bad we could barely see in front of us. I missed the last step on his porch. He caught me. We kissed." I stop.

"Becca?"

"Well, it was the kind of kissing that leads to other things. We kissed into his house. We started taking each other's clothes off. We never made it upstairs. I froze."

"Did you like kissing him?" He's no longer searching. He seems unsure of himself. Wow. How did we circle around to *his* insecurity?

"Yes." My honesty pulls his eyes back up to me sharply. "But it was nothing compared to kissing you. No butterflies, no tingling all over. There is no comparison, Gray. You are the one for me."

"Was he gentle or aggressive when he was taking your clothes off? How far did he get? How did he touch you?" He's searching again. His eyelids are doing Morse code.

"Grayson, please. I told you everything. Stop it."

"Tell me!" His nostrils flare down at me.

"Why?"

"Tell me."

"Um, he wasn't gentle or really aggressive. It was more of a sense of urgency," I offer. I feel my face grow warm.

"Where did he touch you?" His jawline is twitching. Why is he acting like this? This is ridiculous. "Becca, answer me!"

I close my eyes, trying to remember. Another rush of heat hits my face as I recall Ray's mouth on my lips, my neck . . . the tops of my breasts. I remember him hiking my summer dress up and lifting me against the wall of his staircase. His hands held my bum, softly squeezing as he pushed up against me to show me how I was affecting him. I remember wanting him. I remember being afraid of that want. I pushed him off of me and told him to stop. He let me down and begged me not to go. He promised he would never hurt me. He just wanted to love me. I pulled myself back together. The rain had stopped. I left. I didn't talk to him for six months.

"Becca ..." Grayson's voice is barely audible. I open my eyes. "Did you make love to him?"

"No. You know I didn't! Why are you asking me? Why are you

asking me any of this? It's in the past. You are my present. You are my future. Please stop, baby."

"Okay, sweetheart. I'm sorry." He pecks at my lips.

"Oh, come now, Mr. James. I think you can do much better than that." I smile coyly.

"Yes. I believe I can!" He scoops me up and tosses me onto the bed. How does he do that? He makes me feel so light. Which reminds me, I never did get anywhere with my whole "going through the back door" routine. What the hell? "Um, Sweetheart, the idea is that two people make love, not one. I'd really like for you to join me here." *Oops!*

"Sorry, I'm very distracted today."

"Well, I'd like to distract you from your distractions, but if I have to reel you in again, I'm going to stop." I can see the agitation all over his face.

"I'm sorry, baby. I'm here, right where I want to be." I run my hand through his hair and kiss his mark. "I'm ready to pray, Grayson. I'm ready to pray really, really hard," I whisper in his ear. I feel the tension in his body leave as he finds my mouth with his. I give him my full concentration. He takes me to church, over and over again. Our love-making has a soporific effect on me that I slowly succumb to.

I'm awoken by a pounding on the door. I don't know how long I've been asleep or where Grayson went off to.

"Just a minute!" I jump out of bed, grabbing Grayson's dress shirt and buttoning it up. I open the door and pop my head sideways. It's Ray. Oh, why didn't I throw my own clothes on? His eyes start at my top and work their way down. His jawline twitches as he breathes rapidly through his nose—a telltale sign that he's pissed. Probably because I'm in Grayson's shirt and my hair is down and wild, like I've just done . . . well, what I did.

He hands me a binder. "Here are the guys' staff pictures for you to look through."

"Thanks." I take it from him. He holds on and pulls, forcing me forward a little. His eyes scan me again. He's so angry. I've never seen Ray angry, at least not at me.

"You look beautiful." He lets go of the book.

"I'm sorry, Ray."

"For what?"

"If this is hurting you. I never meant for you to get hurt." I'm trying to keep it together.

"Oh, I'm not hurt . . . I think 'destroyed' is the word I'd go for." He purses his lips and exhales cautiously.

"I'm sorry." What else can I say? I close the door.

GRAYSON

"Ray! There you are." I run into him as I'm heading back upstairs.

"Oh, hey. I gave Becca the binder with all of my employee pictures." He's wiping his eyes.

"You all right, mate?"

"Yeah, just some hay fever. Listen, dude, I'll see you tomorrow. I'm late for a meeting." He slaps me on the back and heads off. That was weird. I continue to Becca's room.

"You know, darling, I should just move my . . . stuff . . . Becca? Are you okay? Why are you crying?" Oh, hay fever my arse!

"I'm okay." She tries to smile.

"What just happened between you and Ray?" I'm trying my hardest to stay calm.

"We had some words, that's all. He gave me this binder." She pushes it back a little further on the table near the window. "I was waiting for you so we could look at it together."

She's changing the subject.

"Becca, I want to know every word of your conversation!" Yeah,

I'm done being calm. "Now, Becca!" I hit the table.

"Stop bullying me! You're making a mountain out of a molehill. We didn't say anything important."

She sounds defensive.

"We'll see!" I head out the door. "Melissa, I need you to tell me what was said between Ms. Campbell and Mr. McNeil, please!" She looks up at me, unsure of where her loyalty lies. "You are in my employ," I remind her. She proceeds to tell me what they said, how they reacted to each other. "That's everything?"

"Yes, sir," she says, and glances past me. I turn to see Becca in the doorway of our room. She's looking at us as if we've stabbed her in the back. I walk back to her.

"Let's have a look at those pictures, love."

"Your room is over there, Mr. James." She jerks her head toward it.

"Becca, don't start. Let me in." I'm trying my hand at being calm again. For my efforts, I get a door slammed in my face. I can't do this right now. I'm just going to go downstairs and see about Morgan. Make sure she's getting on all right.

Becca doesn't leave her room for the rest of the day, so I send Morgan upstairs with dinner for her.

"Mommy says he's not in here," she says when she comes back, and hands me the binder.

"Oh, okay. Thank you, little sweetheart. How is Mummy?" I haven't seen her in five hours. It's killing me. Morgan shrugs indifferently.

"Grayson, I think you and I need to have a talk," Aunt Hazel whispers in my ear. Oh God, this can't be good.

"Right now?" *Please say no.*

"Yes. Morgan will be fine with Tanya." Tanya nods in agreement. I get up and follow my aunt into her room. "Gracie, I've noticed some things I don't particularly care for. Becca won't say anything to you, but I know they're bothering her as well." She plants herself in a chair and points to the other seat. I sit.

"What is it, Auntie?" I ask, feeling a bit irritated.

"You're moving so fast with Becca. You haven't slowed down to do the simple little things that matter."

I wait for her to finish, but apparently, she has.

"Spit it out, Auntie. I'm not a mind reader!"

"Watch your tone with me, Gracie!"

"Sorry. What is it? What have I not done?"

"How about showing her a good time outside of the bedroom?"

"I haven't taken her out because she can't leave this place! I wanted to go out to dinner with Becca and Morgan last night, and we couldn't. The day before, we were going to see a movie, but she had to stay here. I'm not planning a romantic evening with her until she has the goddamn staff to cover her arse!" I've gone from irritated to furious. *Women!*

"Okay. That's fair," she says thoughtfully. *Well, good.* "How about the whole 'I want to marry you, let's pick a date' thing? No proper proposal. No ring. Yet you're telling everyone she's your fiancée."

"She's complained to you about this?" I feel my heart sink. She's right.

"You're so quick to make sure you have what you want that you are forgetting she is a person. Not an item or company you want to acquire."

Ugh! I'm a complete idiot!

"Auntie, you're right. I will fix this."

"Now tell me—why is Becca avoiding you today?" She slaps my knee. I tell her about Ray, his history with Becca, and what Melissa told me. "So you went behind her back to find out about a conversation she had and told you not to worry about?" she asks, tapping her chin with her finger.

"Yes."

"Do you trust her?" She opens her eyes wide.

"Of course I trust her." What kind of question is that?

"Don't you think that may have come across as you not trusting her?" Becca's right—Auntie is like Nancy Drew.

"Do you think that's why she's been avoiding me for so long?"

"What do you think?" She sips her tea.

"I think she's confused about Ray, to be honest." There, I said it.

"I think that's your green monster talking. She could've had Ray a long time ago."

She almost did, I want to say, but I don't.

"Well, she won't talk to me. What can I say? I'm not going to beg outside her door. I'll let her sleep on it tonight. Give us both some space."

"That may be a good idea, Gracie." There's my Auntie again, complete with her loving smile. She is a beautiful woman, even at seventy.

"Auntie?" I turn back to her as I'm about to leave.

"Yes, dear?"

"If Becca isn't confused about her feelings for Ray, why was she so upset?"

"Grayson, Ray is one of her dearest friends—probably her best friend next to Stacey. I think she got upset because she truly would never do anything to hurt him. She loves him, Gracie, just not in that way. He's always been good to her. He respects her."

"Christ, Auntie, you don't have to sell him to me!" I laugh. "I think the guy's great. We're going out for a few pints tomorrow."

"That won't be awkward for you, given his feelings for Becca?" She seems shocked. I don't blame her.

"Auntie, he's a man of great character and honor. Sure, there may be moments of awkwardness, but we genuinely like each other." Her eyes are still wide. "I know. I find it kind of crazy, too!"

We head back out into the hall, and I see Becca walking with

Morgan. My heart leaps at the sight.

"Off to bed so soon, Morgy girl?"

"Mom and I are going to watch some TV before I go to bed." She gives me a hug and a kiss.

"I'll be in to say good night, sweetheart." I mess her hair. I try to grab Becca's hand, but she pulls away forcefully. All right then. Melissa gives me a sympathetic look. I shrug. What else can I do? "I'm going to head up to my room. Good night, Auntie." I give her a quick kiss before heading up.

A few mindless TV shows later, I hear Becca's feet on the steps. I rush to open my door, but before I can even open my mouth to speak, she puts her hand up to dismiss me.

That rude fucking . . . ugh! I am pissed now! I charge after her, pushing Melissa to the side and crashing through the door. "How *dare* you?" I yell. "I have this team in place to protect your arse, and this is how you treat me? You disrespect me in front of my employees? What do you have to say for yourself?" I feel crazy. She's got me absolutely mad!

"Get out!"

"That's it? Get out? Sweetheart, you better take a moment and really think about if that's what you want, because I've about had it! I walk out this door and we are done! Finished! Do you understand me?" I try to calm down. I take a breath and realize what I just said. I didn't mean it. My eyelids are going a mile a minute, and she's just standing there in disbelief. "Well?" I can barely speak. I feel as if I'm going to boot. She looks down. I feel dismissed. "Right," I manage, and head toward the door. But I stop. I so badly want to turn around and tell her I didn't mean it. I take in a shaky breath and turn the knob.

"Gray!" she yelps. I close my eyes, thanking God, and close the door in front of me. I turn and race to her. She steps back.

"Becca, please, you have me terribly confused." I sit on the bed and rest my head in my palms.

"You didn't trust me. You don't trust me. How can we be together if you don't trust me?" *Ah, she speaks.*

"I trust you. I've become a very jealous man since I met you. I've never felt this way about anyone before. I don't have control, and I think that's where the jealousy comes in." Good, we're talking. We communicate very well when we take the time to do it.

"Well, there's no reason to be jealous. Honestly, I don't get it. I'm not that great. I don't even understand why you are attracted to me!" *Did she just wave her hands down her body?*

"For the same reason Ray, and Will, and a half a dozen other guys in this town are! Becca, you're fucking beautiful—outside and in! I can't believe this. You haven't once given me any indication that you are self-conscious about your body. Where is this coming from?" This is not the Becca I've been with the past several days.

"I've always been this way. I just haven't said anything because I know guys hate listening to women complaining about themselves."

"Well, you're right. It's absolute nonsense. If I wasn't attracted to you, I wouldn't be with you. I obviously can't keep my fucking hands off of you! Do you know what I see when I look at you?" I stroll over to her and guide her to the mirror.

"What?" She looks away. I bring her face back.

"I see a woman. Beautiful curves. *Fantastic* bum. I don't like twiggies—they look like teenaged boys. It's gross. When I'm in bed with a woman, I want to feel a *woman*. Look at Catherine Zeta-Jones, Sofia Vergara . . . gorgeous women . . . real women. Look at you, doll. You make things stand that don't have feet!" Ah, there it is. I love her laughter. Best sound in the world—besides the obvious, of course.

"I'm worried about what your friends will think of me." She looks down.

"If they are smart, they will think the same as I do. And if they are really smart, they'll keep their bloody hands off of you! Oh, Becca, please squash these thoughts. I'm so head over heels for you, darling."

"You were going to leave me." Her eyes fill.

"I was bluffing; cursed myself out once I made the threat. Honestly, I thought I was going to boot! You know me with vomit—that would not have been a good situation." I cringe at the thought. "Are we good, sweetheart?" I palm her face. "I'd really like to kiss you now. You know how selfish I am."

"Yes. We're good." She places her hands on top of mine.

"Good, because I haven't kissed you in eight hours or so. It's detrimental to my health. I feel weak." I peck at her lips softly.

"Well, we wouldn't want to do anything that would jeopardize your health."

"Becca, I'm truly blindsided by your insecurity. You carry yourself with such confidence, and you don't come off that way in bed, either."

"Yeah, well, I guess I'm a great actress." She shrugs. "C'mere, baby, let me give you an Emmy performance." She smiles and leads me to the bed. She gazes up into my eyes, and before I know it, buttons from my shirt are flying everywhere.

"Ugh! That was my favorite shirt!" I tease.

"Really? Get over it!" She removes it from my body harshly. Her eyes are on fire. I know what she's doing. She wants to give me aggressive. She knows I like it. I grab her wrists and spin her around. I hold them, her arms crisscrossed in front of her, as I slowly run my mouth down the side of her neck and shoulder.

"Lift your arms," I whisper as I grab the hem of her camisole. She obeys and I pull it over her head. My mouth continues its journey across and down her back. I slide her bottoms off and bite playfully at her bum. *God, I love her arse!* I take the rest of my clothes off and turn her to me. My mouth finds hers. I can feel her trembling with anticipation, and I nudge her onto the bed. I follow her lead as she moves backward on her elbows, our mouths connected. The moonlight coming through the window is just breathtaking on her skin. "God, I'm so in love with you, Becca," I confess. She kisses my mark and nudges my hip with her leg. I press my lips to hers and enter her. For the first time, I make love to her at a slow, agonizing pace. It is the sweetest torture I have ever experienced.

Chapter Eight

BECCA

Six in the morning. Again. I am *so* never getting up this early when I hire staff.

"Rise and shine, sweetheart!" Why the hell is Grayson so chipper this morning? Oh, yes. I remember. *(Mental blush.)*

"Good morning, baby." I greet him with a smile that widens when I see a cup of coffee in his hands.

"You have a few extra people to feed this morning." He grabs my hands to pull me out of bed, then steals a kiss.

"Yeah, just a few." I roll my eyes and grab the coffee off the nightstand.

"The lawyer is coming today. He was in court yesterday, which worked out better for us anyhow. Um, Ray is stopping by to go over your plans for the hall and stable. Are you up for that?" I just nod. "Sure?"

"Yes."

"Oh, and my finance guy will be here later to go over your

stuff," he adds.

"I'm sure you've already sent him my numbers and bills so he's all organized, right?" I smirk.

"Uh. Yes. Are you angry?" Morse-code lids, activated. I laugh as I watch them. *Beep-beep, beep-beep, beep-beep.* "Are you laughing at my eyelids?" He rubs his eyes.

"Sorry. I keep thinking I should learn Morse code." I giggle again.

"Morse code?"

"Yes. That's all I hear when I see you do that." I do the *beep-beeps* for him.

"Oh, that's easy, sweetheart. You don't need to take a course. They are simply saying, 'Mayday, Mayday, she's going to blow!'" He laughs.

"Interesting. They weren't doing that the other night when I was getting ready to blow."

"Ooh . . . you're a naughty one, aren't you?" He wraps me in his arms.

"Only when I want to be." I pat his arm, indicating he should let go so I can get dressed. "I'll see you downstairs later?"

"C'mere." He pulls me to him for a kiss. "I'll be down in a couple of hours. I'm going to try to get some more sleep."

"Okay. See you then. Love you!" I open the door. Melissa perks up.

"Melissa, please don't tell me you've been out here all night."

"Oh, no. I just came on duty." She yawns. "Sorry."

"Coffee?"

"Oh, yes please!" Her eyes shoot open at the thought.

"Well, we have plenty made. Let's hit the kitchen. I have to get started on breakfast." We wave to the other detail as we head in.

So begins my morning routine. The menu for this morning is eggs Benedict, waffles, hash browns, and the usual mixed cereals, breads, granola, and yogurt.

"How do you do this every day? It's only seven o'clock and I'm exhausted from watching you."

I've decided in the past hour that Melissa is a lovely girl. We have a lot in common as far as music and interests. She's from a small town outside of Wichita, Kansas. No husband, boyfriend, or kids. She is the third youngest of ten children, and she has twenty nieces and nephews. Her parents are still alive and own a little country store.

After I learn all of this, Melissa teases me about my interrogation skills, saying I should've been in the service.

Just then, Ray pops his head into the kitchen, startling me.

"Becca, are you all done setting up for breakfast? I'd like to meet with you now."

"Um . . . yeah, I'll be right out."

"Are you okay?" Melissa asks once he's left. She places her hand on my forearm.

"Yeah, I just don't know why he's here so early." I look at her, feeling very nervous.

"Probably to get it over with so he doesn't drive himself crazy all day," she offers.

"Well, let's go." I sigh and we head out. We catch up with Ray, and I decide to try my hand at conversation. "Isn't this early for you, Ray?"

"I have a lot going on today," he states flatly.

"Well, you know what they say. 'The early bird catches the worm!'"

"Apparently not, Becca!" he snaps. I don't try again.

"What do you want here?" he asks tersely once we reach the hall. I ramble off everything.

"So, basically, everything Grayson fucking said yesterday?"

"Um, yeah, except I would like a small area for the croppers to shop. Not a whole other store. Just big enough to hold the usual items they tend to buy." I try to ignore his anger.

"How big?" he asks impatiently.

"Well, um, I don't know. Maybe as big as my office?"

"Don't ask me! It's your renovation; you should know what you want."

This time, I've had it.

"Raymond McNeil! You have never been disrespectful to me in all of the years I've known you. Just because things didn't happen the way you wanted them to doesn't mean you get to be now! Knock it off!"

"You're right. Sorry, Becs. Ten by ten should be more than big enough for what you need. Let's head over to the stables."

Once we reach them, I try again. "Do you have a recommendation for out here?"

"No, Becs, I really don't. I can talk to Charlie and do some research on stables to find out what the newest trend is," he offers.

"Thanks, Ray. I really don't know what to do out here." I pause. "How's Annie?" Our daughters have always been common ground for us.

"Really, Becca? Really? 'How's Annie?'" His petulant tone returns. "Is it the money?" he asks, and I could slap him.

"Wow. Yeah, that's me! I'm a gold digger, all about the Benjamins!" I snap. He laughs.

"Ghetto Becca strikes again. All about the Benjamins?" He chuckles again. *Oh, my friend.*

"Well, you know how I likes to roll." I thumb my nose.

"Becca, why him? Why not me? I like Grayson. Irony is, I see us becoming great friends. I just don't understand. I've been waiting patiently for a whole year . . . ever since that day. Should I have been more persistent? What could I have done differently?" He leans against the stable wall.

"Ray, you're just not British enough for me." I try to make light of it. I get a half smile. "Honestly, I don't have the answer. I'm still trying to figure this whirlwind out myself. Grayson is a good guy.

You know, I see an aspiring bromance between you two." *Anything?* Nope. Okay, staying serious. "I didn't know you still felt that way until I saw your face in the office yesterday."

"So I was too cautious? You do—did—find me attractive?" *Wow, this was in question?*

"Ray, I never would've kissed you like that if I didn't." Let's lay that puppy to rest.

"Are you still attracted to me?" He grazes my cheek with the back of his hand and moves closer.

"Ray, please don't . . . please."

"That day still haunts me. I can still feel your mouth on mine." His breath is hot in my face.

"Ray, please." I beg. *Oh no. No. No. No . . . not butterflies! Oh God, really—because my life is not complicated enough?*

"I love you, Becca." Just as he pulls my face to his, Rocco neighs loudly and kicks his stall door. *Impeccable timing.*

"Rocco, what's the matter?" I pull away quickly, before Ray's lips reach mine, and look in on my horse. "Whoa. Whoa, boy!" I say, trying to calm him down. Charlie rushes in and joins me.

"Becca, what is it?"

"I don't know. Something spooked him, I think." I have one guess. "Charlie, when you get him settled down, Ray would like to go over your thoughts on the renovations." I turn to face my old friend. "Thanks for stopping by, Ray. I have to get back inside now," I say, and take off like Julia Roberts in *Runaway Bride*. He follows me.

"Becca!" He grabs my arm outside the stable doors, pulling me to him. "You felt that too. I know you did."

"Ray, I'm engaged. You have to stop!"

"Really? You know, Becs, if you were engaged to me, people would know it because you'd *have a goddamn ring on your finger.*" Butterflies . . . again? *Oh, yeah.* Probably because Ray's tongue is suddenly in my mouth, playing nicely with mine. I can't pull away.

I feel completely paralyzed.

"Oh, Becs . . . baby, please don't marry him. You belong with me," he begs against my lips. I feel the panic rising inside of me. Grayson! How could I let this happen?

"You're fired." I start to cry as I pull away from him.

"What?" His nostrils flare.

"You're fired." My verbal delivery of his pink slip is weak, but to the point. "Melissa, let's go." I turn, and we head back toward the inn. I start to sob. "I'm going to be sick to my stomach."

"Yeah, that makes two of us," Melissa says.

We get inside and I rush up the stairs, only to run into Grayson. His eyes are red. He glares at me angrily.

"Becca!"

"Grayson, I fired him." That's all I say as I continue up the stairs. He follows me into the room. I sit on the bed, waiting for the wrath of Grayson James to be unleashed.

"Explain to me why you are crying, because I want to be fair and not come to my own conclusions," he says through his teeth.

"Because I'm mad as hell. I'm mad at myself. I'm mad at him. I don't know, Grayson, because I know I just blew it with you!" I lean down and sob into my hands. A thought pops into my head that steals my breath away. "Did you know he was coming this early?" He says nothing. "You set me up?" Nothing, again. I feel my heart shatter. "This was a test?"

"And you failed miserably." He looks away.

"I'm sorry." I get up and walk around him, trying to catch his gaze. "I'm sorry that I disappointed you. I will do anything for your forgiveness."

"You fired him without any hesitation, so that's a start. I need to go talk to my aunt. Please move out of my way." He won't look at me.

"Grayson, please, can't we talk this through?"

"Becca, please. I'm so mad. You need to let me leave this room."

His fists are pumping.

"He kissed me! I didn't initiate. Ask Melissa!"

"Oh, I plan on getting a full report from her!"

"Good! Then you will find out that I was turning his advances down the entire time!"

"You kissed him back, didn't you?" he asks through gritted teeth.

"Yes, but it was one of those moments where you don't realize you are doing something until you're in the middle of it. The moment I realized, I pushed him away and fired him! Please, baby, I love you. I didn't mean for this to happen. I was trying to avoid it. I swear!" I'm full-blown sobbing now. I try to reach for his face, but he grabs my wrist and squeezes it so hard I feel like it might break. "Baby, you're hurting me." I lean into him and cry. He pulls me angrily to our bed. I'm happy and scared all at once as he practically rips my clothes off. "What do you want, baby?"

"Lie down on your stomach, Becca." He's stern.

"Okay. What are you going to do?" I ask nervously. He says nothing, and I obey. My obsequious nature greets me like an old friend. I swallow hard and scrunch my pillow with my arms. Before I can even think about what he has planned, I feel a painful sting on my right bum cheek. I yelp.. "Oh God, Grayson. Please . . . don't!"

"Shut up!" he snaps, and his hand comes down again. I bury my face in the pillow and cry. *Submissive Sybil takes over and I respond to his harsh spanks with groans.* I don't know how many times his hand has hit my backside.

He pulls my hips up, forcing me to my knees. He opens my legs and thrusts himself inside of me with such rage, pounding into me so hard I can barely catch my breath. He pulls me up to him so my back is flush against his chest and tugs fiercely at my nipples. There's a fine line between pain and pleasure, and Grayson has me crossing both over and over.

"Oh . . . oh God, baby." I pray as I finally give in to the intensity.

I feel his pace slow down. He's gritting his teeth. I tighten around him. Grayson gasps then releases himself inside of me. "I love you, Gray." I rest my head back on his shoulder.

"Get off." He pats the side of my right thigh. I pull away from him and lie down on my side. He does the same so we're face to face.

"I love you. Please." I try to touch his face. He stops me. I just lay there with my eyes closed and cry. I can't help but wonder when his acrimonious behavior toward me will end—or if it will at all.

"I liked spanking you. I love how you reacted, how wet you were when I entered you. Did you like getting spanked?" I open my eyes to see his face. His glacial stare is no longer. He's warm now, as if nothing happened.

"I like how you spanked me the other night. This time it really hurt, Grayson." My voice trembles.

"But then you liked it." He encourages me.

"Yes. Once I got over the shock of what you were doing. I felt myself accept it and give in."

"That is so hot. You're so hot, sweetheart." He runs his hand down my side.

"Are you going to leave me?"

"No. I'm just going to make you pay for what you did until I feel that you've more than made up for it. So you can expect a lot of this!" He slaps my bum harshly again, and I give him the reaction he wants. "Christ, sweetheart! So fucking hot ..." His mouth is on mine. I welcome him eagerly. He slaps me again, and I release a sob from my throat. He rolls me on my back and pushes my knees apart. Before I know it, he's inside of me again. But he's not harsh; he's making love to me. Soon I find myself praying, loudly, for the whole world to hear. This pleases Grayson. I'm on my way to redemption.

"Gray, I have to get Morgan ready for school." I try to climb out of his arms. He pulls me back.

"You're not going anywhere, darling. You're on bed *ar*rest."

"Gray, I'll come back to bed as soon as she's off to school. Besides, we have the lawyer and your finance guy coming. We really can't stay in bed all day." Mad or not, he's being unrealistic.

"So you're refusing my wishes, is that right?"

"It's not that I'm refusing them, it's just not a good day to stay in bed." Why am I allowing this behavior toward me again? I've more than made up for kissing Ray, so says my sore, welted ass!

"You do realize the thin ice you're on, correct?" He hovers over me.

"You do realize that I've already had one man treat me this way and that I will not go down that road again, right?"

"Oh! So you are comparing me to George again? Well, you know, I'm starting to see his side of things. You probably deserved half the beatings he gave you!" I gasp as I feel my heart plummet. *How could he say that?* That's it—I'm done!

"We're through, Grayson. I need you to leave," I say through my tears. He kisses them away.

"You don't mean it, darling. You love me and I love you. We'll work through this." He trails his kisses down my face and neck.

"I'm done, Grayson. Get off of me! I need you to leave. I don't want to be with you!" He ignores me and holds my hands above my head. "Stop! No! Stop it, Grayson! I don't want you to!" He doesn't listen. He enters me with one swift thrust. I just lay there, defeated, while he has his way with me again.

"Sweetheart, move with me. I love you. Please, I'm sorry," he pleads. I'm numb. I can't even look at him. He stops and climbs off of me. I run to the bathroom to get dressed and finish my crying before I see to my daughter.

Opening the door, I find Grayson with his head in his hands. He looks up and his eyes are rimmed with red. "I went too far, sweetheart. Please forgive me. We both stepped out of line today. Please don't say it's over. Let's just back up and slow down. Let me take you on a date tomorrow night. I'll give you the rest of the day, night, and tomorrow until our date. I won't get in your way. I'll give you space. Please, for our sake and Morgan's. I don't want to lose you. I'm so sorry for what I said, and did. That was unacceptable." He grabs my hands and kisses the top of each of them.

"I can't go tomorrow. Claudia is working tonight for Morgan's swim meet," I say flatly.

"All right, we'll go to her meet tonight. Then we'll bring her back and go on our date. I promise I won't try anything, sweetheart, until I get the okay from you. You have my word." He squeezes my hands.

"Your words hurt," I murmur.

"Yes. I'm an arsehole at times. I'm going to try harder. So, to-night?" He shoots me a hopeful smile.

"Okay." I sigh and pull my hands away. I leave him to his thoughts. *Country Sybil appears in my mind with a picture of Ray.* Yes, I know—Ray would've never treated me the way Grayson did this morning. Ray . . . oh God, he's going to be there tonight with Annie. This should be interesting. Maybe they will duke it out at the swim meet like the two guys from *Bridget Jones's Diary* (the most hysterical part of the movie). Ray is Mr. Darcy, and Grayson is Daniel Cleaver! Hmm, there's some food for thought.

What is it with men, though? I find it absolutely amazing that a woman can be single for years, and then as soon as one man is in the picture, several come out of the woodwork pining for her affection. Do we send out extra pheromones? I need to look this up.

"Mommy, pay attention!" Morgan yells. Jesus, I didn't even re-alize I was already in her room.

"Sorry, baby." I smile and get her outfit.

"I hope I win tonight against Ashley. Please tell me Daddy is coming!" She grabs my arm with a sense of urgency.

"Yes, Morgan. Grayson is coming." She jumps around in a cir-cle at my words. "Morgan, I understand why you are insistent on calling Grayson 'Daddy,' but I really need you to stop." I try to be as stern as I can be.

"Why, Mommy?" She sticks out her bottom lip.

"It's not fair to anyone. You shouldn't call him that until we are married. What happens if we don't work out? Honey, you are possibly setting yourself up for a disappointment that I can't help you avoid." I'm trying to explain this to her so that she *really* gets it.

"You can help by making sure you don't screw things up!" she snaps.

"Morgan Alexa, how dare you talk to me like that?" *What the hell?*

"I'm sorry, Mama." Her chin quivers.

"I need to go for a walk," I say as I rub my temples with my fingers. I head out of her room and slam the door. Why is everybody treating me like shit today?

"What's the matter, love?" Grayson reaches for me.

"Go fuck yourself, Gray!" I say vehemently and walk away. "Hazel, I'm going out." I grab my keys.

"But Claudia is not coming in until this afternoon."

"Tell Grayson to help. I'm sorry, Hazel. I can't stay here." I walk out and get into my truck, wincing at the soreness of my ass cheeks when I sit. Melissa runs after the truck, waving for me to stop. I ignore her and head down the long driveway.

Where am I going? Normally, when I have a problem, I go to Ray. I tell Ray everything. He's my best friend. So . . . Ray's place it is. I don't care what anyone thinks about it, either.

I take all of the back roads to Orchard Drive and turn down his long, winding driveway. His truck is here and I know Annie's already off to school.

As I pull up to the house, Ray steps out onto his front porch. "Becca?" he calls, and heads down the steps to meet me. I grab his hand and lead him into his house.

"Annie at school?" I ask.

"Yeah, the bus just picked her up." He's staring at me, partially in shock and partially like I'm crazy. Maybe I am. I have to ask him.

"Ray, if I was your girl and . . . well, let's say . . . if you were Grayson and he was you, and you saw me kiss him, what would you have done?"

"He saw? I'm sorry, Becca." He looks down.

"What would you have done?" I ask again, tears forming in my eyes.

"I don't know, Becs. I would've been angry. I would probably be beside myself."

"Would you have listened to me about what happened?" I take my coat off.

"Well, yes, but I would've still been pissed."

I take a deep breath and turn around. "Would you have done this?" I ask as I pull my yoga pants down.

"Becs . . . oh God. Oh God, look at what he did!" He kneels down and touches my skin. I wince at his touch. "Come with me." He pulls my pants up gently and grabs my hand, leading me upstairs. I don't argue. I don't care anymore. I know I'm safe with Ray. "Lie on your belly, Becs." He points to the bed. I slip my shoes off and do what he asked.

Ray goes into the bathroom and comes back carrying a tube of aloe lotion. He eases my yoga pants down, then squirts the lotion into his hand and rubs his palms together before slowly rubbing it on my bum.

"God . . . I could fucking kill him for this. How could he do this to you? I would never do anything like this to you, Becca. A man is supposed to protect his woman, not hurt her." He gently pulls my pants back up. I can't help but sob into his pillow. "C'mere, baby." He rubs my back and uses my sacred word. It sounds so right coming from him. I wince as I sit up. Ray pulls me onto his lap and I bury my face into his neck. I feel safe. I feel his hand on my arm, running up and down. He smells incredible.

I don't know why I do it. Maybe it's because I'm past caring. I kiss his neck once . . . twice. I hear his breath catch. He pulls my chin up and I stare into the dark blue-gray storm that is his eyes. Beautiful. I love them. He leans in and softly pecks at my lips, waiting patiently for me to open my mouth and welcome him in. *Butterflies.* When I finally do, he takes my breath away.

"Becs . . . baby, please tell me you're really here and I'm not dreaming." He pulls away and looks at me. Oh God, he really loves me. I can see it in his eyes. I'm so confused. I don't know what to do. I love Grayson. I love Ray. Christ, what the hell is wrong with me? "Shh . . . please don't cry." He kisses my tears.

"I'm so confused, Ray. Maybe you should stay away from me for a while. Until I can figure things out, I don't want to hurt you." I try to get up.

"No! No!" He holds me tight. "What is there to figure out? He hit you! There are welts all over your ass! Don't be stupid, Becca. Please. You're smarter than that."

"I shouldn't have come here, Ray. It's not fair to you."

"It's fair if you stay. Just spend the day with me. I won't expect anything from you. I won't try anything. Just give me the day. I'll clear my schedule." He flashes his boyish grin at me.

"Okay." I smile. "But let's go somewhere. And I need to be back in time to get Morgan."

Ray pulls out his phone. "Gwen, clear my schedule for the day," he instructs his secretary. He smiles and kisses my forehead as he listens to her response. I think I've lost my mind. "Oh, great. Thanks!" He hangs up and rises with me in his arms. "Can I give you a kiss?" I nod. Our lips meet, and then he puts me down. "C'mon, Becs." Hand in hand, we head down the stairs with a little spring in our step— only to find my detail waiting for me outside his front door. "Oh, hey. Becca won't need your services today. And as far as Grayson goes, please tell him I said to go sit and spin!"

"Raymond!" I slap his arm.

"I'm sorry, Mr. McNeil. My instructions are to stay with Ms. Campbell," Melissa says.

"Well, good. Maybe you should video this, then, so Mr. James can watch and see how a guy really treats a lady." He opens the truck door and helps me climb in.

"Ray, she's just doing her job. She's a good kid."

He opens his window. "Sorry that you're caught in the middle of this, Melissa. I mean no disrespect to you." He smiles, rolls up his window, and we're off.

I feel a terrible pang of guilt in my heart. Right now, Grayson is helping Hazel feed my guests breakfast—and I'm out with another man. I feel like a whore. Am I being a whore? I'm not sleeping with another man. Nope, I'm not being a whore! I'm just spending time with my best friend who happens to be male. Who happens to be in love with me. And whom I will let kiss me several times today. Okay, I'm an apprentice whore.

"Becs, where are you at, babe?" Ray smiles over at me. Wow. He is indeed very handsome.

"Oh, just fighting the forces of evil in my head."

"Stop it. We're going to have fun today!" He slaps my knee gently.

"Where are we going?" This is exciting . . . a date!

"You'll see."

I guess I doze off, because Ray has to wake me. When I open my eyes, I see we're at the train station in North Conway, about a half an hour away.

"Let's go. We've got a train to catch."

He grabs my hands, guiding me across the seat to his side of the truck. I grasp his shoulders as I climb out and slide down slowly. His boyish grin greets me, and he plants several excited kisses on my lips. He looks like a teenager in love. My heart melts.

"Are we doing the scenic foliage trip?"

"Yes indeed! We are just going to sit back, hold hands, relax, and take in the scenery." He buys the tickets and we're off to catch the train with only a few moments to spare. He gives me the window seat and, within five minutes, the train is going. It's not long before I feel so at peace—so calm. The scenery is beautiful. I've never actually done this before. Which Ray knew, of course. Ray knows everything about me. "How are you doing?" He kisses the top of my hand.

"Ray, this is just what I needed. Thank you so much." I kiss him and rest my head on his shoulder. We don't say too much more over the next two hours, except for pointing out different things we see. Every once in a while, he kisses me. I welcome it. It's comforting. He feels like home to me. I have a lot to think about.

"So, what do you feel like for lunch?" he asks as we get off the train.

"Someplace simple so we can get in and out."

"Um, okay." He opens the door for me and I climb in. He gets in and starts the truck. I look around. "What?" he asks.

"I haven't seen any of the detail since your house." He shrugs and we're off. "Wow, Ray. Friendly's. You're really pulling out all the stops here!" I tease.

"Well, I thought it was classier than Burger King. Besides, Friendly's is where I take all my favorite girls." He smiles before he gets out. I know his other favorite girl is his daughter, Annie. Yeah, my heart just melted again. I think he likes helping me out of the truck because my body slides down his hands. It's kind of cute.

"Becca, when you passed out again yesterday, I asked Grayson if you were pregnant. He had to stop and think about it. Why is that?" He looks so serious all of the sudden.

"Ray . . . I am having . . . " *God, I feel so uncomfortable.* "Sex with him," I finish quietly.

"I'm not dumb. But you are protecting yourself, right?" He

seems just as uncomfortable as me. I shake my head and his eyes widen. "You have got to be kidding me!" he says through gritted teeth.

"He wants to have a baby with me."

"Wow, Becca! Really? Wow!"

And that's it. He doesn't talk to me for the rest of our meal. I opt to go ahead and order my Happy Ending, because, well, quite frankly—it's the only one that's guaranteed right now. Although, ice cream is not very nice to my bum, either.

Ray pays the bill and takes my hand as we leave. He brings me to the passenger side and spins me around so I'm facing him. "I don't know where the hell your head's been at this week, Becs, but you need to snap out of it! Do you think having a baby with that man is a smart thing to do?" He leans his forehead against mine.

"No." I am being truthful. I know I had moments this week where I was excited, but I've been really impulsive and stupid.

"Becca, please . . . please don't have sex with him again. Please tell me that today cleared your foggy, beautiful head." He kisses me and a sob escapes my throat. I kiss him back with every bit of passion I can muster. "God, Becca," he gasps when he pulls away. "C'mon, we have one more stop." He helps me in, then climbs in on the driver's side and flashes me his gorgeous smile before starting the truck up and putting it in gear.

We head down the street about two blocks before he pulls into the parking lot of a Rite Aid.

"I'll be right back."

I lean against the headrest and close my eyes. After a few minutes, Ray gets back in and hands me a bottle of water. He opens a box and gives me a pill.

"Take this."

"What is it?" He holds the box up. It's the morning-after pill. "Oh, Ray, I can't."

"You can and you will," he snaps.

"What if I got pregnant at the beginning of the week?"

"Take it. Please."

"This is not me. I can't."

"Becs, this whole goddamn week has not been you!" he yells.

"Please don't yell at me."

He puts the truck in gear and we head back in silence. I grab his phone and pull up his calendar. He sighs.

"Sure, go ahead."

"Sorry. I left mine in my truck." I look again at the calendar to figure out my ovulation schedule. "I may be in the clear. If these charts are correct, I won't ovulate for another day or so."

"Yeah, except I'm sure you fucked him this morning, and that sperm can hang out in there for three days." I watch as he cringes at the thought. Suddenly, after feeling like a lady all day, I feel like a whore again. "God, I'm so mad at you!" He hits his steering wheel harshly for emphasis. It worked; my tears have been activated again. "Baby, I'm sorry. C'mere." He puts his hand out to pull me near. I rest my head on his shoulder. He bends his head slightly and kisses my hair as we turn onto his street and then up to his colonial farm-house. I love this house—I helped him pick it out, and took care of most of the décor. That was fun!

Ray tries to move his arm to put the truck in park, but I'm not ready to vacate my comfortable position, so I shift for him then glance at the clock. I have just enough time to get home for Morgan. I start to shift in my seat, resigned to face the inevitable. Ray tilts my face up to his. I open my mouth for him and his tongue quickly darts in. I match his fire and urgency. His left hand slides under my shirt. Butterflies flap their wings erratically as he cups my right breast. His thumb caresses the exposed skin above the lacy hem, and my breath goes wild.

"God, I want you, baby." He puts his forehead to mine.

"I have to go, Ray," I say breathlessly.

"I know." He sighs. I kiss him quickly and hurry out of his truck and into mine. I back out to turn around and drive up his long winding driveway onto the main road.

"Well, once a whore, always a whore," I hear a very familiar voice. I can't catch my breath. George yanks my head back by my hair and I let out a yelp. "Turn here!" he barks. I turn down an old dirt road, my heart pounding in my chest.

Chapter Nine

GRAYSON

I look out the window every time I hear a car pull up, hoping it's Becca. I know she's been with Ray all day. I saw the pictures of him kissing her on the train. I saw how relaxed and how at ease she was with him. He took her to Friendly's, of all places. Really? I'm doing a million-dollar renovation for her, and he takes her to fucking Friendly's? I look at the pictures of them eating lunch. He's mad at her, and I think I know why. Why else would he buy her the morning-after pill? She must've told him we were trying. I think I know Becca well enough on this subject—she wouldn't have taken the pill. But where is she now? Did she trick the detail and go back to his house? No. She would come home for Morgan.

Oh, Morgy girl. Stuck in the middle. I hope she's feeling better. She was so upset this morning, and so was I. Becca doesn't want her to call me "Daddy" anymore. God, that just rips my heart out. More so than her kissing Ray today, over and over again. I deserve her behavior. If she slept with him . . . I deserve it. I can't believe how I treated her. Aunt Hazel went nuts when I told her what I did and said. She literally smacked the crap out of me. Made me realize that I need to beg for forgiveness, no matter what she did with Ray. That's a tough one to chew and swallow. I've become a very jealous man since meeting Becca.

I wish she'd brought her cell phone with her today. I need to warn her that George is indeed alive. He was brought back to the States three months ago. I'm so worried about her. Christ! It's time for Morgan's bus. On my way downstairs, I see poor, exhausted Claudia.

"Here you go, love." I hand her a check. "This is for the extra stuff you've been doing around here. It's under the table, so don't claim it on your taxes." I smile and head out the door. I hear her excited scream as I walk toward Morgan's bus stop. I think ten thousand wiped the exhaustion away.

"Where's Mommy, Da . . . I mean . . . Grayson?" Morgan asks as she exits the bus. Her correction stabs me in the heart.

"Well, Mummy spent the day with Mr. McNeil. I'm sure she'll be home soon. Pizza okay tonight?"

"Sure." She looks down sadly.

"What time is your swim meet at?"

"It's in half an hour, so I have to get ready to leave." She runs into the house. I try Becca again. Nothing.

"Auntie, can you try calling Becca from the store?" I ask when I walk in.

"I just did. Nothing. Grayson, this is not like her at all. I'm very worried. I've got a bad feeling." She fidgets her fingers as her eyes fill up.

"Can you call Ray for me?" I ask, because I just can't.

"Just did that, too. No answer. He'll be at the swim meet," she adds.

"Well, that's it! She's heading over with him! We'll see her there!" I'm trying to be optimistic, but we both know Becca certainly wouldn't do that without calling to tell someone. I feel the panic rising in me. I head to the crop room, where some of the detail are taking their break. "Derek! Does your team know where Becca is?"

"Sir, Johnson said he left Melissa to follow her home."

"Please contact her, because they are not back yet," I say impatiently.

"Yes, sir." He calls Melissa. "No answer, sir. She may be out of cell range. I'll keep trying."

"Yes, please do." *Jesus H. Christ!*

Morgan comes barreling down the stairs.

"I'm ready!" she announces.

"I need extra people on Morgan tonight," I add quietly. Derek nods. I leave the crop room.

"Let's go, sweetheart." I smile at her.

"Where's Mom?" She looks around.

"I'm thinking she may meet us there since, Mr. McNeil will be bringing his daughter."

"Did she call and say that?" I can see the panic on her face. She scans back and forth, the color draining from her cheeks.

"Well, no, honey." I try to remain calm. Morgan pulls out her emergency cell phone and dials.

"Mom. Mom, where are you? Mom? Mom! Are you still there?" She drops the phone, her eyes wide. I kneel down in front of her.

"Morgan, what is it?"

"Somebody has her, Daddy! She said 'Hook'! She said 'Hook'!" She starts crying.

"What does that mean? You heard her voice? Somebody picked up?"

"Somebody picked up. I kept saying her name and all of the sudden she screamed 'Hook'! That's our word for trouble. If we're in trouble or somebody has one of us, we came up with "Hook" because Captain Hook is the villain that is always trying to catch Peter Pan. It's a quick word in case we only have one second to say anything. Somebody has my mommy!"

"Morgan, we're going to find her. Your mother has to be one of the most brilliant women I've ever met." I turn back to the crop room. Derek nods. They heard our conversation. "Morgan, we're going to your swim meet."

"Gracie, why? That's not important now," Aunt Hazel chimes in as she hugs Morgan.

"Auntie, I have to get ahold of Ray. He was the last person with her."

"Oh, right."

"I don't think I can compete." Morgan shakes her head frantically at me.

"You don't have to go, sweetie. I'm just going to look for Mr. McNeil."

"Okay. I'll stay here with Grammy Hazel."

"Okay." I give them each a kiss and head out to the school with Derek and half of his team.

"We still can't reach Melissa," Derek updates me.

"Okay. Hopefully Ray can come up with something." I'm sure he'd like to kick my arse first. Of course, I actually don't blame him. But he's the one guy I want here, going through this hell with me, because I know he loves Becca as much as I do.

We arrive at the school and race into the meet. I search the crowd and we lock eyes at the same time. I wave to him to come down. Oh, he's coming all right! I'm pretty sure his hands are already clenched into fists.

"He's got her Ray!" I shout, before he gets close enough to strike.

"What are you talking about?" He stops.

"George. He's got her. Come on, I'll tell you what we know." I head into the hall. "Before I say anything—I know you want to kick the shit out of me, and I don't blame you. But we need to set aside our differences for Becca's sake. He's got our girl, Ray. We have to find her. Can we call a truce for now, mate, and you can kick my arse when she's home safe?" I extend my hand. He takes it. We debrief him.

Ray sets up childcare with one of the other parents and we head out to his house to start from there. I go with Ray—he knows these roads. But, if I'm really honest with myself, it's also because I don't want him to find her first. Derek rides with us as well.

"Derek, can you track Melissa's cell?" I ask.

"Becca has her iPhone linked to her iPad," Ray states.

Derek gets on the phone. "Check the iPad for Ms. Campbell's phone."

"I should've walked her to her car. I'd normally do that. But she was in a rush to get home to Morgan. She always looks in her back seat before she gets in. This was so out of character for both of us." His nostrils flare.

"Well, don't beat yourself up, mate. You both were focused on getting to your daughters. But I do want to know why her truck wasn't swept before she got into it." I look over my shoulder at Derek.

"Well, I think we were more distracted by the heavy make-out session we had in my truck before she left." He pauses. "And yes— where the fuck were your guys, Derek?"

"Heavy make-out session, *aye*?" I feel my blood pressure rising.

"Just stating the facts, bro." He gives me a wide toothy grin.

"Facts, *aye*? Here's a fact for you. I shagged her three times this morning, mate. You like that fact?" I give him the same stupid grin back.

"Yeah, well, it didn't leave that much of an impression on her, since she was at my house afterward kissing on me. Oh, wait! I'm sorry—you actually left many impressions! The kind I had to rub aloe lotion on!"

"You touched her bum?" I ask angrily.

"No, I rubbed her bum. And that's not the only thing of hers I rubbed today!"

"If you two would please stop focusing on your pissing contest, maybe we can get somewhere here!" Derek yells at the pair of us.

"Are the choppers up?" I snap, trying to pull myself together.

"Yes, Mr. James." His voice is level again. "They won't be able to see too much longer, though. We also have an APB out on her car." Derek's phone rings. "It's Melissa, " he says, and picks up. "Melissa, can you hear me? Shit, she's breaking up. Are you close by? Cabin . . . Northwest 302 . . . dirt road. Can you hear me? We're coming! Ugh, I lost her." He looks up at us, then talks into his earpiece. "Yes, send the choppers onto 302. Look for a dirt road with a cabin. Between McNeil's and home base. Yes, yes . . . we're on 302. Yes. Send backup. Okay, out."

Ray is already hauling ass behind the wheel. "Look, Ray, I know we're itching to knock each other out, but at the end of the day, I think it's safe to say we both hate George far more than each other. Therefore, I suggest we put our best efforts forward to bashing his head in instead of each other's. What do you say there, mate?" Olive branch stretched out. Again.

"I say, when we're done bashing his head in, we pour gasoline on him, light him up, and watch the motherfucker burn . . . maybe roast a couple of marshmallows for s'mores." Ray focuses on the first dirt road he turns down.

"You're a sick bastard . . . I like it!" I laugh. Dead end. Ray spins the truck around like he's doing a stunt in a movie. He travels another mile or so and down the next one. Nothing. He gets back on main road.

"He better not be laying a fucking finger on her, that son of a bitch!"

I find Ray quite scary at the moment. I'm definitely the calmer one here.

166

BECCA

"Get in here!" George pushes me into a cabin.

"What are you going to do, George?" I try to hold the stance I was taught in self-defense class.

"Well, I'm not going to fuck you, if that's what you're worried about. Christ, Becca. You've gained weight. It's such a fuckin' turn off." He's trying to put me down. Really? I will thankfully never exercise again if I get out of this alive. I will never feel bad about myself or want to be a size four. If I could bow down and praise my own fat ass, I would do it in a heartbeat!

"What do you want, George?" I snap. He smacks me. So much for that self-defense class. They should teach a better-reflex class instead. "What do you want?" I repeat, turning my face back to him.

"I want my money, so one of your rich boyfriends better pay up!" he yells.

"What money?"

"The million dollars you got from my death."

"First of all, I'm going to have to pay that back. Second of all, minus the taxes and the almost eight years of child support and alimony, that probably leaves you still owing me. So how about I just write you a check for, say, thirty thousand, and you let me get out of here?" I'm realizing that I'm just not afraid of him anymore. He's so insignificant.

Of course, the gun he presses to my head definitely has some significance.

"I want eight million dollars." Figures. An even number. So unnatural.

"Yeah, I don't think I'm worth even half of that dead, you idiot!" Oh God, Ghetto Sybil's coming out in full force.

"Wow, Becca, you've grown a pair! That's pretty hot. I might have to look past that fat ass of yours. Then you can tell your rich boyfriends what it's like to be with a real man."

"Yeah ..." I look around. "When's he coming?" Damn reflexes! I need to hold my tongue.

"You are going to call your boyfriends and tell them to give me the money, or else I'll kill you." He slowly walks around the perimeter of the room, quickly glancing out of each window.

"What if they say no and you kill me? Then what, genius?" I don't care how many times he hits me; it's worth it just to tell him what a complete moron he is.

"Then I will take Morgan!"

I respectfully try to take his threat seriously at first, but then I think about what he said and find myself laughing hysterically.

"Morgan will run circles around your dumb ass! Besides, she is heavily guarded," I inform him. "Oh, George. Really, you are a stupid, stupid man. What the hell did I ever see in you?"

He grabs my hair and yanks me down to the floor. My adrenaline shoots into overload, my heart pounding—I feel as if it may explode at any moment. He may be a stupid man, but he's a strong one. I feel my fear creep back in a bit as he ties me to the bed posts and kicks me in the side. I try not to show how much it hurts.

"You've evolved, George. You tie a chick up now before you hit her—impressive!" That earns me another kick, which has me seeing stars. I try to ignore the sharp pain as I take in a deep breath. *Hey, Ghetto Sybil, shut up so I can catch my breath and not have all of my ribs cracked!*

Honestly, I don't remember him being this stupid when I met him. Maybe I was just as stupid, but I just got smarter—like most people do?

Several minutes of silence pass.

"So, why didn't you explode? What happened?" Time for the good-cop act.

"I was taken hostage before the explosion," he offers.

"How long?"

"Up until five months ago."

"Did you escape?"

"No, they moved on and left me there to die. Some locals found me and nursed me back to health."

"That was nice of them." *Idiots!* Couldn't they see he was evil?

"Being a hostage was absolute torture," he adds.

"Oh, you don't say?" I snap. *Really—you're going to tell me about being a hostage?* Just as he turns to me, I see Melissa peek in through the window. "George, is that gun really loaded?" I ask, loudly enough for her to hear me—but quiet enough to not attract suspicion.

"Yes, why?"

"I don't believe you. Show me," I demand. Melissa cracks the door slightly behind his turned back. He opens the chamber.

"See?" he snaps.

"I see!" Melissa yells, and kicks the gun out of his hand. He goes after her. As I'm trying to untie my rope to help her, George falls down at my feet, knocked out cold.

"Wow . . . I want to be like you when I grow up," I tell her as she undoes the knots at my wrists. She gives me a half smile and a nod. I think she's a little perturbed with my behavior today. *This* would be why I shouldn't have ditched her. I respect her more for not saying "I told you so." She throws the gun in a Ziploc bag and cuffs him to the bed. We run out of the cabin and down a path to the dirt road.

Just as we get there, Ray and Grayson pull up and jump out of the truck. *Oh my God, who do I run to?*

"Melissa, who do I go to?" I ask frantically.

"I don't know, but can I have whomever you don't pick?" She laughs.

I stop running and walk toward them, looking back and forth. They finally realize my dilemma. Christ, I think I want to run back to the cabin! I walk in between them and take each of their hands.

"You have to know that I want to be in both of your arms right now. I can't choose. So either you guys pick who I hug first, or I'm just going to jump in my truck and go home to my daughter." Oh God, I hope they don't fight.

"Well, I got us here," Ray starts.

"I hired Melissa." Grayson takes his turn.

"I've known and loved her longer."

"I know and love her intimately."

"She has a freckle behind her right ear that's very faint."

"She despises wearing panties to bed."

"Okay, well," I interject, "thank you both for wanting to be my knight in shining armor today, but it looks like Melissa's won the blow job from me! So I'm gonna head home to be with my daughter. Maybe you two can go to a bar and take a shot every time you can name something that you know about me. Then when you're shit-faced and either decide you're both masters of the universe or that you'd like to kick the shit out of each other, please call me because I wouldn't want to miss either event! Good night!" I head down to my truck with Melissa, my new partner in crime.

"I can't believe you said that to them. I almost jumped in to tell you I'd prefer you swallow." We both laugh, and I turn around.

"Hey, guys! Melissa just told me she prefers that I swallow!" I turn back around so they can't see me laugh. I grab at my ribs and wince a little. The pain is seeping in as my adrenaline wears off. As we hop into the truck, Melissa's phone rings.

"Hello? Yes. Oh, no. Okay. Yes, sir. Bye." She hangs up and looks over at me.

"What's the matter?" I glance back.

"Well, you're not getting rid of me yet. George got away. He should've been out longer—damn it!"

"The only person I'm worried about right now is Morgan. We'll beef up security until he's found."

"Right. So, what are you going to do?" She smiles.

"Oh, about Hot and Hotter?" I ask. She nods. "I have no idea. I realized today that I love them both. What am I supposed to do with that? Wait a minute. You're not taping me to give Grayson a report, are you? Are you wired?" I panic.

"No. I'm asking as a friend."

"Okay. So tell me, then, what do you think of this predicament I'm in? You're on the outside looking in," I ask. I really would like another person's opinion.

"Well, Ray is so in love with you. It's all over his face. The way he kisses you; it looks like magic. You and Grayson fight a lot, and he's very aggressive with you. Derek and I reached a whole new level of uncomfortable this morning. We were about to barge in when we heard you crying out in pain, but then you started . . . uh . . . well. I didn't think Derek could blush until that." She gives me a frowny sort of smile. "Put that aside, and you can plainly see his love and concern for you and your daughter. So I don't know. Ray seems more like the married-to-and-in-love-with-forever type. Grayson referred to you yesterday as his wife."

"What?"

"Yeah, that's why Thomas called you 'Mrs. James.' Grayson looked sad when you corrected him—I could tell he loved that you were called that. I don't think I'm helping you." She laughs. "Who's better in bed?"

"I haven't slept with Ray. Though, I must admit, after today, I definitely want to." Damn, I *really* want to. Again, I feel like a whore. "Ray feels like home to me. Grayson feels like a vacation I never want to end."

"Well, eventually, you have to come home, right?" She half smiles, like I found my answer.

"New Hampshire used to be the place I vacationed to, and now its home," I add as a thought.

"Well, I wouldn't want to be in your shoes, but I'd love to have your leftovers." She laughs. We pull up to the B&B. I park the truck and dart out. I run inside to find Morgan, but she's headed straight to me.

"I remembered our word, Mama!"

"I know you did! You brought me home safely!" I hug her tightly and kiss the top of her head. "Will you sleep over in my room, Morgan?" She's the best distraction.

"Yes." She looks up at me, her smile so big. Hazel comes in from the B&B side and rushes over to me, tears streaming down her face. Her powder blue eyes are bloodshot.

"Are you okay? What did he do to you?"

"I'm okay. He hit me a few times, but that was it. My ribs are sore, but I don't think they are fractured or anything." I rub them and wince. "Basically, he wants eight million dollars. That's all." I stop because I realize Morgan is listening.

"Mommy, who was it? Who hurt you?" Her voice squeaks with emotion.

"Morgan, I have to tell you something." I take her hand and bring her to sit on the couch in the lounge. "The real reason for all of the security people is that, yesterday, I could have sworn I saw your father, George, in the parking lot. I told Grayson, and he brought these people in to keep us safe and investigate the situation." I take in a deep breath and wait to see how this information is affecting her. She seems okay so far. "Morgan, your dad was—"

"A bad man, Mom. I know. I remember." She cuts me off.

"You do? I'm so sorry, honey." I hug her.

"So he wants money? What a loser." She rolls her eyes.

"Yeah, well, he's free again, so I need you to make sure you are always with somebody you know, honey! Don't let your guard down at all. Not even to walk out to the stables. Always stay with someone until they catch him, okay?" I put my most serious face on.

"I know, Mom. I will. I promise." She hugs me again.

"I'm so glad that you're back home safe, Becca, I was so worried about you," Hazel says, her eyes teary again. "This hasn't been a very good day for you, has it?" Her quivering chin and the embarrassment on her face tell me she knows what Grayson did this morning. I give her a sympathetic half smile to let her know I don't blame her.

"We'll talk tomorrow," I say with a sigh. Morgan and I both kiss her good night before we head upstairs for our slumber party. I'm actually looking forward to just sleeping tonight. I wonder if Grayson and Ray have each other in head locks right now.

"Do you want to watch *Ever After*, Mom?" she asks, and holds the movie up.

"Oh, not tonight. Let's watch something funny," I say. I need a break from love right now. She chooses *The Parent Trap* with Hayley Mills. Love that movie—it's a classic! We snuggle up, and I don't even make it past the cabin-check scene.

"Becca? Sweetheart?" I hear Grayson's voice. Someone nudges me.

"Becs, baby. C'mon, wake up." Now it's Ray. I open my eyes and see the two of them staring down at me. I look over at the clock. It's two in the morning. "We have to talk to you," Ray says, and Grayson pulls my covers off. I get up and walk out of the room, careful not to wake Morgan as I close the door behind me. I lead them to the room that I use for crafts when I don't want to be downstairs at night by myself. It's safer in here than in Grayson's room. There's no bed.

"You two have been together this entire time?" I ask, kind of in disbelief. "And you haven't mangled each other?"

"Impressive, isn't it?" Grayson smiles.

"Please tell me you two let somebody else drive you here?" It's more of a plea than a question. They are obviously shitfaced.

"Yes. Well, they insisted, even though we waited for the . . . the . . . um . . . until we weren't too drunk," Ray offers.

"Good call on their part, even though it's pretty clear you're not *too* drunk." I sigh with a sarcastic undertone.

"So, after arguing and a few pints, it all became clear to us, darling!" Grayson smiles widely and throws his hands up in excitement. "We're going to share you! See . . . here's the schedule." He hands me a piece of paper.

"That is, until you make up your mind. We thought you could date us both for a month to get your feelings sorted out." Ray adds. I look down at the paper.

Sunday — Grayson

Monday — Ray

Tuesday — Grayson

Wednesday — Off

Thursday — Ray

Friday — Grayson

Saturday — Ray

"Oh, I get Wednesdays off. That's great—a nice break in the middle of the week!" I act excited. The irony hits me right away, of course—I would literally have "Hump Day" off!

"That's what we thought!" They say in unison.

"Are you two out of your fucking minds?"

"Look, sweetheart, we know you are having a hard time, and that you are confused about your feelings." Grayson looks down at his hands, trying to find the right words.

"We realized it when we saw your face today, and obviously what you said confirmed it," Ray says.

"Honestly, this is tough for us, too. We're a lot alike, especially when it comes to our feelings for you. Neither one of us is going to back down. So, instead of fighting over you every day like a couple of bloody idiots—"

"And driving you crazy and away from both of us," Ray cuts in, "we thought we'd give you a chance to explore what you are feeling and decide who you truly want to be with."

"We've made a pact, sweetheart, that the other will walk away peacefully once you've made your decision." Grayson seems very uncomfortable with this. His eyes start their Morse code and he runs his hand through his dark hair.

"Becs, we promise to keep our jealousy at bay when you are with the other. We also agreed not to ask you or each other what happens on our dates," Ray adds.

"You know, guys, I really appreciate that you are trying to find a solution to all of this. I truly do. But I don't think you are taking into consideration how crappy all three of us will feel. You both are very proud men. I don't think you'll be able to handle this. I don't think I'll be able to handle hurting you both. It's just not a good idea." I put my head in my hands. Honestly, it's a brilliant idea on paper.

"So, what's the solution?" Ray snaps. "You continue on with Grayson, and then run to me when he pisses you off? I can tell you right now, Becca, I'm not doing that. It's not fair to any of us!"

"I know, Ray. You're right." The man has a point.

"Becca, sweetheart, we want to do this for many reasons. One, we don't want to both lose you. Two, we don't want you to pick now and then wonder if you'll regret your decision. Three, we both want your happiness to come first, because we deeply love and care for you. Yes, I'm not going to lie, this is going to be very difficult for all of us. For Ray and me especially. But we've agreed it's worth it to us. Can you at least try?" Grayson takes my hand and kisses the top.

Wow. I think this week can honestly go down as the most fucked up week of my life. I look at the paper, then up at their expectant faces.

"Give me a minute to think." The schedule is a little unrealistic. I mean, six nights a week I'm on a date that's probably going to end in sex, which will be over-the-top and exhausting because they are going to want to outdo each other. Plus, I'm running a business—that I've actually neglected this week with just *one* guy around—and I need time for my daughter. *I can't do this!*

"Okay, I'll do it. But—this schedule is ridiculous! You both get two nights a week only. So, I'll go out with one of you one night, then I get the next night off. No one will kiss me or touch me inappropriately if it is not your day. I do not want to be taken anywhere around here—people will talk if they see us. I do not want Morgan to know what is going on. Actually, I will tell her in my own way. And, if I think of any other stipulation to this agreement at a later date, I reserve the right to add it on. Any questions or issues with what I've proposed?" I look up at both of them.

"You seriously came up with all of that in the two minutes you thought about it?" Ray laughs.

"Yes." I'm not laughing.

"Oh. I'm okay with it."

"What time does our day officially start and end?" Grayson asks.

"Um, 5 a.m. to 5 a.m. Does that sound fair?" Both of their nostrils begin to flare. "Any stipulations you guys would like to add?" I raise my brows, knowing exactly why they are upset. Apparently, they never took into consideration the other guy being intimate with me.

"I'd like to add one, but then it would apply to me as well, so I guess I can't." Grayson runs his hand through his hair.

"Okay, so who's going first?" *Oh my God, did I seriously just ask that?* I close my eyes because I feel the urge to change my theme song. It's a toss-up. "Roxanne" by The Police, or "Bad Girls" by Donna Summers? I'm sure it will change to "None of Your Business" by Salt-n- Pepa at a later date.

"Becca? Sweetheart, did you fall asleep?" Grayson touches my arm.

"Nope. Just changing my theme song," I say truthfully. Ray laughs. He knows I do this often.

"Well, um, we need you to decide." Gray looks down at the floor. *Seriously?*

"I'd make a decision based on this weekend's events, but I'd rather you two flip a coin. Just remember, on Saturday, I have that dance expo with Will in the afternoon."

"Bloody hell, Becca! Not that arsehole!" Grayson yells.

"You're still doing that with that jerk?" Ray asks, his voice no kinder than Gray's.

"Will is my friend, and I promised him." I sigh.

"Will is a fucking asshole! Some friend! He goes around town telling everybody how it's only a matter of time before you give him a piece! I outta break his fucking legs!" Ray's fists are clenched.

"Here, here!" Grayson holds up an imaginary toasting glass.

"Well, he's delusional. Flip a coin, you two, I want to go back to bed!" I throw my hands up in the air impatiently.

"Well, I'm going to put my big-boy pants on and get the inevitable over with. Ray, you can take her out Saturday. My mates will be in town. And our mutual hatred for Will has made me feel generous toward you."

"There we go! See you Saturday, Ray. Good night, gentlemen." I get up to head out.

"Becca, wait!" Ray grabs my arm. "Look, I know it's not part of the new rules, but we were both really scared today. Because of the situation we find ourselves in, we weren't able to properly console you—or ourselves." Ray looks to Grayson and back to me. "Can you give us each a few minutes alone in here to do that now? Grayson can go first and I'll wait outside the door, and vice versa." *And so it begins.*

"Um . . . okay." It's two-thirty in the morning. I'm running low on morals.

"If we weren't in love with the same girl, we'd be great mates!" Grayson slaps Ray on the back.

"Just a few minutes, Grayson." Ray says, his smile obviously false. He walks out.

Gray pulls me in his arms and places gentle kisses all over my face until he finds my lips. I open my mouth for him and he deepens the kiss with a slip of his tongue.

"Sweetheart, I'm so sorry for everything." His chin quivers. "I've really been a foolish man, and I've pushed you away when all I wanted to do was reel you in closer. I couldn't even protect you today. I put this whole team in place and he got to you anyway."

"Yes, but because of that team, he didn't have me for very long," I say. "So you did protect me."

"What did he do to you? Did he hurt you?" He's actually crying now. Oh God, I do love him so much, and I know he loves me. This is hard.

"He slapped me a few times, and kicked me in the ribs. I'm okay, though a bit sore."

Grayson's face turns red with anger.

"Incidentally, my ass is too fat for him now. So he found me unappealing." I laugh.

"Well, he always was an idiot, wasn't he?" He chuckles. "I, on the other hand, am very smart and love this fantastic arse of yours!" He grabs it and squeezes, making me wince. The bruises from the spanking he gave me didn't magically disappear. His color drains. "Oh, Becca, I'm so sorry. I will never do that again. I can't believe I thought I had the right to. I was mad with jealousy. Please forgive me." He pecks at my lips. I kiss him back eagerly. "How am I going to keep away from you until Monday?"

"You can do it. Besides, you'll have your mates here. You'll keep busy with them."

Ray knocks at the door and opens it a little. "You've had five minutes, Gray."

"Yes, all right then!" He kisses me again quickly before heading to the door. I turn and look at the pictures of Morgan and myself on the wall, trying to calm the butterflies I feel from Grayson's touch. Woo . . . okay. I close my eyes and take a deep breath.

Ray wraps his arms around me from behind. His lips caress my neck, and I'm up to my throat in butterflies again. He turns me to face him.

"I'm sorry I didn't walk you to your truck. I was in a daze. I should've protected you. What did he do to you, Becca? Are you okay to talk about it?" He searches my eyes. I tell him the same thing I told Grayson. His nose flares and his jawline twitches. I tell him about my unappealing ass. He calls George a certifiable idiot. "I almost died today when you pulled down your pants to show me your ass. It was so hard for me not to make love to you after rubbing the lotion in. I mean, *it* was hard!" He slowly looks down to show me what he meant. I laugh. "I can't wait for Saturday." There's a yearning in his voice, and I know just what his plans are. I feel myself blushing and look away. He pulls my face back to his. "I love you, Becca." And with that, he spends the next two minutes thoroughly exploring my mouth with his own.

"Time!" Grayson shouts, pounding on the door.

"Wow, really?" Ray snaps. We walk out into the hall. Tonight's security team is there, looking at me. I feel a scarlet letter "W" appear on the front of my pajamas. I look down. It's not really there, but it weighs me down just the same.

"Good night," I say to everybody, then head back into my room, where I'm safe from the two men I love.

Chapter Ten

Friday comes and goes uneventfully, which is rare this week. I used it finish the favors for the Miller wedding—my last wedding, maybe?—and am just now climbing into bed at three in the morning. Thankfully, Claudia is coming in early to train one of the new girls I hired. And I have more hiring to do next week. *Ah . . . sleep.*

I wake up when I feel something tickling my face. I rub my cheek with my hand. A man chuckles and I sit up quickly, my heart in my throat.

"Shh, baby, it's me." Ray rubs my back.

"Ray, what are you doing here?" I turn to look at him, but I can't see much because it's still dark. The glowing clock numbers say it's five after five. On Saturday. I lay back down. Really—he couldn't wait until tonight?

"Becs," he whispers as he hovers over me. I touch his chest, and my fingers hit bare skin. His physique is naturally muscular and lean. *Damn, did I hit the jackpot with these two!* I lean up and brush my lips across his chest. His breath hitches sharply. The back of my hand runs down to his happy trail. I turn my hand and allow my fingers to play, slipping them under the elastic of his underwear. Oh, God—I'm going to be a very sore girl today. Ray attacks my lips. *Horny Sybil is half asleep, shaking her ass. Country Sybil is shaking hers too, begging for her pigtails to be pulled. She must have been hanging out with Submissive Sybil.*

My top flies off and his mouth is on my breasts. There's such a sense of urgency. He's devouring me, and my moans only encourage him more and more. He kneels in front of me and yanks my bottoms down. I pull off his boxer briefs. I hear him fumble with the condom packet. I guess he's going right for the kill. I raise my legs, bending them at the knees, and open wide for him. He slowly enters me.

"God . . . Ray," I cry out as he takes his time to fill me. It hurts and feels good all at the same time. His lips attack mine, sucking the lower one; savoring it. My tongue darts out to tease his. He slowly pulls almost all the way out only to slam into me harshly. "Ray!" I cry out and grasp at his back.

"Fuck, baby," he grunts, "you're so tight." He grabs the back of my left thigh, squeezes it, then positions it around his waist as he grinds deeply into me. He pulls back again and slams into me even harder. He kisses me again to quiet me as he unleashes a series of quick, harsh thrusts. My hands grasp his ass as my own lifts off the bed to match his efforts. He pounds harder with each thrust, burying himself deeper. Just as I feel myself rise, he pulls out of me.

"Ray?" I pant.

"Shh," he whispers near my earlobe before nipping at it. His mouth travels down my neck.

"Ray . . . please." I push my hips up against him.

"Uh-uh." I can hear his smile as he cups my left breast and teases my nipple with his mouth. He licks. "You like that?" *Crap, his voice is sexy.* He bites. "How about that?"

"Ray," I moan, and let my chest rise up to meet him. His hand slides down the side of me and across my belly. It continues its journey down to the center of my heat and I ride his hand, wanting that release—aching for it.

"Tell me what you want, Becs. Tell me what I've wanted to hear for five years now. What do you want, baby?" he asks in that same sexy voice, his hand now guiding what I want up and down my center . . . waiting for my words. "Tell me, baby." He presses the tip at my opening.

"You, Ray . . . I want you." Ray wastes no time giving me what I want. My nails rake at his back as he stretches me over and over again. I relish in the ache of having him inside of me and the familiarity he brings. *Home*.

"Becs, that's it baby . . . come for me," he says just as I reach the edge of glory—which is, incidentally, my theme song at the moment. He slows down as my legs begin to shake and I whimper at the build. "That's it, baby, let it happen," he coaxes me. My back arches as the tightening travels up and explodes deep inside my core. I seize my pillow with my right hand, grasping it to my face to muffle myself as I pump my hips up to him quickly, working through my orgasm. I tighten around him and feel his body twitch as his own sounds escape his throat.

"Oh, Becs." He grits his teeth as I squeeze around him as hard as I can. "*Fuck!*" He groans as he pumps a few more times and lands on my chest, breathing rapidly.

It's now a quarter to six and I've already been thoroughly shagged. Ugh! Why did I have to think that word? Now Grayson is on my mind. He has no idea I've just been with another man. A pang of guilt hits me. I'm glad he's with his friends and not here. Ray climbs off of me and disposes of the condom. He pulls me into his arms and I fall fast asleep.

"Mom. Mom, open up!" Morgan pounds on the door. Ray and I jump out of bed.

"Hold on, honey. I'll be right there!" I shout. "Ray, go hide in the bathroom," I whisper urgently as I throw on my PJs. He collects his clothes and runs into the bathroom. I go and open the door. "Hey, honey. Did you forget your key?" I let her in and thank God she did.

"Yeah. Mom, it's nine o'clock. We have to leave in an hour for your expo." She goes to my closet and pulls out my dance costume.

"Thanks, honey. I was up late working on the Miller wedding and didn't get to bed until three." I sit back down on the bed.

"Okay, Mommy, everything is ready. Don't forget your gym bag of clothes for after. Hurry up—you have one hour." Some people have stage moms. I have a stage daughter—and I think she may be even more fierce and pushy.

"Okay, honey." I kiss the top of her head. "I'll be down in an hour. I have to take my shower."

"You rhymed!" She smiles and leaves.

I see Melissa in the hall, so I grab her arm and pull her into my room once Morgan is out of sight.

"What time did you get here?" I ask.

"An hour ago, and I've already been told. Where is he?" She looks around.

"Hiding in the bathroom." A nervous giggle bursts from my mouth.

"This is so unprofessional, but did you?" she asks like a good friend would, her eyes wide. I nod and giggle again. "Oh my God, I'm so jealous. How was he? Oh God, sorry!" She cringes.

"Well, let's just say my decision's no easier. Listen, can you make sure nobody comes in here while I'm getting ready?" I then proceed to tell her very quickly of my arrangement with the guys.

"I have one question for you, though," she says in a strangely serious tone, given the context of our conversation.

"What's that?"

"Can I have them on your nights off? I totally won't mind your 'sloppy seconds.'" She touches my arm as if she's trying to be sincere. I stare blankly at her until I watch her shoulders start to shake.

"Oh, you!" I smack her arm and giggle with her. She's my kind of girl! We're going to be friends for a long time; I can just sense it. She leaves and I head to the bathroom.

"Sorry, Becs. I wasn't thinking about Morgan." He pulls me into his arms.

"It's okay. Do you want to shower with me?" I look to the side, feeling very shy. After this morning's shenanigans, it seems kind of silly.

"I'd love to." He brings my face back to his. "Are you okay?" He leans down and plants a soft, sweet kiss on my lips.

"Yes." I bite my bottom lip and look up at him. He frees my lip from my teeth with his thumb and kisses me again. "Shower, Ray," I remind him. He pulls my top off and I my bottoms. He takes the sight of me in.

"God, you're beautiful," he says. Honestly, I don't know what the hell these two are talking about.

I walk into the shower, leaving him to undress himself. The water beating on my face feels so good. For a moment, I let the steady stream carry my worries away. I feel a soapy facecloth at my back. Ray is taking it upon himself to wash me. I let him.

What am I doing with these two? How am I going to continue with this cloud of guilt lingering over me? I'm not going to lie—the sex is great. I feel like I'm getting away with murder, having them both. Ray turns me around to rinse my backside off and starts on my front. I keep my eyes closed as I lather my hair. I'm too lost in my thoughts to look at him.

"Becs, are you sure you're okay? Open your eyes, baby." I obey and shake my head.

"I feel so guilty. It's a lot for me to handle. You can't tell me you're going to be okay when it's his day and I'm showering with him."

"Becs, Gray and I really had a heart-to-heart the other night. We understand that we are both going to be hurt on some level, but we agreed to put you first. Because, in the end, you are what we both want. It's worth it." He palms my face and grasps my lips. I give in. He backs me to the wall and lifts me like he did that hot, rainy day a year ago.

"Oh . . . oh, Ray ..."

He moves inside me at an agonizing pace. I hold onto him and bury my face in his neck to muffle my sounds. God, he's so strong. I love his shoulders, the sun-kissed freckles dotting them. I feel myself rising. *All Sybils have their choir robes on. They sing "Amen" in unison.* I attack Ray's mouth with my own as complete bliss blankets me.

"Oh God, Becs ..." He grits his teeth and pulls out before he comes.

"What do you prefer, Ray?" I ask quietly as I slide down his body.

"What are you talking about?"

"I want to help you finish. Do you have a preference?" He stares at me, wide-eyed in his disbelief. I offer him a slight smirk and a peck on the lips before I sink to my knees and take him into my mouth.

"Oh, God . . . damn, Becca." He groans and places his hands on the wall to steady himself. I am amazed at myself. I used to hate this. I guess it's different when you love someone and you're not being forced. I pull back, sucking purposefully, then push forward, filling my mouth with him again. He gasps harshly at the intensity of his release. I pick up the pace, turned on by the sounds that escape his throat. I cup his balls and gently pull back on them as I work him through his last few quakes. His knees weaken from the pleasure. I circle my tongue around the tip, licking up the last drop, then plant a little kiss on it. I travel back up his body. He still has his eyes closed. I condition and rinse my hair, swish some water around in my mouth, and step out. I grab my towel and wrap it around myself on the way to the sink.

He doesn't say a word. I'm very proud of the place I've just brought him to—and I've made a decision. If I'm going to feel like a whore anyway, I might as well let my freak flag fly in the bedroom.

"Are you okay?" I ask Ray as I brush my teeth. I didn't even realize he stepped out of the shower. He stands behind me, water dripping down his chest to his toweled waist, watching me in the mirror with a look of bewilderment on his face. My insecurity is rising. What is that look about? "Are you upset with me?" I shoot him a puzzled look after I spit the toothpaste out. He shakes his head. I rinse my mouth and turn to him. "Cat got your tongue?"

"I just never, um . . . pictured you to be the type to do that."

"I never was. I've decided not to hold back. Is that okay with you?" I reach up to touch his face. He takes my hand and kisses my palm.

"Did you like doing that to me? Letting me, um..."

I find his shock amusing. Ray has never been one to be at a loss of words.

"I loved it, Ray." I lick my lips before I lean up to kiss him. "The sounds that came from you were driving me wild. You tasted good, too."

"Do you have any idea how fucking hot you are, baby?" He searches my eyes.

"I was getting ready to ask you the same question." I smirk and lean forward to bite at his bottom lip playfully. He throws me over his shoulder and carries me into the bedroom. I glance at the clock. "Ray, you have ten minutes . . . not even. I have to get ready." With that, he tosses me onto the bed and pulls my towel off as well as his own. He grabs a condom packet and rips it open with his teeth.

"On your knees, Becca," he commands. I obey and grab my pillow, ready to scrunch it under my face for support as I'm surely about to be transported into next week.

He enters me, and five or so minutes later, collapses onto the bed. His breathing is shallow and quick—he sounds like he's practically having an asthma attack. *Holy shit!* How am I going to dance in an hour?

"Sorry, Becs." He rubs my back and leans back over to kiss my shoulder. I smile at him and slowly climb off the bed. Well, I did do my best rumba the day after I did the horizontal mambo with Gray. I just hope Will doesn't think it's him again. Ugh!

"Are you going to come and see me dance today?"

"Yes, I'm coming. I want to make sure Will keeps his claws off of you." He slides his underwear on.

"He made a pass at me the other day. Gray went crazy."

"Hey, Becs, don't talk to me about Gray like that. Like, in a boyfriend sense. Please." He tries to fix his hair in the mirror.

"Sorry," I murmur as I walk out in my dance costume, which is red, glitzy, and backless.

"What the hell is that?" he asks flippantly.

"My costume."

"Let me guess. Will fucking picked it out?"

"Um, yes." I smile sheepishly.

"After today, you are done with him!"

It amazes me how the mere thought or mention of Will brings on this irascible behavior from both Ray and Grayson.

"I agree." I had been thinking the same thing all week.

"You agree?"

I guess he was waiting for a fight.

"Yes." I smile, kiss him, and tap his cheek. "Ready?" I grab my bag.

"Yeah, let's go." He takes the bag from me and plants a kiss on my temple before we leave the room. His mood is back to calm seas.

"Where's Annie?" Morgan asks, looking past Ray when she sees him.

"She's with her grandparents for the weekend."

"Oh."

"Ray's coming with us today, honey," I say as I put my coat on.

"And where's Dadd—I mean, Grayson?" Morgan corrects herself quickly.

"He's with his friends for the weekend, baby. You'll see him in a couple of days." I avoid Ray's eyes. I'm sure his nostrils are flaring again. It's a perpetual habit for him when he's pissed. Tanya, her protective detail, waves for Morgan to come to the truck with her. Morgan looks from her to me and shrugs before she heads off.

"What the hell was that about?" Ray asks angrily. "Do you realize the kind of damage you could do by having her call him 'Daddy'?"

"It's a long story. I didn't tell her to call him that." I sigh impatiently.

"Becca, it is very irresponsible of you to allow her to continue."

"Ray, I don't think it's the most irresponsible thing I've done this week—or today, for that matter. She corrected herself, didn't she? I have an idea, why don't I start being more responsible right now? Would you like that?"

"Let's go." He sighs.

"Yeah, that's what I thought." I shove past him.

"Hey." He grabs my arm and pulls me back. "Don't, baby. I'm sorry." He grazes my face with the back of his hand.

"What is it with men? Just because you're having sex with me doesn't mean you get to talk to me like that, or take control over situations!" My voice is hushed, but my irritation screams loudly.

"You're right. I'm sorry. In my defense, I've always given you a 'what for' when it's needed." He chucks my chin. He's right. I'm just being overly sensitive because of our new relationship.

"C'mon." I smile and kiss him. We walk hand in hand to my truck. Ray opens the door for me, and I climb in. I nod to Morgan and Tanya as I buckle in and wait for Ray to jump into the driver's seat.

"I hope you fall on your butt, Mom!" Morgan snaps. I turn to her. She's mad. Oh . . . she saw us kiss. *Damn it.*

"That's not a very nice way to talk to your mother, young lady." Ray says sternly. *Oh, Ray, your heart's in the right place, but that's not a good idea.*

"You are not my father!" she yells.

"Well, neither is Grayson!" he barks back.

"Stop it, you two!" *This is not good.*

"I'm telling Grayson on you." She crosses her arms and looks away.

"Morgy, honey, Grayson knows. I'll talk to you about everything later." I don't know what else to say to help her understand. Tanya's in the truck, and I really don't want her to know more than she needs to.

"Why did you break up with Grayson?"

"I didn't, sweetie. We're just trying to figure things out. Please, I will talk to you about this later." I reach for her hand. She looks out the window, ignoring my gesture. Ray places his hand on my knee and squeezes. When I look at him, he mouths "sorry." I give him a half smile.

At the expo, Will keeps his lips and thoughts to himself. He does ask me where my boyfriend is, though, and I tell him "with his friends." Ray seems irritated by this. Ray, Morgan, and I have lunch together, and my daughter's reticent behavior has me feeling uneasy. She didn't even cheer for me during the dance. I study Morgan for a while, hoping to see some sort of change in her mood, but when I don't notice anything, I glance over to Ray. He gives me a sympathetic smile and reaches to rub my back a little. Morgan watches him and rolls her eyes.

"I want to go home," she finally says.

"Okay. I need to get back to work anyway."

"Yeah, that would be nice, since Grammy has been covering for you all week. She's exhausted!"

"You're right. I haven't been doing my share lately," I say. "I know you're angry with me, Morgan, so I'm going to give you one free pass right now. However, do not think for one moment that it is okay to talk to me like this just because you are angry. Do you understand me?" I try to be as calm and clear as I can be. Ray looks as if he wants to say something, but I shake my head at him.

"Can we go now, please?" Morgan asks, her attitude in check.

"Yes."

When we arrive home, Morgan jumps out and runs to the inn with Tanya chasing her. I put my head in my hands. Ray opens my door for me. I didn't even notice he got out of the car.

"Come on, baby." He rubs my leg. I lift my head and look over at him. "Aww, Becs, don't cry." He palms my face and thumbs away my tears.

"She's so disappointed in me. I'm like the wicked stepmother to her."

"No, you're not. She'll get over this, baby." He sighs. "I don't get it," he adds.

"What?"

"Not to make this about me, but I've been helping you raise her for the past five years. I'm a little hurt that she's all 'Daddy Grayson' and acting as if you being with me is the worst thing."

"Ray, you haven't seen them together. They are very close. They love each other very much." I don't think anything I'm saying is helpful.

"I love her, Becs! You know I do." He furrows his brow.

"I know. C'mon." I turn my legs to get out, and Ray helps me down. He shuts the door and takes my hand in his. I almost want to pull away to avoid adding fuel to Morgan's fire, but I'm pretty sure that won't go over well.

We walk in to find a disgruntled Hazel.

"Good! You can take over for the night. I'm done!" Great—she's pissed. She shoots Ray a nasty look before she heads off to her room.

Claudia comes out of the dining room and heads over to us.

"Are you mad at me, too?" I ask her.

"Nope! Grayson gave me a nice bonus check. That'll keep me happy for a while."

"What did he give you?"

"Ten thousand," she says. Ray rolls his eyes.

"Well, you deserve it." I hug her.

"What time are you on until, Claudia?" Ray asks.

"I'm leaving in an hour," she says after a brief hesitation, sounding unsure of why he's asking.

"Oh, okay." He sighs.

"How was the new girl today?" I ask to change the subject.

"Alex is great. I think she's going to do well here."

"And when is she working next?" I feel as if I'm slowly losing control over my own business.

"She'll be back on Monday."

"Great."

"Becca, are you okay?" She tilts her head sideways.

"Yeah, Claude, it's just been a very strange week for me. I'm waiting to wake up and have it back to normal." It's the absolute truth.

"Everything is going to be fine," she says, and hugs me. "I'm going to go clean up from lunch."

"Thanks, Claudia." I watch her walk away.

"Sorry, Ray, I guess it won't be much of a date night." I grab his hand. He looks like he's a million miles away. "Ray. Ray?" I shake his arm. He looks at me.

"Sorry. I'm gonna go, Becca. Call me when Morgan's asleep and I'll come over. We'll rent a movie." He kisses me and leaves. Um . . . okay then.

It's a quiet Saturday without croppers. I restock the shelves and place the order I never got around to at the beginning of the week. *Oh no, I never met with the lawyer.* I call Gray.

"Aunt Hazel?" He answers.

"No, baby, it's me." I sigh.

"Oh, I'm still 'baby'?" I can sense his smile on the other side.

"Why wouldn't you be?" *Duh, Becca.*

"What did you need, sweetheart?" He avoids answering.

"I just realized I didn't meet with the lawyer." God, why did I call about this? I feel like an idiot.

"We're meeting with him first thing Monday morning, after we get Morgan off to school."

I miss him. It's hitting me like a ton of bricks.

"Morgan's not talking to me." Why am I telling him this?

"I know. She called me."

"Oh." A monsoon of guilt washes over me. "Are you having fun?" I change the subject.

"Becca, are you crying?"

"No," I lie.

"I know he was there this morning at 5 a.m. sharp."

"Oh." Probably not the best time to tell him it was actually 5:05.

"I know, or at least have an idea of, what you did with him."

"Oh."

"Yes, Becca, I do have a team in place there."

"Of course." I feel like a child. My voice is shaky.

"I still love you. I was hoping for more, but didn't expect any less." I can hear the ice cubes clinking around as he swirls his drink. I say nothing. What *can* I say? "Sweetheart?"

"Yes, Grayson?"

"I'll see you Monday morning."

"Okay, baby, see you Monday." I play with the wire on my retro phone.

"Becca?"

"Yes?"

"Don't call me that. It doesn't feel very sacred anymore."

I balk at this, and try to defend it. "I don't call him that."

"I don't really care what you call him, darling!" He hangs up.

I sit at my desk and have a good cry.

"Mommy, are you okay?" Morgan walks into the office.

"No, I'm not." I try to pull myself together. "C'mon, Morgan, I have to get dinner started." I stand up and wipe my tears away.

"Grammy Hazel told me to remind you that you have people coming tonight for a crop night, and she can't cover for you. She's going out with Charlie. It'll just be us for dinner." Great. I didn't even check the schedule.

"Go on without me. I have to make a call."

"Okay, Mom." She pauses. "I'm sorry about today, Mama. I love you." She hugs me and I feel as if I can breathe again . . . just a little. She leaves and I call Ray.

"Becs?"

"Hi."

"Hi, baby. Is everything all right?" Wow, he's asked me that a lot today.

"No. I have a scheduled crop tonight that I forgot about. Hazel is going out with Charlie and even if she wasn't, she's made it very clear that she won't cover for me anymore." I'm trying to keep my voice steady. Honestly, I'm happy to cancel on him. This guilt is overwhelming.

"Can you cancel the crop?"

"No. It starts in two hours and," I look down at the schedule, "it's almost full."

"Okay, then. I'll see you later."

"Wednesday then?" I ask.

"No, Becca—later!" He doesn't sound happy. "Are you trying to blow me off completely?"

"No." *Yes.* I can't think straight.

"I'll see you later, then."

"I'm sorry, Ray," I offer.

"Becca, I've been meaning to ask you—what were the theme songs you were deciding on the other night?" This puts a smile on my face, which I'm sure matches his. He always loves to hear what my theme songs are.

"Um, it was a toss-up between 'Roxanne' and 'Bad Girls.'"

"But, Becs, those songs are about . . . "

"I have to go." I sigh, feeling our mutual smiles leaving our faces.

"See you later, baby."

"Okay." I hang up.

GRAYSON

She rang. I can't believe it. What does that mean? How could she sleep with him so fast? Do I even have the right to ask that question? She'd only known me for two days when she slept with me. She's known Ray for five years. Still, I didn't think she would do that. I guess I don't know her very well at all. I should just walk away. This is much too painful.

Morgan . . . ugh, my Morgy girl! I wanted to run to her when I heard her voice on the other end of the phone. She's so upset. I didn't really think enough about how this was going to affect her.

I did take all of the blame tonight. She shouldn't hate her mother. *"I want you to be my daddy! You said you were going to be! Why did you lie to me?"* Her words still stab at my heart.

I'm a miserable bloke tonight. My mates have taken off without me. My only friend tonight is Johnnie Walker. Oh, and my security team.

"Hi, are you Grayson James?" I turn to see a tall brunette. She's very attractive. *I should.* I know I could if I wanted to. She's already telling me with her body language. But I can't. I only want Becca. I sign a napkin, smile, and give it to her. She seems very disappointed. I give my team a nod. It's time to leave. I'd head back to the B&B, but I don't think I could handle that.

Hmm . . . I think I may have an idea. Taking in a deep breath, I dial Becca's cell.

"Hi," she says, a hint of surprise in her voice.

"Can I come and pick Morgan up for the night?"

"Uh, Gray, have you been drinking?" How does she know?

"I only had one, plus I have the detail with me. Look, Becca, Morgan's really upset. I think it's best if I just have her with me tonight."

"What about your friends?"

"They're off to the clubs in Boston. I wasn't in the mood." It's the truth.

"Okay. What time will you be here?"

I look at my watch. "I can pick her up in a half an hour."

"Okay, that gives me enough time to pack a bag for her before the crop club comes. Um, thanks, ba . . . Grayson."

"Crop club? You're not going out with Ray?"

"No, I have nobody to cover for me."

"Ray must be pissed." I can't help but laugh a bit.

"Well, he's not pleased." She sighs.

"That's okay—I'm sure he was pleased this morning!" I bite at her, then slap my head. Why did I just say that? I promised I wouldn't do that. "I'm sorry, Becca. I'm a selfish man."

"I know." I can hear the sob that wants to escape her throat. "I'll get Morgan ready. Do you want me to feed her first?" She sounds so distant.

"No. I'll grab a bite with her. See you soon, sweetheart." I hang up. "Derek, we're going to pick Morgan up." He nods and we head out to the car.

BECCA

"Morgan!" I call to her.

"Yes, Mommy?" She comes out from the kitchen.

"Let's pack your bag. Grayson is coming to take you for the night." I reach for her hand.

"Really?" she screeches excitedly, jumping up and down. I help her pack and walk with her over to the store.

I turn the lights on in the crop room and start setting up. Things are a little disheveled, since this has been the meeting room for security.

"Hey, I brought you a salad." I turn to find Grayson holding up a bag. I haven't seen him since yesterday morning. It feels like a week.

"Thank you. You didn't have to do that. I would've made myself something." I take the bag.

"But you never would have gotten to it." He smiles because he knows he's right. "Are you all right, darling?" Why is he asking me this? Of course I'm not all right! I look away and try to blink back my tears. "Becca?" He turns my head back to him. Palming my face, he pushes my tears away with his thumbs. He leans forward to kiss me. I back away.

"You can't touch me until Monday morning." I recite the rules quietly.

"Right!" he says angrily—almost viciously—through his teeth. "Let's go, Morgy girl." His tone is much more pleasant when talking to her.

"Bye, Mom!" Morgan runs in and gives me a hug. I can't help but feel like she's a kid with divorced parents. They walk out the door, but not before Grayson shoots me a look that I swear is armed with a dagger—and it goes straight for my heart. Normally, I could wait here a minute, knowing he'd storm back in claiming to be a selfish man and have his kiss anyway, but he won't do that tonight.

This is not fair to me. They wanted this, and now I'm the fucking villain! I sit down and eat my salad. Why did I allow them to talk me into this again? Oh yeah, because it was two in the morning and I was half asleep. Now everybody is mad at me! I should've just told them both to leave me alone. I guess I'm being selfish, too. I'm not doing this for a month. Not if this is how I'm going to be treated. They have one week. If they can't pull it together, then I'll be done with the pair of 'em!

Tara pops her head in. "Hey, Becca."

"Hey, Tara. Find a seat. Sorry." I grab my salad and bring it to the counter in the store. Eileen comes through the door as well. Slowly all of the croppers trickle in.

"Let me know if you ladies need anything," I say.

"Why don't you pull up a seat and scrap with us? You haven't joined us in a long time." Tara waves me in.

"You know, Tara, I think I will. Let me go and grab some stuff." The ladies cheer and I feel my spirits pick up. She's right; I used to scrap all the time with them. I haven't done any in a month. I run upstairs to my other craft room and grab a box of photos and head back down to join them.

There are two big hurdles when it comes to doing a page. The first is deciding which pictures you want to scrap. I found that scrapping in order only holds you back. The second hurdle is choosing paper. One time it took me three hours just to pick the paper. That was extreme, though—usually it does not take that long.

I fiddle through my box. It seems I chose Morgan's kindergarten year. I find some taken in a pumpkin patch. Oh yes! She lost her top two and bottom two teeth at that time. This is just the therapy I need. I pull them out and run out to the store for paper. After a while, I've decided on brownish-orange, reddish-orange, and green paper. I'm going to make pumpkin borders with my Cricut machine. My title will be "Morg-o-Lantern." It makes me smile.

Excited, I head back into the room, only to find Ray sitting at my table. I giggle at how odd it looks.

"What are you doing?"

"I'm here to scrap. What are you doing?" He looks up from his pictures of Annie.

"I guess I'm going to show you how." I sit down.

"Good. I want to make a book for Annie. I thought I'd start with her baby pictures and work my way up." He shows me pictures of him holding her in the hospital. There are no pictures of Liz holding her because she didn't want to. There are no pictures at all of Liz and Annie. Well, except for one that's framed in Annie's room. Liz decided she didn't want to be a wife or a mother. She left when Annie was only a month old. She never calls or sends Annie cards or anything. I've kind of been Annie's surrogate mother for the past five years.

Luckily, she and Morgan are best friends. I do their Scouts, and Ray and I split up all of their other activities since we're both single parents. That's why I don't fully understand Morgan's behavior toward him today. She loves Ray. I love Ray. He's my best friend. He knows everything about the both of us. I love Annie as if she were my own. At least Annie has her grandparents. Morgan has Hazel, but it's not really the same.

"Becs?"

"Oh, sorry. Is this what you feel like working on tonight? I find it difficult to get too far if you're scrapping something you're not in the mood to scrap. You don't have to scrap in order. I don't suggest you put anything in a book until you're all done anyway." I look back up at him after I organize my layout.

"Actually, I don't feel like doing these. I want to do these." He pulls out several pictures from the carnival last year, right before our kiss. Morgan and I went with them and his parents.

"Hey, you were supposed to give me copies because I forgot my camera." I playfully slap his arm and look back down. There are a few pictures of the four of us smiling. I flip to one where the girls are looking up at me, asking me something, but what catches my eye is the way Ray is looking at me in the photo. *You can see it plain as day.* He loved me so much, even then.

I flip to the next picture. The four of us are walking ahead. Ray and I are in the middle. I have Annie's hand and he has Morgan's. Ray's arm is around my shoulder and my arm is on his lower back. We look like a family, which is why I suppose his mother took this shot. I swallow hard and smile up at him. "This is a beautiful picture."

"My favorite." He pulls out his wallet and opens it. There's a picture of Annie. He flips the page to show me a wallet-sized copy of the picture of the four of us, then one of Morgan next.

"Excuse me. I need a minute." I get up and head quickly to the bathroom. I close the door behind me and let myself have a good cry. *I'm so torn. I'm so torn.* What do I do? What am I going to do? The door opens. It's Ray. He rushes toward me, pushing my back to the wall and attacking my lips.

"I have loved you as long as I've known you," he says, pulling away then diving back in. His kiss is raw and powerful; it renders me breathless. After a few minutes, we pull away reluctantly and try to collect ourselves. I touch my lips gently, reacting to the swelling sensation I feel. Ray leans down and softly pecks at them.

"C'mon, let's go pick out paper for those pictures." I nudge his nose with mine before leading him back out to the store. We pick out paper and sit back down. I show him how to crop the pictures and how to use the Cricut machine. He opts for stickers out in the store instead. I get up to help some of the women. When I sit back down, he's using the "Watching You Grow" page that I have precut and packaged. "Did you finish the other?" I glance over.

"Yeah," he says as he picks out his next set of pictures.

"You're not going to show me?" I tilt my head to the side.

"You already saw, Becs." He smiles up at me and carries on. Um . . . okay.

"Did you journal?"

"Yes." *That's it?* He's being so laconic; so unlike Ray. Guess he doesn't want me to see it. He gets up after about an hour to go check on the Red Sox score.

"He put it under those pages." Tara smirks and points. This is terrible, but I have to look. I go over to his side. "Go ahead. I'll watch the door," she says.

I look. Oh. The title says "Family Fun." I don't see the journaling.

"Under the watermelon," Tara says. I swivel the watermelon around.

> Annie, this is one of my favorite days. We're at the carnival with Nona and Pop and my other two favorite girls, Becca and Morgan. This is our family. No matter what happens in our life. I can't be prouder of moments like these, where I feel I'm actually giving you everything you deserve. I hope one day I can give you days like this every day. I love you so much, honey!

I put it back. God, I think I just fell more in love with him. How is this possible? How can I feel this way about both of them? I sit back down in my seat and try to think about something else. There's only one more hour of crop night and I've managed to get three layouts done. Pretty impressive!

"Are you okay?" Tara asks. What's up with everybody asking me that?

"Yes. It's just been a long day." I start to clean my station up. Ray walks back in.

"The Sox are nailing them! I'm gonna go watch the last inning," he announces.

"Had enough of us?" I tease as I clean up.

"I could never have enough of you, baby." He gives me that boyish grin. All the women hoot and howl. I turn every shade of red. He winks and kisses the air at me before he walks away. We all admire the way his ass looks in his jeans.

"Uh, where did you meet him so I can go and find me one?" Christine laughs.

"Parent-teacher night at the elementary school." I giggle.

"I've been to some of those. I must be going to the wrong school!"

I continue to clean up, emptying the garbage and running the Swiffer vacuum. The last cropper says good night and I lock the door after her. I start to clean Ray's stuff. "I've got that, babe." He rushes over.

"Okay." I rub his back and kiss him on the cheek. "I'm going to put my stuff away upstairs."

"Bec, where's Morgan?"

"She's staying with Grayson tonight." I turn back to look at him. He doesn't seem to have an opinion either way. "You still have to leave by 5 a.m.," I remind him.

"Yes, Becca, I'm aware of that!" He starts throwing stuff in his bag haphazardly.

"You're going to ruin everything you worked on." I place my hand on his arm.

"Who cares?" he snaps.

"I do. Annie will. Stop, Ray." I pick up his stuff and put it into his bag nicely. He stands behind me, runs his hands under my shirt, and rubs my back. I can feel him against me. "Ray, not here. Please." I stop and look up to see if anyone sees us. Ray pulls his hands away then grabs his bag.

"I'll see you in a few days." He sighs and leans forward to graze my lips with his.

"Oh. You don't want to stay?" I'm so confused.

"No, I don't." He heads toward the door. "'Night, Becs."

"'Night, Ray." I follow him out the door. "Ray . . . please, wait." I grab his arm. "I don't understand."

"Don't get upset, Becs. I just can't do this tonight. I don't want this. I want what's in that picture." His right hand palms my left cheek and he inches closer to me. "I don't like how all of this makes you feel. I shouldn't have done what I did this morning. I was self-ish." He closes his eyes and shakes his head with disappointment. "Do me a favor." His eyes open again and stare into mine. "I went through a lot of trouble to make sure my schedule was clear so that I could have this time with you. Please bestow the same courtesy on me for Wednesday. This really sucked, Bec. I had a whole night planned for us." He steps back and pulls his hand away.

"I'm sorry, Ray. I honestly forgot about this tonight." He just nods. "It meant a lot to me that you came and did this with me." I move closer to him and nudge his nose with mine. "Can I have a real good-night kiss?" I put my arms around his neck.

"Baby, if I kiss you, I don't think I'll be able to stop." He rests his forehead on mine.

"Then don't." I challenge him.

"Good night, Becca." He kisses me quickly and pulls my arms off of him. He walks backward away from me, then finally turns on his heel to head to his truck. "See you Wednesday!" I smile and lock the door once again. Once inside, I call him on his cell.

"Yeah, baby?" he answers.

"Call me when you get home so I know you got there safe."

"Okay, babe."

I hang up and do the usual nightly routine of turning down lights, putting up the sign, and making sure the breakfast setup is ready to go. My cell rings just as I turn the kitchen light off.

"I don't think it's fair that he knows every move I make with you but I don't know what he's doing with you!" he says. No *Hello,*

I'm home safe.

"I agree. He tried to kiss me today when he picked Morgan up, but I pulled away and reminded him that he can't touch me until Monday. That's all I can do, Ray—be honest with you." In the lounge, I turn off the TV and light that he left on.

"I want you to be at my house with me tonight," he says.

"You know I—"

He cuts me off. "Yes, Becca, I know you can't! I'm gonna go. I'll see you Wednesday. I love you."

"Okay." That's all I've got. He hangs up. *Country Sybecca* (because that's her real name) *is shaking her head.* I call Ray back.

"Hi," he says quickly.

"I love you, too," I say and hang up. I go upstairs with a heavy heart and a bottle of wine. I see Melissa heading down the hall toward me.

"Hey, I'm taking a bath in a minute, but would you be interested in watching a chick flick and hanging out?"

She looks like she's about to say *yes*, but one of the other guards gives her a look.

"I can't, Becca. I'm sorry."

"Okay." I shrug. I head into my room and pour my wine. I may drink the whole bottle tonight. Okay . . . maybe only two glasses. I do have a full inn, and I'm the only person here. I disrobe, light a few candles, and sink in. Josh Groban sings softly to me out of the iPod, trying his hardest to calm my nerves. Yes, it's all so romantic . . . I mean, relaxing . . . all by myself. I take a sip of wine, lie back, and close my eyes.

"*Jesus Christ, Becca!* Wake up!"

My eyes fly open. Ray is there, bending over the tub to hit the drain. I'm freezing. He yanks me out of the water.

"Are you trying to drown yourself?"

"No. I just closed my eyes for a minute." *What's eating him?*

"Becca, Melissa said you got in the tub over an hour ago, which is why the fucking water is cold!" His nose flares. Yup' he's a little furious!

"Oh. I must've fallen asleep." I sigh. *So what?*

"God, Becs, if anything ever happened to you ..." His voice softens as he kisses my forehead.

"What are you doing here?" I start drying off.

"I felt bad about how I acted tonight. Look at you. You're like a big prune." He chuckles.

"Can you give me that?" I point to my robe. He bites his lip and shakes his head. "Please. I'm cold." I go to reach for it, but he blocks me.

"I'll keep you warm, baby." He wraps me in his arms and kisses my nose. "C'mon ..." He pulls me into the room. I seriously need to do lingerie shopping if I'm going to keep this up. I'll need a Gray drawer and a Ray drawer. Oh God, why do their names have to rhyme?

"Something sexy or something comfy?" I ask quietly.

"How about nothing? Why are you whispering?" He cocks his head and points his thumb toward the door. I nod. He opens the door and sticks his head out. "Hey! I don't want anyone hurting themselves trying to listen, so you can go ahead and let your boss know that I am indeed here to bang her. Thanks and see you at 5 a.m. sharp!" He closes the door, that boyish grin intact on his face.

"That wasn't very nice, Ray." I try to act shocked, but I can't help giggling. He pulls off his shirt and whips off his belt. He grins as he unloads the wad of condom packets in his pocket. Jeans unzipped and off. Goodbye, underwear . . . hello, big guy! He grabs a packet and rips it with his teeth. Okay. He's not wasting any time. I pull the duvet down and slide back on the bed. He hovers over me, mirroring my actions. I bring my knees up at his sides.

"Sorry, Becs," he whispers against my lips, then enters me at once. As he has his way with me, I hear Sting in my head: *Roxanne!* Donna Summer "hustles" in . . . *toot toot, hey, beep beep.* Ray stops.

"Did you just whisper *beep beep*?"

"Did I?" I ask, then giggle.

Ray chuckles as well. "Tell Donna Summer to get out of there. You're not a bad girl . . . you're a very, very good girl." He sets his hips back in motion. I close my eyes and try to focus, but calling me a "good girl" during sex is definitely a trigger for me. *Just breathe. Just breathe.* Ray stops again. "Becs, where are you?" *Georgia, ten years ago, being a "good girl" for George after he beat the shit out of me.*

"Ray, I'm sorry. You have to get off of me." *Shit.*

"What's the matter?" He climbs off.

"George." I say, then quickly explain the different triggers. "I'm sorry. I don't always know what's going to trigger the flashbacks, but that's definitely a major one. I hope you understand." I don't even understand why this keeps happening to me. I *so* want to be over it!

"Becca, why wouldn't I understand? I'd be a complete asshole if I didn't. That was a very traumatic time in your life." He moves a strand of my hair out of my face.

"I feel so ridiculous. So mad. God, it's such a killjoy!"

"Wow—*killjoy*? That's, what . . . circa 1992, maybe?" He laughs at me.

"Yeah, well, I like to recycle shit every once in a while, except for *not*. I cringe whenever somebody says that." I look over at him. His blue-gray eyes are mesmerizing. He's beautiful. I touch his face and lean forward to kiss him. I kiss him once . . . twice . . . *mmm*. He rolls me onto my back and looks into my eyes, searching. I just stare back.

"I love your green eyes. I love how amazing they look when the sun hits them. I love how rich the color turns when you cry. I love that you called me back tonight to tell me that you love me. I love how you love Annie, how you make her feel so special. I love that you saw how beautiful that picture is. I love how you responded to its importance to me. I love how you made me feel this morning. I love how your nostrils flare when you're trying not to cry. I love you, Becca—everything about you." He kisses my fallen tear away, then my lips ever so softly, then down my neck.

I close my eyes as he continues to travel down, bathing me in his kisses and his words. Oh God, I love him. Oh God . . . *oh God!* Uh . . . oh um . . . okay. I grasp on to the sheets and feel my eyes roll back into my head. *All Sybeccas* (their newly appointed name) *are at their pole stations, shaking their asses. Except for Ghetto Sybecca . . . she's bouncin' hers!* I feel myself rising. Ray holds my legs steady as my hips go wild. Holy shit! *The power of Christ compels me! The power of Christ compels me!* I drop my head back after my last quake and stare at the ceiling, wide-eyed in amazement.

I hear him ripping another packet, and he pulls me up to sit astride him. I bury my face in his neck as I expand around him. He brings my face to his as I slowly move my hips. I bite at his lips, tasting myself on them. He deepens the kiss with the slip of his tongue. His mouth moves to my chin, along my jawline, and to my ear. He buries his left hand in my hair, his right at the small of my back. "Theme song?" he asks, his lips against my ear.

"Toss-up between . . . 'Let Me Take You for a Ride' . . . Joe . . . McIntyre . . . or 'Big Green Tractor' . . . Jason Aldean." I try to steady my breath.

"What?" He chuckles.

"Shh . . . focus, McNeil."

"Yes, baby." He captures my lips again. We're in perfect rhythm with each other. It feels like forever and not long enough when we finally come undone. I rest my head on his shoulder and he on mine, our chests heaving. "Did you like the ride on my big green tractor?" He laughs.

"Mm-hmm." I smile against his lips. I slide off of him and lie down while he disposes of the condom. He collapses next to me.

"I'm scared, Becca, that you're not going to choose me."

Raw honesty is not something I've ever found Ray to be low on.

"Please, sweetie. Don't do this. It's only the first day." I palm his face and kiss him. I lie on his chest, set the alarm for twenty of five, and try to go to sleep.

"Have you had anal sex with him?"

"Raymond!" I yell in a whisper.

"Just asking," he says, all innocent.

"Go to sleep!" I slap his chest.

"Okay, baby, but you'd tell me if you did, right?"

"Good night, Ray." I say in a sterner tone.

"'Night, Baby." He kisses my hair.

I've barely even closed my eyes when the alarm goes off.

"It's too early," I grumble. "Ray, c'mon, honey. Wake up." I nudge him.

"You're fucking kidding me. I have twenty more minutes," he complains.

"Okay. I just didn't think you wanted to run out of the room in a mad dash at five." I yawn.

"Becs, I'm too tired to drive." He turns over. I think for a moment.

"Hey, Ray, give me a kiss now. I'm going to go sleep in Grayson's room." I smack his butt. He rolls onto his back and pulls me on top of him. I kiss him. "I love you. I'll see you on Wednesday." I kiss him again.

"Hey . . . I have ten more minutes."

"Ray, we're both so tired, we'll only end up falling back asleep. Give me another kiss." I grab his face with my hand and plant another one on him.

"See you later, baby." He smiles and smacks my butt. I go to Grayson's room and go back to sleep.

Chapter Eleven

"Hey, Becca, sweetheart." Grayson shakes me. I open my eyes and smile up at him. "I'm happy to see you eager, but you are a whole day early. Must I remind you of the rules?" He touches my face and I remember.

"No, baby." I yawn.

"Don't call me that," he snaps lightly.

"Sorry. I forgot." I sit up and study him a bit. He's sitting on the edge of the bed as if he's about to stand. He's facing forward to avoid my eyes, I guess. He looks lost in his thoughts. I yearn to know just one of them, one little thought crossing his mind. The silence is killing me. "Is your aunt still mad at me?"

"I didn't know that she was." He seems surprised.

"Of course she is. I can just imagine what she thinks of me." I feel my chin quiver at the thought. I decide to climb out of his bed and head for the door. This is all too awkward—all of it! How did my life get so fucked up in one week's time?

"Thank you for not staying with him past five." He pulls me back by my waist and stands up behind me, slamming my back into his chest. An electric current goes through my body, sending me into sensory overload. *Damn my erratic breathing!* Pull it together, Becca. *Thespian Sybecca steps onto the stage, dusting off her script and clearing her throat.*

"Well, I knew it would be in your full report if I did," I say sarcastically.

"Bye!" His voice thick with irritation, as he shoves me forward and releases his grip on me.

"Okay, then ..." I murmur, and glance back at him as I open the door. He's standing there, hands on his hips and watching me. A combination of anger and disgust blanket his face. I feel my nostrils flare. Funny, I never noticed I did this to hold back my tears until Ray mentioned it. Gray sees the effect he's having on me and his face softens. He looks down. I close the door behind me and head to my room.

Ray is gone, but I see he's left me a note on my bed.

Morning, baby,

Thanks for not kicking me out! You are so amazing ... I hate leaving you, but I have two new songs to listen to! Wednesday can't get here fast enough. I love you!

Always, Ray

PS. Just in case ... morning, mate!

And I'm sure, as Ray predicted, Grayson read my note. I toss my hair up, deciding not to wash it as I walk into the bathroom for a quick shower.

After drying off, I throw on my dark blue jeans and formfitting olive-green shirt. I wipe the steam off the mirror to see what's what. My locks are rocking the wavy look today, so I decide to go with it and just clip my bangs back. I brush my teeth and decide a little makeup is in order today.

"Christ!" I grumble under my breath. I put my eyeliner down and pick up the tweezers to groom my eyebrows a bit. I need to go for a waxing this week. I simply cannot put it off any longer. Okay, stragglers gone, makeup is done, underarms have a secret, and my neck has a hint of sophistication. I am determined not to feel bad or cry at all today. If anybody tries to make me do either, I will simply smile at them and silently sing *Fuck you* by Lily Allen. Love that song!

It's almost lunchtime. I take in a deep breath before I open my door to head downstairs. I lock it behind me and, with a new purpose in my step (new defense mechanism, maybe?), I travel down and head to the kitchen. Hazel looks at me, then away again. Ugh, here we go!

"Hazel, how long are you going to be mad at me for?" I walk over to her.

"I don't know, Becca. I can't even look at you right now. I'm so disappointed in you." She spoons tuna salad onto a croissant.

"I'm sorry you feel that way." Lily Allen blasts in my head as I go to the fridge and pull out the pastries. We work in silence for the next half an hour. I start putting trays out, then head to my office. Grayson is in there on my computer.

"What are you doing?" My irritation level is through the roof. There are only so many times you can sing a song in your mind before it loses its powerful effect.

"I'm checking your finances to see how long it will take you to pay me back for renovations in case you don't choose me." Honest bastard, isn't he? Oh, that's right, England produces "blunt chaps."

"Well, I'm sure Ray won't charge as much."

"Because you're shagging him? Do you think I'm going to give my money to Ray? I would literally be paying him to fuck you! You are turning out to be quite the whore, aren't you, love?"

I slap his face as hard as I can. He stands, and I run out of the office and up to my room.

Oh God, how could he say that to me? He wanted this! He wanted me to "give it a try." Ray would never, ever treat me like this! My door opens and Gray walks in. I keep my distance.

"I'm sorry, sweetheart. I'm trying not to be jealous. I'm not doing a very good job. That's all I wanted to say." He leaves. I take several minutes to pull myself together before heading back downstairs.

I realize it's in my best interest to just avoid Grayson and Hazel for the rest of the day. As soon as there is a break in my schedule, I decide that a shopping excursion and movie with Morgan is an even better idea.

"Uh, who are you and what have you done with my mother?" Morgan asks, wide-eyed with excitement at my offer as she grabs her coat. Funny, I've been asking that same question about myself all week.

My alarm goes off quietly at five of five. I set it last night so that I wouldn't be surprised when he came in. Five comes. Five-thirty. Six. Seven. Resolved with the idea that he's not paying me a visit this morning, I climb out of bed and get dressed. I need to get Morgan up and ready for the bus. First, I head downstairs and into the kitchen to get my coffee. Grayson is at the table, dressed and ready for the day.

"Morning, Gray." I wrap my arms around him from behind and lean over to kiss his cheek. I linger there for a moment, taking in the intoxicating smell that is Grayson James. He continues to read his paper, or at least pretending to. "Oh, baby, baby, baby . . . what am I going to do with you?" I whisper in his ear before I kiss it.

GRAYSON

Christ! I could think of a million things I'd love for her do with me. Why isn't she mad? I thought she would be when I didn't go to her. *She smells so lovely.* I'm being foolish. Why am I pushing her away? Ray wasted no time.

"Morning, Gracie," Aunt Hazel says, and gives me a kiss.

"Morning, Auntie," I say cheerfully. I'm being an idiot. Becca sits next to me with her coffee.

"So, what are we doing today?" She's smiling that gorgeous smile, and I'm being an arsehole. All I can do is stare at her. "C'mon, mate! What do you have planned for us?" She's trying her hand at my accent again. I give her nothing. "Chim chiminey, chim chiminey, chim chim cher-ee . . . I sees what I likes and I likes what I sees ..." she sings, and even Aunt Hazel looks like she's fighting to hold back a smile.

I clear my throat and turn the page. Becca takes the paper away from me, slides onto my lap, and sings a few lines from "Boys Don't Cry" by The Cure. She kisses my mark. God, I'm so mad at her. I close my eyes and rest my head on her chest.

"Grayson, you asked me to do this. I told you it was going to be hard on all of us."

"I know, sweetheart. I just feel like Ray is gaining and I'm losing. You were all mine not four days ago. How did this happen? Please, just get off, Becca." I honestly think I'm going to be sick.

"Gray?" She palms my face.

"I just can't. I can't do this. I have to leave." That's it. I've made the decision for her.

"Oh, no. Please don't do this. I don't want to lose you," Becca begs. "Please, baby . . . please." She kisses me.

"I can't, Becca. I feel sick to my stomach." I try to push her off.

"Grayson, what if I'm pregnant?" She whispers in my ear.

"I'd guess we'd get a paternity test, then." I didn't even think about that.

"It would be yours, Grayson—I can assure you!" She sounds hurt.

"Well, then, I would take care of it." I try to nudge her off again.

"What about Morgan?"

"Oh, funny how you only think about her when someone isn't between your legs!" I shove her to the floor. She sits on the ground, looking up at me, her eyes wide with shock. I get up and leave, ignoring both her and my aunt's indecisive glare. Christ, my heart feels as if it just smashed into a million pieces for the umpteenth time since I've met her.

"Daddy, where are you going?" Morgan asks, running up and hugging me. She started calling me "Daddy" again the other night. Christ! What am I doing? Am I really giving up without a fight? This is not me. I haven't been me all week. No. I'm not doing this. I'm not giving up.

"Morgy girl, stay out here a minute." I kiss her head and go back into the kitchen. Becca is still on the floor, crying.

"Get up, sweetheart. Morgan's coming." I pull her to her feet, but her sobs don't lessen. "Come with me." I pull her into the stock-room. She turns away from me and cries by the wall. "Shh, shh," I kiss her hair. "C'mon now, let's get Morgy ready for school and bring her down to the bus stop together." I wrap my arms around her from behind.

"Grayson, what are you doing to me? I don't know if I'm coming or going with you." She turns and cries into my chest.

"Oh c'mon, surely you can tell when you're coming with me, love." Ah! There's my giggly girl.

"You're paying for my therapy bill." She smacks my chest.

"Fair enough, sweetheart. Now dry your eyes and give me a kiss." I wipe away her tears and lean in to do what I've been dying to do for three days. She returns my kiss with so much passion I feel my knees weaken. Oh, I am going to make her pray all day today.

"All better now, sweetheart?" I pull away.

"Yes, baby." She breathes deeply, and we head back into the kitchen.

"Got your breakfast already, little sweetheart?" I smile and kiss Morgy's head.

"I'm hungry. You had me waiting forever!" she says, then turns to Becca. "Mommy, is Grammy Hazel still mad at you?"

"Why don't you ask her?" Becca takes a sip of her coffee.

"Grammy Hazel, are you still mad at Mommy?"

"I'm a little upset, yes." My aunt keeps her back turned.

"Well, get in line." Becca waves her arm, clearly frustrated. I grab her hand and squeeze. She gets up and leaves the kitchen.

"Are *you* mad at Mommy?" She looks at me before taking another bite of cereal.

"I love the little freckles you have here, Morgan." I kiss her nose and smile. "Hurry up; you don't want to be late." She lets out a big sigh and shakes her head. I guess we adults are very difficult and confusing. Morgan finishes her breakfast and we walk out to the store, where we find Becca cleaning the counter.

"C'mon, love, let's get our girl off." I put my hand out. She grabs her jacket.

"Do you have your lunch, Morgan?"

"No, Mom. Daddy gave me lunch money."

Oh, brave little one, testing the waters. Becca says nothing. We walk out the door and are greeted by a very brisk sunny day.

"I love the smell of fall," Becca says. She closes her eyes and inhales deeply. Christ, I don't think I've ever seen her in a moment where she doesn't look beautiful.

We get to the end of the driveway. The three of us hold hands and wait for the bus. I'm amazed at the comfort such a simple gesture brings me. We see the yellow lights, which turn red when the bus stops. Morgan gives us both a kiss and gets on. We wave and head back.

"Is she the reason you changed your mind this morning, or was it just a show for her?" Becca stares straight ahead when she asks.

"I'm just as confused as you are, Becca. I love you. That's the one thing I'm not confused about." I pull her close as we walk up the driveway and inside. "What's on your schedule this morning?" I ask, grabbing it off the store counter.

"Grayson James, followed by a lawyer, then Grayson James. Then I have two interviews to do. Then I have Grayson James, lunch . . . followed by Grayson James. That's my schedule until Morgan gets home. What does your schedule look like?" She smiles.

"Oh, about the same, except I have Becca Campbell to deal with . . . ugh! That woman drives me mad!"

"Oh yeah, that's tough. Maybe we should introduce her to Grayson James; he's impossible."

"Is that so?" I throw her over my shoulder.

"Grayson!" Her yell is full of laughter. I run up the stairs, and Melissa opens Becca's bedroom door for us.

"Thanks, doll." I smile at her. She blushes as she closes the door for me and I toss Becca onto the bed. "No, no." I pick her back up and open the door. Melissa's eyes widen. I nod to my door. She goes and opens it, then closes it behind us.

I throw her onto my bed and pull my shirt off. She bites her bottom lip.

"I'll have you know," I say, "I spent many extra hours in the gym this weekend." I let my jeans fall.

"Mama likes." She grins and kneels on the bed to pull her shirt off. Her jeans are quite loose on her.

"Sweetheart, have you lost weight, or are those old jeans?" I pull at the waist.

"No, I bought these two weeks ago. I do have a new workout regimen myself." She smirks as she unbuttons and unzips them. She's wearing a matching powder-blue and cream lacy bra and panty set. Now I'm biting *my* lip. "You like? I bought these yesterday, just for you." She leans up for a kiss.

"They look great. They'll look better on the floor."

She stands on the bed to unfasten her bra. She towers over me. I caress her stomach with my mouth as I pull her panties off. She slides her body down through my hands and captures my mouth with hers. I lose my left hand in her hair and let my right explore her sex. She moans against my lips as my fingers dive deep inside of her.

"Oh, sweetheart, you're already so wet for me," I say against her ear as I find the sweet spot inside her. I want to hear her sing her prayers first. I can feel her body start to quake. "Pray for me."

"Oh God, baby!" she cries. Still the best sound in the world. I do this to her four more times. "Oh, please, Grayson—I need you," she whimpers into my neck. I bend down to my jeans and pull a condom out. Her eyes open wide.

"Shocked?" I ask. She nods. "Lay back, sweetheart," I say, trying to keep my resolve. I never wanted to wear one of these with her. She lays back and waits, and I can't help wondering if she'll feel the same to me.

"Gray?" She pushes herself up on her elbows. "Are you okay?" She seems nervous and unsure of herself. I climb on top of her and stare down into her eyes. She nudges my hip with her leg, just like she always does when she's ready for me. Part of me wants to run. I feel like I can't come home again. I close my eyes. She leans forward and kisses my mark. "I love you, baby."

I grab her leg and enter her, burying myself as deep as humanly possible and listening to her soft cry under me. We're so entangled, devouring each other—I can't tell where she starts and I finish. She still feels like home. Oh God, I can't get close enough to her.

Becca cries beneath me. It's a good cry. I know because she holds onto me, desperately trying to meet my thrusts, and calls me "baby."

"Becca, oh God . . . sweetheart." I hold my teeth together to keep some sort of control. I land on her chest.

"I love you. I love you so much," she says through her tears, then plants several kisses on the side of my face. For the first time in five days, I feel complete contentment. I pull out and bring her to lay on my chest. We're blissfully spent. I rub her bum and take in the scent of her hair. "Go ahead, baby. I know you want to." She eggs me on. I close my eyes and give her bum a good slap. I take in a sharp breath at the small sob she releases next to my ear. "Again, baby . . . please," she begs. I slap her again.

"Sweetheart, that's enough. We only have fifteen minutes until the lawyer gets here." I'm begging her now, because I can feel myself getting wild under her.

"Just one more," she says against my lips. I oblige and she bites my lip to muffle her sounds.

"Becca, please, you're driving me crazy!" I turn her onto her back. "You have to stop," I say quietly, and stare into her eyes. Does he do this to her? Does she ask him? No, no. He was pissed about it the other day. This is ours. Only I do this to her. And with the exception of that day, she loves it.

"What are you thinking about, sweetie?"

"How terribly in love with you I am."

Her eyes turn sad, and I know the guilt of all of this is really weighing heavily on her heart.

BECCA

I can't believe that just happened. I really thought he was done. I'm so all over the place—and no closer to deciding. If anything, I think this is all making it worse.

"Come on, sweetheart," Grayson calls from the other side of the door.

"Okay, ready." I smile and step out from the bathroom.

We head downstairs to meet Richard Brown, Attorney at Law.

He's a chubby man of about fifty, balding, but with blond on the sides and a moustache to match. We go over the details of my situation. He asks me if George is still an active member in the service, because if so, our divorce would fall under the Service Members Civil Relief Act. This entitles active-duty service members to delay a divorce or any civil litigation.

"He is active for another month," Grayson offers.

"Well, then you might want to wait that month." Mr. Brown sighs.

"Here's my other question. I built up my business—using his life-insurance policy—under the assumption that he was dead. I'm aware that I will probably have to pay back the money I received, but how will the divorce affect my business?" I'll be pissed if I have to give George anything after what that son of a bitch did to me.

"Well, Mrs. Campbell—"

"Ms. Campbell." Grayson and I correct him in unison.

"Ms. Campbell. Given the situation with him going AWOL and kidnapping you, this whole thing will most likely play in your favor. You said the authorities are looking for him now?"

"Yes," we both say.

"Well, let's do the paperwork for the divorce and custody. When he is caught, we will file immediately." He has me sign some papers about being his client, petitioning for divorce, and sole custody of Morgan. "Are you sure you don't want support?"

"I want nothing but to have him out of my life." I sign my last document. Our meeting is then adjourned, and he leaves.

"Ugh! I need to sit down and do a budget. Thanks for cosigning that loan for me, baby. I'm going to be paying the insurance company for a long time." I turn to my computer and pull up the new software he installed. "Maybe your finance guy can help me figure out the tax situation with that. No, I'll probably have to get a tax attorney. Won't the government have to pay back money to me and to the insurance company? Damn . . . this is such a mess."

"Sweetheart, I'll take care of it." Grayson grabs the mouse and closes the screen.

"No, this is my mess, baby. You're not taking care of this."

"Well, let me at least get my people on it to find out what needs to be done. You have enough to worry about." He rubs my shoulders.

"You and your people." I laugh. "I wish I had 'people.'" I do the air quotation marks.

"You'll have them once you decide I'm the man for you. My people will become your people. Just one of the many perks to marrying me." He helps me out of the chair. "C'mon, let's go shopping for Aunt Hazel's birthday gift."

"Oh God, Gray, I almost forgot! Ugh . . . I've been terrible this week. Let's send her and Charlie on a cruise. She always talks about going on one!" I'm getting excited, as if I'm going with her.

"Spending my money already?" He arches a brow.

"No. No, I'll pay for the cruise. I want to. The refinance has freed up a lot of my money, so I can do it. I'll worry about the insurance company when I have to. I want to do this for Hazel, she's done so much for me over the years." *I can't wait to see her face!*

"Well, we'll see." He humors me. "We should make sure it's okay with Charlie. What if he doesn't like cruises, love?"

"Ooh, you're right. Let's go ask him. C'mon!" I practically pull him out the door. We head up to the stables.

"Hey, Rocco, my handsome boy. We'll go for a ride tomorrow. I promise." I kiss his face, and he snorts at me. He's pissed. I scratch his neck and turn to Charlie. "Hazel's birthday is next week, and I'd love to send you two on a cruise. Would you be interested in doing something like that?" I ask as I feed Rocco an apple.

"Uh, sure. When, where, and uh . . . how much is my share?" He pulls off his cowboy hat, slides his hand across the top of his head, and puts the hat back on. He seems like he may be uncomfortable with this.

"Well, I was going to look into all of that, but I wanted to make sure you'd like to go. Do you have a preference as to when or where? Maybe you could get Hazel's top destination out of her nonchalantly and we could go from there. Your share is whatever you want to spend on the trip. I certainly wouldn't send Hazel alone so, your fare is included." I try to stay focused as Grayson walks away in the midst of a heated discussion on his cell.

"Oh, Becca, I couldn't let you do that." Charlie shakes his head.

"Besides Morgan and my aunt and uncle, you and Hazel are my only family. You are like parents to me. I love you both so much, and you have been so good to us over the years. Please let me do this. I can, and I want to. It would bring me so much joy." I grab his hand in both of mine and squeeze. I meant every single word. I don't know what I would ever do without them.

"Becca, honey, you really know how to get to an old man." His smile is small—he's giving in, but not wanting to.

"It's not just the ole chaps, Charlie! She's got us young ones blindsided, too!" Grayson slaps him on the back.

"Oh, whatever. Now, Charlie, remember: your job is to find out where in the world she most wants to cruise to." I give him a big hug, and Gray and I head out.

"We only have about an hour and a half, baby. I have two women coming for an interview," I remind him.

"Sure, sweetheart, I'll drive." He nods to Derek and Melissa, who hop in a black Escalade to follow us. We climb into his Range Rover and wait for their signal to go.

"Didn't you have a car a few days ago?" I ask as I start messing with buttons.

"Yes, but I wanted something more rugged without getting a truck." He taps my hand.

"I love my truck. It's shit on gas, but I love it." I have a good old Ford F-350 King Ranch.

"Well, this is shitty on gas, too."

"Where are we going?" I take his hand.

"Jewelry store. I saw one downtown the other day. We'll see what they have." I close my eyes and lean my head back. Grayson turns the radio on, and Enya pipes through the speakers.

"You listen to Enya?" I smile over at him.

"It's calming," he answers simply.

"It is." I close my eyes again. "Is this one of your songs, love?" I do the English accent.

"No." He chuckles. "I haven't written for Enya." He brings my hand up to his mouth and kisses the back of it.

A few minutes later, I feel Grayson kissing my lips. I open my eyes. I must've dozed off. I smile against his lips and welcome them a little bit more.

"Mm . . . c'mon, love." He kisses my forehead. Just as he pulls away, I see Ray standing on the sidewalk in front of the Java Joint, on his cell phone, staring right at us. He shakes his head and walks away. My cell pings. I pull it out to find a text from Ray.

September 31, 2012 10:03 a.m.
Ray: No dates allowed in this area . . . remember?
Me: Not out on a date. We're getting Hazel's b-day gift. XOXO
Ray: Date or no date . . . PDA . . . not a good idea! BTW, he saw me and did it on purpose. I saw u were asleep. XOXO Miss you! :p
Me: :-o I'll talk to him. XX
Ray: Theme song?
Me: You say he's just a friend . . . Biz Markie . . . LOL
Ray: LOL! You're perpetually stuck in the 90s, babe! I love you!

"Becca! Tell Ray I said to fuck off and let that be your last god-damn text!" Grayson snaps.

Me: Gray said to fuck off, Ray . . . that's the last thing I'm allowed to say today . . . the fact that your names rhyme is fucking gay! G'day!

I hit "send" and press the circle at the bottom of my phone. Grayson takes it from me and tries to read my texts. "Where are the other ones?"

"I deleted them." I look in the glass cases at the jewelry. I was so busy texting, I didn't even realize I'd walked into the store. I can see why people get into accidents while texting and driving.

"Why did you delete them?" he asks through his teeth.

"I always do, baby. It's a habit. Go ahead and look. You won't find any texts on there." I point at the phone to encourage him. He looks, just like I knew he would. "I'm going to buy you a pair of purple pants."

"What the hell for?" *Yes, I have five heads!*

"Because that's what the Hulk always wears."

"Becca, what the fuck are you talking about?" he asks in an irritated tone.

"Forget it, Grayson. I don't want to argue. What are we looking at for your auntie?" I say the last word with his accent.

"Oh, I don't bloody know. You pick something!" He walks over to the watches. I hear my phone ping. Grayson looks at it and starts to text, smiling to himself, then walks the phone back over to me. I move to put it in my purse. "You're not going to read what I texted?" he asks in disbelief . . . or is it disappointment?

My phone pings again. "Here, it's for you." I hand it over. I decide to go and look at the pearl necklaces while Grayson has a texting war with Ray. Even pissing contests have become technologically advanced!

I find a string of pearls with a beautiful diamond-accent clasp for Hazel. Eric, the jeweler, takes it—and the matching bracelet— out of the case for me. I know how much Hazel loves pearls, and this necklace is quite different from the one she already owns. I look over to see Grayson still carrying on with Ray, so I decide to add on the Mikimoto pearl bracelet, necklace, and earrings for myself.

"Credit card, please, baby," I say to him. He walks over to me and hands me his black AmEx. I hand the card to Eric, who has graciously helped me spend a lot of money today.

Grayson's pissing contest has just cost him about six thousand dollars. I sign "Becca James" on the monitor, hand him the printed slip with the card, and walk out to the car with the goods. He follows me, looking at the slip as I put my new earrings on. A slow, satisfied smile crosses his lips. I bend over near the passenger mirror to check out my new earrings, and my theme song changes to "Material Girl" by Madonna. I stand upright again to find Grayson practically on top of me.

"I was going to yell at you for spending all of this money on my aunt, buying her two of everything. Then I realized you bought yourself stuff . . . without asking. Then I saw," he caresses my cheek and slides his fingers back, playing with my earring, "your signature. Sweetheart, I will buy you that whole store if it would get you to make that signature legal." He leans down and collects my lips with his own. His tongue beckons to me, asking for permission to deepen the kiss. I comply. *Ping. Ping. Ping.* Grayson laughs as he pulls away and sends another text on my phone. "I think you have a stalker, *Mrs. James.*"

"Let's go home, baby," I say, trying not to show my guilt. I don't want him making a spectacle out of us in front of Ray for hours.

"If you promise to read the texts." He hands me the phone.

"I don't want to be in the middle of your pissing contest." I sigh and look away.

"Oh, but you are, sweetheart." He pulls my face back to his and grasps my lips again. *Ping.*

"Let's go, please. I'll read them."

"Okay, then." He smiles wickedly and unlocks the door for me. I get in, take a deep breath, and look down to read the epic novel between these two assholes.

September 31, 2012   10:15am

Ray: You are so fucking cute, babe!

Gray: Yeah, you should've seen how cute she was this morning when she begged me to slap that fine arse of hers.

Ray: George liked to slap her around too. U guys should go out for a pint and compare notes!

Gray: You're a funny "little" man, aren't you? Probably why Becca begged me not to leave her this morning.

Ray: Hmm . . . yeah, I don't think she would agree with you. It seemed to me that Becca could barely take all of me in.

Gray: I think it was that she could barely take you. I had her crying tears of joy this morning. I'm sure it was pure relief to be with a real man.

Ray: She was probably crying because it wasn't me. She sings with me . . . beautifully.

Gray: She prays with me! She'll be praying again once we get home. I love taking her to church several times a day.

Ray: She's probably praying for it to be over! She begs me. Can't get enough of me, loves the taste of me in her mouth. Remember that the next time you do PDA in our town. U know Becca doesn't want that attn. u asshole!

Gray: Speaking of assholes, I think I'll be bringing hers to church tonight!

Ray: I swear to God, u better not do anything to her she doesn't want u 2 do! U R not going to win, Gray! I know her better and longer! U R delusional if you think she'll chose you!

Ray: No PDA!

Gray: She just spent $4,000 of my money on herself and she signed the slip BECCA JAMES, BITCH!

Ray: That's all you're good for!

Ray: PDA!

Ray: Becca asked us not to do this!

Ray: You're an asshole!

Ray: Becca I love u! See u Weds. Baby! XX

"You guys are fucking idiots!" I throw my phone into my purse.

"Well, let's not talk about what you are." He clears his throat and looks away. My heart sinks. I face the window and just let the tears forming in my eyes fall freely. That's what he wants, to make me feel this way. "Becca," he says after few minutes. I ignore him and run out of the car as soon as he parks at the inn. I walk into the store and wipe my face. Claudia walks around the desk when she sees me.

"Becca, are you okay?"

"Claudia, would you feel comfortable doing the interviews today?" I ask.

"Absolutely. I'll do them. You know, Becca, you don't cry when you're with Ray," she states, not caring that Grayson has just walked up behind me. I look over at Hazel. She's looking at Grayson. You can see the disappointment all over her face.

"I'll be back later," I say and start for the door.

"Where are you going?" Gray snaps.

"For a ride on Rocco."

"The only thing you are riding today is me!" he says angrily and throws me over his shoulder.

"Grayson, you put her down right now!" Hazel yells at him, getting right up in his face. I just sway on the other side, completely mortified.

"Auntie, get out of my way!"

"Grayson, I'm ashamed of you!"

"Auntie, move!"

"It's okay, Hazel." I try to comfort her.

"Becca, I'm sorry." She shakes her head and walks away.

"Sir, we are here under your orders to protect Ms. Campbell. Please put her down now." Derek says.

"Christ, people—I'm not going to hurt her. I love her. I wouldn't hurt her." But he does put me down. "We're just arguing. It's not the end of the world! C'mon, Becca." He grabs my hand. I go with him because I feel the need to hide. When we get up to his room, he locks the door.

"Grayson, I don't think you can handle this. You're getting crazy, and you're scaring everybody—including me." I have to try to talk some kind of sense into him.

"I want to know everything you did with him." His jaw twitches.

"I'm not doing this!" I yell. "You need to snap out of this jealous rage. The only thing you are doing is pushing me away. *You* came to me with this 'great' plan. I didn't want this!" *I really can't go on like this.* "You've got your aunt upset. You made a spectacle of yourself downstairs in front of everybody. Even your security team is trying to protect me from you! Do you know that they were two seconds away from beating down the door the other day when they heard you hurting me?" I've got to lay it all out for him. He just sits on his bed, staring at the floor.

"I don't know what to say. I'm having a hard time keeping myself in check. I'm not used to not having control over situations. I feel helpless, and I don't like it." He confesses what I already know about him.

"Do you know why I wanted to take Rocco out?" I sit on the floor in front of him, crossing my legs and putting my head in my hands.

"You were mad at me."

"For?"

"For implying."

I look up at him. "Implying what, Grayson?"

"That you're a whore. Becca, I was angry about the texts," he explains, sounding defensive.

"First of all, you *both* did exactly what I asked you not to do! You are not supposed to discuss what I do with either of you. I bit my tongue and ignored it, and you made me rub my nose in it! Then you got mad at me and make me feel like shit about following through on a plan you partly came up with. Do you know how it makes me feel to be with both of you? You *absolutely* do . . . and you use it to make me feel shittier. You want to know what Ray does with me? I'll tell you one thing: he works real hard at trying to make me *not* feel that way. So who do you think is winning?" There. I've said it all.

"I'm going to take a shower." *That's it?*

"What the fuck, Gray?" I head downstairs, grab my coat, and walk out to the stables.

"Um, I don't know how to ride a horse," Melissa says nervously.

"Is there anyone who does? I'd bring you and go slow, but I just need to take off." I feel terrible, but I just need time to myself.

"I can ride, ma'am. Hi, I'm Ryan." A tall, good-looking man reaches out to shake my hand. He has light brown hair, hazel eyes, and a great smile. *Yeah, Bec, why don't you add him on?* God, what is wrong with me?

"Great. Come on." I grab Rocco's saddle and riding blanket. Charlie gives Ryan Butterscotch. Once the horses are ready to go, we mount up and head down to the field. Ryan's cell phone goes off. He answers.

"Okay. Yes, sir." He hangs up. "Ma'am, I'm not allowed to ride with you. We have to wait. Mr. James is on his way."

"I'm not waiting, Ryan. Sorry." I give Rocco a little kick and we take off.

"Becca! Bloody hell!" It's the last thing I hear from Grayson.

The brisk air bites at my face. I love it. I love the fall, and I know Rocco does, too. We have our best and longest rides at this time of year. "You'll protect me, ole boy. I don't need them." I pat his shoulder. We head through our favorite trail, where there are great jumps to be had over fallen trees—it's nature's obstacle course. We get a good canter in as our first tree comes up. Rocco leaps into the air with such grace. I could stay out here all day. I feel free. We leap over the next one. "Good boy, Rocco!"

We come out of the first part of our trail and into the meadow. There's a bubbling stream on the right that we usually stop at on the way back. In the spring there are gorgeous wildflowers, but now the grass is blanketed in orange and red leaves. It's like a painting.

I give Rocco a little kick and we race through the meadow to the second part of our trail. I lean forward to hug him and pat his shoulder. "I love you, Rocco. You're the only guy who truly understands me." I get a snort for this, as if he's saying, *I told you so!* I giggle. "Yes you did."

We head back after a few hours. Horse therapy is the best. I so needed this. I'm sure I'll get a "what for" from Grayson for going without anyone and taking three hours away from him. We trot slowly back to the stables.

"Becca!" Grayson yells as I dismount. "What in God's name were you thinking?" He gives my bottom a good wallop. *Really?* "Why didn't you wait for me? I wanted to ride with you as part of our date." He looks truly hurt.

"I thought you were only coming because another guy was riding with me." It's still very obvious to me that this was the case.

"Well, yes, but going for a ride was part of my plan today."

"I needed time to myself." I hang Rocco's saddle up and grab his brush. Charlie pops out of one of the stalls and waves to me.

"Leave it, Becca. I'll brush him and pick his hooves!" he calls.

"Thanks!"

"Becca." Grayson brings my attention back to him. "You can have that tomorrow. This is my day," he reminds me, his voice a touch too loud.

"And you've been an asshole for half of it!" I widen my eyes for emphasis.

"You're right. I have been, and I'm sorry. I've apologized to everyone inside. Can we start over? I do have something planned for tonight that you will like." He palms my face.

"Okay." I let him kiss me.

"C'mon, I'm sure you're hungry. I know I am." He gets a wild look in his eyes. I bite my lip.

In the two hours 'til Morgan gets home, we eat lunch, make love, make love again, then head downstairs for some hot cocoa in front of the fireplace.

"It's four o'clock, love. Let's go get our daughter." Gray sighs and slaps my knee. I grab his outstretched hand and stand up. I look into his eyes as he wraps his arms around me. "I love you, Becca. With all my heart, I do." His voice is soft. He leans down and plants a gentle kiss on my lips before releasing me.

We head out of the inn and reach the bus stop just in time. "Hey, Morgy girl!" Grayson picks her up and swings her around. I think he does this partly because he loves her so much and partly because he knows their relationship melts my heart. "Listen, Mum and I are going on a date tonight, so Grammy Hazel will take care of you." Morgan jumps around and squeals. I'm guessing she's thrilled.

"Where are you going?"

"Boston, and we're leaving soon." He grabs her backpack for her. These are the moments I love—us as a family. No insecurities flying around, no anger or arguing. It feels so natural. "Sweetheart, you'll want to go and put something nice on. And wear the new jewelry I bought you. I'd like to actually see it."

"Okay. Morgan, do you want to help me before you do your homework?"

"Oh, yes!"

"Gray, what type of 'nice'? You're not taking me to a club, are you?" *Oh God, please say no.*

"No, no club. Not really my thing."

"Me neither."

"Something nice and classy, but just . . . oh—we're going to the theatre, Becca. Dress accordingly!" I can see he's frustrated at having to give away the information.

"Okay. What are we seeing?" I feel giddy.

"Go and get dressed!" He smacks me lightly on my bum. We race off, and Morgan runs right to my closet.

"Mommy, wear your new little black dress!" she calls to me.

I go into the bathroom for a quick shower. After drying myself and my hair off, I spray it so I can tease it for an updo. Morgan brings my chiffon dress, and I put on my black self-adhesive bra and matching panties before ripping the tags off of it. It's backless with a slight cowl-neck, and it hugs my every curve.

"Morgan, can you get me that bag from my nightstand?" I ask. She runs and grabs it, and I pull out my new jewelry, then work my hair into a ponytail and fan it under to look like a bun. I set the necklace so that it trails down my back, then slip on the bracelet and earrings. I dust my face with makeup, and Morgan brings me my black heels with the faux diamond buckles on the side. I look in the mirror. Wow—I clean up well!

"Mommy, you look beautiful." Morgan's eyes are wide. "Who are you wearing? Somebody may ask."

"No idea. I doubt anyone will ask me, sweetie." I giggle. We head downstairs. Grayson is facing his aunt as she inspects his suit. Morgan clears her throat. I blush. Why do I feel like I'm going to the prom or something? Oh yeah, this is actually our first date! Grayson turns around. His eyes scan me over.

"Oh, Becca." Hazel covers her mouth with her hands. "You look stunning." I smile sheepishly and turn at Morgan's beckoning. I feel Grayson's hands on my upper arms and his lips at the back of my neck.

"God, you are so beautiful," he says softly in my ear. I actually can't believe I'm wearing a backless dress. I'm so worried a "problem area" will show in public. I turn to him, and he takes my coat from Morgan to help me into it. He sweeps my lips with his own.

"You look very handsome, baby." I kiss his mark and inhale deeply the lovely scent that is Grayson James.

"The car's here, darling. Let's go." He grabs my hand and leads me out the door.

We step into the limo. Grayson opens a bottle of Cristal and pours me a glass. I sip it.

"Mmm . . . delicious." I raise the glass to my lips again. For some reason, the butterflies are going wild in my belly. I know it's our first date, but it's not like we aren't already "acquainted" with each other. I finish my glass. He pours me another. I start to feel warm, so I take my coat off. The privacy window goes up. Grayson takes his jacket off. I finish my second glass and hold it up to him for more. He smirks playfully at me and shakes his head as he pours me yet another.

Why am I so nervous? What is wrong with me? I start on my third glass while Grayson's lips gently paint my neck with soft kisses. His hand slowly slides up my dress, his fingers brushing against my inner thigh. I close my eyes, relishing in his touch.

"Thank you for not wearing stockings," he whispers. Why does he sound more British than usual? The champagne must be hitting me now. "I can't keep my hands off of you, Becca. This dress is driving me wild." My eyes remain closed as I listen to his words. Honestly, I don't think he even has to touch me at this point. He can just talk. It's intoxicating. "I want you to pray for me, baby." The words are soft in my ear as his fingers push my panties to the side. They enter me and find the area that always takes me to church. "Are you going to pray for me?" *Oh, keep talking, you beautiful British bastard!*

"Yes, baby, I will." I lick my lips and allow my breath to get erratic.

"C'mon, sweetheart, c'mon, let me hear you. Pray, darling." His

British command has me undone. *Our Father . . . who art in Heaven . . .*

"Oh God, baby ..." He muffles my cries with his mouth as he works me through my last quakes. He removes his fingers and I watch as he places them in his mouth, sucking my taste off.

"Mmm . . . some people like strawberries with their champagne, doll, but I find you much sweeter." He flashes me a mischievous grin then leans in for a kiss. I finish my third glass and rest my head back. I feel intoxicated on so many different levels.

"Sweetheart, we're here." He kisses my eyelids. Why do these men exhaust me so? I can't even manage a simple car ride lately without falling asleep.

"Where are we?" I look around.

"The North End, for dinner." He helps me out. *Oh, yum.* We head inside Giacomo's and Grayson gives his name.

"Follow me, Mr. and Mrs. James," The host says. I look over at Grayson at the mention of "Mrs. James." He gives me a quick wink and a crooked smile. I shake my head, trying not to smile. We are seated in a secluded, dimly lit area in the back.

"Shall I order for you, darling?" he asks as we look over the menu.

"You can once I tell you what I want."

He looks up over the menu at me. "I know what you want, or at least what you are thinking about," he states with confidence.

"Really? Please, enlighten me. What am I thinking about having?" I'll play.

"You, my dear, are looking at the pumpkin tortellini because it's fall. You love fall. You love pumpkin, and there are no interesting dishes with eggplant in them. How am I doing?" he says all of this without even looking up.

"God—you are so hot." *Did I just say that out loud?* This warrants a fabulous smile from him. The waiter comes over.

"Mrs. James will have the pumpkin tortellini and a glass of the

Shiraz. I will have tonight's steak special—medium. And, actually, just make that a bottle of the Shiraz for both of us." He hands the waiter our menus.

"So, what are we going to see?" I'm so excited. I love the theatre.

"It's a surprise. I hope you like it. I was going to choose something else, but I have better tickets for another night. So we'll be back down here next week." He reaches across the table for my hand.

"I wonder if Charlie was successful at getting a location for the cruise."

"Becca, I don't want to talk about anybody but us. We're on a date. We should be learning about each other." He leans forward and rests his head on his fist. I mirror his stance.

"Yes. You're right. So, how did you get into writing music for a living?"

"Christ, Becca, you still haven't Googled me?" He chuckles.

"Nope. No, sorry. Besides," I add. "I'd rather learn about your life from you, not a tabloid or magazine article."

"Well, as you know, I studied business and music. I started writing some songs just because I could—hidden talent, I guess you could say. A friend of mine had a friend of a friend who was friends with Simon Lewis."

"You started with Simon Lewis? What song did you write for him?" Wow, that's a pretty big start! Simon Lewis is from the U.K., but he exploded over here.

"I wrote 'Every Day' and 'Winter's Baby.' Oh, and 'Sorry Now.'"

"Grayson, I love those songs! You're really talented. There's so much meaning behind them." I squeeze his hand.

"Thank you, but not really. I just wrote them. They didn't mean anything to me."

"Well, they're beautiful, and I'm sure they mean a lot to other people. Wow, can you imagine what will come from you when there *is* meaning behind it?"

"I wrote a song last weekend, but I haven't been able to write again since." A couple across the way laugh loudly, and he glances over.

"Well, it will happen. Inspiration hits at the funniest times and places." I squeeze again. "So, it just had a domino effect from there?" My wine arrives, and I sip it.

"Yes. I've written for many people and earned a lot of my money at it. I invested well and now have my own label. Enough about me, though. Tell me more about you. Where are your parents?" He dips bread into the seasoned olive oil and takes a bite.

"Same place as yours. I lost them when I was twenty. Car accident. I have my aunt and uncle, as you know." I have a piece myself.

"I'm sorry. I definitely know how painful that is. No siblings?" he asks.

"Nope."

"Yeah, me neither. I guess Mum had a hard time carrying. I was lucky."

"What was your favorite age, and why?" I ask, anxious to tell mine. Our dinners arrive.

"Eleven. That was the year we finally got a piano at our house, and I would play all the time. Mum would sing. She had a beautiful voice. It was my last carefree year as a child." My heart sinks as a blanket of sadness comes over his face. He shakes it away. "What about you?"

"Seventeen. I got my driver's license and a new sense of freedom. That's when my best friends and I started taking road trips to Boston. We went to a few New Kids concerts and finally got to meet them. It was the only year of my youth that I actually acted my age. The music was great, too. Definitely was my favorite year." I love thinking back to that time.

"Wow! New Kids on The Block, aye?" He chuckles.

"Yes, I am a Blockhead . . . and if you know what's good for you, you won't say anything negative about them."

"Actually, I like them. They're a lot of fun. I've worked with them a few times. Who's your favorite?" he asks.

"Why, so you can kick his ass because I had a crush on him?" I laugh.

"Well, it all depends. Do you still have a crush on him?" He acts jealous jokingly for once.

"I love them all. I'm not telling you any different." I smile and take a bite of tortellini. "Mmm. Gray, you have to try this." I hold up a forkful for him.

"Yeah, no thanks, love." He makes a face.

"You don't like pumpkin?" I feel destroyed.

"I do, just not for dinner." *Phew.*

"Oh, good, because I make a lot of pumpkin baked goods in the fall."

We continue getting to know each other. He talks about his other business ventures. I talk about the places I want to visit. Before we know it, it's time to pay the check and go. Our limo pulls up and we climb in. He asks the driver how long it will take to get there.

"Only a few minutes." I answer instead. Grayson wastes no time attacking my lips.

"God, I can't wait to get you home," he says with deep urgency. He acts as if he hasn't had me a few times today already. We pull up to the theatre.

"*Les Misérables.* Oh, this is my favorite!" I smack his leg.

"I know, and if you do that again, you won't make it in there." He arches his eyebrow.

"Oh, c'mon," I say. He climbs out first and then reaches for my hands. We head inside to take our seats just as the lights blink. I love this musical. It's been so many years since I've seen it. It's the only one that's ever made me cry. The music is so powerful.

Chapter Twelve

GRAYSON

Thank God this is almost over. I just want to get her home and back into bed. She looks so goddamn beautiful tonight! I had to give so many men the staredown during intermission. I admire her lack of jealousy, as some of the women out there stared at me. Yet, I wish it did bother her a little. This is why I had no idea of her insecurities—she doesn't show them.

I look over at her watching the musical, tears coming down her face as she mouths the words to the song. I give her my handker-chief. She doesn't even look at me as she takes it. She's completely mesmerized. This has been a wonderful date! I'm looking forward to next week's excursion down here. I think she'll get a kick out of seeing *Mary Poppins*. I couldn't resist!

When the play ends, Becca stands, clapping like crazy. I quick-ly place her jacket over her shoulders. She smiles toward me and mouths *thank you*.

We are finally able to leave our seats. I charge through the crowd, holding her hand and elbow until the brisk city air hits our faces. Our limo is right up front, and we climb in. I let the driver know we are going directly home and yank the privacy window up.

I reach up Becca's dress and pull her panties down. She stares at me in shock. I part her legs and, flash her a wicked smile, and dive into my personal paradise. She moans lightly and places her hands in my hair to encourage me as she moves her hips against my mouth.

"Oh, Grayson. Oh God, baby, you know how to drive me wild." I insert my fingers to caress her sweet spot. Her hips move a little more erotically. She pulls my hair, and I bite her. She gasps. "C'mon, baby, make me pray." She eggs me on. God, she's so bloody fucking hot!

"That's it, love, pray for me . . . c'mon, sweetheart." I'm relentless. She's rising, but she's not getting there. I glance up and see she's looking at the privacy window. I hit the stereo so it blasts. She grabs my shirt collar and finally lets go.

"Oh God, baby. Oh God . . . Oh, baby . . . stop . . . stop, please . . . no don't, don't stop . . . Oh God!"

She finishes, pushes me away harshly, and closes her legs, then pulls her knees up to her chest. I'm at a loss for words. *What did I do?*

"Becca . . . sweetheart?" I lower the stereo. "Becca?" *Should I touch her?* "Becca?" She grabs her panties and slips them back on without looking at me. Bloody hell! I sit back, put my hands in my hair, and close my eyes. *What did I do wrong?* I feel her touch my legs and open my eyes quickly. She's kneeling in front of me.

She undoes my belt and my pants. She reveals my manhood and returns my wicked smile as she takes me into her mouth. Oh, bloody hell! *She. Is. So. Fucking. Good. At. This.* I inhale sharply, holding my tongue against my top teeth as her tongue swirls and caresses the most sensitive area of my head before plunging back down. Her emerald eyes lock onto mine. She twists her hand and increases the intensity of her suction as she pulls back. The heat of her stare.

Watching myself sliding in and out of that lovely mouth of hers. It's my undoing.

"Oh God, sweetheart," I groan. *Jesus H. Christ, she's good at this!* "Becca—God! Oh, Becca, baby, that's it." I touch her cheek softly as I empty into her mouth, gasping when I finish. I watch her as she licks my tip for the last drop. Her eyes stay connected with mine. "You are so fucking unbelievably hot, sweetheart." She kisses me there then licks her lips. She leans in for a kiss but pulls back, teasing me. I grab her and attack her lips. She straddles me.

"Why is it taking so long to get home?" she whispers in my ear.

"Oh, sweetheart, don't you worry. I'll be fucking you hard in no time." I slap her ass.

"Promise, baby?" She bites her bottom lip.

"Becca, you stir something in me that I never knew existed." I stare deeply into her eyes.

"I think I just tasted it." She giggles.

"I love you. I love you so much. I want you every day. I want you for the rest of my days. I need you. It's why I get so crazy . . . it's why I keep hurting you. I'm scared, Becca." I pour my heart out to her. I need her to understand where I'm coming from—that it's not all about having control. It's about my vulnerability.

Her eyes turn sad again. She kisses me and leans her forehead against mine.

"Let me put myself together, darling." I pat her bum. She gets off and I fix myself. I put my head back, close my eyes, and hold her hand. I can't believe she just did that to me. God, it was amazing! But . . . is that what Ray meant by his comment about his taste in her mouth?

"Gray, baby, what's wrong? Your nose is flaring."

"Nothing, Becca!" I snap. It's a better reaction than the one I want to have, which is to say something nasty to hurt her again because I'm upset. It's childish, and I need to stop.

"What are you thinking about?" she asks.

"Becca, please stop and let me get over it." I let go of her hand and lean forward into mine.

"Okay, baby." She rubs my back. Suddenly, I know just what I'm going to do. I'm going to piss *him* off instead. I sit back and pull out my cell.

September 31, 2012   11:35 p.m.
Me: Wow—she was thirsty! It was mind-blowing as well!

There, I feel much better now.

"Who are you texting, baby?" Becca asks as she puts her arm through mine and hugs it.

"Business associate, sweetheart." Well, it's not a lie. I did rehire him for the renovations . . . but only because no one else is as good or available. *Shit.* Her phone just pinged. I didn't think that far ahead. "Give me your phone, sweetheart. There's only one person who would be texting you this goddamn late!" I put my hand out for it.

"Who—your business associate?" She tries to hide her smile. I can't help but laugh. Clever girl.

"Why would my business associate be texting you?" I try to pull myself together as I look at the text. It's from Stacey.

September 31, 2012   11:36 p.m.
Stacey: So, you're swallowing now, Becs? That's nasty! What are you doing to my Ray over here? I came for a surprise visit. I guess you're indisposed until 5 a.m. I told Ray he could practice on me until it's his turn again, but he thinks I'm joking! Clear your schedule tomorrow to fill me in. I'll see if I can get Ray to fill me in in the meantime! ;p Love you!

I turn to Becca. "Stacey has a thing for Ray?" She grabs the phone and reads. I feel my eyelids start their "Morse code," as Becca likes to claim. She giggles and shakes her head. I lean over her and watch what she texts.

Becca: Come by for lunch. I promise to only put food in my mouth!

"Did you see it all? Can I press 'send'?" She looks to me with a smirk.

"Yes." I kiss her cheek. "So, answer my question. And do you think Ray would go for Stacey?" I would love to play Cupid.

"Stacey's married, Gray." She playfully taps my face with her palm.

"Well, she certainly sounds like she wants him." I am hopeful.

"That's because he's a great-looking guy. I'm sure she'll be changing her panties tomorrow after she meets you." She giggles.

"I could help her with that," I say thoughtfully. Becca just laughs at me. No sign or hint of a jealous spark. It does piss me off.

Finally, we arrive home. I give the driver a tip and we head inside.

A woman's voice calls out. "Becs!"

"Stacey? What are you doing here?" Becca looks surprised.

"I texted you that I was here." Stacey's an attractive blonde with brown eyes. She's between twiggy and curvy. Her hair and makeup are flawless, even at midnight.

"I know, but I don't have any rooms." Becca looks like she's caught off guard, but that's probably because Ray has just walked in.

"Becs, I always stay in your room."

"Right. Sorry. Are you settled in?" Becca hugs her.

"Yes, but I'd be more settled in if Ray would spend the night with me." She teases him.

"Yes, Ray! Why don't you have a go?" I slap him on the back.

"Oh, I will, Gray . . . on Wednesday." He slaps me back.

BECCA

Awkward! This is so awkward I can't even think of a theme song for it right now. Of course, "I Had a Dream" from *Les Mis* comes to mind, but I don't think I've yet hit the dramatics of that song. Besides, it's the type of song you must actually belt out loud when it becomes your theme song. Probably not a good idea after midnight, on a Monday, at the bottom of my B&B staircase. I mentally push the song down.

"Becca, you okay?" Stacey asks.

"She's deciding on a theme song," Ray pipes up and chuckles. "I had one today, Becs. 'Me and Mrs. Jones,' except I changed it to 'Me and Mrs. James' since that's how you're signing your name these days." I open my eyes to his boyish grin and find myself giggling. I glance over to Grayson and instantly feel the cold chill from his glacial stare. Again, herein lies the difference. I give Grayson a disappointed look.

"Good night, everyone." I feel melancholy. I just want to go to sleep.

"Becca!" Ray calls as Grayson places his hand on my back to walk me up the stairs. I turn to look his way. "You look breathtakingly beautiful tonight, baby. I love you."

"Thank you. G'nite." I give him a weak smile and turn back. Grayson lets his hand slip down to my ass—on purpose, I'm sure. I go to his door and wait for him to unlock it. We walk in, and Gray immediately starts working on getting my dress off. "Lock the door, please," I say quietly. Gray is back in front of me, trying his hand at peeling me—literally—out of my bra. His fingers caress my belly, igniting the sleeping butterflies. This area of my body seems to be the only one that cooperates in the gym. I think he likes it, too, because he's always touching or kissing it. I'm having a hard time bringing my eyes up to his. Are they still like ice? His touch says *no*, but I really can't go by that.

He leans down and speaks softly in my ear. "I want to spank you, sweetheart."

"Please don't hurt me," I beg. I don't want a repeat of the other day.

"I won't. I didn't mean it like that, darling." He curls his finger under my chin, bringing my eyes up to his. "I need you to focus on me, Becca. This is *my* time. I should get an extra fifteen minutes in the morning for their intrusion. I love you. Please don't stay in this place; you wanted me so bad not twenty minutes ago." He grasps my lips with his. I return his kiss eagerly. He's right. I've never in my life come so hard as I did twenty minutes ago. It more than took my breath away. I felt like I was having an out-of-body experience. I wanted him to somehow quiet my explosion, but instead, he made me have little explosions on top of the big one. I can't . . . I need to stop thinking about the things I wanted him to do to me at that moment.

I rip Grayson's shirt and tank top off. I attack his chest with my mouth, biting his nipples. I feel very raw and violent toward him. I push him down onto the bed and pin his hands above his head, then nip at the skin across his shoulder, neck, and chest. I bite his lip a little harder then I should.

"Ow, Becca!" He pushes me off and flips me so that I'm on my stomach. I feel his hand come down hard on my ass and it makes me go wild. I twist my back and circle my arm around his head, bringing him down to kiss me. His hand meets my bum again.

"Oh, baby," I whimper. He bends my right knee to allow him access, then situates himself between my legs and enters me harshly from behind. My sore bum smarts against the slapping from his body.

"Becca, I want . . . to come . . . in your mouth again," he pants as he pounds into me.

"Yes," is all I can muster. He pins my arms and bites at my back as he slows down to an agonizing pace.

"Oh, Becca . . . Becca, oh God."

"Grayson, get out. Please. Let me finish you in my . . . Grayson! Damn it!" I snap as he pumps his last few times.

"Oh, sweetheart, you're so good. You feel so good." His breath is erratic at my back.

"Get off of me!" I jerk my body. He complies and flips me over, but holds my arms down above my head. "Get off of me!" I yell again through my tears. He doesn't listen. Instead, his right hand goes in between my legs. He pins my legs down with his as his hand plays in my wetness, swirling the come that has seeped out over my lips and up and down my center. My hips betray me. My breasts, too, as they rise to meet his mouth. His hand moves around with ease in my, as I like to refer to it at this time, "Slip 'n Slide." *Oh, it feels so good.* He inserts his fingers and I gasp at how he's stretching me. My hips continue their betrayal more eagerly. His mouth comes up to comfort my cries. I feel myself climb and climb. He pulls his fingers out and enters me again. He brings my legs all the way back, leaving me fully vulnerable, and slams in to me over and over as if his life depended on it. I try to push him off when I realize my hands are free. He grabs them and places them behind my knees, holding them and my legs in place so he can have me the way he wants me. I close my eyes because it's the only thing on my body he can't control. I feel him slow down and spill inside of me again. He climbs off to rest on his back. I bring my legs down slowly, feeling as if they may have popped out of my hip sockets. I have nothing to say to him. He's a selfish man. I've known that since day one.

"Do you feel sore, sweetheart?" Grayson rubs my belly gently and kisses my forehead.

"Yes." I swallow.

"Good. Come, now, let's get some sleep." He pulls me to him. I don't fight. I'm too tired to fight sleep, too. He slaps my ass one more time. I feed him the sound he wants from me and then I fall asleep.

It's a quarter of five and Gray's phone is ringing. It's "Chim Chim Cher-ee" from Mary Poppins. I can't help but laugh.

"I thought you would like that." He pulls me into his arms and kisses my forehead. "You still sore, sweetheart?"

"Yes." I close my eyes and breathe him in.

"Good. Darling, I want you to think about me all day, even when you don't want to." He nudges my chin so I'm facing him. "Are you mad at me for being so selfish?"

"Yes, I am." I'm honest.

"Okay, but I won't apologize for what I did. I have no control anywhere else in this relationship." He looks up at the ceiling.

"Well, trapping me in a relationship with you is not the way to keep me." I sit up to get ready to leave.

"Uh, I believe I get an extra fifteen minutes for the interruption last night." He pulls me back.

"Does it turn you on to make me mad?" I'm very serious.

"Maybe a bit." His fingers graze my cheek and trace over my lips.

"Why?"

"I don't know. I haven't figured that out yet, darling." He kisses me deeply. We make love—he's even a good boy and wears protection this time. I pray . . . again. I grab one of his T-shirts to put on, kiss him, and head to my room.

Stacey's passed out in my bed. I jump into the shower and take a super-fast one. I'm thankful for the break today from both men. It looks like I won't be spending any time with Rocco either, thanks to Grayson. I'm so glad I was smart enough not to go along with their original schedule. I wouldn't be able to walk! I step out of the shower and wipe down the mirror. Hmm. Do I look like a whore? No. I guess I don't. I dry off and throw my hair up in a messy bun. Today is going to be a comfy-cozy-cotton day. Love my yoga pants! After getting dressed, I head down to make breakfast.

I run into Grayson in the hall. He pulls me to him and backs me up to the wall. He lingers over me like he's about to kiss me, but holds up my phone instead. "You forgot this."

"Thank you." I stare into his chocolate-brown eyes.

"No, Mrs. James, thank you." He winks, then turns to head downstairs. I turn my phone on. There are several texts from Ray.

October 1, 2012   12:45 a.m.
Ray: I'm sorry if I made things worse today.
Ray: You were beautiful tonight.
Ray: Please clear your schedule for Weds.

October 1, 2012   5:05 a.m.
Ray: You better be out of his bed.
Ray: Did he hurt you?
Ray: I better not see any marks on you!
Ray: I love you!

I now have a chance to reply.

6:30 am
Me: Obsessed much?
Ray: Are you okay?
Me: I'm fine! Why R U up so early?
Ray: Worried about u! I'm going 2 bed now!
Ray: Wish u were here! Theme song last night?
Me: I had a dream Les Mis. 2 dramatic. I couldn't come up with anything else!
Ray: I'm sorry that u could only think of that! ☹
Me: Go to sleep. I love you! ☺
Ray: Still?
Me: Of course! ;)

Grayson rips the phone out of my hand. I haven't deleted anything. He reads every word, then throws the phone down, his nostrils flaring. I pick up my phone and text him.

October 1, 2012   6:38 a.m.

Me: A true Brit would stick his nose high in the air as it flares. R U sure ur British and not just faking it?

Gray: A true lady wouldn't go around and tell half the men in town that she loves them!

Me: Hmm. Certainly U R not referring to me, sir. I have said that to 2 men and 1 horse. But, there are indeed more than 4 men and 2 male horses in this town. Incidentally, my horse will be neglected by me once again. I'm terribly sore from riding one of my men instead! I am a silly woman!

Gray: Dear silly woman, it seems that you are very confused as to who actually did the riding! I do enjoy the way you buck!

Me: If I recall correctly, sir, I believe you also enjoy the way I s—k!

Gray: Oh . . . u do indeed know how to drain a fellow don't u, love? ;p

Me: See what happens when you're being a VERY GOOD BOY?

Me: BTW, extra turned on last night by your accent! You could've commanded a prayer without any touching! ☺

Gray: Well, I'll be sure to be a good boy from now on! Today I will be extra British around U and watch you come undone!

Me: I love you Baby! You are my BBB!

Gray: BBB?

Me: Hmm?

He looks up from his cell phone at me. I smile and go about making the quiches.

"Is it three different words, Becca?"

"Yes."

"Well, what do I get if I figure it out?" He picks up the paper to read.

"I don't know. Do you think you're going to figure it out?" I giggle.

"Of course I am, darling. I'm quite the erudite man, you know." He rattles the paper as he turns the page.

"That's true. You did fall in love with me." I smile widely, thinking I got him out of his foul mood.

"Yes. That was probably the stupidest thing I've ever done," he states, with much more levity than the words call for.

My smile dissipates and I bite my lip. Why does he always say things to hurt me? I know it's a defense mechanism, but still—why does he have to do it so much? Would it end if I left Ray for him? No. No, he was sort of doing this to me before Ray. So why would I continue seeing a man who hurts me so much?

"Becca? I'm being an arse. I'm sorry, sweetheart."

I say nothing. What's there to say?

"Good morning." Morgan grumbles, coming into the kitchen as I put in the last few quiches.

"Morgy girl, what are you doing up so early?" Grayson hugs her as she sits on his lap.

"I couldn't sleep, Daddy." She yawns.

"Stop calling him that! He's not your daddy! He's not going to be your daddy, so just stop!" I yell at her.

"Becca?" Grayson sounds as if the air has been knocked out of his lungs. "Becca?" he says again.

I look up from wiping the counter. Morgan has tears in her eyes, and Grayson's not far behind her. "Sweetheart?" His chin is quivering. I walk out of the kitchen and head to my office. I quickly sit at my desk. I feel like I'm hyperventilating. Did I just make my decision?

"Becca?" The door opens. "Becca, sweetheart, can I talk to you?" Grayson is speaking softly, like he's fighting for calm.

"Grayson, you just keep going out of your way to say and do things that will hurt me. I don't think I need a month. I've already had one abusive relationship. I can't go there again. I can't do this. It won't change. I'm sorry. I think you need to leave." I turn to look at him.

"No," he says, as if he's answering a simple question. "I'll do better. I'll show you." He walks away. I get up and follow him out of the office.

"Grayson." I grab his arm to turn him to me. He looks around at the people staring at us, including Morgan and some of the detail.

"I said—" he starts.

"I know what you said. It's not good enough. I don't believe you. You want things to be so, because that's what you want. It doesn't work like that, Gray. I'm done. I can't go on like this anymore." I search his eyes, hoping to see acceptance. He shakes his head. He swiftly throws me over his shoulder and heads up the stairs, with me pounding on his back the whole way. He tosses me onto his bed and holds me down.

"You love me!" he cries.

"I do, but not enough to allow you to treat me like this."

"Becca, please, I'm going to really try. I know you're serious, darling. I'll shape up. Please. I can't lose you, sweetheart." He tries to kiss me, but I turn my head.

"You can't lose *me*, Grayson, or you can't lose?" I snap.

"Becca, I can't lose you or Morgan. I love you. Please . . . please give me one more week! What's one more week? I promise I will do better."

"Get off of me." I try to push him away.

"Sweetheart, one more week." He kisses my neck.

"Or what, you lay on top of me for the seven days?" I'm beyond aggravated.

"I'd love to do that, minus our clothes, of course." He smiles and kisses me.

"It's not your day." I turn my head.

"So I get another day?" His eyebrow arches. I say nothing. He kisses me again and again. I don't know how it happens, but all of a sudden, we're making love.

"Shit, the quiches!" I sit up in a panic.

"What every man loves to hear from his woman after making love." He chuckles.

"I'm staying over Ray's tomorrow, and he gets extra time in the morning." I put my clothes back on. I watch the smile leave Grayson's face.

"Okay, sweetheart." He gets up as well and dresses. I leave his room and run downstairs to the kitchen.

"Where's Daddy?" Morgan asks.

"I'm right here, Morgy girl. Why don't we give Mummy some space. I'll teach you how to play your keyboard," Grayson offers from behind me. She sticks her tongue out at me and grabs his hand to leave.

I start bringing the quiches out to the dining room and am greeted by a frantic Ray. *Oh, for the love of God.*

"Are you all right?" He grabs my arms.

"Yes. Why?"

"Claudia called me and told me you and Gray were having a fight and he threw you over his shoulder and went upstairs." He's out of breath.

"I'm okay. Good news for you, I don't have to leave at five on Thursday. I'm staying over and staying longer." I smile and hug him.

"Why? Wait. Did you . . . did you let him have you just now? Get off of me!" He pushes me away. He shakes his head and throws his hands up into the air before stomping toward the door. I stand there in my oven mitts, feeling like a truck just ran me over. Ray turns back to me.

"You're not staying at my house. I'm not doing to Annie what you are doing to Morgan! I have a better idea. Why don't you just stay here and get abused by Grayson, since that's what you like so much, *Mrs. James*!"

I just stand there and take it, in my big red puffy oven mitts.

"Will you stop thinking about a damn theme song?" he yells.

"I'm not. There are no songs out there about having your heart broken while wearing oven mitts," I say calmly. Ray stares at me. His body starts shaking. I bite my bottom lip, trying not to smile, and hold up my gloved hands. He breaks into a hearty laugh and takes long strides toward me. He sinks his hands into my hair.

"Ugh—I can't stand you!" He shakes my head gently before attacking my lips. I kiss him back fiercely. I hear somebody clearing their throat. I break away. It's Grayson.

"Morgan's heading this way," he says quietly, then leaves the room.

"I have to go. I'll see you tomorrow." He kisses me again quickly. I head back into the kitchen to bring out the other quiches.

"What can I help you with, sweetheart?" Grayson asks. He seems very melancholy.

"Um, can you grab that tray?" I point to the pastries and bagels. He does so. "Thank you."

"Of course." He follows me out to the dining room.

"Uh . . . Grayson," I stammer. "I'm sorry you saw what you saw. I'm sure that wasn't very easy." He gives me a silent nod.

"I've noticed you two mention theme songs a lot. I realize it's an inside joke, but would you mind telling me?" He glances over at me.

"Oh, no, I don't mind at all." I smile. "For as long as I can remember, I've had a 'theme song'—a song that pops into my head, something that covers how I'm feeling or a situation I'm involved in. If I get quiet in the middle of a conversation or, well, anything, it's usually the CD in my brain changing." I laugh at myself.

"That's very cute, actually." Grayson chuckles a little.

"Would you like to know some of my theme songs since I've met you?" I glance back up.

"Becca, I'd love to. I find this very interesting." He pulls up a chair for me, then sits as well.

"Okay, let me think. Okay. The day we first met, when I came out of my office and ran straight into you?"

"Yes, of course, I remember. Oh my God, you were changing your theme song when I thought you were going to pass out?" His eyes widen. I nod.

"I avoided you for three hours and I had to teach a class on *distressing*, of all things." I laugh.

"What was the song?"

I really have him intrigued.

"'Ironic'—Alanis Morissette." He laughs his hearty laugh. "Then, at some point last week, I changed the lyrics of 'She Drives Me Crazy' to 'He Drives Me Crazy.' I'm trying to think of the moment, but I can't." I pause. "Oh, and when you two came to me about your plan? It was a toss-up."

"Yes, I remember you saying you were changing your theme song. What was it?" He sips his tea. I tell him the other three songs. "You really feel that way?" He grabs my hand.

"Yes, and you've encouraged those feelings, haven't you?" I can't help it. It's the truth.

"Yes, yes I have. I'm so sorry, sweetheart." He's blinking a mile a minute.

"Um, yesterday's was 'Material Girl,' as I was putting on my new earrings." I change the subject. He relaxes a bit and smiles. "So far, I think that's it. Which is actually a lot of theme-song changing for only—what? Barely two weeks?" I stretch out in the chair.

"Weeks. Becca, it's crazy. I feel like we've been together for at least a few months."

"Yes, well, I think we've squished a few months of emotion into these weeks. Maybe that's why everything is so stressful. This hasn't been a traditional relationship by any means."

"And the whole situation with Ray has not helped."

"No, it hasn't. But we were having some issues before that. I think we've moved at light speed, and it's biting us in the ass." I play with the napkin on the table, trying to make something out of it. I took a class on creating napkin animals and shapes six months ago, and never got around to utilizing what I learned.

"Sweetheart, I don't think either one of us said 'oh, let me get involved in a relationship where I have no sense, no filter for my feelings, and no willpower.' Did you? Because I didn't." He sounds defensive, and he shrugs and moves his hands throughout the whole speech. His eyelids are blinking fast, but not rapidly like when he's nervous. He's just passionate about what he's saying. "Becca, are you listening?" He waves his hand in front of my face.

"Yes, sorry. I was watching a very hypnotic, beautiful British man speak. He is a lovely man." I lean forward on my arms and look up at him with a smile.

"Oh yeah? Do I detect a crush, Ms. Campbell?" He arches his brow.

"Crushes are for schoolgirls, Mr. James." I sigh nonchalantly.

"Very well then,—what do you think it is?" He leans on his arms as well.

"I think he's drugging me, truth be told," I say, with a secretive edge to my voice.

"No! What gives you that idea?" He sounds shocked, matching my disposition.

"Well, every time he comes around me, I get completely intoxi-cated by his smell. I can't think straight and I find myself following all of his commands. Once I'm away from him, my thoughts are clear again. What do you make of that?"

"Ms. Campbell, you're on to something. He is definitely drug-ging you!" He taps his index finger on the table for emphasis.

"What do you think it is? What drug is it?" I sit up, alarmed.

"Love!" He points into the air matter-of-factly. "It's crazy, mad-dening, intoxicating love! Yes, I've heard of this type of love before.

Tell me, Ms. Campbell. Does your heart beat fast?"

"Yes!"

"Do you feel what people call 'butterflies in your stomach'?"

"Up to my throat in them."

"Do your knees get weak?"

"I've passed out!"

"Is your breathing erratic?"

"Only around him."

"Do you find yourself unable to stop your thoughts about him the moment you're apart?"

"Yes! It's quite annoying."

"I'm afraid this is a very dangerous situation you've got yourself in. Believe me—I know!" He widens his eyes and taps the table again.

"Well, how do you know, Mr. James?" I reach for his arm.

"I suffer from the same ill fate."

"No! Is she British as well?"

"Worse—she's American! I've been behaving strangely ever since I met her."

"No! Mr. James, what are we to do?" I look down and shake my head.

"I don't know, Ms. Campbell." He grabs my hands, caressing the backs of them with his thumbs. "We'll just have to stick together. Help each other. Eventually a plan of action will present itself." He brings my hands up to his lips. His eyes close. He seems sad. I lean forward and kiss his mark softly. He turns his head and captures my lips. I kiss him once . . . twice . . . mmm. *Damn rules.*

"Grayson, we can't keep doing this. It's not fair to Ray." I turn my head. I know I've killed a very sweet and vulnerable moment, but fair is fair.

"I have to say ..." He looks up to the ceiling and takes in a deep breath. I can see he's fighting to remain calm, and succeeding. "That I don't particularly care about Ray's feelings and what is fair to him.

I am a different man, Becca. I am persistent—selfish, to say the least—but very persistent. And I find nothing more irritating than a man who sits back and does nothing until somebody threatens to take away something that was never his in the first place. Ugh. Bloody hell. Forget it. I'm not going to sit here and waste time explaining. You're a smart woman, Becca. I'm sure you can see it. I just . . . I can't lose you, sweetheart. I won't give up!" There's so much passion in his voice; so much purpose.

"Grayson, I understand where you are coming from. I get it. But Ray is a different type of man than you. He wasn't sitting back because he thought I was already his. He was waiting for me to be ready. His approach was more subtle. Holding my hand at the carnival with the girls. Back rubs and dinners when I had a stressful day. Scheduling who was going to take the girls to what. He knew what I went through with George. He didn't want to do anything to push me away. He wanted me to feel safe, loved, and needed. He's my best friend, and while that seems like a big advantage for him, it has also become a big disadvantage." I take a deep breath. "I don't know if it's just that I was finally ready, or if you woke my body up, or what. Last year in the rain, I was going to have sex with Ray. That's all it was going to be. I knew it—and that's why I was able to stop. I didn't want to lose my best friend, and I would've. But now, I do feel something. I didn't go to him last week to make things more complicated. I went to him because I needed to talk to my best friend. But, he's already transformed to another level . . . something more. I don't know if I'm making any sense. Does any of this make sense to you? I feel like I'm babbling." I put my head in my hands. This is so frustrating—the whole situation is.

"I think it does," he says quietly. "Becca, I think we need to revise the plan." He chucks my chin so I'm looking at him.

"How—what do you mean?"

"The way it is set up now, I don't think it helps any of us." He rubs his face. "I hate saying this, but I think we need to make it strictly dating only. You know, we can kiss and touch—a *little*," he says with emphasis. "But sex is making it complicated for all of us."

"Uh, yeah, including Lady Marmalade over here!" I point to myself.

"Stop it, sweetheart, it's not your fault. Especially with me. I am a selfish man." He smirks.

"Yes . . . that has been established." I giggle a little. "Well, if you two can handle it, I'm so on board. I completely agree. It's not helping."

"Well, we'll sit down with Ray later and go over it."

"You know, I don't think he'll believe you're going to comply with the new rules." I try at the napkin one last time.

"That's because he knows you're mine. Sweetheart, what the hell are you trying to do?" He points to my project just as I finish my last fold.

"I did it! Look, it's a swan! Yay! I took a class awhile back and haven't tried it since! Look!" I show him excitedly.

"You have to be the strangest, most lovely woman I have ever met." He leans forward and kisses me again. Guests begin entering the dining room, ready for breakfast.

"C'mon, let's bring the rest of the stuff out." I slap his knee. He helps me with the entire meal service.

I spend the morning training new staff, paying bills, placing orders, and sorting through more resumes, and time flies by. I hear a knock at my office door.

"Hey, Becca, it's lunchtime!" It's Stacey. "We need to get out of here before I start dry humping your hot Brit." This sends me into hysterics.

Stacey is just the medicine I need. We've been best friends since middle school and have been through just about everything. She's the only friend I've ever had that I can be completely myself around.

She gets me and I get her. Of course, she's crazy as hell—in a good way.

She took us in after George "died" and helped me organize a business plan. It was then that I finally told her about everything George did to me. As a matter of fact, she's the only one who knows *everything*. She was so pissed I didn't come to her while the abuse was going on. But like I said, she's crazy—crazier than Ghetto Sybecca! Lord only knows what she would've done. I just wish Steve, her husband, didn't have to relocate them to Tennessee. Morgan and I miss her so much.

"He might like that!" I get up and stretch.

"Ray told me he hits you." She says it like a statement, but it's really meant as a question.

"Well, no. He spanks me. Ray is referring to the morning when Grayson caught us kissing and did it a lot harder than usual." Amazing, I'm not even blushing.

"Well, he can spank me any day of the week!" She fans herself. And this is why I'm not blushing, because I really can tell her anything. "So, does he have a red room?" She giggles.

"Oh my God—stop it! No, that's as far as it goes. It is pretty hot, though." I bite my lip, thinking about last night. "Let's go to lunch. You can tell me everything Ray has told you so far, and I'll correct it and add in the rest." I grab my purse and coat before we head out.

Melissa and Ryan are our detail for the day. Which reminds me—I need to try to hook those two up. I've seen them secretly checking each other out.

"You know, you really should get a car for non-farm shit!" Stacey complains as she climbs into my truck.

"Sorry, I don't get out enough to worry about having a 'social' car." I do the air quotes.

"Well, what's Moneybags driving?" She looks around the parking lot.

"That Range Rover over there. Why?" No sooner than I say it, she's out of the truck and heading back to the B&B. A minute or two goes by before my cell rings. It's Grayson. I answer.

"Do you know what you so-called best friend just said to me?" He's trying to sound shocked.

Stacey's yelling in the background. "He's lying! I would never!"

"Oh God—what did she say? Wait, do I really want to know?" I put my head on the steering wheel.

"Well, she gave me an ultimatum, sweetheart. Wait, I'm sorry, this came from you."

"What?"

"Let's see. If I let you have the car for your lunch date, I could . . . what is it? Oh, right. Drop, I believe . . . a load in your mouth." *Oh my God—she is an asshole!* "And if I don't, you will drive to Ray's to let *him* drop a load in your mouth. Now—what do you have to say for yourself, sweetheart?" I sense his smile on the phone.

"Well, I have a better idea. If you let me cart Stacey's ass around in your car, I will let her dry hump you like she said she would earlier. Please do tell her I said that." I totally want to go inside to see her face. I climb out of the truck. Pretty sure I won't be driving it to lunch. Grayson, laughing his ass off, repeats to her what I said. I head inside.

"She's absolutely fucking mad, this one!" He says to me on the phone.

"I know," I say, standing right behind him. He turns around.

"I don't know if I feel comfortable letting the pair of you out of my sight." He smiles and hangs up his phone.

I hold out my hand. "Please, or she'll drive me crazy." I half smile.

He holds the keys out of my reach and pulls me close with his other arm. "What do I get in return?"

"I already told you what you'll get. Oh, all right. You can spank my ass, too." Stacey pats his shoulder and grabs the keys from him.

She heads out to his car and leaves me in his embrace.

"Becca ..." He looks a little embarrassed, which seems odd for him.

"Ray said something, so I had to correct it. Sorry." I palm his face. He searches my eyes and leans down for a kiss. It's soft and reluctant. I run my hands behind his neck and pull him to me, encouraging a deeper kiss. He complies willingly.

"I love you, Becca." Another quick kiss, and he pats my bum. "Go on then, love."

I stare up at him. "What is it, Gray?"

He shakes his head and nods to the door. "Go."

I hug him and head out.

Stacey smiles when I get into the car.

"Now, this is much better," she says.

"Stace, can you please watch what you say around him? Everybody's getting this impression that he's this jerk. Yes, he can be arrogant and selfish, but he's sensitive as well." I put the Rover in reverse and proceed to head out.

"Geez . . . sorry." She sighs. "He was laughing with me."

"I know, but I think he was thrown off by the whole spanking thing. It's personal, but it's become less so thanks to Ray." And suddenly, I find myself pissed off at Ray.

"Well, you have a whole hell of a lot to fill me in on, sister!" She smacks my arm. I begin to tell her everything about when Grayson and I first met: the electricity between us, my new subconscious multiple personality disorder that has come about, my constant theme-song changes. Even about Morgan, Ray, and the personal stuff I don't want to say in public. We've sat outside the restaurant for forty minutes now.

"Becca, I think I may need a panty change." She laughs, but I think she may be serious.

We finally head into The Break Room, a new local place that's been getting a lot of buzz. A little on the pricey side, but Stacey and

I don't get to see each other that often. We order some wine and continue our conversation.

"So what are you going to do?" She sips her wine.

"I don't know. It's very confusing. When I'm with one, I feel very loyal to him—but I drift off in thought about the other. With Grayson, I think, 'Well, Ray wouldn't be like this!' and when I'm with Ray, I just feel absolutely guilty and upset that I'm doing this to Grayson."

"Becca, you just said your answer!" She springs her previously clasped hands apart for emphasis.

"What are you talking about?"

"Becca, you don't feel guilty about Ray when you're with Grayson, right?" I stop and think about it again. No, I don't feel guilt. I only think of how he wouldn't say or do some of the things that Grayson does.

"No. I've felt guilty twice: the morning he brought me the binder after I saw George, and then the other night, when he made his scrapbooking page."

"But when you're with Ray, and you think of Grayson?"

"I feel sickened with guilt." Something is starting to click.

"Becca, you love Ray, but you are *in love* with Grayson. He's the one you are supposed to be with." I can tell she thinks she's a genius.

Our food comes. Stacey has ordered the grilled chicken salad with toasted walnuts and raspberry vinaigrette. It looks delicious. I went for comfort: angel-hair pasta with chicken, roasted red peppers, eggplant, and sun-dried tomatoes in a butter garlic sauce. Grayson would've selected it for me because he knows. *He knows.* Oh, God. Stacey's right! My heart is beating a mile a minute. I pull out my cell to text. "Sorry, I have to do this."

October 1, 2012   1:05 p.m.

Me: Hey, baby! We're at The Break Room. Look at the menu.

What have I ordered? Love you!

"What are you doing?" Stacey knows I'm up to something. I tell her about last night. "Jesus, I've been with Steve for twelve years and he wouldn't be able to or even care to do that." Her smile fades.

"What's wrong?" I reach for her hand.

"Becs, this isn't just a social trip. Steve and I are getting a divorce." She downs the last of her wine. I quickly signal the waiter for a refill.

"Stace, what happened?" I had no idea they were even having any problems.

"Out with the old, in with the new! I'm thirty-five years old. I thought we were okay. We were even talking about getting IVF. Turns out, by the way, that we haven't been able to get pregnant because of him. He has a very low sperm count, but he lied about it. When I found out, he said it was because he was embarrassed. That's when we—or, I guess, *I*—started talking about IVF. Seeing a doctor kept getting pushed off. Late nights at work, you know." She winks. "Then bam! Out of nowhere, divorce papers. He didn't want to have a baby, at least not with me." Her eyes dart upward and she brings a napkin up to blot underneath and stop her tears. "I'm so mad. How could he do this to me? I helped him become who he is in his career. I gave him my best years!" And now they run free down her face.

I hand her a cloth napkin. "No, you didn't! Your best years are going to be the ones where you are finding yourself. You're only thirty-five! You still have time for kids. You still have time to be happy. You're beautiful, smart, and funny. You'll have somebody under your spell in no time." My cell pings. I apologize and glance at it.

Gray: You are my favorite trivia question! You have ordered the angel-hair pasta dish with eggplant, roasted red peppers, and sun-dried tomatoes in a garlic butter sauce.

Me: You are so fucking HOT!

Gray: Don't say things to me that will trigger a response I can't have under the new plan. Please! ☺

Me: Fuck the paperwork!

Gray: Reciting your favorite book, huh? Incidentally, I am reading and thoroughly enjoying it! Many ideas . . . many!

I look up at Stacey. I can feel my eyes grow wide.

Me: I have no idea of what you are referring. :-o

Gray: Hmm . . . maybe I should show you what I'm referring to. ;p

Me: Mr. James, I can attest to your high degree of knowledge in the bedroom. Therefore, I do not believe it necessary for you to acquire any more ideas. ;-)

Gray: I can assure you that I will always want to acquire as many ideas as possible to keep Mrs. James very happy in the bedroom!

Me: OH GOD, BABY! You can even make me pray by text, that's how skilled you are!

Gray: . . .

Me: What was that?

Gray: You've made me textless.

Me: Eye roll . . . thanks for playing my trivia game. Must get back to Stacey!

Gray: Does she hate me yet?

Me: Nope . . . actually, she is on team Grayson! She's very persuasive. You may want to hire her as your campaign manager! Love you!

Gray: Really? Okay . . . I'll let her dry hump me then!

Me: LOL! See you soon!

Gray: XXXXX . . . because 3's not enough and 4 is just not right!

Me: ☺

"Um, hello!" Stacey says. I hand her my phone so she can read the texts—a reward for her patience. "Holy shit, he is fucking hot! Ray is fucking hot, too. Why do you have all the luck?" she whines. I suddenly feel the urge to push her and Ray together.

Wow. This is why a girl needs her best friend, who incidentally should also be a girl or a gay guy—somebody who isn't in love with her—to show her the light. I'm dying to get home to Grayson.

"So, Becca, I was wondering if I could stay with you until I find a place and a job. I want to come back home." She also suffers from ADD, which makes us even more interesting together.

"Absobloodylutely!" I hold my wine glass up to her.

"Maybe Ray and I can give each other a sympathy fuck!" she says excitedly.

"Well, you know, they say a sympathy fuck is the cornerstone to all great relationships." I laugh.

"Who are 'they'?" She does the air quotations.

"Who are 'they' indeed?" I mirror her pondering look. We laugh hysterically. Not only are we best friends, we're a couple of ass-holes, and we love that about us!

"Dessert?" the waiter asks.

"Oh, no, I have dessert at home." I laugh because Stacey and I both know I'm not talking about what's in the fridge.

"I'll have the tiramisu to go, please. I don't have an English biscuit to sink my teeth into at home."

"Very well." He's a very serious guy.

"Oh, and I'll take the check, please."

"Your husband has taken care of everything, Mrs. James. Do you not want the tiramisu he ordered for you?"

"Um, sure, I'll take it home as well." I smile then look to Stacey, whose eyes are wide. The waiter nods and walks away.

"Mrs. James, if I were you, I'd be licking that tiramisu right off of that man's chest!" She fans herself with her hand.

"Really? I don't think the waiter is that attractive." I let puzzlement cross my face, but laugh when she hits me.

"I think he knows you better than you know yourself." She shakes her head in disbelief.

"It's a little scary, but I think you're right." I bite my lip. We get our desserts and head out to the car.

"What's wrong?" Stacey asks after a few minutes of silence.

"I can't believe how clear I feel. You know, I tried to break up with him this morning."

"Why?" She plays with the buttons in the car. I hit her hand and laugh because Grayson did the same thing to me.

"He said something that hurt me again, and even though he apologized right away, I still went through the whole 'Ray wouldn't say that' scenario. I thought that was my answer. But you made me see how I really feel. I wasn't seeing my own signs." I feel butterflies as we get closer.

"What did Grayson do?" She plays with the sunroof. Total ADD!

"He wouldn't let me. He told me he'd do better, that he can't lose me or Morgan. You know, he wants to be her father so bad. They already have an amazing relationship." I smile.

"Persistent, isn't he?"

"Yeah . . . thank God," I say as we pull in.

"Becca, I keep forgetting to ask you—why all the security?" *Holy shit.* How the hell did I leave this out? I thought Ray told her.

"Oh, yeah. George is alive. He kidnapped me the other day, but Melissa kicked his ass. He got away, so Grayson beefed up the security."

Stacey's mouth is open wide. "I can see how that would slip your mind!" she says sarcastically. "Are you fucking kidding me?"

"Nope."

"Wait, is that the George you mentioned before, when talking about Ray and the binder?" She shoots me a puzzled look.

"Yeah, why?" What's she getting at?

"You said it so cavalier, I had no idea it was *the* George!" She smacks my arm.

"Ow! Geez, lady! Sorry!" I rub my arm.

"Well, Christ, Becca! This is a bit serious! What happened? How did he kidnap you?" *Oh, crap.*

"It's a long story that I totally promise to tell you, but can I do it later? I really want to get to Grayson." I smile and I clutch my purse, eager to go.

"You'd better! I don't blame you—if you weren't my best friend, I'd be knocking you down to get to Grayson myself!" She laughs as we get out.

Chapter Thirteen

I run inside. Ray is there. *Shit! What is he doing here?*

"Um, hi. Have you seen Grayson?"

"He went upstairs. By the way, he told me of the new plan. I think it's a great idea, Becs!" he yells after me as I run up the stairs to Gray's room. I open the door quietly and slip in. He's lying on his stomach reading a book—probably getting ideas.

"Hey," I say quietly as I climb up his back. He jumps.

"Jesus, sweetheart! You startled me. Did you see Ray downstairs? I told him about the new plan." He swivels his head, looking for me.

"Um, yeah . . . about that." I pull off my shirt. "I don't think it will be necessary." I let him flip over. He's wearing his glasses—so hot.

"Becca?" His voice matches the yearning in his eyes. His eyelids are going mad.

"I prefer *Mrs. James*." I unhook my bra.

"It's over? You're mine?" He sits up, keeping me astride him. I bite my lip and nod. "Did you tell him, sweetheart? Does he know?"

He touches my face.

"I didn't tell him, but if he didn't realize it on his own, I'm sure Stacey is clarifying it for him right now. And possibly offering her, uh, *services*." I laugh.

"How do you know? You were calling it quits on me this morning. Forgive me for being a little confused. And hesitant," he says in between my kisses.

"I've always known. I just didn't see the signs. Stacey helped me." I kiss his mark.

"What were they?" Yeah, he's really not sure if I'm sure.

"The biggest one is that when I'm with you, I only think of Ray if you say or do something to hurt me. I think how Ray wouldn't say or do that. When I'm with Ray, I think about how much I'm hurting you or what you're doing—how I should be with you." This warrants a very powerful kiss from him. "I don't call him 'baby'—only you." I look into his eyes and play with his hair a little.

"Well, what did you say to him?"

"When I came in, I asked him where you were. He said upstairs. I ran up as he was shouting that he liked the idea for the new plan." I kiss him again. "I didn't respond, I just continued to run to you. That should be a big hint."

"I'm definitely dry humping your friend, darling!" His smile is huge. "Becca, I love you so much."

"I know . . . and I . . . you." And that's it—he devours my body.

GRAYSON

I'm intoxicated by her smell, her touch, her love. She's mine. I listen to her pray as my mouth and fingers make love to her. I want to keep her in my bed all day today.

"Grayson, please ..." she begs as I bring her to her peak again. Oh, I love the way her hips get wild beneath me. "Please, baby."

She's breathless, running her fingers through my hair. "I need you, baby, please." I hear the love in her voice. I wipe my mouth with my forearm and attack her lips. I pull away and stare down into her face. God, she's so beautiful. Her green eyes are gorgeous. *Oh my God.* A theme song just popped into my head. The song she was dancing with Will to. I don't know it, but I remember the woman singing about believing in the other person's eyes and not caring what that person has done before. I keep hearing her singing it over and over.

It's exactly how I feel. I don't care what Becca has done with Ray. Her eyes are full of love for me—only me. I can see it. I can feel it. I enter her and watch her face and her eyes the entire time, making love to her in that sweet-torture kind of way. I muffle her cries with my lips. We are so in sync. It feels like hours of focusing on just each other. The first wave hits me. I grit my teeth as she squeezes around me.

"That's it, baby . . . c'mon." She lifts her hips to meet me, pushing me even deeper inside her. I feel her reach climax. I love when we come together. Our prayers are so beautiful, I'm sure there must be an angel or two weeping to the joyous sound of them.

"Darling, what . . . was the name . . . of that song . . . you danced to . . . with Will?" I'm trying to catch my breath.

"'L'Amour Toujours' by Gigi D'Agostino. Why?" She plays with and kisses my hair.

"That was my theme song. I was looking into your eyes and that woman started singing in my head over and over again." I smile at her. Becca starts to softly sing the song to me. I lay on her chest, finding myself hypnotized by her voice. "Becca, sweetheart, your voice is lovely. Please don't stop." I kiss her when she pauses. She smiles and carries on with the next verse.

"... and I'll fly with you," she finishes. "Then it's the same lyrics again," she adds, rubbing my back.

"I can't believe how perfect that song is at the moment, sweetheart." I look up at her.

"Yes it is, isn't it?" She leans forward for a kiss. "I'll download it on your iPod."

"Okay. By the way, I will be using your voice to help me with some of the songs I write."

"What? No—you're not recording me!" Her face is slack with panic.

"First of all, your voice is so lovely. It should be recorded. But since you're not interested in doing that, I'm more than happy to keep it for my own listening pleasure. What I meant was you could help when I'm writing just by lending me your voice, sweetheart."

"Oh, okay." She exhales dramatically and relaxes.

"Did you have a theme song?" I feel weird asking her. I want to know, but I feel like it's a "Ray thing."

"Yes. 'Emotions' by Mariah Carey." She giggles. Love that sound. She looks over at the clock. "Shit, we have to get Morgan, and I have to start dinner." She closes her eyes. She doesn't want to leave my bed. I wrap my arms under her and hug her to me tightly. She reciprocates.

"I love you, Becca."

"Oh, Grayson, you are everything to me. I love you."

I feel my heart explode. I attack her face with kisses until she is hysterical.

"Gray, come on, she'll be getting off the bus in ten minutes!" I let her free and we get dressed. We both seem very calm and content. I grab her hand and allow her to leave the room first.

"Ray, what are you doing?"

I close my door and see Ray just leaving Becca's room.

"I'll pick you up at about seven, Stacey," Ray says through the open door behind him.

"Ray, did you and Stacey just . . . uh."

I watch Becca closely. Is she jealous?

"Becca, I don't think it's any of your business what I do, or with whom!" he snaps. She grits her teeth and tightens her fists. My heart sinks.

"Ray, it is my business when it's my best friend! She's in the middle of a divorce. She's vulnerable. I swear to God, if you hurt her . . . if you're doing this to make me jealous, then you're an idiot. It won't work, Ray. I'm not the jealous type, and I'm not in love with you. I'll be damned if I let you use Stacey to get to me!" Oh, thank God. It's about Stacey. She's not jealous. She told him she's not in love with him. Everything is getting squashed right now.

"Don't flatter yourself, Becca! You're nothing but a fucking whore!" he says through gritted teeth. His eyes are filling up. I clench my fist, but Becca beats me to the punch—literally!

"How dare you!" she yells.

"Ooh . . . ouch, mate, I caught one of those myself last week! It'll take a day or two before it stops smarting." I wince in sympathy.

"What is going on out here?" Stacey opens Becca's door.

"Short version, doll?" I ask her. She nods. "Ray is letting Becca believe he had his way with you. Becca is concerned about him using you to get to her."

"Well, that won't work. Becca's not the jealous type."

"Yes, we know—or I do, at least. Ray called Becca a whore, and ..."

"Ghetto Sybecca came out to slap a fool?" Stacey finishes, and I have to laugh. I can't help it, but it warrants an elbow from Becca, so I stop.

"Well, nothing happened. He followed you up here. I followed him. We stood outside the door listening to, apparently, a very moving church service. By the way, Becca, I had no idea you were so religious." She laughs. Becca bites back her smile and shakes her head quickly. "Theme song?" Stacey asks her. *Oh, it's not just a "Ray thing."* Becca nods.

"I have to go and get Annie!" Ray shoves past Becca and me.

"Bye, José!" I couldn't help it.

"He's not José. Stop it!" Becca slaps my arm.

"Well, he sort of is, sweetheart."

"José didn't get that far," she reminds me.

"Yes . . . well, I don't care about that anymore, sweetheart. Now, let's go get our daughter." I kiss her sweetly and hug her to me.

"Grayson, sweetie, I don't think you need to read those books. Sounds to me—and everyone else out here—that you know just what to do!" Stacey says, and pats me on the back. "Steve never had me praying like that, only B.O.B." She sighs and looks down. Becca is hysterical.

"C'mon, Gray." She pulls me along and we race out.

"Who's Bob, sweetheart?" I ask as we head down the driveway.

"'Battery operated boyfriend.'" She smirks. I am overcome with giggles that surely make me look ridiculous.

"What was your theme song?" I break from my giggling fit.

"'Closer' by Nine Inch Nails, because you get me closer to God."

I laugh again and pull her into my arms as we walk.

"We'll have to play that one tonight! It's very inspirational in the bedroom." I kiss her hair.

Morgan and Tanya greet us halfway up the driveway.

"Sorry we're late, love." I put my arms out, and Morgan runs to me.

"That's okay, Daddy." She hugs me and ignores Becca.

"Morgy, please don't ignore your Mum. She loves you very much."

"Hallo, Mummy." She tries her hand at my accent. I laugh—I love this kid!

"Hi, honey, how was your day?" Becca asks.

"Fine." And she runs up to the B&B with Tanya in tow.

"I've really messed things up with her." Becca's voice is shaky.

"It'll be all right, love, once she sees that it's just us. It will be all right." I hold her close.

"I hope so." Her smile is an unsure one.

"Have I said how cool this is?" Morgan asks as she settles in to her seat on my private jet.

"Yes, little sweetheart, you mentioned it on the way out here." I yank on her ponytail playfully and pick up my phone to call Becca.

"Hey, baby!" she answers.

"Sweetheart, we'll be taking off here in a few minutes. We'll see you about ten-thirty tonight, okay?" I get seated.

"Can't wait! I miss you." She sighs.

"Miss you too, sweetheart." I hang up.

"I still can't believe she didn't come out to California with us." Morgan shakes her head.

"Come now, Morgy, you know she wanted to. She had to stay back for the wedding. It's her last one. You're going to see a lot of changes from now on. You're going to have much more time with Mum. We've hired a few more people and, in the spring, we'll have all the remodeling and renovations going on. Big things coming, sweetheart!" I hug her.

It's been a wonderful two weeks. Becca and I are beginning to balance our relationship better. No arguing. No running away, scared-of-what-we're-feeling nonsense. We've embraced our situation and have been nurturing it.

Ray's company is still doing the work, but he's having one of his project managers handle everything. Which is understandable. If it wasn't such a large amount of money in a lousy economy, I'm sure he would've walked away. Stacey's been checking in on him. Becca's hopeful about this. Becca's been playing Cupid a lot lately! She's got Melissa and Ryan dating as well.

Aunt Hazel and Becca are back to normal—thank God! She and Charlie are very excited about going to Greece in the spring. Everything seems to be going perfectly—of course with the exception of my life back in California. I hate having to fly across the country at the spur of the moment like this, but I have been a bit neglectful. I couldn't put it off any longer, and we'll have to fly back out again next week. I'm hoping Becca can come.

"I wish we could've stayed until tomorrow. I didn't even get to see anything!"

"Oh, Morgy, we'll be taking lots of trips out here. Don't forget, California's going to be your second home." I put my arm around her. "Now, which movie are we watching?" I ask as we hit the runway and take off.

"Let's do a *Harry Potter* marathon!"

"*Harry Potter* it is."

BECCA

"Hey Stace! Where are you going?" I smile as I hang up Guest Services sign. She's all dolled up.

"Uh, I have a date," she says nervously.

"With who?" I'm so excited for her.

"With me." I turn around to find Ray. He glances back and forth from me to Stacey. "You look beautiful, Stace." He walks up to her and gives her a kiss on the cheek.

"Hey, well, you kids have a great time!" It looks like my handiwork has paid off.

Stacey gives me a hug. "Don't wait up for me," she whispers in my ear. I'm distracted by the way Ray is staring at me.

"Theme song, Ray?" I ask him, puzzled.

"No. I don't think they've come out with the song 'Fuck Off, Becca,'" he says sarcastically. I can't help it—I laugh.

"Becca, it was meant as an insult." Stacey grabs my upper arms to stop me.

"I know. But it was pretty funny. If it was someone else, I would've been insulted. But, from Ray, I'll take it." I tap her hands.

"You took it from me quite a few times, didn't you?" He takes another leap.

"Yeah, I did, Ray. Shall we sit on the sofa and go over it play-by-play for Stacey? Because that's great first-date conversation." I smile. I'm not going to be nasty. He's pissed—I get it. But this isn't fair to my best friend.

"Let's go, Stace." He holds out his hand for her.

"Bye. Have fun." I wave.

Hazel walks out of the kitchen, "Becca, honey, do you want to have a cup of tea with me?"

"Sounds great." I follow her.

It's just us two this weekend. Charlie went to go visit his son, Frank, and his family in Connecticut. He's spent the last week train-ing Gary, our new stable guy, even though he can't seem to under-stand why we hired so early given the fact that the new stable won't be complete until the beginning of next summer. I told him I wanted to make sure we had the right person in place so we're not going cra-zy then. I also mentioned that he could go and visit his family more without worrying about things. This did the trick, since he does have a new namesake—Frank and his wife, Regina, named their daughter Charlotte, but call her "Charlie" after her grandfather. He's only seen her twice and she turned one this weekend, hence his visit.

"So, who were you talking to out there? Stacey?" Hazel asks as she dips her tea bag one last time then squeezes the water from it.

"Yes, and Ray," I say as I do the same.

"Ray?" She looks up sharply.

"Yes. Calm down. He was here to pick Stacey up for a date." I add milk.

"How do you feel about that, Becca?" She's quiet, which means she's nervous.

"Well, if it's for the right reasons, I'm happy about it. I just don't want Stacey to get hurt. Whether she wants to admit it or not, she's very vulnerable right now. I just don't know what his motive is. Is he really interested in her? Or is she the closest thing to being with me?" I spoon my sugar in. Maybe Grayson was right. Pushing them together was probably not such a great idea.

"Well, did he say something that would make you question his motive?"

"Yeah, actually, he did." I tell her.

"That was inappropriate! I don't care if she's your best friend and knows everything that's happened. He shouldn't have mentioned it!" She slams her cup down.

"That's what I thought. I feel terrible. Gray was right, Hazel. I shouldn't have tried set them up. Not so soon after . . . well, you know." I look down into my tea.

"Becca, this is none of my business, but it keeps gnawing at me. Why did you sleep with Ray?" I can tell she is still hurt for her nephew and disappointed in me.

"I've taken a lot of time to think about that, because honest-ly, it was gnawing at me as well. This is what I've come up with. When Grayson and I met, we threw ourselves into each other, and you know how freaked out I was about everything. Moving so fast caused a lot of issues for Grayson and me. We argued about holding back, about not holding back—it was just crazy. I felt so all over the place, so overwhelmed. Ray confronted me with his feelings, and that was kind of the 'platform' to the roller-coaster ride I was on. With Grayson, there were all of these twists and turns coming up so fast I couldn't see them. With Ray, I knew I could stand still and take a breath. He was my *known*, Grayson my *unknown*. Honestly, at the end of the day, I was scared of my feelings for Grayson. I know Ray. He's safe. I was trying to make myself feel for Ray what I was really feeling for Grayson. I fooled myself easily, too, because I do love Ray. He is—was—my best friend. But I'm *in love* with Grayson. There's a difference. Stacey helped me realize I was missing my own signals. Does any of this make sense? You know how I can babble." I wince, unsure.

"Perfect sense, dear! I'm sorry that you lost Ray as a friend. I know what he meant to you." She holds my hand.

"I wish I wasn't such an idiot. I wish I didn't sleep with him for all of our sakes. Grayson held it over my head when it happened. He hasn't done so since, but I'm always worried that it's going to pop up again. You know," I take a deep breath, "it's unbelievable how I can push away men for seven years and the moment I budge with one, I end up in a love triangle *and* my dead husband resurfaces and kidnaps me! I mean, *really*?" I laugh . . . and she joins in.

"What is going on with the whole George thing? Why can't they find him?"

"I don't know. I'm just worried about Morgan's safety. Grayson's getting pissed. He wants to get married, and I have to wait 'til they catch this son of a bitch to get divorced. Actually, Attorney Brown said that once George is classified as a civilian, we can approach the divorce quickly by putting a notice in the paper that I am seeking a divorce. I have to run this notice for three weeks. If he does not answer it, then I can proceed without him. So, actually, it would be better if he's not caught. He'll be considered a civilian in two weeks. Hopefully, by Christmas, I will again be a free woman." I do a two-armed first pump.

"Becca, what if he kidnaps you again and hurts you like he used to?" Tears spring to her eyes.

"Well, the last time, he said I was too fat for him and that it was unattractive." I laugh. "So I don't think I have to worry about that."

"Well, first of all, you are not fat! As a matter of fact, you've been losing weight. So I wouldn't be too sure."

"I was a size four when we were married. I wasn't allowed to gain any weight. If my clothes got tight, he would . . . well, you know. As far as me losing weight now, um, yeah, I've been on a new fitness regimen called 'Grayson James.'" I giggle. "Oh . . . sorry!" Sometimes I forget that he's her nephew, and that she still calls him "Gracie" like he's five. "It has been nice not busting out of the seams of my size-twelve pants. I've even bought some tens! Grayson doesn't like it, though. He's afraid I'll lose my curves." What a breath of fresh air that thought process is. "So, how are you and Charlie doing?" I change the subject, because if I think about Grayson anymore, I'm going to need my B.O.B.! Hazel's face beams at the mention.

"Oh, Becca. I feel like a teenager experiencing love for the first time! He's just so . . . I'm so . . . we're so ..." She clasps her hands and smiles.

"You two are pretty damn cute, I have to say!"

"Becca, who would've thought at seventy years old, I'd feeling this way again?" She bites her bottom lip—a habit I think she may have picked up from me.

"Well . . . so?" I nudge her.

"What?" She laughs, then turns red. "Oh, Becca, be serious! We're too old."

"Oh my God, you are not! What are you talking about? I've seen you two making out. He so wants in your pants!" I slap her lap.

"Knock it off. You are so sex-crazed!" She laughs.

"Um, have you seen the man in my bed?" Ugh . . . mental head slap! Why do I keep doing that? Of course she's seen him; she's raised him since he was fifteen. "You're not too old. Just make sure to have some K-Y around."

"Becca, stop!" She hits me, but she's still giggling. Oh my God, she has *so* been thinking about it! *Go Charlie.*

"So, have you heard from Will?" She changes the subject, probably because she doesn't have a B.O.B. to turn to. God, I am sex-crazed. Then again, I *have* seen the man in my bed. *Shut up, Becca! Focus.*

"Um, I ran into him the other day. It's kind of weird. We were . . . well, I thought we were good friends. But I guess not. He was basically going around town, telling everyone I was going to be his girl; he was 'breaking me in' slowly. Stupid stuff like that. I guess he's being teased about it now, since everyone knows Grayson and I are together and I won't dance with him anymore." I am hurt by

Will. I really did think we were friends.

"Well, Becca, there are quite a few men in town with broken hearts over you." She smiles.

"What are you talking about?"

"Um, well, let's see. Tom . . . Henry . . . Will . . . Ray . . . Bob."

B.O.B.? Oh, not that one. Mental chuckle.

"You're crazy!"

"You're oblivious, dear!"

"I'll give you Will and Ray, but come on—Tom is fifty!"

"Uh, that's only fifteen—"

I cut her off mid-sentence with a slap to the table.

"Shut it!" I say, and warn her with a laugh. "Henry? Isn't he gay?"

"Nope."

"Oh, well, Bob is married!" I put my hands in the air.

"Only until he can have a chance with you, as he says around town." She arches a brow.

"That's absurd! You know, I'm not the only single woman around here."

"No, that's true, but you are the trifecta." Her smile is proud. I miss that sort of smile.

"Trifecta?" I admit—she has me intrigued.

"Smart, funny, and beautiful," she holds three fingers up. "Of course, I like to add warm, caring, and thoughtful, but that's a mother's perspective." My eyes fill. It's been a few weeks since she's referenced herself as a mother to me.

I hug her and kiss her face. "I love you, Mama Hazel."

"I love you, too." She hugs me again.

"Well, these men will have to move on from their schoolboy crushes, because I am way off the market!" I declare. A terrible thought occurs to me. "Hazel, Ray is so angry. I would never question his character before any of this happened, but do you think he will mention to anybody what happened?" My heart breaks at the thought. That would be the worst betrayal of all.

"You know, Becca, I don't know. I want to say *no* because Ray is the only one in town who never, ever talked about you like that, even though everybody knows how much time you two spent together. When people asked, he would just say you were a great friend to him. They were starting to wonder if he was gay. You know every single woman in town wants him, even the twenty-year-olds!" She taps the table for emphasis like somebody else I know.

"Well, that doesn't surprise me. He's the male trifecta of the town. He should've been off the market a long time ago. It's all because of what Liz did to him. How could she just walk out on a great guy like Ray and their daughter?" Suddenly I feel like the wind's been knocked out of me. "Oh God, Hazel, I left him too! What if I'm the 'straw'?" Air quotations provided. Now I'm nervous that Ray is going to crack.

"Becca, come on, that was a long time ago."

"Yeah, but it was very traumatic. Do you think Ray's talked to his parents about us? Should I call them?" My thoughts are going a mile a minute.

"Becca, just leave it alone for now, honey." She pats my hand. "You may be making a mountain out of a molehill."

"I may not be, though." I tell her about the picture from the carnival last year and how he keeps a copy in his wallet, and about the hidden message to Annie behind the watermelon that he didn't want me to see.

"Humph, well, I say go *slowly* through the backdoor." She leans in as if somebody may hear "The Plan." "See what he mentions to Stacey. Ask if he's mentioned . . . no, refer to things as adjacent to Annie and how it affects her. Don't make it seem like you're pining for answers or info. Do you know what I mean?"

"Yes." I did that with Grayson to see if he wished I was thinner. I didn't do a very good job, and I didn't get my answer until I blurted out my insecurity. "That's a great idea. I'll try that. I am worried about him. He doesn't seem the same to me, but then again, he is pissed at me."

"So, when is my nephew going to put a ring on that finger?" She grabs my hand.

"I don't know. I wish he would so Morgan will stop being so irritated with me." I roll my eyes.

"I'm surprised she's still being this way." Hazel pours us some more tea.

"Thank you. This is good . . . hits the spot."

"Well, Grayson said it's your favorite."

"Hazel, I don't have a favorite tea. I have a favorite coffee, but not tea. What is it?" Just as I ask, I know exactly what she's going to say. "Twinings English Breakfast," we say in unison. My shoulders start shaking from laughter, and I can't help it. I snort.

"What is so funny?" She laughs, too.

"Your nephew is a perpetual asshole!" I shake my head.

"Why?"

"He read my favorite trilogy, and now likes to surprise me with little, subtle things from those books. This tea is the main character's favorite tea, not mine. You'd have to read the books to get why this is so funny, but I think you may have a heart attack if you did." I add a silent prayer, begging her not to read them. "Hold on," I say, and pull out my phone. They should be landing.

November 2, 2012   10:03 p.m.

Me: I've been enjoying a delicious cup of tea with your aunt. Apparently, it's my favorite!

"Sorry. Yeah, so, the other day when the interior designer was here for the remodel, he told her we'd like to make my craft room upstairs into the 'Red Playroom'! Clearly she had read the books, because she spit her coffee out all over the place. I could've killed him!" It *was* really funny, though.

"What's that?" She seems intrigued.

"It's the sex room, but like hardcore—a what-goes-where kind of room?"

"I'm not following," she says, confused.

"Yeah . . . never mind. It's just something he's been doing to get a reaction out of me." I grin because I have something up my sleeve for tonight. My cell pings.

Gray: I thought you might like that! We're here! C U soon!
Me: Okay! XXX

"They're on their way home now." I smile.

"Oh, good. Morgan's going to be so tired. Good thing she's off from school tomorrow. I'll turn down her bed." Hazel gets up, finishes her tea, and heads off to Morgan's room. *Ping!*

Stacey: Are you okay with me being out with Ray? ☹
Me: Of course, Stace! He's a great guy! I just don't want you to get hurt. I'm not 100% sure where his head is at.
Stacey: Do you think he's using me?
Me: That would be stupid. You're such a gr8 catch! If he is, I don't think it's intentional.
Stacey: Do you still have feelings for him?
Me: Stace . . . you know how I feel. Why r u asking?
Stacey: Just making sure. I don't want to hurt our friendship! ☺
Me: Theme song! "Sisters" from *White Christmas*! I love u. Have fun!
Stacey: TY! He's a great kisser!
Me: Yes, he is! Have fun and be safe!
Stacey: Would u b mad if I slept with him?
Me: No. Be smart, please. You're going through a lot right now!
Stacey: Do you know what he likes?
Me: Not really. R U texting in front of him?

Stacey: He's in the bathroom. U can't tell me anything?

Me: Idk! I only slept with him a few times. Oh wait! He likes to get right 2 it.

Stacey: What do you mean?

Me: Wham bam . . . now erase all of these before he comes back!

Stacey: Um, okay. G'nite.

Me: Nite!

Grayson walks into the kitchen as I finish my last text. He looks at the clock, then me. I smile and hand him my phone. He starts reading. *Hello to you, too!*

"They're on a date?" I nod. "Becca, this sounds to me like he's feeding her these questions." He sounds irritated.

"I was thinking the same thing," I say with disappointment.

"Why would she do this?" He sits down and continues reading.

"I'm not sure, but she's not in her usual state lately, so I wouldn't hold it against her."

"Does he kiss better than me?" He looks up. I shake my head and sit on his lap. He holds me with one arm as he continues.

"I've missed you," I whisper in his ear. He pecks my lips softly, then turns back to the phone.

"Bloody hell! It's so fucking obvious! Poor Stacey!" He lets go of me and starts texting.

Gray: It's Gray. Tell Ray I said he's got a beautiful woman right in front of him and stop being a pathetic arsehole!

Stacey: You read our texts?

Gray: Yes, and it's very obvious to both of us who's asking the questions! U wouldn't ask Becca these types of questions because you know her well enough to know the goddamn answers! Do yourself a favor and come home!

Stacey: God . . . you are fucking hot! Sorry, Becca! XX

I grab the phone to reply.

Me: I agree!

Gray signals me to pass it back.

Gray: Come home. I'm worried about you! Take B.O.B. out for a spin instead! You can call out my name!

Stacey: LOL! You're an asshole! I'll be fine! Gotta go, I'm being rude! Love you guys!

I decide to send one final text.

Me: Knock when u get home. I'll probably still be saying my prayers ...

"Where's Morgan?" I ask.

"In bed. I had to carry her in." He kisses my neck, and his hands slowly climb under my top and bra. He finds and plays with my nipples. *Horny Sybecca rises on her pole and gyrates her hips.*

"Grayson, not in here, please." I push his hands down and try to collect myself.

"Ugh! I can't wait 'til we have our own home!"

"Let me kiss Morgan and we'll head up."

I go to Morgan's room and kiss her forehead as I pull the covers up to her chin—the way she likes it. She curls up and turns onto her side, clutching her quilt. I stare at her for a moment and really take in how much she's grown. I can't believe she's almost eleven. I feel myself get *verklempt*, like I always do when I take moments like this to freeze-frame life. It's so precious, so quick—sometimes quicker than it should be. I release a long sigh as I close her door.

"'Night, Mom." I smile at Hazel. She returns the gesture and waves. I run upstairs to give Grayson my surprise.

I walk into the room. Lit candles are everywhere. Enya is softly playing on the iPod because, well, it's calming. Grayson walks out of the bathroom in nothing but his boxer briefs. He's wearing the shorter, formfitting ones. So hot. He's so beautiful. I could come undone just looking at him. I walk toward him.

"Can you give me two minutes in there?" I kiss him.

"Don't—" he starts.

"I never do." I smirk.

"You know what I was going to say?" He looks shocked.

"Yes. Now move so I can close the door." He bites his lip and complies, and I lock the door. Geez, I knew about not peeing before sex to increase my orgasm a long time before those books ever came out! Although, I don't know how I knew. Not something I was concerned about with George. The only thing I was ever concerned about with him was when it was going to be over. *Come on, Becca, focus!*

I go to the linen closet and search for my surprise, then get undressed down to my panties and put it on. It was surprisingly hard to find. I had to go to several stores! I turn off the bathroom light and open the door. Grayson throws my phone at the wall and runs his hand through his hair.

"Grayson, what's wrong?"

He's on the opposite side of the room, facing the built-in bookshelves. I look from him to my broken phone on the floor.

"Please tell me he is lying," he says quietly. I quickly put my robe on and turn off the music.

"What is it?" I place my hand on his back. He turns and grabs my upper arms harshly.

"Did you sleep with him this weekend?" He squeezes my arms so hard, his eyes wild.

"*No!* Grayson, baby, look at me. Look into my eyes. Sweetheart, I am surrounded by your security detail. I can barely pee by myself. Please think about it! You would know. It would be reported to you. If you don't believe my word, think about that. Grayson, I'm sick with love for you. I just want you. I'm sorry that everything happened the way it did. I wish I could change it, baby, I do. Please, you have to believe me. I love you, I want you, I need you . . . please." A sob releases from my throat. He loosens his grip and places his forehead against mine.

"I'm going to make love to you in your bum, sweetheart," he says quietly.

"No—no, you're not!" I pull away.

"Why?" he yells. "Because that's what Raymond does with you? It's only for him?"

"What?"

"Yes, that's what he said!"

"He's a fucking liar! Ask Stacey if you don't believe me!"

"Why would I ask Stacey?"

"Because she's the only person in the whole world who knows what George did to me. She knows everything!" My voice carries louder than his, powered solely by my sobs. I sit on the bed and place my head in my hands as I lose control. I feel Grayson sit beside me. He rubs my back and kisses my shoulder.

"What did he do, sweetheart? Tell me, please." He's so calm now. So loving.

"That's how he would punish me for bad behavior. He. Would. Beat me. Up. Then. He would . . . and. He didn't. Use anything. To ease it. It. Was. So. Painful. I had—" I take a minute because I'm sobbing so hard I can't even finish a sentence. I exhale. "I had to have surgery because he . . . oh, God, he stabbed me there. I almost bled to death." I'm shaking with sobs in Grayson's arms. And he's crying with me.

"I'm sorry, Becca. I'm so sorry, sweetheart. Oh my God, how could he do that to you? I'm going to kill him!" He brings my face up to his. "I'm sorry I let Ray bait me. I'm so sorry, sweetheart, please . . . please forgive me." He kisses away my tears.

"I'm so getting you those purple pants!"

"And I will parade around town in them if it means you will forgive me."

I smile at the thought.

"It's official . . . I fucking hate Ray." I sigh and kiss Grayson.

"Welcome to the club, sweetheart. I'm Grayson, your president." He chuckles.

I grab the remote and turn the music back on. I take a shaky breath.

"Now . . . Mr. James, you are looking extremely sexy in only your underwear, sir. Something must be done about that." I smile wickedly as I trace the outlines of his muscles.

"Becca, we don't have to. I just fucking traumatized you. I shouldn't be rewarded." He holds my hand.

"And I shouldn't be punished just because you were being an arsehole." I arch my right brow. He tugs at my robe, and a playful smirk crosses his face.

"Well, what do you have going on under here, sweetheart?"

"Uh-uh, Mr. James. Please go and take your position over there, and I will re-enter the room. Oh, and try not to text or take any calls. Please." I tap his nose with my finger. He grabs it, bites it lightly, and sucks on it. *Um, goodbye, dry panties!* He gets up and goes to the built-in bookcase. I run to the bathroom, take off my robe, and clear my throat. He turns to find me in nothing but my panties and a gray tie. He falls to his knees.

"My God. You are so fucking hot." He grabs at his hair. "C'mere, sweetheart—you gorgeous, crazy little thing!" He stands up. I walk very slowly toward him, holding on to the tie and working my hips. I may have to start referring to his guy in there as "The Incredible Hulk," 'cuz he's busting out of his shorts. I should mention that he totally called me "little" . . . big step up from "elephant in the room."

"Oh, Becca, sweetheart, you are positively the most amazing woman on the planet. I can't even stand how in love with you I am."

"Ooh, Gray, that's a good line for one of your songs!" I probably just killed the moment, but that's ADD for ya!

"Which line?"

"'I can't even stand how in love with you I am.' Hurry! Write it down!" I slap his arm.

"Becca . . . later." He starts kissing me.

"No. Now!" I pull away and grab a pen and paper. Grayson runs his fingers up and down my back, his "Hulk" against my backside as I write the line.

"Are you done, sweetheart?" He reaches around and grabs the tie to pull me back to him. "Hmm—I like this." He smirks. He loosens it and pulls it off of me. His fingers then trace over my belly, spurring the butterflies into action. "Come. Lay down. Let me look at you." His voice is so soft and vulnerable.

I oblige and lay on the bed for him. He pulls my panties off and runs his hand up my leg and over my hip. He leans down and caresses my stomach with his lips. His tongue slips into my navel, sending an erotic sensation to my . . . oh . . . uh . . . um. My hips are moving, my hand in his hair. His tongue sinks into my navel over and over again. *Really?* He's going to make me come this way? *No. Way.* Oh, God . . . oh, yes . . . he is! *You have . . . got . . . to be . . . kidding me!* My belly button? Seriously?

"Oh God . . . oh God, baby!" I cry. My hips gyrate through the last quakes.

Grayson lifts his head and looks at me. "Really?"

"Uh. Yeah. You didn't know that was going to happen?"

"No! I had no idea! You?"

"Uh. Nope."

"Bloody hell, Becca, that was fucking hot!" We're both bewildered. "Well, let's see what happens when we do this." He starts again, but this time he parts my legs and his fingers search inside of me. Those talented little fuckers know right where to go . . . *oh . . . oh, my . . . oh, Jesus*.

I am wild under his touch. I can't control myself. My arms are flailing. He holds me down with his free arm because I think I'm trying to escape. It's so intense. I'm saying crazy things, *yes . . . no, yes . . . no*. I think I just sang in Italian. Grayson's body shakes when I say I need an exorcism. *Finally, Porn Sybecca takes over and gives in to the intensity. Her performance will surely win her this year's MVP or Emmy for Best Porn Star Actress in a Real-Life Situation.* My last quake ends.

"Well that was a record breaker, love." He smiles up at me. Yes, I should also receive the award for the longest orgasm in the history of orgasms! "Do you mind if I have a go now?" He chuckles lightly and climbs between my legs.

"Sure. Step inside my Slip 'n Slide!" My hand points there. Grayson goes into stitches.

"You're mad! Do you know that?" He hovers over me. I hold his face and tease his lips with mine as I nudge his hip with my leg. He knows the signal well and enters me. I am lost in the intoxicating smell and feel of Grayson James.

Chapter Fourteen

GRAYSON

I wake to Becca thrashing in bed. She hasn't done this in a while. I pull her to me.

"Becca, sweetheart, it's okay."

"Wh . . . huh?" She's disoriented.

"Shh, just sleep." I kiss her head. She lays down on my chest and falls back to sleep.

I can't believe I let him bait me last night! I've done so well with not bringing up what happened. It's been hard to not think about his hands on her. Ugh! I need to stop. I don't want to be in a sour mood today. She let such a huge wall down last night. I can't believe George did that to her—that sick, twisted bastard! I need to talk to Stacey today about all of this.

Becca clears her throat. "What time is it?"

"It's a little after five, sweetheart. Go back to sleep." I rub her back.

"Are you okay?" She raises her head to look at me.

"Yes," I lie.

"No . . . you're not. What's going on in that beautiful head of yours?" I feel her fingers trace my jawline. It sends a signal to an area I don't want signaled right now.

"Becca, don't . . . I . . . you don't need my crap right now." I peck her lips.

"Well, I think it's best if we talk it out. Are you thinking about last night?"

"Yes. I'm sorry." I hug her.

"Are you thinking about how you reacted?" she continues.

"Yes." I feel like an idiot.

"Well, I think it was a reaction that was bound to happen . . . incidentally, another good line for a song." Man, does she get sidetracked!

"Why?"

"Because it rhymes."

"No, why was it bound to happen?" This is utterly frustrating.

"Because you were secretly waiting for the other shoe to drop. It's not going to, baby. I'm completely committed to you." She rubs my nose with hers and kisses me.

"You really think so?" The thought hadn't occurred to me.

"Well, sure, why not? I panicked in the beginning of our relationship, and I sort of ran." She leans her head on her hand.

"I don't want to feel that way, Becca. I don't want to feel scared that I'm going to lose you and Morgan." I can't believe my own ears as I spew out my vulnerabilities.

"Grayson, that fear of loss stems from losing your parents at such a young age. I know. I've had that feeling ever since Morgan was born. I've had to work on it in therapy. You haven't finished grieving. We're not going anywhere. I promise. You might want to see a therapist to help you through the grief from your parents. I can try to help, but I'm not sure I can."

"Becca, how do you just know all of this stuff?" I am amazed.

She really is a very insightful and intelligent woman.

"Honestly? I've studied a lot of psychology, and I've had more therapy than one person should." She giggles a little.

"Thank you, sweetheart. I'm feeling much better now." I hug her.

"Good. I'd like to make your Hulk feel better now." She runs her mouth across and down my chest.

"My Hulk?" I chuckle.

"Yeah, he was ready to bust out of your shorts last night . . . and . . . he's pretty incredible." And with that she fills her mouth with me. Oh dear God, I think *I* will need an exorcism! After about fifteen minutes or so, I finish my prayers and Becca makes her way back up my chest. "Relaxed now, my love?" She touches my face.

"Absobloodylutely, sweetheart." I hug her and kiss her shoulder. It doesn't take long before I'm asleep again.

I hear a ruckus in the hallway. I open my eyes and look at the clock. It's a few minutes after ten. I hear the shower going. I'm going to call a realtor today. We can't live like this anymore. There's no real privacy. I get up and join the future missus in the shower.

"Becca, sweetheart." I walk in. "Becca? Becca, what's wrong?" I run to the shower. She is on the floor, crying. I lift her up. "Becca?"

"I'm sorry, Gray."

"Sorry for what?"

"For sobbing in here like an idiot. I had a bad nightmare. I woke up and wanted to wash it away. I just don't want to dream about it anymore! Why do I have to keep reliving it over and over again? Am I cursed? What did I do to deserve this? I hate him! *I fucking hate him!* I want him to go to prison and have everything he did to me done to him!" I have never seen Becca this angry. I don't blame her, and I can easily match it.

"He will get his, sweetheart. I promise." I crush her in my arms. "Come now, let's get you washed up." She stands under the water.

I grab her facecloth and lather it, then wash her body down. She's losing weight—it's my fault, of course. She has more time to go to the gym now. She and Stacey have been going at least three times a week. Then you add in the workouts I give her daily. At least she still has her curves. I love her curves. I love her bum. I wish he didn't do that to her. *Oh God, her bum is fantastic.*

"Uh . . . baby . . . I think I'm all clean there." She giggles.

"Yes, love, but now I'm feeling very dirty." I attack her neck as I let my Hulk (I totally love that she named him that) make his presence known at her backside.

"Gray . . . um, I don't think I can do this right now. Please." I've denied her the right to stop me before, and she was okay. But today is different. Today I will stop.

"Sorry, sweetheart. I'll stop." I wrap her in my arms.

"Thank you, honey." She lays her head back on my chest.

"Okay. Let's finish up in here and, for goodness' sake—keep your bum away from me, darling!"

We finish up and head out to the room for the morning ritual of Becca getting pissed that we're in my room and most of her clothes are in hers. She doesn't want to lose another room by giving Stacey her own, and I don't want to sleep in her bed because she and Ray . . . well . . .

"Becca, I'm calling a real estate agent today. I will try to get us as close to the B&B as I can, but sweetheart, we cannot continue to live like this." I throw on my jeans and a light, formfitting navy blue sweater. Becca stops and stares at me. "What?" I look down as I fasten my belt.

"I can't even stand how fucking hot you look right now!"

"Becca, are you turning me into a piece of meat?" I laugh at her.

"A big ole juicy steak, baby—yum!"

"You are a wicked one, aren't you?" I walk up and grab her.

Her breath instantly becomes erratic. I love that I affect her like this; it's such a turn-on. I attack her lips and give her bum a really good smack. She moans against my mouth. The Hulk awakens once more. I slap her again, triggering another moan and a rescue mission of the Hulk from my pants. We wrestle over to the bed and I show her just how incredible he is. Morning prayers are said, leaving both parties thoroughly shagged and ready for the walk of shame.

"All of that from an outfit, aye?" I smile breathlessly over at her.

"Apparently." She mirrors me. I cup her face and kiss her once . . . twice . . . hmm, I'd love another go. "C'mon." She pushes me off gently. I groan in disappointment and get up with her.

"Grayson, please let security know that Ray is not permitted on our property. I'd ask you to fire him, but I don't want to take away from Annie or any of the crew that is depending on this. He just . . . he went overboard, and I don't want anything to do with him at all." She looks up at me. She really is hurt by his actions. I nod and take her hand, and we head out of the room to start our day. Mine begins with a debriefing in the crop room—our security headquarters at the moment—and Becca's with her morning staff meeting.

BECCA

I can't believe everything on my checklist is done . . . by my staff. This is so weird for me. I'm not used to this.

"Hey, baby," I say as I head into the main foyer. "Oh, sorry." He's on the phone. I didn't realize.

"I just got back yesterday. Jesus H. Christ! Sorry, Carol, it's not your fault. I'll be there tomorrow." He hangs up. "Becca, we have to be in L.A. tomorrow. I'm doing a secret deal that I can't let go. It's going to be huge news. And it has to be done tomorrow, or it's a bust. Go pack your things, sweetheart. We're leaving tonight." He gets back on the phone right away. He looks at me with an arched eyebrow, daring me to fight him on this. "Smitty," he says in a clipped tone to his pilot. "Yes, we need to leave tonight. Five o'clock. Great. See you then." He hangs up again. "What, Becca?" he snaps. I bite my bottom lip and give his body a thorough scan. I run my hands up his chest.

"Are you done with your phone calls, baby?" I palm his face.

"No, I have one more. But it can wait. Why?" He licks his lips and holds my hips.

"Oh, good. I need your help upstairs." I reach up on my tippy-toes to kiss him.

"What if I say no?" he teases.

"Oh, I'll just have to see B.O.B. then." I turn to walk away. Grayson spins me around and throws me over his shoulder. He sprints up the stairs like I'm not 170 pounds. Well. I may be 160 pounds now.

Over the next hour I pray to God, Jesus, the Holy Mother, and all of the saints. I'm not even Catholic. "Your Aunt Hazel is right." I steady my breath.

"Oh yeah? What's she right about, love?" He rubs my bum, which he has thoroughly spanked. I'm still so surprised at how much I love it when he does that.

"I am sex-crazed." I snort.

"She said that? What did you say?" He's a little shocked.

"I asked her if she's seen who's in my bed . . . then I did a mental head slap for obvious reasons." I lean on my arm. He flashes me a smile and continues with the rubdown.

"Sweetheart, is it okay that I've done this?" He nods to my bum.

"Yeah, I'm a huge fan. Never thought I would be, given my history, but I love when you do it. It's quite the turn-on." I lean forward for a kiss.

"Did . . . um . . . did he . . . you know?"

"Ray?" I ask. He nods. "No. I don't think I would have let him anyhow. It's our thing." He seems relieved. "How old are you,

Grayson?" I finally ask.

"Coming in from left field, are we, darling? And a whole month later!"

"Yeah, I've been a little distracted." I laugh.

"Thirty-four, sweetheart, which makes you most definitely my old lady!" he barks. I hit him.

"Not funny! Damn it. Why am I suddenly older then everybody?" I'm actually pretty serious. This sucks!

"Well, I think you're overreacting. Now get yourself together. We have to pack."

"How long are we going for?"

"Rest of the week—now, come on!" He slaps me again.

"Ow. Baby, that's enough." I wince.

"Sorry . . . sorry, sweetheart." He rubs and kisses where he slapped. We get dressed and I head over to my room to pack before I deal with any scheduling issues.

Stacey is just getting up.

"Hey, what time did you get in?" I'm careful to keep my face as blank as possible.

"Well, I was home in time to hear Grayson. Guess Ray was wrong." She smiles.

"What do you mean?" I pretend not to know.

"Ray said he was pretty sure I'd come home to find you two broken up."

"Do you know why he would think that?" I tread lightly.

"No. I came back from the bathroom and he just said it."

"Well, Ray is no longer allowed on these premises. So if you want to see him, you'll have to meet him elsewhere. I'm not sure why you let him talk you into texting those questions to me, but if I were you, I'd stay away. He obviously does not have good intentions toward you." I sit beside her.

"Well, his intentions were very good last night," she says, sounding sarcastic and defensive. "I'm a grown woman, Becca. Maybe I have my own intentions right now!"

"Did you sleep with him, Stace?" Oh God, she's going to get hurt and resent me for it!

"Yes, I did. To get back at Steve. Plus, I have my own agenda, Becca," she says quietly and avoids my eyes. Something tells me she's not too happy she did that.

"Well, I think you should know why Ray thought what he did." I sigh, then proceed to tell her.

"How could he do that, Becca? What an effin' liar! Does Grayson know the truth?" She touches my arm.

"Yes. That's why Ray's plan didn't work. He doesn't know everything that's happened. I don't know what he's playing at but, his behavior is very disturbing." I pause and then add, "Do you really want to be a part of that behavior?"

"Becca, are you jealous that he's with me now?" she snaps.

"Wow, Stace . . . really? Who are you and what have you done with my friend? Go ahead and be with him. I just don't want you to get hurt." I'm appalled. Honestly! I get up and pull my suitcase out to pack. She looks at me.

"Where are you going?"

"Grayson and I have to go to L.A. for business . . . and pleasure, as always." I laugh.

"Yeah, you two woke me up this morning with your daily prayers." She laughs as well and straightens out her nightgown on her lap.

"Sorry. So, we'll be gone for a few days. Will you help Hazel with Morgan?"

"Yes, of course." She half smiles.

"I don't know what to bring with me. Ugh." I pick up the phone and call downstairs. "Can you put Grayson on for me, Claudia?"

"Sweetheart, are you okay?" he asks once he gets on the phone. I usually don't call him in the house. What can I say? I had quite the workout this morning, and I'm too lazy to run back downstairs.

"Yes. What kinds of clothes should I bring?" I push the pieces in my closet around.

"It's still warm there, so summer stuff, but bring something for an evening chill. Maybe a dress if we go out. Don't go crazy, doll. Anything you need, we'll get out there. Now, hurry!" I hang up, pull some summer stuff out, and call it a day. Everything has gotten so big on me—I'm pretty sure I'll need to go shopping. Oh, darn!

I turn when I hear Stacey's phone pinging like crazy. She looks at it and starts giggling uncontrollably.

"It's Ray. He wants to know if he rocked my world last night." She looks up. I just flash her a smile and head to the bathroom to get my toiletries.

Something is not sitting well with me. This is very out of character for Stacey. Either Steve has sent her for such a loop that she can no longer smell bullshit from a mile away, or . . . or . . . I don't know. I've been best friends with her for twenty-three years; this is not the same girl. I really don't get it. There is only one thing I can think of, but I'll talk to Grayson about it when we're on the plane later. I don't want anyone in earshot.

I don't like that I suddenly feel like I need to secure all personal stuff away from my best friend. I feel like I'm going to be sick. I need to find Gray.

"See you downstairs?" I ask as I roll my suitcase out. She just waves as she continues to text. All righty then. I put my suitcase in Grayson's room, turn, and run right into him.

"Need to say your prayers again, sweetheart?" He laughs and hugs me. Actually, I would love to, but I need to stay focused. I shush him and close the door. I turn the iPod on in its dock and bring him to the bathroom.

"Don't get any ideas. I just need to talk." I stop him from trying to undress me. Geez, we really are like jackrabbits! Ah, new love . . . may it always be this way. *Focus, Becca!* "Can you sit so I'm not straining my neck?" I bring him to the tiled edge of the tub and move the candles out of the way.

"What's going on, sweetheart?" He pats his leg for me to sit on his lap. I comply. I fill him in on my conversation with Stacey and watch his nose flare and jawline twitch at the mention of Ray trying to break us up. I tell him how Stacey seemed to be upset that Ray lied like that, but then she was texting him and giggling like a schoolgirl as she told me what he was saying.

"Baby, something's not right. That's not my friend in there. I don't even feel comfortable leaving personal shit around. I've never felt that way! There are only two things I can think of." I take a deep breath.

"What, sweetheart?"

"Either she has really lost it because of what Steve did—well, I think she has, because the other thing would have to be a part of that. Because she would never."

"Spit it out, Becca!"

"Sorry! Gray, I know she flirts with you around me, but has she ever done it *not* around me and made you feel uncomfortable? Well, maybe not uncomfortable. But you might have thought she went too far?" I ask. He taps his fingers on his lip, contemplating my question.

"Well, yes. Recently there have been a few instances, but I sort of brushed them off thinking it's just how Stacey is. The other day, she said out of the blue, 'You know, Grayson, I'm a good Catholic girl and I bet I pray a hell of a lot better than Becca.' She was very serious, but I thought she was just trying to get me to have a good laugh or to see if I'd cheat on you or something. It was very bizarre."

"What did you say?" I swallow hard, feeling a pang of betrayal.

"I said, 'We should have a go at it, then'!" His grin is huge, and I smack him because I know he's teasing me. "No. I said, 'Well then, Stacey, I'm definitely not man enough for you, because I can barely handle Becca!'"

"Well played, baby."

"Yes, but then she said, 'I hear how you handle Becca, and

you're definitely man enough to handle me.' And then she winked, blew me a kiss, and walked away shaking her hips." I look down. I think I may be right. "What's the matter?" He chucks my chin.

"They're working together to break us up. He wants me to turn to him, and she wants you to turn to her." I try to keep my chin from quivering.

"Well, sweetheart, that won't happen." He hugs me.

"I know. I'm upset because she's been my best friend for twenty-three years! Could Steve leaving her drive her to the point of betraying her best friend? How could she keep playing along with Ray after what he triggered last night? She's Morgan's godmother! I mean, this is so . . . so juvenile, like high school. Not even, because high school Stacey wouldn't do this. Something's not right with her, Gray. This is not my best friend."

"Well, first, we're going to beef up security around her. We'll just tell her we have reason to believe we should do so. To make it look less suspicious, I'll increase security for everyone. Ray is not allowed on the property, so that takes care of help looking through personal things. Now, should you call Steve? Does he know she's here? What if she's not even telling the truth?" He looks to me as I stare at him. He's gone totally James Bond on me. I suddenly feel the need to pray. *Focus, Becca!* "Focus, Becca!" He repeats my thoughts.

"I don't think she's lying about Steve. I do have most of my important papers in a safe, but what about the computer and all the info on there?" I ask.

"Why are you worried about that stuff again?" He looks at me, puzzled.

"You know, I don't really know. Maybe I'm being a little crazy. The security is a good idea." I kiss his cheek.

"C'mon, let's grab Morgy and take her for lunch. We also have to get you a new phone. Some arsehole broke yours." He smiles and pats me so I'll get up.

We head out to the bedroom and turn off the iPod before heading downstairs to the ship that is smoothly sailing without me. Still not sure if I really like that. I am from Jersey—if there's enough time to get everything done and no crisis happening . . . well, then it's boring!

I tell Hazel I'm going with Grayson to L.A. and ask her if she minds taking care of Morgan.

"Oh, Becca, don't be ridiculous! Of course I will!" She pushes away at the air in front of her.

"Well, I didn't want to be rude and not ask. Thanks!" I hug her then head off to find Grayson. He's in the crop room talking with the detail again. I go and find Morgan to tell her we're going out for lunch and to the mall.

"Hey, what's going on down here?" Stacey asks, seeing the crop room full.

"I don't know. It must be serious, though, because he's already had a morning debriefing. There's never two in one day." I plant the seed. Stacey shrugs and heads for the dining room. I see her start to text like mad. I feel my heart break even more.

Grayson comes out. "All set," he whispers in my ear before he heads toward Stacey. "Stacey, love." She turns quickly. "Listen, I have to beef up everybody's security as a precaution. There may be some evidence as to George's whereabouts. I'm sorry, I know this is all a pain in the arse, but I wouldn't want anything to happen to you." He touches her face and plants a kiss on her cheek. I watch her close her eyes and relish in it. *I fucking hate being right sometimes!* Why is he letting his fingers linger on her cheek? "You understand, right, sweetheart?" He palms her face.

"Um . . . yes," she says quietly. *I'm his sweetheart. Not you, bitch!* Whoa, Becca . . . what was that? *Sybecca looks at her green body and purple pants and shrugs at me.* No! Me? I never get jealous. I know that he was baiting her. I take a deep breath.

Refocusing, I walk up behind them to play along.

"Uh . . . Grayson?" I question in a confused, *What am I seeing here?* sort of tone. He pulls away sharply.

"Ready, sweetheart?" He acts nervous.

"Um, yeah." I look back and forth between them. "Everything okay?" Same confusion.

"Yes. Just letting Stacey know about the extra security." He picks at a speck of nothing on his sweater.

"Do you really think it's necessary, Grayson?" She stares longingly at him, like an actress in an old black-and-white movie. I fight the urge to roll my eyes.

"Oh, Stace, please. I'd just die if anything happened to you. You're my family . . . my sister. Protecting you is my top priority. I couldn't live with myself if anybody hurt you." *Thespian Sybecca matches her dramatics.* I see the guilt swarm over her face. "I love you, Stacey. Let me take care of you like you took care of me and your goddaughter so many years ago." I hug her hard.

"Okay, okay . . . stop." She pats my back.

"Mummy, Daddy? I'm a bit hungry, can we get going now?" Morgan walks in, trying out her almost-perfected English accent.

"Yes, little sweetheart, let's get going." He turns around to give her a piggyback ride.

"Where are you all off to?" Stacey asks.

"Lunch and shopping. I need a new phone." I sigh and roll my eyes.

"Oh. Why?" Stacey asks, with more interest than is necessary.

"Oh, because it's Monday. Who knows? Grayson is always buying me something new." I shake my head.

"Oh. Well, see you guys later." She sips her coffee. We head out with our extra detail in tow.

"Sweetheart, you were brilliant!" He leans over and kisses me once we're in the Rover. I hug him and cry into his neck. I know I should try to keep it together, especially with Morgan in the car, but

I'm so deeply hurt.

"Please, don't ever call her 'sweetheart' again," I whisper in his ear.

"Becca Campbell, are you—"

"Yes. Now shut it!" I warn him.

"Yes! Yes! Yes! Yes! Yes!" He does a few side fist pumps and hits the steering wheel once with each hand. He then pulls out his cell and takes a picture of me.

"What are you doing?" I'm glad he's so fucking pleased with himself!

"Let's see. I have ten Grammys, seven Moonman awards, and twelve AMAs, but they are all shit compared to the day I made Becca Campbell jealous! This picture is going on a plaque and taking over my award shelves." His smile is absolutely ridiculous. I feel myself getting pissed. "Oh, come on, sweetheart! Don't be mad. I mean, I don't want you to be all *Fatal Attraction* on me, but it does do my heart—and, of course, my ego—good to know that you care enough to be jealous, even if it is just a smidge." He backs out of the parking space and heads down the driveway, that huge smile plastered to his face. He grabs my hand and kisses the back of it.

"Sorry. I've just never experienced that before." I manage a half smile. I'm experiencing and learning a lot of new things about myself and relationships. I look at Grayson and I see this tall, strong, confident, beautiful man, and I forget that he still has a lot of insecurities, too. I need to remember to nurture them. "I love you, Grayson. Congratulations on your newest award." I run the back of my hand across his cheek.

"I'm sorry she's hurting you," he says quietly. Thankfully, Morgan's plugged into her iPod. Grayson bought it for her and made her a playlist of all his songs that are acceptable for a ten-year-old to listen to. I don't really want her to know what's going on, or even get a hint of it. I'm glad she wasn't in the room for our theatrics.

"Grayson, the only thing that's helping me keep it together is the fact that I *know* something is off. You don't know Stacey in any light other than what you've seen in the past two weeks. This is so out of left field for her. When we're on the plane later, I really want to dissect this behavior of hers."

"I'll help you, sweetheart." He laces his fingers with mine, and I turn to look into the backseat.

"Tanya? I'm sorry, I feel like we're being rude."

"Oh, no, ma'am."

"Eck." I wince. "'Becca,' please."

She laughs. "I feel the same way."

"Anyway, have you noticed or heard Stacey make any strange comments to anyone—most importantly, Morgan?"

"What, Mummy?" Morgan looks up and takes an earbud out.

"Nothing, sweetie. I was talking to Tanya. Go back to Daddy's music." Her smile once again tells me that I am the most fantastic and wonderful mother in the world because I referred to Grayson as "Daddy." Grayson squeezes my hand, too, and I squeeze back. Morgan puts the bud back in.

"Actually, Becca, I was getting ready to say something to you after you two were done talking." She leans forward and lowers her voice. "A few days ago, she and Morgan were talking about, you know, normal, everyday things. Well, Morgan mentioned a boy she has a crush on at school."

"What?" Grayson cuts her off (typical Dad response). I squeeze his hand and shush him. Tanya smiles and shakes her head a little when I give her an eye roll.

"Uh, so anyway, Stacey said to her, 'Oh, I bet Ray won't like you having a crush! He'll want to know who this boy is!' Morgan asked her why Ray would care. I was wondering the same thing. Everybody knows Mr. James is Morgan's Daddy. She makes sure of that." She smiles huge and glances over at Morgan, who's rocking out to her iPod. Grayson squeezes my hand so long and hard it feels like a death grip. I glance over at him, and he's fighting tears back.

God, I love him. I love that he loves my daughter so much. I love how proud he is to be her "Daddy."

"Stacey said something to the effect of Ray being like a father to her for the past several years, helping you raise her. That he loves her so much, and it's never just 'Annie this' or 'Annie that,' it's always 'my girls.'"

"What did Morgan say?" I'm once again appalled.

"Well, my little girlfriend here was like, 'Ray's not my Daddy, Grayson is. Mommy and Grammy Hazel have been raising me, not Mommy and Ray. Ray only bothers with me when he has to pick me and Annie up from somewhere or when we all go together some-place.' Then she said, 'it's never been "my girls."' She totally did the air quotations, too!" Tanya laughs. "She said, 'When he picks us up at a swim meet or dance or anything and Mommy's not around, he always asks how Annie did. Never me! When Mommy picks us both up, she always asks about both of us. Ray is fake, Aunt Stacey. I feel sorry for Annie. She always wishes my mom was her mom, and with good reason, because I have the best mom in the world, but also be-cause my mom treats Annie like she's her mom, too. But I don't feel that way about her dad even though I didn't have one 'til Grayson."

"Is our daughter brilliant or what, sweetheart?" Grayson is beaming with so much pride.

"She most certainly is!"

"Oh, I'm not done." Tanya puts her hand up. "Then Stacey said it's a fact that Grayson is known to not only dislike children, but definitely does not want to have any."

"Jesus H. Christ!" Grayson hisses through gritted teeth.

"Do you know what your brilliant daughter said to her?" She laughs. I can tell Tanya has really fallen under Morgan's spell the past few weeks. Of course, who wouldn't?

"What?" we ask in unison.

"'Oh, Aunt Stacey, you've Googled the wrong Grayson James. My daddy's a very private person. All of the articles complain about it. It's very rare to see him with a serious girlfriend, only dates. That, of course, is because he was waiting for my mother, with whom he'd like to have lots of babies. Try again. You probably spelled his name wrong.' She then spelled out your name for her. Stacey said, 'See, he obviously has commitment issues.' And Morgan said, 'Nope. He's been committed to my mother ever since she told him she was awesome!' and she walked away. Stacey seemed completely shocked that she was just outsmarted by a ten-year-old!" We all start laughing.

"What is so funny?" Morgan asks with a curious smile.

"Oh, just grown-up talk." I reach my free hand toward her. "Morgan?"

"Yes, Mommy?" she asks, and takes it.

"Daddy and I love you very much, and we think you're pretty awesome."

"Must run in the family," she says, and we're all in stitches again.

Gray turns the car off. I didn't even realize we were here. "I do, you know." He takes my hand again as we walk into the mall.

"What?" I look over at him.

"Want to have lots of babies with you." He pulls me to him, but then he stops walking suddenly. I look up at him. My smile fades when I see how serious he is. His eyes go wide.

"What?" I feel sick. I don't like this look.

"He didn't . . . Ray used ..." He can't finish, but I know what he's asking.

"No, he used protection."

"What if he tampered with it?"

"I don't think he did." I shake my head.

"Did you take that pill?"

"No, Grayson, I would never. You know that." I feel tears filling my eyes. If I wasn't such a complete idiot, we wouldn't be having this conversation.

"Becca, why are you crying? Is there something you're not telling me?" He leans closer to my ear so no one will hear.

"No!" I grab his face. "No, baby, I'm just upset with myself. I feel like the stupid mistake I made is going to haunt us for the rest of our lives. How could I be so stupid? I'm . . . so . . . sorry." *Tears brought to you by annoying sobs!*

"Mommy, what's wrong?" I shake my head. She turns to Grayson. "What happened, Daddy?"

"Mummy's just a little upset with herself. She'll be all right, sweetheart. We all do stupid things in our lives that we wish we could take back. Mummy's feeling that way right now, and it's got her awfully upset. We love her no matter what, Morgy, right?" He hugs me.

"Right! Mama, it's okay." She hugs me too. People are walking by slowly, watching us.

"She missed the big sale at Macy's! It was over yesterday . . . don't you hate when that happens? It's all right, sweetheart, they'll have another one-day sale next month!" My body turns from shakes of sobbing to shakes of laughter. I haven't raised my face for him to see, though. I'm still buried in his chest. "Look, sweetheart! Bath & Body Works is having a grand sale! Five for $15! Come now, let us get some antibacterial soap! Hormonal . . . may be on the nest!"

"Stop it!" I smack his chest and look up so he can see I'm laughing. Christ!

"Morgy, love, please go with Tanya." She listens. Wow—if he could bottle that up!

He palms my face quickly, "Yes. I may, from time to time, remember and feel hurt by what happened. It is very difficult for me to swallow."

"Not for me."

"Becca, damn it, stop. I love you. I'm in love with you. Nothing will change that. I know you regret it. I know where your heart and your loyalty lie, but it is okay for me to feel this way, especially when it is so recent. I feel guilty about having had a hand in it all. You did not go behind my back and betray me. I love you no matter what. I need you to always feel sure of that. My confidence may have a relapse here and there, but I won't ever let it make me push you away again. Do you understand me?"

"Yes," I whisper, and welcome his lips on mine.

"Hey guys . . . stop. Everyone is looking!" Morgan says with exaggerated embarrassment.

"Sorry, love. Come. Let us have lunch at ..." He looks around. "Bertucci's?"

"Sounds good." I put my arm around his waist and hug him. His left arm goes around my shoulder and his right hand out to Morgan as we head to the restaurant.

Chapter Fifteen

"What do you mean you're going back to L.A. tonight? And without me?" Okay, so she's a little upset.

"Morgan, you have school. Grammy Hazel will be with you." I push her hair behind her ears.

"I'm sorry, Morgy girl. It's last minute. You know we want you to come." He reaches for her hand.

"Is Aunt Stacey going to be around?" She's flat. Normally this would be an excitement-worthy question.

"Yes."

"Mommy, she's been acting so weird. I don't get her. One minute she's flirting with Daddy, which, by the way . . . puke city." She sticks her finger in her mouth. "Then the next minute, she's telling me he's going to leave us, and that's why he hasn't given you a ring. She keeps pushing Ray on me. Mommy, I don't really like Ray. I don't *dislike* him, but I don't know. Aunt Stacey isn't the same." She sighs and sucks down her chocolate milk.

"Flirting with?" I raise my eyebrow at Gray.

"Oh, I think that's something you'll have to pray about later."

He bites his lip and I feel his hand traveling up my inner thigh under the table. I smack it. "Sweetheart, I think Morgan has the flu and can't go to school this week," he whispers in my ear.

"I agree. She definitely looks peakish." I feel Morgan's forehead. "Morgan, I think it's settled. You are too sick to go to school. Terrible flu."

"Really?"

I nod. She does a little dance in her seat.

"Grayson, Tanya hasn't seen her kids in a few weeks. Can we . . . you can say no, but can we bring her family out to meet her there? Maybe we can all go to Disneyland one of the days?" I ask quietly. "She's so good to Morgan."

"No, sweetheart. I'm sorry, but that wouldn't be fair to everyone else." He seems adamant.

"Okay." I give him a half smile.

"Tanya, are your children in school?" Grayson asks.

"My twins are in the first grade, and my daughter is in preschool." I can see from the look in her eyes that she misses them terribly. I place my hand on Gray's leg.

"Where do you live?" he continues.

"Virginia, sir."

"It's terrible how they've come down with the flu. I think they need their Mum. Please call your husband and have him prepare for a trip out to California. There's a special doctor there they must see with their Mum. Doctor, err . . . what's his name, sweetheart?"

"Disney?"

"Yes, Dr. Disney has the only cure for this flu!" He then gets on the phone with Smitty, telling him the jet will need to head to Virginia to pick up the Smith family. "Tanya, please email me your address right now so I can forward it." She just sits there, staring at him with tears rolling down her face. "Come now—hurry it up before I fire you!" She laughs and pulls out her phone. "Okay, Smitty, I'll email it to you in two minutes. Please set up a car for them. Thanks. Bye."

"Mr. James."

"Grayson," he corrects.

"Grayson. I don't know how to thank you. Can I hug you?" She stands.

"Oh, if you must." He waves her on, and she wraps her arms around him. "Jesus, Tanya! You're supposed to protect me, not crush me to death!" he teases.

"Sir, I would take a bullet for you and *not* complain about it!" She laughs, but I sense she's very serious.

"Don't do that. You have three children counting on you. Besides, my fiancée is the brains behind this operation. We're both grateful for the protection and love you give our daughter, right, sweetheart?"

"Right, baby." I hug Tanya. She then sits back down and calls her husband. I can tell he's thrilled on the other end. He's been home, taking care of the kids and unable to find work like a lot of other people right now. They could use a carefree vacation. "Tanya!" I try to get her attention. She tells her husband to hold on. "Make sure he knows all expenses are paid. We just want you guys to enjoy yourselves." She mouths *thank you* and proceeds to tell her husband.

"Anything else you want to spend my money on?" Grayson says sharply in my ear.

"I'll pay for them," I say quickly. "Her husband's having a hard time finding a job. It's been really tough on them. I'll pay for it, baby." He looks forward and taps Morgan on the head with the menu, ignoring my comment.

The waitress comes back for our order. "We should have something big now, sweetheart, since we'll be busy traveling later."

"Okay." I nod.

"I'll have the filet mignon, medium. My wife will have your Chicken Domani, and my daughter will have . . . pizza or ravioli, sweetheart?"

"Ravioli!"

"And that's our party, too." He points to the table with Tanya, Derek, Melissa and Ryan.

"Separate bills?" she asks.

"Nope. I'll pay for everything." He sighs nonchalantly, then crosses his arms and rests his head on them. She smiles and heads over to their table.

"Hey," I say quietly near his ear.

"What?" He turns his head toward me.

"You okay? Tired? What's going on? Your mood went south." I prop my head on his arm.

"I'm going to be working a lot the next few days. I've been so focused on our family and your business that I've kind of dropped the ball with mine." I love that he said "our family."

"How can I help you, baby?" I kiss his arm.

"I'll focus on my business. You just focus on me, if you know what I mean." I laugh at his Shelley impersonation. "Okay?" he asks.

"Oh . . . sorry, yes, gladly." I play with his hair.

"I'm probably going to be very frustrated when I come home at night. I need you to know that it's not you, it's my work. Okay?"

"Yes, baby. I'm excited to see your house." He just smiles. Why is he acting so weird? His phone pings. He quickly checks his email.

"Damn it!" he says angrily and puts his hands in his hair.

"What?" I rub his back. He slides his phone over to me. I read the email.

From: Carol Praxton
To: Grayson James

Regarding: Ethan McCaw
November 3, 2012 1:05 p.m.

Ethan McCaw signed with Sony. PR meeting set for 8 a.m. Lots of fires to put out!

Carol

Carol Praxton
Assistant to Grayson James, President and CEO of GBM Records

"Why? What fires?" I turn to him.

"I've been gone a month with no reason. Rumors start flying around." He sighs.

"But you were on vacation." I defend him.

"Yeah, for three weeks. I'm on my fifth week now, and I've let a lot of things slide at my company."

"I'm sorry, Grayson. I had no intention of pulling you away from your obligations." He has been super focused on me and my career. I feel terrible.

"Oh, sweetheart, you and Morgan are my number-one obligation. But now that you're squared away, I have to throw myself back in and do damage control. I'm going to have to have some sort of press conference. I'll need you there, wearing something nice. I'll be introducing you to the world." He leans forward and kisses me.

I wince. "Is that really a good idea?"

"I don't know, you tell me!" he snaps.

"Um, how are you going to introduce me? Who are you going to say I am to you?" It will be very strange to announce that I'm his fiancée when I don't have a ring. Even Duchess Kate got a ring, so I know they do that in England!

"Becca, don't ask me questions that you know will aggravate the piss out of me!" he says through his teeth. I'm just going to be very patient with him. It's not me; it's work. I kiss his arm again.

He calls Carol and tells her to have a personal shopper pick out clothes for Morgan and me. When he gives her our sizes, I feel my eyes grow wide.

"Grayson . . . honey, I'm not a size eight." I pat his arm and my heart sinks. Does he want me to be a size eight?

He tells her to hold on. "Sweetheart, I've told her to buy in two sizes. You've been losing a lot of weight, and I don't want you to look frumpy. By the way—eat up, please, because I'll cry if you lose those curves." He smirks. I'm relieved to get a glimpse of my Grayson, and I kiss him. He gets back on the phone and tells her to have a hair and makeup stylist for me, too. *Country Sybecca reluctantly pulls out her pigtails.*

Our food arrives and Gray gets off the phone.

"Mummy, how does Daddy know what you want to eat when you didn't even say anything?" Morgan asks, looking puzzled as I dive into keeping my curves.

"He just knows. Hidden talent, I guess." *Among many!* I feel Gray's hand slowly slide up my inner thigh as if he heard my last thought. "Doesn't Daddy look handsome in this outfit?" I ask Morgan, keeping my eyes on him. He licks his lips before biting at his lower one. Oh God, I can't wait to focus on him!

"Daddy is always handsome, no matter what he wears!" *Or doesn't,* I add in my head and wink at him. "All of the girls in my class have had a crush on him ever since he came in for Parents' Day!"

Grayson beams. I remember him on that day. He was so excited and nervous. He wanted to make Morgan proud.

He brought everyone in the class an autographed picture of himself and gave out iTunes gift cards so they could download music . . . preferably his, but it was their choosing. The kids were so excited to hear about the singers and bands that Grayson has worked with. Thank God he was the last parent, because he would have been a tough act to follow. The only tough question he got was from Ashley—that little bitch!

"How are you Morgan's daddy all of a sudden? We've never met you or heard about you before." I know Grayson wanted to strangle her. Morgan was very upset by this question.

"Well, Ashley, it took me a long time to find Morgan and her mum. I was very busy doing what I talked about."

"So are you her real father?"

"Yes."

"Why doesn't she have your last name?"

"She will. Now, enough with the personal questions. Who wants to hear about Justin Bieber?"

He adamantly hates Ashley. I do, too. Morgan was so proud, though, especially when he said he was her real father. She could pass as his. They have the same eyes and dark hair. Even her teacher said she could see the resemblance. Grayson loved that.

"I can see why. I've had a crush on him ever since he walked into the store." I grab his hand and kiss his cheek. He nods to my plate and I comply, finishing everything.

"Dessert?" The waitress asks. I shake my head along with everybody else. Grayson opens his wallet for his credit card and I see he has only one picture in there. It's of him and Morgan on Parents' Day. I feel that jealous pang again, but push it away. We need to take more pictures together.

"What?" He must have noticed my face.

"I love that picture." I touch it.

"Me, too. I'm a very proud father." He pulls my hand up to his lips and kisses the inside of my palm, then my wrist, and then he lays his head in my hand.

"Everything's will be all right, baby." I pull his face to me and kiss him once . . . twice . . . "Guys . . . stop! Geez!" Morgan complains.

"Morgy, your mother and I are very much in love. When two people are in love, they kiss a lot to tell each other with no concern of who is watching. You're going to have to either get used to it or learn how to ignore us, because I certainly don't want to hear this rubbish coming from you every time I kiss your mother." Grayson is blunt and to the point—as usual. Morgan's gotten used to him being stern with her when she's out of line, and no longer questions if he still loves her.

"Sorry, Daddy." She looks down.

The waitress comes back with the slip. Grayson is back on the phone with Carol, so at his nod, I take it. I tip twenty percent and sign "Becca James." I love that. I can't wait to make it legal.

At the AT&T store, I hand the remnants of my broken phone to the clerk. He shoots me an odd look, but quickly turns his eyes back down to his screen.

"Okay, Mrs. James," he says. *Mrs. James?* I didn't tell him my name. "You can use your husband's upgrade." *What?* Wait, I didn't get my bill this month, come to think of it. Oh, Grayson.

"Give her the newest model, please, and the accessories for it," he tells the clerk. "A laptop, too," he adds.

"Daddy, can I have a new phone?"

"No!" Grayson and I both pipe up.

"Ugh! Can I at least have an iPad?" I refuse again, but Grayson nods to the clerk and Morgan starts jumping around. She hugs her daddy, and he smiles. After twenty minutes or so, everything's ready to take home. I would've spent a buck on a new 3G model, but instead, the bill is slightly over two grand. I start to hand Grayson my credit card, but he almost knocks it out of my hand when he slaps my wrist and offers up his Black AmEx. I gasp and look up at him in shock. That actually hurt. He shoots me a glance that should come equipped with daggers, but his eyes soften as I rub my wrist. He grabs it and kisses it tenderly.

"Okay, Carol, great!" He hangs up. "Disney is set for Friday, love, and the Smiths are staying on Disney property. Everything's booked and all set." He kisses me. "Don't ever embarrass me like that again," he whispers in my ear.

"I'm sorry." I kiss him.

"Mrs. James, you're all set," the clerk says. Grayson signs, hands me my phone, and grabs the bags. My new phone pings. I look at it. Ten unread texts. I see Grayson's jawline twitching like mad. I sit down on the sofa in the store, and he holds out his hand for the phone as he sits beside me. This is something I find incredibly sexy about him, and yet, I'm nervous he will find reason to get angry with me. He hits the message cloud. I put his arm around me and wrap my arms around his waist to lay my head on his chest. He relaxes a bit.

I put my hand over the cell screen.

"I have no control over what these messages say or who they are from. Please don't take it out on me. Think before you react," I say softly in his ear. He's already in a foul mood about work. He doesn't need to get heated over any of this nonsense.

"I promise, sweetheart," he says flatly, and moves my hand. The first two messages are about my new phone. The rest are from Ray. Oh, God—here we go!

November 3, 2012   1:30 a.m.
Ray: Are you okay?
Ray: Did he hurt you?
Ray: Do you need me?
Ray: I love u. I'll come 4 u. No questions asked.
Ray: WOW! Really? I guess u love 2 b abused!
Ray: Does he taste as good as me?
Ray: I'm sorry! I didn't know! Please forgive me. Becca, I love you. I'm so haunted by your touch, your sounds. I dream about our lovemaking every night.
Ray: That's it? After all of these years, you're throwing me away? I've meant nothing 2 u? Well, I'll be waiting 4 when u come around to your senses. He'll hurt you!

Grayson deletes them all and blocks Ray's number so he can no longer call or text me.

"Let's go home," he says, and pats my leg. I get up and feel his arm back around my shoulder. He holds Morgan's hand and we head out to the car. But he is quiet all the way home.

"Aunt Hazel, Morgan is coming with us. She has the flu." Grayson winks. "Claudia, Becca won't be here for the next week. Please take her off the schedule. You can reach her by phone, email, and text if needed. Tanya, would you mind helping Morgan pack while Becca and I finish?" She nods.

He's barking out orders to get last-minute details situated, but I know what he's really up to. I head upstairs to his room. I undress myself and get on the bed. The door opens swiftly.

"Becca!" he yells, but then he sees me waiting for him. He slams the door shut and locks it. God, he's so angry. He pulls his sweater over his head and tosses it on the chair. He stares at me. *Daggers.* He undoes his belt and pants then heads toward me, stark naked and looking like a lion ready to pounce on its prey. I part my legs for him, and before I can think of nudging him with my knee, he's inside me. It's rough and harsh. I do my best to keep up, but I mostly just hold on for the ride, turn my head, and bury my face in his palm. I feel him slow down and he grits his teeth. I squeeze around him until he crashes onto my chest.

My body shakes with sobs, but he doesn't look at me. He just trails kisses down my chest to my belly. His tongue finds my navel. His hand explores my wetlands (previously known as my "Slip 'n Slide"). His fingers command my sobs to turn into moans. After several minutes, I'm saying my prayers with such conviction, I feel I should have the audience of a deeply moved congregation fanning themselves with one hand and praising Jesus with the other.

He gets up and pulls me with him to the shower. Once the water is running, he backs me up to the wall and kisses me with such passion my knees go weak.

I think this trip will be good. He can focus on work during the day, his family at night, and none of the other bullshit that's been going on here.

"I want Stacey out of here as well." He speaks . . . finally.

"I'll tell her," I say.

"I'm sorry. I'm all over the place today." He rubs my shoulders.

"I know. I think this trip will be good for us." I kiss his chest.

"Becca, if I said we'd have to move you guys out to California, what would you say?" He's staring straight ahead, blinking a million miles a minute.

"I'd say you are my home. Wherever you need to be is where we need to be." I cup his face to bring him to look at me. "I could start this up out there. I would do that, Grayson."

"Thank you. It may come to that, sweetheart." He closes his eyes.

"Okay, just let me know." I play with the stubble on his chin. He gives me a quick kiss and we finish our shower.

Once we're dressed and ready, he grabs my suitcase.

"Do you have everything you need?"

"Yes, but I'll have to do a little shopping out there. My summer clothes are too big." I tie my hair back.

"Okay. Let's go then." He sighs and we head downstairs.

In the lobby, Stacey runs up and grabs my arm.

"Becca! Annie's been hurt! Ray has her at the ER now."

Panic rises in me. Grayson's hand is crushing mine.

"What happened?"

"She fell out of a tree and her arm and leg are broken. Her belly hurts, too, so they're checking for internal bleeding. She's scared and is calling for you."

"Well, Stacey, you should go and tell her that I love her and I'm sorry I can't be there. We're leaving now." I look at Grayson.

"Becs, you're the only mother she's ever known!" she yells.

"I'm sure her grandmother is with her. That's the mother she should have there. I'm going with Grayson," I say again, and we head out to the car.

"Mom, Annie's afraid of heights. She wouldn't climb a tree for anything!" Morgan says.

"Yes, sweetie, I know. But Aunt Stacey does not realize I do. I'd say we're two for two, huh, baby?" I look at Grayson.

"Yes. And I think it's safe to say that we—you guys—are moving to California. I am not putting up with this shit any longer!"

"Daddy?" Morgan has tears in her eyes.

"Get in the car, sweetheart!" he snaps. She listens.

"Hey." I grab his arm. "I understand that you are pissed about many things right now, but please don't make comments like that in front of her and then snap when she gets upset."

"If you didn't go and act like a fucking whore, none of this would've happened!" he yells through his teeth. I feel my heart shatter into a million pieces.

GRAYSON

Oh no. No. No! What did I do? What did I say?

"Becca . . . Becca . . . please, sweetheart, I'm sorry!" I grab her face. "I'm having a bad day with all of this on top of everything else. Please get into the car. Please. I see that you want to run, and I'm begging you not to!" I kiss her face. "Please come with me." She closes her eyes and pulls my hands off of her face. Oh no. Oh God. Wait . . . she's getting in? She's getting in. I follow her. "Morgy, sweetheart, I'm sorry. I'm a little off today." I kiss her head.

The driver backs out of the parking space and heads down the long driveway. Becca sits quietly, staring out the window as we head to the airport. I grab her hand and bring it up to my mouth. I kiss her knuckles over and over again, silently continuing to beg for forgiveness.

"Mummsies, me thinks Daddsies would likes to gives you a kiss!" Morgan and her accents!

Becca starts giggling. She looks to me, and I waste no time.

"I'm so sorry. I love you," I say against her lips.

"Please, you have got to stop doing this to me. I know how you feel sometimes, but I need you to keep it to yourself. I don't know how much more I can take. I know you know how sorry I am about what happened," she whispers to me. Yes, I do know, and I'm so mad that I let it—him—get to me again. He knew I would read her texts, just like I did last night.

"I do. You're right. I really am sorry." I kiss her again and sit back. She lets me hold her hand for the remaining fifteen minutes it takes to get to the airport.

We climb out of the car and board my plane. Morgan grabs her favorite seat, and I take Becca's hand to give her a little tour.

"Can you just show me where the bathroom is?"

"It's right over here." I walk her down toward the back and open the door to bring her in. Her eyes widen.

"This is big for an airplane."

"Yeah, I hate plane bathrooms. This was the only thing I put in the design. The plane is small. My new plane will be ready in about a month. It's much bigger and will have a bedroom." She's so distant now. "Becca . . . I—"

"Grayson, can I have some privacy?" She cuts me off.

"Um . . . yes. Yes, of course." I nod and leave her to her business while I go and meet with Smitty, my captain.

"We should be in L.A. at 8 p.m. Pacific time. Weather will be good all the way." *Blah biddy blah, blah, blah.* I thank him and take my seat. Becca comes out and sits across from me. She buckles up and closes her eyes.

"Do you get nervous about flying?" Maybe that's it.

"No." She doesn't even look at me. Morgan glances over from her *Bop* magazine.

"Mommy flew planes, smaller ones, when she was a little girl."

"Really?" This woman never ceases to amaze me!

"Yes. When she was a little girl, my grandfather would take her out to the island to visit her aunt."

"Which island?" I ask.

"Uh, Long Island." I truly feel that she wanted to end that answer with a *duh*. "Anyway, they would go to the tiny airport there where you could pay to ride in a Cessna plane. Mommy called them 'chestnut planes' because that's what she thought they were saying." She giggles. "Well, the one woman pilot would take Mommy up in her plane and let her fly it once they were in the air. That's one of your favorite memories from when you were little, isn't it, Mommy?"

"Yes." Becca smiles, her eyes still shut.

"The lady told Grandpa that he should encourage Mommy to fly as she got older because she was a natural at only seven years old, right, Mommy?"

"Yes." Still smiling.

"She said that Mommy had just the right touch and was so confident. No nerves, like she'd been flying for twenty years. She wanted to be a pilot for a long time. But then her aunt moved back to Jersey and Mommy never flew a plane again. It's too bad, Mommy. I bet you would've been a great pilot." Morgan goes back to her magazine.

"Thanks, Morgan." Becca sighs, looks through her purse, and gets out a mint.

"That's fascinating, sweetheart. Why didn't your parents get you flying lessons?" I try to engage her.

"The rent was more important." She's flat.

"Um, does flying a plane still interest you?" I'm not giving up.

"I don't know. It seems all very advanced now. There's a big difference from the simplicity of thirty years ago." She takes a book out and starts reading. I breathe deeply to calm the anger that is brewing. Oh, we are having ourselves a bad day, the pair of us!

"What are you reading?" *You are not going to shut me down!*

"The latest by Jennifer Chiaverini." Flat and still reading.

"What's it about?" *I'll do this the whole way, sweetheart!*

"Well, I just started reading this one, but all of her books are based around quilters. I love them, especially the ones that take place years ago, during slavery. Some of the Underground Railroad stations used quilts that were actually maps to the next station. The runaway slaves would study them until they knew them by heart. This was a way to keep the station masters safe as well. It's all very interesting!" Her face lights up, just like it does when something is of huge interest to her.

"Have you ever gotten into quilting?" I don't want to lose her now.

"Well, I'd love too. I did try once, but I didn't stick with it. I'm not that great at sewing. Hazel tries to teach me, but by the time we get to it again, I've already forgotten what I had learned. I love quilts, though. They're so beautiful."

"Would you like to take quilting classes?" Mental notebook, ready for ideas.

"Yes. Eventually, I think I would. I'd like to make Morgan a wedding quilt for her hope chest." She glances over at our daughter.

"Well, does this book go back in time?"

"Um, not sure." She looks at the back. "No, I don't think so."

"Becca?"

"Yes?" She looks up just as the plane starts picking up speed on the runway. I watch her turn her head to glance out the window. A small smile appears across her lips as we ascend. She closes her eyes. She's remembering. It does still interest her! Mental note with several exclamation points! After a few minutes, we level out in the sky. She opens her eyes and wipes the corners of them. Why is she crying?

"Grandpa, Mom?" Morgan asks.

"Yes. Grandpa." She smiles. I sit back hard. Flying to her is like playing the piano to me. Her father . . . my mother . . . our favorite childhood memories. She looks down at her book. Morgan puts her iPod earbuds in.

"Becca?"

"Yes?" She looks up.

"Why are you sitting away from me?" I unbuckle, scoot forward in my chair, and put my hands out for her to hold.

"I don't know. I just sat here. I'm across from you—it's no big deal." She ignores my hands and goes back to her book. I rub my face in frustration and get up to sit next to her.

"Becca?" I start again.

"What?" she snaps. I take in another deep breath.

"Why did you cry earlier . . . in bed?" I whisper, just in case. "Did I hurt you?" I kiss her shoulder.

"Yes." She starts reading again. I take the book from her. "What, Grayson?" she asks, a thick layer of irritation in her voice.

"Becca, you were fine afterward. You didn't tell me it hurt."

"Do you know why I turned my head?"

"Because it was intense." Usual reason.

"No! Because you—" She's starting to cry again. She takes a deep breath. I glance up at Morgan to see if she's watching us, but she isn't. "You were looking at me with such disgust and hatred. I could almost tell what you were thinking. And then you confirmed it outside. You have never looked at me like that. Not in bed, at least, and certainly not while you were . . . well, you know. Now, can I have my book back? I would like to escape from my reality, please," she says through her tears.

"What? Escape? You are not a prisoner, Becca! You can leave anytime you want too!" I slap the book into her lap.

"That's not what I meant! Damn it, Grayson!" she yells, then gets up and heads to the bathroom.

"Daddy, please go after her." Morgan nudges me.

"Ugh, bloody hell!" I get up and bang on the door. "Becca, open up! Don't make me break the door in!" I yell. She unlocks it. Wow, that was easy. She's sitting on the toilet cover, crying into her hands. I stop inside and lock the door, then pull her up to me. I don't want to argue. I don't want to talk about feelings. I just want to kiss her. I just want to be lost in her. I move her fallen hair off of her neck and slowly kiss her there, savoring her taste. "Lift your arms up, sweetheart," I command. I want to pull off her shirt.

"No, I don't want to do this." She matches my calm.

"Arms up, Becca," I say again, and run my hands under her shirt. I unhook her bra and fill my hands with her. I gently roll and tug at her nipples as I bring my mouth over to her face.

"I said no, Grayson. I don't want to." She tries to push my hands off. "Stop it!" She shoves my shoulder as I lift her by her bum and press her against the wall. I go to kiss her, but she puts her hands up, blocking my face. I let her back down. She fixes herself. I want to ask her if it's over between us. That's what it feels like right now. But I'm afraid.

"I'm sorry, sweetheart." It's all I can say.

"Maybe you should just have that tattooed on your forehead so you don't have to say it so much!" she snaps.

"Good idea. Should I get that in black . . . or blue?" I try to get something out of her.

"How about green?" she suggests sarcastically.

"Green it is!" I smile. She doesn't bite. I open the door and wave toward it. "After you." She shoves past me.

"All better now?" Morgan looks up.

"No, little sweetheart. I've pretty much made a mess of things today. Maybe Mummy will go to sleep tonight and miraculously forget how much she hates me right now when she wakes up tomorrow," I say with sincere hope.

"Mommy loves you. Stop it." She slaps my leg. I glance at Becca for some indication of this. Nothing. Ugh, it's going to be a long flight. I turn the TV on to do something other than stare at Becca.

"Gray . . . Morgan . . . wake up." I hear Becca's voice and feel a slap on my knee.

I open my eyes. "What's wrong?"

"Nothing. We're here. I didn't want you guys to get startled by the landing." She puts her book away.

"Well, that's nice, love. Several hours ago I got the feeling you wanted to open the door and throw me off the plane." I try to rouse a smile. The one I get is slight, but it's quite the improvement.

"Be careful. I still might."

The landing is smooth. I shake Smitty's hand when he comes out of the cockpit and thank him for the nice flight. We head down to the car that is waiting for us.

Becca stares out the window with Morgan's head resting on her lap. We sit in silence for the half-hour journey to Calabasas.

"Becca, we're here." I reach forward and touch her cheek after noticing she's dozed off. Her skin is always so soft. She opens her eyes as we pull up to my gate. Sam keys the code in and we head up the long driveway to my Mediterranean-style ranch.

"This is all for just you?" Becca's eyes are wide as we drive around the fountain of my circular driveway and stop by the front door.

"Now it's for our family." I grab her hand and squeeze it. She just rubs Morgan's head. I let go and sit back. I'm really not sure of what to do here. I keep trying. "Morgy girl, wake up. We're home." I tap her knee. She sits up and smiles at the house. We climb out of the car and head in. Morgan heads straight to her room—the one she picked when we were here the last time—greeting the staff on the way there.

"Can I give you a tour?" I hold my hand out.

"I'm tired. Maybe tomorrow. Where did Morgan go?"

"To her bedroom."

"Where is it? I'll share her room with her." She starts to head down the hall.

"Becca?" I can hardly find my voice as I grab her arm.

"I don't want to do this tonight, Grayson. I'm very tired. I just want to go to sleep." She tries to pull out of my grip. I lean in toward her ear.

"Don't embarrass me. You will sleep in our room. I won't touch you," I say through gritted teeth. I'm really ready to lose my cool now.

"Fine." She sighs sharply. I lead her down the hall to our room.

Inside, it's lit by a hundred candles. Rose petals are everywhere and soft music plays in the background. Her silk nightie waits for her on its hanger. I'm immediately embarrassed—I forgot that I asked my staff to do this.

I was going to propose tonight. Properly, with a ring. It's not exactly how I wanted to do it, but I tried to make it as romantic as possible. This way, I could introduce her tomorrow. I guess I can scratch that off the list.

"I'm sorry. I had all of this done before I turned into a complete arsehole today," I stammer, watching her take it all in. My eyelids are wreaking havoc as she walks over to the Cristal and strawberries. She traces the cork with her finger and looks up at me.

"Can I have a glass?"

"Eh . . . uh, yes. Of course, sweetheart." Again, I stammer. I feel so nervous. I grab the bottle and pop the cork.

"I'm going to get changed," she says. I nod. "Which door?"

"The one on the right." I point. She smiles and I turn back to the champagne, but out of the corner of my eye, I see her take the nightie with her. Oh, I hope I can redeem my earlier behavior. I fill her glass as much as I can without being too obvious of my intent. Should I ask her tonight as planned? Should I do it before or after? *Grayson, don't get ahead of yourself! There may not be a before or an after.*

"This one mine?" Becca pipes up, startling me.

"Christ, sweetheart, I didn't even know you came in." I hand her the glass and look at her, instantly intoxicated by her beauty. Her hair is down and wavy, hanging over her shoulders. Her face is fresh and clean of all makeup. I love that about her. Most women do the opposite and glop more crap on. Her robe is open, and I can't help but let my eyes fall to her lovely breast.

She sips her Cristal and I place my hands on her hips because I love them . . . because I can't help myself. I lean down and smell her hair and neck. I feel her breathing become erratic. I circle around her, leaving my right hand on her stomach as I move her hair away from her neck with my left. My lips caress her neck.

"Grayson." She turns to me. "Why did you do all of this?" She looks around, then back at me when I palm her face. I shake my head and lean in for a proper kiss from her. It's been about eight hours, but if feels like a hundred years. She matches my passion, which ignites something so deep in me. Her stubbornness has been killing her, too! "Grayson, why?"

"Becca, I want . . . I need to make love to you." I lean in again.

"You didn't need to do all of this to be able to make love to me." Her eyebrow arches.

"Clearly today I did . . . or do, I should say. It's a welcome-home sentiment." It's a tiny lie.

"Oh." Flat. Disappointed. She was hoping for her ring. Which, by the way, should piss me off on a whole other level. But that's not really Becca's character, and I am done with us being pissy today.

"Theme song?" she muses.

"Huh? Oh. No. Becca, can we be done with talking now? It's really killing the moment, darling." She nods and her hands find my belt. I pull my shirt off. Her fingers admire my efforts at the gym. I help her robe to fall to the floor. My Funny Valentine pipes softly through the speakers.

"Frank?"

"Yes."

"I like Frank."

"Yes, me too, sweetheart." I pull one strap off her shoulder and kiss the skin I've uncovered. Becca giggles. "What's so funny?" My mouth explores across the top of her chest to her other shoulder.

"I remember him on *The Tonight Show Starring Johnny Carson.* Johnny said that a lot of people play his records when they want to make love. Then he waited and said something like 'I was just wondering . . . who do you put on?' It was very funny." She giggles more. Honestly—she has got to be fucking kidding me.

"Becca?"

"Yes."

"I love you, sweetheart, and I'm glad you got a kick out of Mr. Carson, but could you kindly shut the fuck up now? We are in the middle of something here." I almost cringe as I say it, but I honestly couldn't help myself. I pull away from her shoulder and look down into her eyes. I'm searching to see if my bluntness has gotten me into trouble. Becca bites her bottom lip to hold back a smile. She glances at my eyelids.

"Beep. Beep. Beep. Be-beep. Beep," she teases.

"Stop, sweetheart." I caress her lips with my thumb before I collect them with mine.

I pull the nightie's straps off and let it fall to the ground. My jeans and underwear follow suit. I walk over to the bed and pull the duvet back. Rose petals fly everywhere. I place my left hand on her right hip and lose my right hand in her hair as my mouth finds hers again. Slowly, I guide her onto the bed, our mouths never leaving one another's.

I pull away from the kiss and let my fingers caress her cheek as I stare into her eyes again. I'm so in love with her. I'm so in love with learning more about her, hearing about all of the things in her past that piece together who she is today. She's the most amazing woman I never even knew I was waiting for. How did I get so lucky?

"You are, indeed , very awesome," I say, and grasp her lips again as I enter her.

BECCA

What is he doing? I don't want to open my eyes. I know it's not time to get up yet—there's no alarm. *Oh my God, he's totally slipping a ring onto my finger!* I guess I'm so awesome, I don't require an actual proposal. Humph. No . . . wait, this may actually be brilliantly sweet. He already knows my answer. We've established that we are indeed getting married. Yes, okay, I totally love this! Should I nonchalantly stir in my sleep and wake to find a ring on my finger? No. I should wait a few minutes first. No . . . hmm. If I can't look at it yet, I want to at least feel what it looks like. He's still holding my hand kissing the ring. Is he chanting? Oh . . . he's praying (the usual way people pray . . . not our way). Shit. My eyes fill up. I nuzzle my head into his neck. He turns his head and kisses my cheek.

"Mmm . . . I love you," I whisper. He lets go of my hand and rubs my back. I quickly run my hand up under his pillow to meet my other hand so I can hug him and, well, check out the ring.

Grayson starts chuckling. "Copping a feel of your new ring, sweetheart?" I can't help but giggle.

"Oh, Grayson." I gasp when he slaps my bottom.

"First things first, then we'll have a look." He pulls me astride him, slaps me again, and enters me. I can't stand how wild he makes me feel.

By the powers invested in Grayson's hips, I now pronounce myself thoroughly shagged for the third time this evening. The twenty minutes I just endured were both pleasurable and torturous. I find myself wondering if sex is his superpower. Christ. Where does he get the energy? Then again, where am *I* getting the energy?

"Come. Let us see what we have here." He pats my bottom— my very sore bottom—and pulls himself up to turn on the light. It takes us both a few minutes to focus.

"Oh, Grayson, it's gorgeous!" I hold my hand up high, then out straight, then on his chest. It's beautiful from every angle.

"See, these three round diamonds represent you, me, and Morgan. Then the diamond ropes wrapping around them represent the intertwining of our lives. Do you like the design? I thought Neil did a great job." I look up at him. He sort of reminds me of a child who is excited about something, but isn't sure you will love it as much as they thought you would.

"I love it, Grayson. It's perfect. I love the sentiment. I love the antique look to it—it's classy and beautiful. It takes my breath away, just like you." I lean up and kiss him.

"I'm glad. I started working on the design with Neil a few weeks ago. I got it so fast because I told him I'd be introducing you to the world. He wanted to make sure his name was on that ring." He plays with it. I am overcome with tears—my usual reaction to everything lately. "Shh. What's the matter, sweetheart?" He looks worried.

"I just . . . I thought I hadn't gotten a ring yet because you didn't trust me, and here you were, trying to design it the entire time." I just shake my head in disbelief.

"I'm sorry you thought that, sweetheart, but did you honestly think I was just going to pop into the mall and pick out whatever looked good?"

"Um . . . yeah, that would be the normal thing to do." I smile and roll my eyes.

"And this," he pinches the ring, "is not normal?"

"Well, not the usual," I say.

"Oh, you want the usual? Have you met us yet? Hi, we're Grayson and Becca . . . not your usual sort. But if you want me to give this back and run to the mall, by all means." He goes to pull it off.

"No!" I slap his hand.

"No?" He asks.

"No." I shake my head.

"Well, come on, love. We have to get up in five hours." He turns off the light and scoots back down. I nuzzle into his neck again and plant a kiss there. "You know, it's official," he says softly.

"What's that?" I close my eyes.

"I'm going to be slapping this fantastic bum well into our nineties!" He slaps me hard for emphasis.

"Oh God, baby, please stop now." He's been slaphappy tonight, and not in the way that word is defined.

"Yes, sweetheart." He kisses my head and I'm off to dreamland after he chuckles at me for asking who the fuck Neil is. Apparently, he's the jeweler to the stars. I guess I've got a lot to learn about who's who out here in La-La Land!

Chapter Sixteen

It's seven in the morning and I can hear the buzz going on in the house. Grayson needs to be at his office in an hour for his public relations meeting. I'm not quite sure about all these little fires he has to put out. I've seen him on the phone over the past month handling things—or so I thought.

I climb out of bed and join him in the shower. *Damn, he is quite the sight.* Oh, wow, he has one of those showers where there are five million heads coming out of the wall. I foresee many hours of my future eaten away by me just standing there, letting wasted water pelt away my stress. I walk in and move my hands up his back to his shoulders. He's tense. Christ. One would think that, after last night, he'd be so relaxed he'd seem drugged.

"Hey, baby, you okay?" I turn him toward me.

"I'll be all right, sweetheart. I just have to save my company today. No big deal, really." He tries to smile.

"Gray, how can so many problems arise in five weeks? I really can't understand this." Maybe I should be Googling . . . no. I shouldn't have to Google my own fiancé!

"Well, I haven't been on top of my game lately. I guess I just got sick of all the bullshit, and I loosened my grip on the reigns a bit. I am back, though, and ultra-focused. With very good reason, of course." His smile finally widens.

"What can I do? I'm ready to help in any way I can." I wrap my arms around his waist and look up into his chocolate-brown eyes.

"Sweetheart, I told you what I need from you." He smirks and slaps my ass. That's it? That's all I'm good for? I feel the steam rising—and it's not from the shower! "What?" He lifts my chin. "Sweetheart, the only thing you can do is to be supportive and encouraging and, for heaven's sake, try not to get mad at me every two minutes!" He laughs at this, which, of course, makes me mad. "Please, Becca. I just need to get lost in your love after work. And I don't mean only sex, so stop looking at me that way and give me a kiss, please."

I comply (how unusual). Normally, one thing would lead to another, but this morning is not the time for that.

"What time will you be home?" I try to get us focused.

"I don't know. Not soon enough. I just want to be with you. When you were mad on the plane yesterday, I missed you terribly. I thought you were going to say it was over. You've never fought me off before. Not like that. You wouldn't even kiss me." He furrows his brow and looks down, avoiding eye contact. He looks so vulnerable to me right now.

"I'm sorry you felt that way, but you really hurt me." My heart was shattered, but I don't tell him that.

"Why . . . what made you come with me?"

"Because 'I belong to your life,'" I giggle, reciting his first theme-song moment. "I reminded myself of what you said in the mall. I knew that between the stress of work and Ray, you had a momentary lapse of intelligence."

"You mean judgment?"

"*No*. Intelligence!"

"Why did you have a change of heart last night?" His thumb runs over my bottom lip.

"I realized you put a lot of thought into the room, and I needed to stop being mad. I didn't want to ruin all your hard work. I . . . um . . . I . . . uh, Gray, I . . . oh, forget it!" I stop talking and give in to his kisses.

Now, some people like to sing in the shower, but Grayson and I . . . we like to pray! *All Sybeccas are on deck, with thoroughly fucked hair, disheveled robes, and smiles on their faces. Praise Jesus!* It's a quick but very powerful prayer.

"Oh, Becca, why can't I get enough of you?" His breath is heavy as he allows my body to slide down his. We finish—or, uh, *start*—our shower, then head out to the bedroom after drying off.

"So, after discussing things with Carol, early this morning—"

"Do you two ever sleep?" I ask, trying to figure when he talked to her.

"No, not really." He smirks. "Anyway, we've decided to get some other things wrapped up before I introduce you to the press."

"What things?" I pull clothes out of my suitcase.

"Nothing for you to worry about, love." He pats my bottom.

"Should I just stick around here today?" I ask as I get dressed. It's a bittersweet moment when my favorite pair of shorts makes me look like I'm going for the "gangsta look." Only a few months ago, I was fighting to get these puppies buttoned.

"From the looks of those shorts, I'd say no. You're gonna go shopping!" He grabs the waistband and looks a little concerned. I still find this very interesting and comical—it's so completely opposite of the norm. I mean, it's not like these shorts are a size two. They are a twelve, and I was busting out of them! He's sort of ruining my inner "woo-hoo" dance. Suddenly, the CD changes in my head and I laugh. He smiles. "What?"

"Uh . . . Sir Mix-A-Lot got sent to my head instead of yours." I start to sing. "I like big butts and I cannot lie . . . " Grayson rolls his eyes and shakes his head at me.

"I don't like *big* butts." He stretches his arms out for emphasis. "I like your butt. And, actually, I do favor these shorts for easy-access purposes." He grabs my bum and demonstrates.

"You're going to be late, Mr. James!" I pull away.

"Well, I doubt I'll get fired for it, sweetheart. I mean . . . it is my company." He bites his bottom lip, stifling a mischievous smile.

"Focus, Mr. James. And put a damn shirt on so I can focus around here, too!" I slap his chest. He groans disapprovingly, then palms my face and smacks his lips against mine. He finishes getting dressed and I turn on my phone. Of course, I'm greeted by the now-dreadful ping of texts. Actually, my phone sounds as if it will explode between the texts, voicemails, and emails. I don't even turn around. I hold my phone over my head and, just as predicted, Grayson tears it from my grasp. I'm left to ponder who is worse: The Possessor, The Stalker, or The Betrayer?

I turn to find Grayson lying on his stomach and looking at my cell. I settle in next to him to see what kind of shit I'm going to have to deal with today.

"Voicemail was from Aunt Hazel; we forgot to call her. Texts are from Stacey and your Aunt Tess, both asking if we made it here all right. And emails, let's see . . . junk. Junk. Girl Scouts. Junk. Oh, here we go! I was beginning to get disappointed. Raymond, how lovely to hear from you!" Nothing like making a sarcastic comment to a cell phone.

"Are you sure you don't want to check the Girls Scouts email first?" I give my own sarcasm a whirl.

"You know, sweetheart, you did give me your phone." He tries to be terse, and it makes him seem extra British. Yum.

"Uh, did I have a choice?" I let my finger trace his jawline.

"No, but you still gave it to me."

"I've given you a lot of things, Grayson."

"Stop distracting me." He pulls back on the smile that was forming. *Yes, we must be serious now!*

To: Becca Campbell

From: Raymond McNeil

Date: November 3, 2012

Dear Becca,

I'm sorry. I'm not very proud of the way I've been acting. Because of me, you weren't there for Annie when she really needed you. I know you sent your love and that meant a lot. Annie has a broken leg, arm, and two cracked ribs. It was a nasty fall! She fell through the floor of a new friend's tree house. Thankfully, there was no internal bleeding!

Becca, you're my best friend, and I miss you terribly! Yes, I wish things were different and that you were in my bed instead of his, but that aside, I miss my best friend. I know I've been a jerk, but you need to think about something. You didn't even give me the courtesy of pulling me aside and telling me you had made your decision. You texted me that morning saying that you loved me, then told me a few hours later that I broke your heart because I was mad at you for being with him again. You kissed me with so much passion my knees went weak! A few hours later, Grayson told me of the revised plan, went upstairs, and you practically knocked me down to get to him! I ran upstairs to make sure everything was okay, and I heard you two going at it.

Now, think about all that. Can you see why I've kind of gone crazy? How could you disrespect me like this? I've been by your side for almost five years, waiting for you to "come around." Patiently, I might add. How could you treat me like this, like I don't matter, like our entire relationship over the past five years meant nothing? I'm sorry for my behavior since that day, Becca. Are you sorry for yours?

I miss you terribly, and I love you with all of my heart. No matter what. Please don't block me out of your life, Becca.

Please don't block Annie.

    Love always,

    Ray

    P.S. Grayson, please let her read this!

"What do you think about that?" I ask after clearing my throat.

"I think that you should extend him the courtesy of a reply because you did indeed behave that way, and it's only fair. But then, Becca, you're done—at least until we are certain he has moved on. Okay, sweetheart? Oh, and when you're done emailing him, please block him." He hands me the phone and kisses my cheek before he gets up. "Becca, do you understand me?" Now he's terse.

"Yes, Gray." I understand his reasoning, but it still seems a little harsh to me. This Ray, the one who emailed, is my friend, and I love and miss him, too. I feel terrible that I did this to him. I never even thought about it. I guess some of Grayson's selfishness has rubbed off on me.

"Becca—are you crying?" He seems aggravated.

"Yes." I look to him. His jawline is going at it again, and his eyelids match the beat of the twitch.

"Why?" he snaps, and puts his cuff links on.

"I hurt my best friend and didn't even think about it."

"Please do as I say. I don't need any of this shit while I'm out here. I have enough to worry about without the theatrics of Ray Mc-Neil adding to it!" He fidgets with his collar. I get up and help him.

"I love you, Grayson. You are the one for me. Please don't worry." I pull him to me. He searches my eyes—for the truth, I think. His face softens and his lips fall to mine, gently caressing them.

"I love you too, sweetheart. I'll call you later."

"Okay." I hug him.

"Block him, or I will, Becca."

Like he has to remind me. I grab my laptop as Grayson heads to the door. I can feel his stare as he walks out. I lay on the bed, open my laptop, and click on the email icon. I hit reply on Ray's email and stare at a blank screen.

To: Raymond McNeil
From: Becca Campbell
Date: November 4, 2012

Dear Ray,
I'm sorry I hurt you. I've been terribly selfish and irresponsible in handling this whole situation. I will never forgive myself for the way I treated you.

And then I delete everything. Ray has not been himself. I want to say this stuff to him, but not by email. I can't trust him not to leak these emails out. I don't want to say anything he could use to confirm what he said. Grayson is getting ready to announce our engagement to the world.

So I block him. I lay on the bed and have myself a good cry, because it's not like me to be this cold. I just can't take the chance that he'll use this to publicly humiliate Grayson.

"Sweetheart?" Gray sits on the bed. I didn't even realize that he came back into the room.

"Yes?" I look up and wipe my tears away. He glances from me to the laptop. "I didn't email him. I started to but, then I thought, *what if he leaks the emails?* I don't want you to have another fire to put out so, I just blocked him." As I'm telling him this, I get a funny feeling that he already knows I blocked Ray.

"I thought of that, but I didn't want to ask you not to respond. I didn't think it would be very fair of me. I know it was hard for you, and it does mean a lot to me that you did that." He kisses the top of my head. "Now, come, let's have some breakfast before I go." He holds out his hand to help me up. We make our way down to the kitchen.

The walls in the main corridors are a warm amber color. The door frames are made from dark wood, which enhances the rustic appeal of this Mediterranean-style home. There are several framed pieces of artwork along the wall. I recognize most of them as Renoir, my favorite artist. I'm not familiar at all with the others—maybe they're by local artists. I'm not sure.

"What's upstairs?" I ask, remembering the fancy staircase we passed on our way in last night.

"Oh, that just leads to my office. It's the only part of the house with a second level." He looks over his shoulder. "Sorry I haven't given you a complete tour yet." He smiles thoughtfully as we walk into the kitchen—a huge gourmet kitchen. Not only am I in love, I'm completely jealous. "All yours, sweetheart," he whispers in my ear as he comes up behind me and wraps his arm around my waist.

I think I might come undone, looking at it all. The creamy off-white cabinets are inviting—comforting, if you will. I almost feel as if I'm in a completely different house. I thought there would be all dark cabinetry in here, but instead, it's a much lighter atmosphere. The detailed woodworking and French-lace knobs are perfect.

Against the back wall, cushioned by the cabinets, is a restaurant-style stainless steel stove. There are double wall ovens to the left of it, just before the archway to another room. The left wall of the kitchen hosts two large windows above a very large Fireclay Farmhouse sink. The cream-based granite countertop stretches to the wall on either side of the sink. To the right are more cabinets and granite, leading up to the stainless steel wine fridge . . . the huge, "ready to party when you are" wine fridge. *All Sybeccas get on their knees and bow to the almighty wine fridge.*

Smack-dab in the middle of the kitchen is an oversized island in dark cherrywood. The color picks up the dark specks in the countertops. A bronzed metal chandelier hangs over it. Yes, I can see myself spending many a happy hour in this very room!

"What would you like to eat?" I ask as I open the massive fridge on the right side of the stove. Its French doors are paneled to match the cabinets.

"Uh, sweetheart, I have staff for that. Come sit down." He leads me over to the small kitchen dinette. Its creamy legs and cherry top complement the room well. "Susanna will make you whatever you'd like," he adds as he pulls out a chair for me.

"Right . . . of course you do! You have 'people.'" I tease him.

"No. *We* have people." He holds up my ringed hand. I admire it again. It is beautiful.

An older woman walks in. She's dressed as if she's heading out for yoga (kind of how I look most of the time).

"Oh, good morning, Grayson . . . Ms. Campbell," she says.

"Becca, please," I smile.

"This is Susanna, sweetheart."

"Nice to meet you, Susanna." I quickly reach for one of the plates she's taking out of the warmer. *Totally love this kitchen!* She's a little taken aback by my offer, but allows me to take mine as she brings Grayson his.

I catch Grayson's boyish grin as she pats his shoulder. He glances at me quickly. He seems proud of himself for something as he opens his napkin and places it on his lap.

I look down at my Greek omelet. It's filled with spinach, feta cheese, onions, tomatoes, and black olives, and I feel as if I may have an unexpected drooling accident. Just in case, I raise my napkin to my mouth before placing it in my lap. Susanna places a side of crispy bacon next to my plate and pours me a cup of coffee.

"Pumpkin?" I stare at her in amazement as the sweet aroma greets my nostrils.

"It's fall, sweetheart. All pumpkin, all the time, right?"

I flash him my pearly whites and dive in to my omelet. I think I may be having my second orgasm of the morning.

"Oh my God, Susanna, this is the most delicious omelet I've

ever had!" *I think I just moaned.* Everything is so fresh, light, and powerful.

"Thank you, Becca." She smiles at me over her shoulder. "While I have you here, do you know what you and Morgan would like for lunch?" She's very busy cleaning the already immaculate kitchen. Her OCD, I decide, is the perfect match to my ADD.

"Um, probably this again . . . it's so good!" I take in another mouthful. Grayson glances over at me and a smile hits his eyes as I do my happy dance. It's slight, a little dance I do in my chair whenever I'm eating something I really love. I never even realized I did it until Grayson pointed it out a few weeks ago.

"Susanna, she'll have grilled chicken salad and Morgan will probably want your—"

"Pizza bagels," Susanna finishes. "And to drink?"

"Diet ginger ale, with a splash of cranberry in it." It still amazes me. How does he know what I'll want? I don't even know. I don't think he's ever seen me drink diet ginger ale with cranberry, but I do like it!

"Theme song?" He arches an eyebrow and gives me a crooked smile.

"Huh? Oh no, I'm just fascinated by how you seem to always know what I like and want." I take another bite.

"Feeling's mutual, sweetheart." His voice is soft and seductive. He shoots me an air kiss to confirm my suspicions. He's not talking about food.

"Good morning, Susanna!" Morgan runs into the kitchen and into Susanna's arms. I pull my eyes away from Grayson's thoughtful stare to watch Morgan and Susanna.

"Good morning, sweetie. I'm so happy to have you back here! Would you like your favorite?" Morgan nods. "I thought you might. Go have a seat. It will only take me a few minutes." She kisses her forehead. Suddenly, I think she remembers that I'm in the room. She looks up at me, unsure of how I will respond to her familiarity with my daughter. I smile, and she relaxes.

"Sweetheart, hurry up. I need to debrief you quickly before I leave." Grayson doesn't even look up from his cell phone as I bring my attention back to him. He's keying in something. Hmm, I wonder what's going on. "Morgy, be good for Susanna and Mummy today. Susanna, let Sam know I'll probably be about another fifteen minutes." He stands up.

"Grayson, you're already cutting it close." Susanna looks at the clock.

"Yes, but this matter can't be put off," he says quickly, and reaches for my hand.

We move hastily down the long hall to his—our—room. He pulls me in, shuts the door, and locks it.

"Is something up?" I ask, feeling a bit nervous.

"Yes, something is definitely up!" He grabs me and attacks my lips.

"Grayson, wait . . . you said you had to debrief me." As I say it, my shorts come right down.

"That's exactly what I'm doing, sweetheart." He chuckles lightly as he kisses me again and dances me back to the bed.

"Grayson, you can't keep avoiding the situation at work." I try, but my efforts are futile as he unzips and lowers his pants.

"Yes, darling, but a situation's come up at home that needs my immediate attention."

"Is that so, Mr. James?" I smirk and lay back on the bed.

"Yes." He rotates his finger in the air to tell me to flip. "Sorry, sweetheart, it's going to be a bit of a 'wham bam, thank you ma'am' situation." For my compliance, I get an ass slap before I am brought up to speed on the situation at hand.

Horny Sybecca's the only one left to come forward for morning prayers. Her lipstick is smeared and the heel of one of her shoes is broken. She limps away after Grayson finishes his last pump.

"Christ, Becca! I can't keep my bloody hands off of you!" He almost sounds angry about this.

"Grayson, you need," I stop to catch my breath, "to go to work. If nothing else, my body needs a break." I am sore beyond comprehension. I attempt to get off of the bed.

"Becca, you okay?"

"Yeah." The room spins and I lose my balance a bit. Grayson gasps and grabs me.

"Jesus H. Christ, Becca!"

"I'm fine." I grip his upper arms to stabilize myself. "I just got up too quickly." I kiss him. "Come on, honey. Pull yourself together. You have to go." I help him tuck his shirt into his pants.

"I'll call you later. Your credit card is on the dresser there." He nods toward it before giving me five kisses on my lips. He heads to the door and opens it halfway. He lingers there, staring at me, before he nods and leaves. I finish putting myself back together and go to head out myself.

Your credit card is on the dresser there. Grayson's words repeat in my mind. Oh, yeah. I go back to the dresser to find my very own Black AmEx. Huh? I pick it up. It says Becca K. James on it. Uh, how? Um. All righty then. I grab my purse and toss the card into one of its pockets for now. I turn on my heels to head out again. My phone rings as I reach for the door. It's Gray.

"Did you forget something, baby?"

"No."

"What's the matter?"

"Nothing. I just wanted to hear your voice. I love you, Becca." I can almost hear his eyelids.

"Everything is going to be fine. I believe in you." I give him a kiss over the phone and head down the hall to see if Morgan's done.

"Thank you, sweetheart. I'll call you later. Bye."

"Bye, baby." I hang up and find Morgan eating blueberry crepes.

"That looks delicious." I kiss her head and look to where I was sitting. *Damn it.* The rest of my omelet is gone!

"Becca, you were pulled away and I wasn't sure if you were finished. I have the rest of your plate in the warmer." Susanna points as she starts to head over.

"Susanna, I think I love you already!" Honestly, I could give this woman a huge hug. She laughs and brings it over. It's kind of sad that I'm this excited over an omelet, but it is *so* good! "Why don't you sit down and eat with us?" I pull out a chair.

"Oh, Becca. Thank you, but I've already eaten in the staff kitchen." Staff kitchen? *Fuck.* Well, I have a "staff kitchen" at my inn. Of course, I am the "staff," and it is the *only* kitchen. I guess my point doesn't really have a point. *Fuck.*

"Well, sit and have some coffee or tea. Take a break!" I pat the seat.

"I told you so!" Morgan says to Susanna.

"Told her what so?" I look to Morgan.

"I told her that when you're here, you'll probably end up cooking for her. And you would never see yourself as above her because you work in hospitality, too. I don't think she believed me." Morgan takes her last bite and then sucks down the rest of her milk.

"Oh, Morgy, I didn't say I didn't believe you." Susanna blushes. She's an attractive older woman with salt-and-pepper hair—more pepper than salt still—pulled back in a short ponytail. She has gorgeous olive skin, and not a single wrinkle that I can see. Blue eyes so deep they're almost violet. She's thin with the exception of her pot belly, which, incidentally, is a terrible way to describe a stomach! I'd say she doesn't have any more than twenty years on me, and that's going by the hair. She could be younger.

"Come and sit, then." I wave her over. She's hesitant at first, but she gives me an *oh, what the heck?* look and has a seat. "Coffee or tea?" I ask and get up.

"Oh, stop, I have some already. I'll get my mug."

"Morgan, please go—"

"I got it!" Morgan cuts me off and hops up.

"So, you and Grayson seem to have a close relationship," I start, not lending any time to awkwardness.

"Oh, Becca, it's completely professional." She looks uncomfortable.

"Wait, no," I say. "Before you even bother, I just meant that I can see that you are friends as well. You care about each other." I touch her hand.

She looks at my hand on hers, then back up to my face. "Grayson is right. You really are a rare breed." She places her free hand on top of mine.

"Well, that's the pot calling the kettle black, aye?" I giggle, and she can't help but join me.

Morgan brings out Susanna's coffee and announces she's going to find the video-game room.

"Uh, he has a room just for video games?" I wonder aloud. I have one of those, too. I simply call it "Morgan's bedroom."

"Oh, that's what Morgan calls it, but it's actually the rec room. There are a bunch of things in there. Grayson and my husband, Sam, usually play pool in there a few nights a week." I can tell she's at ease now. I'm glad.

"Sam—the driver—yours?"

She nods. "Yes. As a matter of fact, I'm meant to tell you that he will be bringing you shopping today when he gets back from dropping Grayson off."

"Yikes! Lucky him." I roll my eyes. She laughs.

"How did you know I'd like this omelet?" I take my last bite—sadly, I might add.

"Grayson texted what you wanted this morning." I laugh. "What?" she asks.

"He never asks me what I want. He just orders for me. Funny thing is, he will order exactly what I'm looking at, or he'll just pick what he somehow knows I will like it. It's crazy! I have never had a Greek omelet in his presence before." I'm passionate about this.

Five weeks later, it still amazes me.

"Well, I can tell you, he's never done that with one of his regulars." As she says it, her eyes widen in alarm.

"Regulars? You mean girlfriends, or ..." Or what? *Why would you say "or," Becca?*

"Uh, no, there weren't, um, girlfriends. I've never known him to get serious with anyone. That is, until you. I've never seen him in love before. He knows what you want and what you will like because he's interested in everything about you. Those other girls—" she starts laughing. It's my turn to give her a puzzled look. "Oh, every once in a while, one of them would get on my nerves acting like she was the 'mistress' of the house. Bossing me around and everything. I'd lay into him and tell him he needs to stop wasting his time on these girls. To go and find himself a real woman, a good girl who wouldn't put up with his crap—but would love him like hell." She sips her coffee. "He'd say, 'But Susanna, you're already married!'" I laugh with her. "Then I'd tell him, 'You'll find her. You won't be looking and *bam*! Cupid will shoot a big fat arrow into your ass!' And he said, 'Well, in the meantime, I shall continue to practice on these shallow women so that I never disappoint this good girl who's coming.'" I roll my eyes and laugh with her, but I kind of feel sad. I haven't exactly been the good girl Susanna was thinking of.

"Well, I finally convinced him to visit his Aunt Hazel. With all of the trouble that was going on here, he needed to get away. The first day he was there, he called me and said, 'Bloody hell, Susie! I believe that fat, diapered, winged bastard hit me straight in the arse. I'm mad, I tell ya!' Then he went on talking and talking about you." She clasps her hands and shakes them. It reminds me of Hazel—she does that.

"You ever notice he talks in rhymes and doesn't realize it?" I giggle.

"All the time," she agrees. "Well, I knew it was extremely serious, because two days later a new bed arrived for his room." She taps the table for emphasis, just like Grayson and Hazel.

"Why would a new bed mean anything?" *Huh?*

"Um, because the one he was tossing was only a week old, but he had company before he left." Table tap. Come to think of it, that is *so* Grayson. My bed is new, but ever since I slept with Ray in it, we have stayed in his room.

"He's never just randomly changed beds before? Maybe it wasn't comfortable," I offer.

She shakes her head. "It was the same exact model."

"Oh. Well, he sure doesn't lack confidence, huh?" I let my eyes do the giggling. Arrogant bastard!

"Most things, no." She smiles.

"Susanna, what's going on with his company? He hasn't told me too much, but it seems like a lot more then he lets on." I am very worried about him, especially after his phone call this morning.

"That's right. He told me you won't Google him. You didn't even know who he was! I joke with Sam that you had Grayson at, 'Who the hell are you?' He's not really used to that. As far as his company, you either have to Google him or ask him. It's not my place to tell you." She pats my hand. I nod with disappointment, but I understand.

We continue our conversation for the next twenty minutes, branching out to my bed-and-breakfast and her two sons, Matteo and Luca. Both boys are away at out-of-state colleges. Matteo is becoming a software engineer, and Luca is trying to find himself—and taking every girl he can along for the ride. Susanna cracks me up. I already love her!

The house phone buzzes and Susanna gets up for it. "Yes? Hi, Sam. Yup, I'll let her know. Love you too! Bye-bye then." She hangs up and turns to me. "Sam is waiting for you and Morgan. I'd better get back to work. You have fun . . . you dear, dear girl!" She hugs me. *Yeah, I'm in!* She pages Morgan over the intercom system, asking her to meet me at the front door. *Sweet!* I could definitely get used to this house. I grab my purse and head down to the front door to meet Morgan.

Sam is very pleasant and, like Susanna, has built quite the rapport with Morgan already. He brings us to the first store and tells me to ask for Erica. This happens for the next four stores. After the fifth store, I tell Sam I've had enough and to please bring us home. Morgan checked out two stores ago!

"Well, Grayson has three more stores he would like you to go to," Sam says uncomfortably.

"Did he say it was extremely important for me to go to them?" I really just can't.

"Well, no."

"Then please, Sam, I'm tired and I'm hungry. I need to go home."

"Yes, Becca."

Ah, finally. *Ping!* I grab my phone and hit the cloud.

November 4, 2012   1:18 p.m.

Gray: Why R U going home and why haven't U bought anything?

Me: I'm tired. How do U know? What? I bought a shitload of stuff!

Gray: I've got people ☺ I have no alerts of you buying anything.

Me: Maybe your people don't care about what I buy. BTW, how R U?

Gray: No, Becca, I'm not getting any alerts from AmEx. Done. Mentally that is.

Me: You can do that? Well, I didn't use that card. I'm sorry it's been a rough day ☹

Me: When will you come home?

Gray: Why didn't you use that card? Oh Becca, Becca, Becca!

I'll be home late. Wait up!

Me: Let me know when u r leaving and I'll fix u something to eat.

Gray: I promise to chew slowly ;-p

Me: And savor the taste . . . ☺

Gray: Mmm ...

Me: I love you and I miss you! XXXXX

Gray: Love u 2 Sweetheart! XXXXX

GRAYSON

God! I want Sam to come and bring me home as well! It's two in the afternoon and my day is nowhere near getting ready to slow down. So many interviews, all with the same tedious questions over and over again. *Were you tipped off? Do you think they have a case? If you're not guilty, where have you been? Are you selling the company? How do you feel about Ethan McCaw's departure? Have you written anything new? What do you see for the future of GBM Records? Are you going bankrupt? Blah. Blah. Bibbity blah blah blah* . . . ugh, I can't stand it!

I get mad at Becca sometimes for not knowing about any of this crap that's going on. But then again, a part of me is glad she doesn't. After talking about it all day with these imbeciles, I most definitely do not want to discuss it at home. She has to know, though. She's going to get hammered with most of these questions, and it wouldn't be fair for her to get railroaded like that. Plus, it would be embarrassing. For both of us.

I better tell her about Mackenzie and her false claims before she hears about it elsewhere. As soon as the amniocentesis is done, that'll be squared away. It's not the first time some woman I've slept with has tried to claim me as the father to her child. Thanks to Becca, it will certainly be the last!

"Grayson." Carol interrupts my thoughts, "Your next interviewer is here."

"Yay." My voice is dry. Carol offers me a sympathetic smile.

Tyler from the BBC walks in. He's going to be all, *Hallo, mate! How ya been?* like we've been friends forever and plan to go out for a pint after. Then the bloody camera will turn on and he'll turn into Barbara bloody fucking Walters, trying to make me cry!

"Hallo, mate!" he says. Oh, Christ! Is his P.A. too terrified of him to give him a goddamn mint? His breath smells as if he has already eaten someone's arse! Honestly, did he eat a shit sandwich for lunch? I'm British, for God's sake—I already make faces that look as if I smell shit. Now I'm going to look like a real aristocratic arsehole!

"Hallo!" *You fake bastard!* I give him a good manly handshake and a huge smile that says, *Kiss my arse.* "Hold on a minute, mate." I pull out my phone.

November 4, 2012   1:59 p.m.

Me: Carol, please bring mints in here and encourage Mr. Riggins to have 1. TY.

Me: Priceless, sweetheart! The man interviewing me has shit-sandwich breath! What is a disgusted Brit to do? ☹

Becca: Turn that frown upside down. Don't let the people know you're smelling the brown! XXXXX

I'm literally laughing out loud. She's teased me about how I frown when I talk sometimes. Actually, she teases me terribly about it, yet she loves that I do it. I wish I was home with her instead of here.

Me: TY for giving me the courage to smile. ☺ XXXXX

Becca: YW. Just don't let him talk shit! And if he has shitty questions, call him on it! XXX

Me: Our conversation has really gone to the shitters! XXXXX
Becca: Stop texting now and give Shit Breath your full attention, please! XXXXX

"Sorry, mate!" Apparently talking to my fiancée about shit for five minutes is more interesting than talking to you! Good thing people can't read your mind.

Carol walks in to save the day, only to have Tyler politely decline. He opens his mouth to show her he already has one. I fight the childish urge to pull out my phone and update Becca on this latest shocking development! Instead, I grab a mint so I can try to nonchalantly blow peppermint up my nose.

The cameras go on, and he's off . . . right into serious mode. Thank God for this Altoid burning the fuck out of my tongue, or I'd probably be laughing.

Same questions . . . surprise, surprise! "Well, Tyler, as you know, I am not allowed to discuss the specifics of the case. What I can tell you is I have no reason to be concerned. I was visiting family and falling in love." You're in love? Is Grayson James off the market?

"Yes and yes." I smile. For good?

"Yes. I am engaged."

"Becca."

"No, I'm not going bankrupt."

"No, not selling."

"Yes, I have been writing."

The same questions. The same answers. This continues for the entire day.

It's half past nine and I'm done . . . finally! Sam brings the car around. I call Becca.

"Hey, baby! How are you?" I can hear her shuffling things around in the background.

"Same. Happy now that I'm on my way home to you." I loosen my tie.

"Hungry?"

"Starved. For many things, sweetheart." I close my eyes and think about holding her.

"Well, you'll be home in no time, baby. Let me go so I don't burn your dinner." I hear sizzling.

"What's my dinner?" It's so nice to come home to a woman who loves me and wants to take care of me.

"You'll see. Love you!"

"Love you." I hang up and call my tech guy, Chris.

"Hey . . . well?"

"Nothing all day."

"What about the other two?"

"Well, you guys were right. I'll have that pulled up for you tomorrow."

"Thanks, Chris!"

"Yep!" We both hang up. I close my eyes. Damn, I'm wiped.

"We're here," Sam says. As soon as he stops the car, I hop out with a new sense of purpose. I walk through the door and head right for the kitchen.

I lean up against the doorframe and watch her plate my dinner. She's in a silk robe with, I'm sure, a matching nightie underneath. She spoons some sort of cheese out carefully. So full of love in everything she does.

I walk up behind her, place my hands on her hips, and smell her hair. Her breath catches. I love that I affect her like this.

"What's for dinner, love?" I move her hair and kiss her neck.

"Um . . . steak gorgonzola salad. Is that okay?" She looks up at me.

"Smells lovely. Thank you, sweetheart." I caress her lips with mine. She pulls me closer to deepen the kiss. God . . . this is the best place in the world.

"Come and eat, baby." She grabs my plate and the glass of red wine she's already poured for me. I follow her to the table and take a seat. The salad looks nice enough to be pictured in a magazine.

"You don't want it? I can make something else for you." She looks at me with a bit of disappointment.

"I do want it. It just looks so perfect and beautiful. I hate to eat it." I smile up at her and watch her frown dissipate. A small smile pushes her shy dimple into view. You'd never know she had one. Only certain facial expressions showcase it.

"Baby, eat." She nudges my hand lightly. I place a forkful into my mouth. An explosion of flavor hits me that, quite frankly, I was not expecting.

"Oh, Becca. This is delicious, sweetheart!" I would've said that even if it was crap, but it is divine. I am in culinary heaven!

"Thank you. I'm glad you like it." She leans on her hand.

"Talk to anyone today?" I ask, but of course, I already know.

"Hazel. Everything is fine. Ship is smoothly sailing." She waves her free hand. I can see it kind of bothers her. I'll talk to her about it tomorrow. She tells me that she and Susanna have become fast friends. This makes me so happy to hear. I take my last few bites. A little quicker than I normally eat, but I want to get to relaxing with Becca. She gets up and grabs my dish as I wipe my mouth. She plants a kiss on the top of my head before she walks the dish over to the sink.

"Leave the dishes, sweetheart." I sigh as I hear the water running. I stand up and wait for her to comply. *Good girl!* I hold my hand out to her as she walks back to me. We lace our fingers and head down the hall to the family room to lounge on the couch.

I lay my head back and close my eyes. Becca stands behind me and rubs my shoulders and neck.

"You're so tense, baby." She sighs and tries to work out a knot.

"C'mere, sweetheart." I pat her hand. She comes over to me. "Sit astride me, love." She does. I lean forward, placing my head on her chest and holding her to me tightly. I breathe in the sweet, calming smell of my future wife. This is where I've wanted to be all day. I love feeling her play with my hair. She's so comforting.

After a few minutes, I bring my right hand back and slowly graze over her left nipple. She sucks in a sharp breath at my touch. Her reaction is such a turn-on. I continue to circle around her peaked nipple and look up to see my effect on her. Her eyes are closed and she's biting her lip. I untie her robe and pull it off her shoulders. Her strap automatically falls, as if it knows it needs to give me access to her. I pull her nightie down a bit on that side, freeing her left, very teased, breast. My tongue and mouth ignite a moan from her throat.

"Oh." She cries out softly when I bite her nipple.

"Oh, Becca, I love to hear you, sweetheart." I bite a little harder, a little longer.

"Ow! Grayson . . . stop!" I look up at her, shocked. She's holding her breast. I sit back and stare at her. I slide my hand down her body to rest firmly on her hip and bum. "Are you . . . are you mad at me?" She tilts her head.

"Should I be?"

"No."

"Why are you so sensitive tonight?" I've bitten her aggressively before.

"I don't know. Maybe I'm just not turned on enough yet."

"I don't think that's it." I contemplate her seriously. Suddenly, a lightbulb comes on and she looks more beautiful to me than ever. "Becca, do you ever have irregular periods?" I place my hand on her stomach.

"No. Never. Why?" She looks at me, puzzled. Her face then drains of all color. Her reaction not only angers me, but actually breaks my heart a little.

"You know, Becca," my right hand cups her chin, grasping her face harshly, "saying you want to have my baby is a pretty big thing to fucking lie about!" Her eyes widen, and her breaths become sharp and rapid. I let go of her face and rest my head back, closing my eyes. I listen to the sound of her breathing and feel the vibration from its shakiness. I open my eyes to find her looking upward. She shakes her head as she fights off tears.

"Becca, c'mon." I pat her bottom. "Let's go to our room." My anger abated, I soften my eyes toward her. She gets up and allows me to take her hand in mine. I bring it up to caress the top with my lips. *What is wrong with me?* I'm home barely an hour and I've already made her upset. I'm so worried she's going to turn to Ray, and yet here I am, pushing her to do so!

"I'll be out in a minute." She looks at her hand, waiting for me to let go so she can head to the bathroom.

"Becca, I ..." How can I even say *sorry* to her again? Once again, I've behaved inimically. If I don't stop this, I'm going to lose her for sure.

"I know." She comes back to me and stands on her tippy-toes. She brushes her lips against mine. *I don't deserve her.* I hold her, laying my forehead on hers. "Gray, let me go."

"Never, Becca." *Never.* I caress her lips with mine.

"Grayson, I have to go. I promise not to escape out the window." She smiles meekly.

"The way I'm behaving? I wouldn't blame you." I sigh, shaking my head slightly, and let her go.

I get ready for bed, cursing myself left and right under my breath. Christ, I could jump out of my skin! Between work and the whole Ray situation, I am all out of sorts. *Pull it together, Gray!* Becca—sweet, loving, and adoring Becca—is trying everything she can to keep me levelheaded. And I'm fighting her with my acrimonious theatrics again! She doesn't need this. Neither one of us does. I was doing so well. It's the added stress. It must be.

The door opens and I hear the faint sound of the light switch being flicked off. Becca comes out, her face freshly cleaned. I love that. She gives me a small, sheepish smile and climbs into bed. *Damn it.*

This is not how I expected my day to end. I climb in and immediately pull her to me.

"Ow! Grayson! Why do you have to be so damn rough all of the time!" She smacks my chest, her voice full of irritation.

"Sorry, love, I wasn't trying to be rough. Can I have a kiss good night, at least, or is not kissing me part of my punishment for bad behavior?" My fingers trail up and down her back. How is it possible that she can manage to take my overbearing personality and slap me upside my head with it when she really wants to? Christ, she knows how to turn the tables! I can't believe I'm begging for a good-night kiss. *Fuck this!* I flip her on her back and search her eyes. Her breathing is instantly erratic. She likes to pretend that my aggressive behavior appalls her, but I know better. She loves this about me! *I know just how to prove it.*

I dance around her face with mine. Her chest rises quickly, anticipating my kiss. I pull back playfully when she tries to kiss me.

"Oh, would you like to kiss me now?" I bait her, which I know she hates. She doesn't like to beg, either. I go to kiss her again, but then quickly pull the strap of her nightie down and fill my mouth with her breast. I play slowly, gently with her nipple. I can feel her hips working in small circles beneath me. I bring my face to hers and finally devour what is mine.

"Gray . . . Gray." She tries to pull away from my mouth. "Go easy."

I stop and look at her. "Sweetheart, I'll stop. Do you want me to stop?"

"No, just go easy tonight. Please." Her lips are back on mine after her request. I am slow, calculating, and very thorough. She prays so sweetly.

"Are you okay?" I look up at her after a beat.

"Yes," she says, but I'm unconvinced.

BECCA

Grayson goes into the bathroom to brush his teeth for bed while I lie here and wonder what the hell that was all about in the living room. My face still hurts! Why did he think I don't want to have his baby? Yes, I had a moment of panic, but it wasn't like *Oh God, I don't want this!* It was more, *Oh God, I didn't think of that!*

"I'll get a test tomorrow." I sit up and watch Grayson walk around to his side of the bed.

"The doctor will be here at nine in the morning to give you an exam." He climbs in and pulls me to him.

"What doctor?" How the hell did he do that?

"My personal doctor. I pay him to make house calls." He pulls the duvet up. "Becca, how do you truly feel about all of this?" Now he asks! *Typical Grayson.* He always acts as if he's got control over everything, including his insecurities, but I know better.

"Baby," I inhale deeply. "You are so quick to think the worst." I look up at him. His eyes stare deeply into mine as his fingers reach up and lightly caress my cheek. "My reaction was based solely on the fact that I didn't think of it, not because of the possibility. I wish you would stop doing that. I know where it comes from, but at some point, you have to try to get over it. We both need to."

"God, Becca, I just know you'll run to him the moment I let my guard down!" *Wow . . . he'll never trust me.*

"I don't know what to tell you, Grayson. That hurts me. Will you not ever be able to trust me? I only did what you guys asked of me. This is not fair." I sit up again. Is it work feeding into this bull-shit, or is it like a twenty-four-to-forty-eight-hour bug that makes him bring this all up again? "Grayson, I know you are under a lot of stress from work, which is adding to all of this. But I need to be honest with you. Until we resolve this issue you are clearly having with me, I am not walking down the aisle. Trust is huge! If we don't have that, we don't have anything." *Since I'm on a roll, I need to nip something else in the bud as well.* "And another thing! If you ever, ever grab my face in anger—or any part of my body, really—again, we will be done!" *How's that for blunt, Mr. James?*

"G'nite, Becca," he says and rolls over, turning off his light. *Is he serious?*

"You'll never change," I murmur.

How does this happen with us? We had two wonderful weeks. We didn't fight once! Then Ray started his shit, and *poof!* I lie back down and turn away from Grayson. I absorb from the cloud hanging over our heads and let the rain pour out of my eyes. Grayson grunts with irritation and climbs out of the bed. He leaves the room. That's so unlike him. I am quite worried about him—he hasn't been himself all day.

After half an hour, I get up to venture after him. I turn down the corridor on the right when I reach the end of the main one. I can see light beaming out from underneath the door at the end. Once I reach the room, I open the door slightly and discover Grayson's home gym. He's in there, beating the shit out of a punching bag. He's full of sweat and anger. *Cautionary Sybecca is walking down the line, handing out new panties to each of the girls. She changes hers as well.* All that sweat accentuates his muscles. God, look how beautiful he is. *My beautiful British bastard.*

Suddenly, I hear a theme song play in my head for Grayson, and I laugh to myself. I walk over to his iPod and download the song I wish to bestow onto him. I can feel him watching me and I notice my breath hitch. *Oh, how he affects me.* I turn the volume up. The beat starts—it's "Eye of the Tiger" from *Rocky*. I watch him in the mirror. He's trying to ignore me and not smile, both very difficult things to do. I walk up right behind him. He stops.

"I must break you," I say with a Russian accent. Oh, he's fighting hard! I can see the smile peeking through.

"Remember when we was face to face, and you thought you was so fucking great? But I kept giving you lip, and you kept trying to give me the slip." I do a little thrusting motion for that line of my revised *Rocky* poem. "That was our first date and after that, every day was great. So now I want you to know, that wherever you go, L.A. or in the snow, don't worry about a thing, 'cuz as long as I got this ring—" I hold my hand up. "My bum, you will be spanking . . . cha, cha!" I finish my *Rocky* impression, leaving Grayson in stitches.

"Ugh—I can't fucking stand you!" One second he's laughing, then it's as if he remembers something that squashes it. "Becca, go to bed."

"C'mon, Grayson, I had you back for a moment. Where did you go?" I come around to stand in front of him. "Please don't stay in this angry place." I place my hands on his chest and look up.

"Becca, get off of me and go to bed!" he says venomously through his teeth.

"Come with me, please. Grayson, please." I let my fingers wander down to his happy trail. I had my Gracie for a moment. I can pull him back out from his cloud of anger.

"Becca, please. I'm so angry. Just go to bed." His tone is sharper.

"Why are you angry with me?" I cry. *Damn it. Enough is enough!*

"*Because you slept with him!* How could you? How could you let him touch you? How? Why? Why wasn't I enough for you? You're such a fucking whore, Becca! You're such a fucking whore! How could you do this to me?" He screams through his tears, squeezing the shit out of my upper arms. He lets go, sits down on the bench, and his head falls right into his hands. He's sobbing.

My mind is racing, competing with my increased pulse. I'm very upset—for an extremely good reason!—but the logical side of me knows he's stressed out and can't control his feelings anymore. He needed to purge them. I rub his back and kiss his shoulder.

"I've thought a lot about what happened. When you are ready, I will tell you why I think I did it. Grayson, you have always been more than good enough. I regret my behavior terribly, and I wish I could take it back. But I'm not a whore. I made a mistake that you and Ray backed me into." I'm trying my hardest to remain calm.

"You could have said no!" he yells.

"You're right. I wish I did. But I would have had to say no to you, too, and you know how hard it is for me to do that." I kneel in front of him so he can look at me. I grab his hands and rest my head in the palm of his left.

"You begged him to spend the night. Do you not think I got a full report on every detail?" His voice has softened now.

"Grayson, I was confused and scared of what we have. I hadn't so much as looked at a man in this kind of light until you came along." I continue to explain to him what I said to Hazel. "Grayson, I'm so in love with you, and I'm not scared of it anymore. I don't know what else to do to prove to you that I don't want him. I've completely cut him out of my life. What else can I do?" I feel my chin begin to quiver. My nostrils flare to stop impending tears. I close my eyes and relish in the feeling of his hand on my face. "I can't keep on doing this. We're trying to add to our family. We need to do something to get past this hurt." Suddenly, a thought occurs to me. "Grayson." I open my eyes to stare into his reddened ones. "Do you still want this with me? Do you still want a family?" Maybe he doesn't. Maybe that's why he's pushing me away.

"Of course I do! I wouldn't have put this on your finger if I didn't." He taps my ring and pulls me up to sit on his lap. "I don't like how jealous I've become. I don't want to be like this. I don't want to say things that hurt you. I'm just really mad about everything that happened." He runs his index finger down my jawline. "I was just thinking about what you said. How Ray was your *known*. Becca, I'm afraid I've brought you out here to stand in the middle of this huge shitstorm with me. You have no idea what you are about to be hit with. I'm afraid that you will run to what is safe—*known*—to you." Wow . . . okay, we are getting somewhere. "Ray feels like a huge threat to me . . . to us. Again. Thing is, I wouldn't blame you for running to Ray. Hell, if *I* could run away into the safety of Ray's arms, I would." I know he's exaggerating, but the thought makes me grin.

"Wait. Hold for the mental picture, please." I put my hand up and envision a gay man's dream ending to this triangle.

"Oh, Becca. Stop it, sweetheart!" He chuckles.

"Grayson, I think I need to tell you something that I can see you are not aware of." I move his sweaty hair off of his forehead.

"What's that?" His eyelids quicken their pace.

"You are my safe and known now. Let's go to our room and take a shower, and then you can fill me in on this shitstorm so I can stand strong in the middle of it with you. Knowledge is power, baby. I need to know everything. You can't leave me alone to figure this all out. I don't want to Google it; I want to hear it all from your mouth." I squish his lips for emphasis, then kiss him.

"Fair enough, sweetheart." He pats my bottom to ask me to get up. "Becca, I do know how wonderful you are." He swings my hand as we walk down the hall. "I don't really want to push you away. From the moment I left this morning, all I thought about was getting home to you. I'm not happy with my behavior tonight. If it makes you feel any better, you are actually the only woman to drive me into complete madness."

"Yay me!" I raise my arms in victory as a tease. He pulls me ahead of him and smacks my bum as we head into our room. "Go take your shower. I'm going to read." I head toward the bed.

He pulls me back to him. "Read this," he points to his face. "It says, *I want you in the shower with me.*" He pulls at my nightgown.

"No. No, you go and hurry up! If you want, I'll sit in there and you can start talking."

He gives me a pouty face. "C'mon then, I'll start in there and finish out here." He raises an eyebrow. I laugh and follow him into the bathroom.

Grayson pulls his shorts off. I wince from the pain of biting down too hard on my lip. He flashes me a knowing smirk before stepping into the shower. *Arrogant bastard!* The sound of the water rushing through the pipes echoes hypnotically off the tiled walls. I'm suddenly second-guessing my decision not to join him.

"I guess I'll start with the biggest thing," he says, pulling me back to focus. "I'm going to court next month for fraud charges filed against me from the Securities and Exchange Commission."

"What?" Uh, yeah, that's definitely something on the list of things I need to know about!

"Don't worry, they don't have a case. I'll give you the short version," he says, and I can hear him rinsing his hair. It takes a moment before he continues. "I was invested in a company that I no longer had interest in. So, like I usually do, I sold all of my shares to reinvest somewhere else. I've always had a knack for knowing when to pull out."

"Really? You could've fooled me!" *God, I'm just as bad as he is.* His laughter pulls me back again.

"Of companies, sweetheart." I can sense his lingering smile. "I never like to pull out of you." *I don't like you pulling out of me either . . . mmm.* "So, moving along here." He sighs. "I have a very strong history of doing this, but this time, two things happened that worked against me. First, a week after I sold my shares, they released a product that bombed in a catastrophic sense. Second, I had just been seen golfing with the CEO of the company."

"Oh God . . . you golf?" I cringe.

"Everybody does, sweetheart! I actually hate it, but it is a good way to do business and catch up with people. You know—keep the networking *up to par*." He laughs.

"I'm rolling my eyes!" I announce in rebuttal to his lame golf reference.

"I knew you would, but it had to be said. Anyway, as much as I dislike golf, I'm pretty good at it."

"Another hidden talent?" I muse.

"But of course, love. I have many hidden talents as, you are well aware." *Egotistical much?* I roll my eyes again.

"So, why were you with the CEO?"

"We're old mates from university. We were just catching up. If I had known this was all going to happen, we never would have gone! Guy is being brought up on the same charges. The media is going wild with it, and several artists have walked away from the label because they are concerned about what's going to happen to my company or how it will affect their career. No one's interested in my songs right now. It's just been a nightmare. My company is losing shareholders. It's starting to affect my other companies, the ones people know I helm." He steps out of the shower.

"Well, why do you think it's open and shut?" I ask, trying not to notice the water dripping down his chest. *Yum . . . focus, Becca!*

"Because, sweetheart, they can only speculate. There's no proof whatsoever. Guy and I get together every few months. Our lawyers will prove our personal history goes back to before we were ever the 'us' of now. Our caddies are our witnesses to our conversation that day."

"Who is your caddy?" I ask quickly.

"Sam . . . why?"

"Our Sam?"

"Yes." He smiles, liking the reference, I think.

"Oh, thank God. It's not somebody that could easily be bought off. What about Guy?"

"Actually, his nephew caddied for him that day. Gee, Becca, I didn't even think of the possibilities if I hadn't had Sam with me. That could've been a disaster! Anyway, there is no documentation that would prove anything, either. In fact, I liquidated my shares of two other companies that day as well. They really don't have anything. We're actually expecting the charges to be dropped soon. That would help me put out all of the fires except for one," he says, running his towel over his hair quickly again before throwing it in the hamper. "All right, come now. Off to bed we go!" He pulls me along.

"Grayson, which fire will be left?"

"Uh . . . well." He turns to me and quickly looks away. "A paternity test."

"What?" My heart sinks.

"It's not mine! This has happened to me from time to time. One of the, uh . . . women that I used to sleep with is pregnant and claiming I'm the father. Becca, you are the only one I've not used protection with. Well, except for an *oops* in school, but that is it. I go through this every other year, if not annually." He finds my eyes. His eyelids are going crazy.

"When will she have the amniocentesis?"

"In a few weeks. Are you all right?"

"Yeah. Thank you for being honest with me." Of course, he's only telling me because somebody may ask me.

"You don't look all right." He grabs my hips and pulls me to him.

"Well, I can't help but feel that you wouldn't have told me about that last thing if you weren't afraid I'd find out elsewhere or be questioned."

"Becca, I have not stopped you from researching me."

"That's true, but you knew I wouldn't," I remind him.

"Oh, sweetheart, c'mon now. Let's stop all of this." He pulls me tighter to him and collects my lips with his.

"Trying to use your favorite distraction?" I pull away.

"What's that?"

"Sex." I move my head back from his advances.

"Well, I'm actually just kissing you good night, but I'd love another go if you'd like to!" *Yeah, right!* I roll my eyes. "No, sweetheart?"

"No. I'm tired, Gray." *Man, am I tired.* Another emotional roller coaster brought to me courtesy of Grayson James.

"Okay, love. Climb in then." He covers me once I get in, then joins me and pulls me to him. It doesn't take me long to fall asleep.

Chapter Seventeen

I shake Grayson. "Baby, cancel the doctor."

"Huh? What?" He grumbles.

"Cancel the doctor," I repeat. "What time do you have to get up this morning?" I lay back down. It's six o'clock in the morning, and I was rudely awoken by Aunt Flo from Red Bank, as we Jersey girls like to say.

"I'm going in late today. Did you tell me to cancel the doctor?" He snuggles up to me.

"Yes, there's no need." I'm a little disappointed, but also glad for extra time with Grayson.

"Becca, you should get checked out anyway. How late were you?" He rubs my stomach.

"Um, I'm guessing two weeks. But stress can do this. This happened to me a lot when I was with Geor—" I stop myself as I feel him tense up. "It hasn't been a typical month for me, between you and Ray and then getting kidnapped. I've been surrounded by security 24-7 and worried about Morgan. It's no surprise this happened. I am sorry, though, baby." He's still tense.

"Becca, last night I . . . um, I know it was wrong, but I will never go further than that and I'm going to try my hardest not to do it again." He holds me tightly to him.

"You are not George, Grayson. What you did last night was like a kiss from George. He was very brutal to me. There is no comparison." I kiss his chest. He says nothing. I concentrate on the sound and rhythm of his breathing and slowly am lulled back to a deep sleep.

November 5, 2012   10:45 a.m.
Gray: Ugh . . . bloody, bloody hell! I miss you!
Me: Please, don't talk to me about bloody hell! Miss U 2! R U the type of man who will buy tampons for your woman? ☺
Gray: For you, I'd buy them and take them out!
Me: Really? But you can't handle vomit? You are a weird sort, aren't u, mate? ☺
Gray: Yes, I find myself willing to do all sorts of weird stuff nowadays! I may even overcome my vomit phobia! :-o
Me: Emetophobia: An intense, irrational fear or anxiety pertaining to vomit. Consider yourself schooled, mate!
Gray: Wow! I'm not sure how I feel about this. You took time to Google vomit fear, but won't take time to Google me? Vomit outranks me? Really? ☹
Me: How did you know I Googled that?
Gray: Because, like you . . . I am awesome as well!

November 7, 2012   9:30 a.m.
Me: You were indeed awesome this morning!! :-p
Gray: TY! TTYL! Love you!

November 8, 2012   4:50 p.m.
Me: Can't wait for tomorrow! Whole day with my man and my mouse!

Gray: IDK . . . may be a bust 4 me. I'm trying!
Me: What?! Sat. then?
Gray: I'm trying, sweetheart! Don't wait up!
Me: I'll be up! Love you!
Gray: LY2!

Grayson has been so busy this week. I just want him to be able to take a break for the day so he can enjoy family time. It is probably a smidge selfish, since he was, for the most part, having family time with us for five weeks before we got here. He's been all over the TV due to the upcoming court date. I feel terrible for him . . . different people, same fucking questions over and over again.

There should be a new rule in journalism. When interviewing someone who is very "hot" in the news, the journalist should just do a recap of the answers that person has already answered then ask something new. If you can't think of a new question, don't do the interview. It's very irritating to the interviewee to keep pretending no one else was brilliant enough to ask that question.

Okay, another five minutes of precious time wasted on ranting to myself. I'm always good at solo debates. I should win the regional trophy!

"Mommy, what are you wearing to Disney tomorrow?" Morgan strolls in and jumps up onto our bed.

"Um, I don't know. What do you think I should wear?" I walk into our closet, which is large enough for two people to share comfortably. I'm slowly adding to my section. Grayson made me buy more clothes. It's pretty comical—most men don't want you shopping that much. I was also read the riot act and am now using my black AmEx card. He gave this whole speech on how it's just easier for him to pay the bill on a joint account than having to link my cards for him to pay. I know I'm not going to win this one, so I've given in. I know he likes to keep tabs on everything I do. He likes the *ping* he gets from his alerts. He knows I obviously know about tracking on the black card, but he doesn't know I know he's already linked my own cards for him to pay off . . . which he did. He also tracks my phone records and anything I do on my laptop. I don't have anything to hide, so it doesn't bother me. It's actually kind of hot. *Ugh, that's so weird!* Why do I find it hot, when other people would be like *what the fuck*? I don't know. Maybe it's because he doesn't know that I know. It's not like he's rubbing it in my face and doing the whole "I'm watching you" hand signal. He's a bit of a control freak, and I like it.

This all reminds me that I have a double session with my therapist when I get back. I've only seen her once in the past month. I completely hit her like a freight train with the triangle and the kidnapping. She didn't have a minute to dissect any of it! I wonder if it pisses her off sometimes when I walk in having already figured out issues that have arisen. Kind of takes her thunder away. I should just have sessions with myself and stick my copay in a jar for donation.

"Mom! Hello! Earth to Mom! Paging Becca Campbell!" Morgan yells through a rolled-up paper.

"Sorry, honey." I laugh.

"Geez, Mom, you were in a galaxy far, far and away! Wear your Tinkerbell shirt." She holds it up. Probably a better choice than my new Dopey tank top. I can just see it now . . . the first time I'm photographed with Grayson and I'm wearing that shirt, the headline would read, "HE'S WITH DOPEY!"

"Good idea, Morgan. Tink it is." I grab a pair of black capris to go with it. I should check the weather for tomorrow to make sure there won't be a chill in the air. "Well, come on, let's go see about your outfit. Wait! Didn't you get the same shirt? Do you want to match?" I put my arm around her shoulder as we walk to her room.

"Mom, you're such a dork." She rolls her eyes.

"Morgan, you're ten. You should still consider that a fantastic idea. Stop growing up so fast!" Seriously! It makes me so sad.

"I'll wear my Snow White shirt." She ignores me.

"Okay. Listen, it's nine o'clock. It's time to get to bed." I pull out her PJs and roll down her bed.

"But I haven't seen Daddy all week!" She stomps her foot. There's my little girl.

"He's been working really hard, honey. You'll see him soon enough. Now, get ready for bed and I'll be back to tuck you in." I leave the room to get my phone so I can call Grayson, but I bump right into him instead.

"Hey, she still up?" He holds me in his arms.

"Yes. She's getting ready for bed now and would love it if you tuck her in." He rubs the side of my arms and kisses my forehead before he knocks and enters her room. I hear Morgan screech excitedly to see him.

I start to head down the hall, but stop when I hear Morgan yell, "No, Daddy, you promised!" She's crying now. I head back to the door and listen as he tries over and over again to tell her how sorry he is.

"Gray, can we go on Saturday?" I pop my head in.

"Becca, I can't. There's nothing I can do. I already feel bloody awful!" His eyes widen, then turn sad. "You two can go with Tanya's family. I'm just swamped. I'm sorry, girls. Good night, Morgy. I love you. Please don't stay mad at me." He gives her a kiss on the cheek. She turns away from him, pouting and hiccupping from crying.

"Becca, I . . . " He looks so confused. I wave him to just come out of the room. He gets up off of his knees and joins me in the hall. "Sweetheart, I didn't want to break my promise to her. She's never been mad at me." He shakes his head before bringing his right hand up to hold the back of his neck. He's upset.

"Clearly, you should receive a medal for going a whole six weeks without Morgan ever getting mad at you." I pat him on the back as we head out to the kitchen. "Look, it will pass. I promise. Now, what can I fix you to eat?" I open the fridge.

"I'm sorry. I ordered in at the office. I just want a glass of wine and you, sweetheart." He wraps his arms around me as he buries his face in my neck.

"Red or white?"

"Will you have a glass with me?"

"Yes."

"Then I'll have red as well. Let me grab the bottle. You get the glasses, love." He kisses my head and releases me. He looks so beat, I notice, as I meet him at the center island.

"Baby, what is going on at work that you are up to your elbows in it? Is it just getting worse?"

"Oh, Becca, it's awful. My companies' stocks are dropping like crazy. I've got people wanting to leave left and right. I wish they would drop the charges already. They have absolutely nothing to go on, and they are single-handedly destroying everything I've worked hard for!" He looks so distraught for such a strong, confident man.

"Can you sue them for what they've cost you?"

"Yes, sweetheart, we're building a case against them. I've had five lawyer meetings this week. *Five!*" I pour more wine into his glass.

"Well, that's our lucky number, isn't it?" I quickly kiss him.

"Yes it is." He grasps my hips to pull me back toward him. "Stay close, darling. I need the double intoxication of you and this wine." He smirks and kisses me again. I lay my head on his chest. After a few minutes, he gives me a little squeeze. "Come, sweetheart. I haven't nearly paid you enough attention lately." He grabs my glass of wine and sets it on the counter.

We head to our room. His thumb caresses the top of my hand, unleashing the butterflies like always.

"Let's have a shower, shall we?"

I nod and we head in.

"I guess you're not flying back with us on Sunday." I've been thinking about that all day.

He turns from getting the shower started. "Sweetheart, you are not flying back there without me. On Monday, call the school and let them know Morgan will be homeschooled until further notice. Find out from them where Morgan is academically so her tutor can take over this week." It amazes me how all of this flies out of his mouth as if he's talking about the weather.

"What tutor?" I look up at his face as he unbuttons my shirt. He looks so tired, like he's aged five years in one week.

"The one I hired today, sweetheart." His finger traces from clavicle to clavicle. He dips down to kiss my neck.

"Gray, what about my business?" I push at his shoulders.

"Everything is running fine. You know that. Becca, had I not met you, I would've been back here a lot earlier. Please don't take that the wrong way," he says quickly as he silences me by placing his thumb on my lips. The rest of his hand palms my face. "I'm at a crucial moment in my career. I need you here, supporting me. I need the comfort of knowing that at the end of the day, I'm coming home to you. I love you, Becca. I need you. Please don't argue with me." He searches my eyes.

That was a lovely speech. However, he and I both know the main reason I cannot go home without him. *Ray.* I can appreciate his effort to avoid an argument by omitting this fact.

"How long will we be here?"

A satisfied smile crosses his face.

"At least a month. No more than two."

"Grayson, I want to have Christmas in New Hampshire, not here. We will stay here with no argument, but that is my one stipulation." I try to be as stern as possible.

"Don't be ridiculous, sweetheart. We're not having Christmas at the B&B with a bunch of strangers. We'll have it here and fly out whomever you want." He pulls my face to his. I allow his kiss.

"Grayson, it would just be us. I always close the inn for the weeks around Christmas and New Year's. We'll have it there. I'm serious!"

"Becca, we are not going to be able to spend two weeks there!"

"I didn't say we had to spend two weeks. Just that I close for two weeks. Why are you being such a jerk about this?" I push him off again.

He pulls me closer. "Now that's not very nice, sweetheart," he whispers against my ear. The butterflies reignite from their short slumber and my breathing becomes erratic. *Damn it!* "We'll put that on the back burner for now, sweetheart, and see what we can do when the time comes. Right now, there is another pressing issue that we must take care of straight away." I can barely concentrate on what he is saying. His accent is so thick, which I think he does on purpose because he knows its effect on me, but I'm also too focused on his light touch and how it tickles my skin. I unbutton his shirt and help him out of it. My lips caress his chest as my fingers play at unbuckling his belt.

"Are you off your—" he starts as he works on sliding my bottoms off.

"Almost. Get in the shower. I'll be right there." I muster the strength to nudge him away. He's so intoxicating. My theme song changes to "Addicted" by Kelly Clarkson.

"Theme song, sweetheart?" He chucks me under my chin. I smile and open my eyes, then tell him the new song. He looks at me curiously and walks over to the iPod dock on the counter and finds the song. "Press 'play' before you come in," he says quickly before he unleashes the Hulk and heads into the shower. I take care of what I need to, then flush the toilet because he irritated me before. He yelps. "Becca! Jesus!"

"Oops. Sorry." I giggle silently.

I hit "play," turn up the volume, and walk into the shower. Grayson immediately grabs me and forces me up against the wall. He devours my mouth. The music in the background has raised the temperature in this shower by at least twenty degrees. Grayson lifts me up and I wrap my legs around him. He wastes no time filling me. His hips quicken and slow according to the tempo of the song. Our mouths are wild. As the song finishes, his mouth and body drop down to a thorough and agonizing pace. Honestly, I don't know how he has the energy or stamina to do all of this, but I am not complaining. I'm just enjoying the ride. Joe McIntyre's song comes to mind, but I push it out quickly—that was a Ray song. *Damn it.* New song! New song!

Grayson slaps my bum hard. "Focus, Becca!" He snaps. "Twisted" by New Kids on the Block. I palm his face and stare into his eyes. The song is blaring in my head and I feel myself rising. The song changes to "S&M" by Rihanna. "Pray, sweetheart," Grayson commands through gritted teeth.

But I'm already there. "Oh God, baby," I cry, "please . . . oh please." It's so intense! I want him to stop and continue all at the same time. He muffles our sounds by attacking my mouth with his until we each have our last quake. I slide down his body, feeling completely over the limit for intoxication.

"Where was this beautiful mind of yours traveling to, sweetheart?" His fingers caress my cheek. I can't even open my eyes yet, I'm so drunk on him.

"Um, apparently I've acquired a CD changer in my head. That was quite the soundtrack." I finally open my eyes to find his curious grin. I then tell him the two songs.

"Hmm, I'll have to listen to those when we finish." He lathers up with his bodywash. I grab my facecloth and do the same. "By the way, that was a very intense theme song you had going at the beginning. It'll be a new permanent fixture on my playlist. Actually, we have quite the array of songs that should go on our 'hot list.'" He spanks my bottom for emphasis. This releases one last quake that I didn't realize was still lingering around. I close my eyes and relish in it. "God, Becca, how you turn me on." He presses his lips to mine as I'm still trying to recover.

GRAYSON

"Mr. James? Mr. James?" Charity Newman's voice snaps me back into focus. She is interviewing me for *Music Now Magazine*. Her skirt is shorter than usual, probably to increase my chances of discovering she has no panties on. I think she's crossed and uncrossed her legs about ten times in the past twenty minutes. It's quite annoying, actually! I'd like to tell her to give it a rest, she's not my type, but I chose to communicate it not glancing down once. God, she's classless and terribly boring.

"So, rumor has it that you're engaged." She uncrosses her legs again.

"It is not a rumor. It is a fact. Tell me, Ms. Newman, is your chair uncomfortable? Because I'm sure we can find you another one." My question catches her off guard and I can tell she's irritated now. Good. Let's get this over with, for Christ's sake! I have better things to do with my time.

She looks down at her notes. "Rebecca Campbell."

"No, my fiancée's name is Becca Campbell." She glances back up at me. Okay, and? Oh, c'mon, lady! "Any more questions, Ms. Newman? I have a very busy schedule." I'm as polite as I can be.

"We've never seen her." Again . . . not a question.

"Never seen who?"

"Your fiancée."

"And your question is, Ms. Newman?"

"How do we know she's real?" *This is absurd!*

"Why would I make her up, Ms. Newman?" I look at her as if she has five heads.

"I think people are just curious about the woman who's laid claim to Grayson James's heart." She tries to save herself.

"Well, everyone will see her soon enough, Ms. Newman. Now, if we're finished here, I have another matter that needs my attention." I stand, giving her no choice but to do so as well. She thanks me for my time and I open the door for her. I pick up my office phone and buzz Carol.

"Yes, cancel the rest of my day. I'm not wasting another minute on these bullshit interviews. No. No, reschedule that. I don't care! Have Sam pick me up." I hang up and pull out my cell.

November 9, 2012   10:55 a.m.
Me: Where R U?
Becca: Disney . . . remember? Cuckoo, cuckoo!
Me: I know Disney, smartass! I'm coming. Be near the gate in 1 hr. LY XXXXX
Becca: OMG! Yay! Can't wait 2 C U! XXXXX
Me: Me too!

I head out of my office. Carol seems frazzled. "Sorry, Carol, that interview was absurd. I just need a break from it all. When you're done rescheduling, go home." This lifts her spirits.

Sam is already here, with clothes Susanna gave him so I can change.

"You have a brilliant wife, Sam." This will get me there all the quicker.

11:15 a.m.
Me: I'll be there in 25 mins.
Becca: Okay. See you at the front gate.

I get into my "play" clothes in the back, then rest my head against the seat. I'm exhausted.

"Grayson, sonny, we're here," Sam says. His endearment is new to our conversation this morning. I can tell he's worried that I'm burning the candle at both ends of the stick. I assured him things will calm down soon.

It better, Grayson! Susanna, Becca, and I are all worried about you! I love that he added Becca in there, like she's been around as long as they have. Ah . . . Sam and Susanna, my surrogate parents. I couldn't ask for better ones! They love and care for me as if I'm their own son. Of course, that does mean that they don't put up with my shit. They are always ready and willing to give me a "what for" when needed. I love that about them.

"We'll call you later, Sam," I say as I rub my face to wake up. I finally climb out and wave him off. I grab my cell to call Becca.

"Grayson, over here!" I turn to find her waving. Morgan yells excitedly and runs toward me. I catch her and twirl her around.

"Hello, Morgy girl!"

"Daddy, I'm so happy you're here." She hugs my neck.

"Me, too." I kiss her and put her down to welcome Becca's hug.

"Daddy, are those people taking pictures of us?" Morgan looks past me.

"Yes, little sweetheart, I'm afraid so." I didn't even think about the paparazzi. "Becca, this may have been a bad idea." I look to her, a little worried.

"It'll be fine, unless you don't want to be seen with us," she teases.

"Well, if they get too pesky, we can just pose for a few pictures. Sometimes they back off a little after that. Let's play it by ear." I grab their hands and we head into the park.

There are perks to being famous. Becca has teased me all day, calling me their "personal FASTPASS." I was right about the photographers, though, at least this lot. We gave them a few shots, and they've pretty much left us alone since. I've loved just having fun with the family for a day. I really needed it. Plus, it was good to see Tanya's family have such a nice time. From what Becca told me of their situation, they really needed this as well. Her husband, Reggie, is going to send me his résumé. I want to see if there is somewhere I can place him in one of my companies.

We find a good spot for the fireworks display. I stand behind Becca and wrap my arms around her. She cranes her neck, beckoning me closer. I lean down.

"I'm so glad you came today, baby," she says. "We had a wonderful time. Thank you!" She kisses my mark.

"You can thank me more when we get home," I say suggestively. She smirks and shakes her head. I am an insatiable man. I can't wait to get her home. I think I've listened to that Kelly Clarkson song ten times this morning. It stirred something so deep in me, and yet, it's bittersweet. I'm conflicted over the words. Does she really feel so tortured by her addiction to me? I feel the same way about her, but in a good way. On the other hand, "Twisted" is definitely us. Oh, Christ, I need to stop before I get myself all worked up.

The fireworks finish and we head out of the park to find Sam waiting with the car. We all climb in, bone tired. Morgan passes out before we even get off Disney property.

"She had a great time." Becca yawns as she plays with Morgy's hair.

"I loved watching her. Did you tell her about being homeschooled?" I check my phone for emails.

"Yes. She's not really happy about it. I asked her if she wanted me to enroll her in school here. She's going to think about it."

"Becca, we're not doing that. It's too much. If this remains our full-time home, then yes. But not for six weeks or so. That's silly." I email Carol back regarding a few of her questions.

"Excuse me, Grayson, but six weeks is a long time for a ten-year-old, and I will make the final decision when it comes to Morgan."

"We are her parents, sweetheart. We make the decision together. Got it?" I'm trying to remain calm.

"I'm her parent, Gray." She whips the words out, stinging me.

"Fuck you, Becca!" I say through my teeth in her ear.

"I'm sure you will." She pats my knee and leans her head back against my chest. *Ha! She has no idea!*

Twenty minutes of silence go by. I grab her hand and bring it to my lips. She leans back to look up at me. I caress her lips with my own.

"Ugh." Morgan groans when she opens her eyes to us kissing. "Thank God we're home." She sighs. We ignore her and just stare into each other's eyes.

Sam pulls around the fountain and lets us out. Morgan is off like a bat out of hell. Becca and I take our time, walking hand in hand to the front door.

"I'm sorry that I said that, Grayson." She places her hand on my chest.

"Don't do it again." I touch her cheek. "It made me feel a little bit *twisted*, if you know what I mean."

"Mm . . . I love my Gracie with a twist." She licks her lips and turns to walk into the house. *And that is* exactly *what you are going to get, sweetheart!*

I yell "Good night!" to Morgan and head to our room for a shower.

A few minutes pass and I feel Becca's touch. "Don't be long, sweetheart." I give her a kiss and a good smack on the bum before I head out with a smirk on my face. I love teasing her. I dry off and head out to our bedroom and to the iPod dock. I've made a special playlist to surprise Becca.

Honestly, I shouldn't have bothered to go into work this morning at all. All of my thoughts were focused on Becca. Becca in the shower last night. Becca at three in the morning. Becca at six in the morning, and then once again before I left. It amazes me that I still can't keep my hands off of her. We've been together just about every day for six weeks, and my need for her just grows. I just can't get enough . . . she feels so good . . . so perfect.

Damn it. What the hell is taking so long? The Hulk is dying

to show her something incredible! I still love that name. She's so bloody fucking cute! Is she seriously blow-drying her goddamn hair? Okay, she turned it off.

I'm watching the clock, and she's been in there twenty-five minutes now. *C'mon, Becca!* I hear the hair dryer again. *That's it!* I get up and charge into the bathroom. She's leaning forward over the sink with her ass—clothed in lacy red panties—sticking out. The bottoms of her cheeks peek at me. Her matching camisole has a slit in the front, letting me view her stomach. I love her stomach. I love to caress and kiss it. I love to fuck her belly button with my tongue. I swear, I think she's the only woman in the world who can come that way.

The camisole gives her breasts nice lift, and I can see her nipples through the lace. She has a satisfied smirk on her face. I walk up to her and wrap my left hand around the back of her neck to pull her close.

"You have two seconds to get this sweet arse into my bed." I slap her bottom and feel it sting my right hand. She closes her eyes and bites her bottom lip. "Another, sweetheart?" I lay my accent on thick. I know what it does to her, and I love it. I softly rub her reddened cheek. Her breathing becomes rapid as I lean into her neck, smelling her and caressing it with my lips. I slap her again, a bit harder, and she gasps with a moanish whimper that drives me mad. I need to hear it one more time—and, well, because three is much better than two. I slap the opposite cheek with just as much intensity and muffle her cry with my mouth.

"C'mon, sweetheart." She follows my pull into the bedroom. I hit "play" and "Lullaby" by The Cure comes on. The first song we ever made love to. I turn to Becca. A tear winds its way down her face. That last one must've really hurt. I drag my bottom lip up her cheek to catch it and kiss her eye. I bring my face across hers and find her lips. Her hands travel up my chest as she gives into my kiss. I lay her on the bed, then explore her neck and across the top of her chest with my mouth. I bite each nipple through the fabric. She rewards me with her moans. I part the camisole to fully reveal her stomach.

"L'Amour Toujours" starts playing. I tease her belly button with my tongue before I slowly lick inside. Her hips jolt up and I know I've touched the sensitive area I need to concentrate on. Her hips rise over and over again. She grabs my hair and thrusts wildly as she peaks and says her prayers. I pull her panties off as she catches her breath. "Still calling this your Slip 'n Slide?" I tease.

"Nope . . . my wetlands," she says with such seriousness, I can't help but laugh. She's a good kind of crazy. Love that about her.

I bite at her inner thigh. She gasps. My fingers slide into her wetlands. Boy, she's not kidding! I caress her most sensitive area inside and begin working her with my mouth on the outside. I try to control her hips with my left arm. For twenty minutes or so, I continue to make her pray. "Addicted" comes on, and I finally give in to Becca's pleas and pull her up to sit astride me. Her hips move at a slow, agonizing pace. I grasp them and guide her down to feel my full potential.

"Oh . . . Grayson." She's barely audible. She leans back, propping herself on her hands and letting her hips go wild. I match her stride and her sounds.

"Ugh ..." I grit my teeth. She takes the cue. Her pace slows and she squeezes around me. My explosion is fierce and intense. I pound quicker through my quakes and slam her down on me as I sail through the last one. "Oh, Becca, sweetheart . . . we're so good together." I hold her to me tightly.

BECCA

"The tutor will be here at nine o'clock this morning, sweetheart. She said she'll test Morgan to see where she's at until you get the info from her teacher." Grayson sits down next to me and opens the paper as Susanna finishes making our breakfast.

"Okay. I'm calling right after we eat." I sip my pumpkin coffee.

"Becca, sweetheart, are you all right? You seem a little distant this morning." He does look very concerned, which tells me he doesn't realize how aggressive he's been the past few days.

I lean in close to him. "You've left welts on me."

A flicker of panic comes across his face. He takes my hand and pulls me to my feet.

"We'll be right back, Susanna."

She nods, smiling, and turns back to our omelets. He brings me to the bathroom in the hallway.

"Pull your pants down, sweetheart." I turn around and comply. "Oh God! I . . . I didn't mean to do that, sweetheart. Please, you have to believe me." He softly rubs my bum and I move to face him. I can see how upset he is.

"Just go a little easier on me, baby. You've been very aggressive, which normally I love, but it's been constant, every time, and—"

"I have been more aggressive," he says, cutting me off. "I'm just trying to escape into you. I'm very frustrated at work, and I've brought it into our bedroom, in a sense. You just . . . being with you, it makes everything all better. I'm sorry, sweetheart. I promise to be more careful." He palms my face. His eyelids are blinking like mad.

"Grayson, I know you didn't do it on purpose. I just wanted you to know because you need to know." I think I'm rambling.

"Have I hurt you in any other way?" I immediately shake my head. He slowly leans forward and kisses me softly, over and over, until I let him deepen it. "Thank you for being honest with me so that I can correct it. I don't want to hurt you, sweetheart. I don't want to lose you." His thumbs caress my cheeks.

"I know. Maybe you should try some yoga to reach your Zen." I smile.

"You are my Zen." He leans his forehead against mine. "Come.

Let us have some breakfast now, shall we?" He leads me back to the kitchen. My Greek omelet is waiting for me.

"Yay—my favorite!" I cheer. Grayson smiles because, as usual, he got my order right. Bet he's glad he chose this!

"Hey, Grayson?" I look up after my first bite.

"Yes, sweetheart?" He glances up for a second, then continues texting or emailing or whatever he's doing.

"Have you gotten any information on the whole Stacey and Ray situation?" Just as I suspected, his jawline goes into a pulsating frenzy. However, due to the mishandling of his fiancée by none other than himself, I am confident he will keep his temper and jealousy at bay.

"Why?"

"Because you said you were going to keep tabs on them," I remind him.

"I have, but there's nothing to report. Stop thinking about it. You won't have to deal with them for a while anyhow." He dives into his omelet.

"Gray, I haven't heard from Stacey in a few days. I'm worried." I'm not dropping this just because he wants me to. Besides, I know he's lying. His eyelids are going insane. What's he keeping from me?

"Maybe she's busy at her new job," he offers.

"She got a job? Where?" I'm excited for her, but disappointed she hasn't called to tell me.

"With Ray." He looks up to catch my reaction. I don't offer much of one, and he seems satisfied.

"I'll call Hazel and ask her what she knows." I sigh and take another bite.

"There's nothing to know, Becca! She's working for him and looking for an apartment. That is it! What are you searching for?" His fist hits the table. I want to tell him I'll be searching for his purple pants in a minute, but given his anger, I decide it's not a good idea.

"I'm worried about her, that's all," I end up saying, very calmly.

"Becca, I just don't need the extra stress of worrying about what's going on out there. I have enough with everything here. You and Morgan are far away from all that nonsense, and that's all I care about right now." He grabs my hand and squeezes it.

"What about George?"

"Becca, goddamn it! You are far away and safe on all counts! Let me worry about that stuff!" He continues to raise his voice.

"Grayson, I am not trying to argue with you. You do realize you are telling me to basically not concern myself with my own life? You get a debriefing every morning about my life, and I am left in the dark." I'm trying to reason with him. I'm pretty sure my efforts will be unsuccessful.

"Your life is here, with your fiancé and your daughter. Stacey, Ray, and George are not your life, just a thorn in the side of it!" *Something is up. It has to be, for him to be yelling like this.*

"Is the lawyer doing the ad today?" After this question, I'll drop it . . . for now.

"It was done on Friday, sweetheart." He's calm again.

"And yet, it's Monday, and I only know because I asked." Point—Becca Campbell! I ignore Grayson's hard glare and finish my breakfast. Instead of sitting in angry silence, I decide to bring our dishes to the sink and wash them.

"Oh, Becca, I'll get those." Susanna comes over and tries to stop me.

"Please, just let me." I look to her. I can feel my eyes filling up. I'm so mad. She gives me a sympathetic smile. She must have heard our argument. Christ, who wouldn't have? He was so loud.

After a few minutes, I feel Grayson's hand on my right hip. He pushes my hair away from my neck with his other hand. I feel my breath catch. *Damn it!* Why does he always have this effect on me? Why now, when I'm pissed at him? Thespian Sybecca moved out a while ago. Horny Sybecca is working the pole. *Damn whore!* Looks like I'm on my own.

"Please stop," I say as calmly as I can.

"Stop what, sweetheart?" He takes in my scent. Maybe if I just hold my breath . . . Grayson chuckles behind me. *Bastard!* He kisses at my neck and lightly tickles my sides so I'll breathe. I try to shrug him off and break free, but he grabs my wrist and pulls me back, then pins me up against the counter with both hands. His eyes are wild and a satisfied smirk appears across his lips. He's totally fucking turned on! What the hell?

He leans in to kiss me. I turn my head.

"Sweetheart, we both know I'm a selfish man. A turn of your head is not going to stop me. The more you fight, the more precarious a position—or, I should say, *positions*—you will find yourself in." I turn back to him to tell him where he can go, except . . . I'm not successful. He invades my mouth with his tongue. Oh, I hate him! *Mmm . . . God, he's delicious. Porn Sybecca steps up to the plate.* I give in and take over, making love to his mouth with my own. I'm aggressive and encouraging, then gentle and reluctant, followed by fierce passion and a final bite of his lower lip. He can't seem to steady his breath. His hands are against the counter on either side of me, as if for support.

I sneak under his arm and slap his ass.

"Have a nice day, Gracie!" I walk out of the kitchen with a smirk on my face and my new "who's in control now, bitch?" attitude, courtesy of Ghetto Sybecca. Of course, I am smart enough to run to any room but the bedroom. He needs to go to work and stew in that! I wish I could call and talk to Stacey. She would laugh her ass off. God, I miss her.

In the study, I start looking over the books while I wait for Grayson to leave. I love this room. It's very feminine. Everything is creamy white, from the wainscoting to the built-in bookshelves. The walls are a cream-based red, and the light fixtures are shabby-chic and white as well. So is the couch. I could spend hours in this room.

I look at the wall on the right and it's filled with Renoirs. I love it! I almost feel as if this room was made for me. Which is absurd . . . but then again, it wouldn't surprise me.

I keep looking at the book spines, seeing if anything catches my eye. Oh wow, he has *A Christmas Carol* by Charles Dickens. I've never actually read that book, but I've always wanted to. I reach for it. This will be perfect to get me in the holiday spirit. *Tippy-toes. Tippy-toes and a jump.* Nope. I try to put the desk chair on the platform shelf. Just as I thought, the shelf is too small to support all four legs, but I can do two. If I hold on as I step on, I can steady it on the two legs.

"Don't you fucking dare!" Grayson snaps as I'm about to climb. He comes over and grabs the chair. "Which book, sweetheart?" He takes my hand to guide me off the platform. I tell him. My choice warrants a smile from him and he retrieves it for me.

"Thank you." I hold out my hand. He starts to pass it to me, but yanks it back.

"You know, sweetheart, you are very lucky I have a meeting I cannot be late for." His eyebrow shoots up.

"Really, baby? I don't know if I'd call that luck." I run my hands up his chest. I'd better stop. The look he's giving me tells me he might just fuck me into next week!

"I'll see you tonight." I pull his face down to mine and offer a harmless, sweet kiss.

"You drive me mad, sweetheart, on so many fucking different levels. I don't know whether I'm coming or going with you." He grabs my hand and kisses my wrist.

"Oh, Mr. James, surely you know when you are coming with me." I recycle his comment from several weeks ago. He chuckles a little and collects my face in his hands.

"Oh, Ms. Campbell, how I do love to come with you!" His lips caress mine one final time before he heads out.

"Love you, baby!" I yell after him.

"Love you too, darling!"

I smile. I can never stay mad at him.

Instead of calling Morgan's school, I dial the number for the B&B. I want to talk to Hazel. An unfamiliar voice answers, which saddens me. I feel like my dreams have been taken from me. I know Grayson is trying to help by making my business flourish and be less overwhelming, but at the end of the day, that's my baby!

I ask to speak to Hazel, and I'm put on hold. I listen to an ad about the B&B and the store. I didn't even know we were recording these. When did it happen? Fifteen minutes go by and I'm still on hold. Oh, hell no! I get my cell from my room and text Claudia.

November 12, 2012   8:15 a.m.
Me: Who is working the store desk? I have been on hold for 15+ mins now!

"Becca?" Claudia picks up the phone right away.

"Claudia, who the hell answered the phone? No one should be waiting on the phone like this!" I'm so irritated.

"Becca, I'm sorry. I don't know who answered. They should've said their name." Claudia sounds just as peeved as I feel.

"I'm sorry everything has been left to you, Claude." That's basically what Grayson did by making her general manager and throwing a pile of shit—my shit—into her lap. He just placed a generous bonus check on top to make it all smell sweet.

"Becca, it's okay. We're doing fine. I'm doing fine. Grayson has been great with approving any changes I make. Our profits are up. We're doing more crops. We have an event at the end of the month for a free 'Make It and Take It' night for new scrappers. I'm just trying to increase our clientele. We're running ads and many more tourists are stopping by! We've even hired a few more people."

"Claudia!" I cut her off.

"Yes?"

"Can I ask why *Grayson* is approving everything? This is *my* business, so I'm a little confused as to why no one is asking me about any of this."

"I'm so sorry, Becca. It's what Grayson instructed me to do. He didn't want you to have to worry about anything. Please don't be mad at me."

I can hear that she is on the verge of tears. I'm like a big sister to her—she's told me so many times—and I love her like family. She's been a good friend and employee, rainbow hair and all!

"Oh, Claudia, I'm not mad at you. You are doing a great job and I'm so proud of you. Really, I am! From now on, though, please come to me. Grayson had no right doing that. Now, what else is going on there? Has Stacey moved out yet? What's up with her?" Claudia will tell me. I know it.

"Becca, Stacey moved out a couple of days after you left. We haven't seen or heard from her since." She sounds a little off—shocked, maybe, that I don't know.

"Has anyone seen her around town?" I was already worried, but now my heart is pounding.

"No."

I feel as if I may vomit. "Did she say where she was going?"

"No. She just left. I guess she told security she didn't want them with her, that it was her right to refuse their services."

"How are Hazel and Charlie?"

"They are visiting family," she whispers.

"Is everything okay?" I ask, because it's almost as if she can't talk.

"Um . . . yeah."

"Anything else strange going on?" I feel like our time is running out.

"Yes, but I can't say."

"Security?" That controlling son of a bitch!

"Yes."

"Okay, ask them if they happen to speak French. But ask like you need help with it." She complies.

"Vous etes brilliant!"

Yes, I am pretty brilliant. I definitely have my moments, at least.

"Okay, tell me what's going on." I'm in complete James Bond mode!

"Il envoya Charlie et Hazel. Il dispose d'une equipe d'experts prendre soin des chevaux. La securite est extremement lourd ici!" I guess Grayson sent Charlie and Hazel away, but she says there's a whole team of experts taking care of the horses. That's good if Charlie's not there. Why is the security beefed up so?

"Claudia, why did he send them away, and for how long?" I knew something was up.

"Je ne sais pas. Il ne me dissent pas. C'était le silence meme tous les chut! Becca, que se passe-t-il? Je suis faire peur. Grayson à securite me suit partout trop! Quand vous etes venue à domicile?" Okay, I have to slow that down in my head. She said they didn't tell her how long or why. It was all hush-hush. She's got heavy security on her as well. She's scared and wants to know when I'll be home.

"Claudia, Grayson is protecting you. These people are highly trained. Do not blow them off at any time. I'm not supposed to come home for a month or so. I'm going to try to get out there sooner, though. I wish I had the answers for you, but he's keeping me in the dark as well. He's trying to protect us, but it's wrong. It leaves us more vulnerable. I will talk with him today. I love you, Claudia. Hang in there."

"I love you, too." I can hear her nerves.

"How are your other languages? Don't say them, because we may have to use them next time."

"Very good. Once again, I need to remind you that you are awesome!" She giggles.

"Yes, I am. I love him but he can go suck it!" I am pissed! She laughs and we say our goodbyes.

I quickly get dressed and head down to the kitchen, where I find Morgan digging in to her breakfast. It's almost nine o'clock. Her tutor should be here soon.

"Susanna, can you let Sam know I need a ride to Grayson's office?" I grab a fresh cup of coffee.

"I'm sorry, Becca. Sam is on an errand a few hours away."

"Where are the keys to Grayson's cars?" I ask cautiously and take a sip.

"Um, in the key cupboard by the garage door. Becca, he's very busy, maybe you should just call." Oh, she can see the steam coming out of my ears.

"Nope, need to see him in person."

Just then, the doorbell rings. I head down to greet Morgan's new teacher. She flashes me a fantastic smile. She must be about twenty-five. She's of average height, with golden-blonde hair, green eyes, and skin that has been kissed by the sun.

"Hi! I'm Abigail Stern!" She holds her hand out to me. I take it and return her smile. "Mrs. James, I presume?"

"Oh, call me 'Becca,' please. And we're not married yet," I offer. I don't know why. She's very nice, confident, personable, and attractive. I summarize Morgan's situation as we head toward the kitchen.

Morgan gets up to greet her new teacher. I can see she's glad Miss Stern is young and very fashionable. Instant hit! I have them follow me to Morgan's study, which Grayson had built over the weekend. There's a wall that was made into a blackboard with special paint, plus two desks: one for the teacher, and a smaller one for Morgan. There's shelving for educational books and two new, shiny computers. Abigail's eyes go wide, and she looks thrilled. I don't blame her—I would be, too!

"Well, Morgan can help you figure out what she's been working on 'til I hear back from her teacher at home. I have an errand to run. I'll be back later. Have fun, Morgy!" I give her a kiss.

I grab my purse from my room and head toward the garage.

"Becca, we can't let you leave," Melissa states as I look at the keys. There are so many! She seems uncomfortable, and I'm confused for two different reasons: why I can't leave, and why one person needs so many damn vehicles. Honestly!

"Melissa, I love you and I know you hate doing this, but I am not a prisoner, nor am I a piece of property. I can leave as I choose. I have a question for you, though." I smile.

"Um, what's that?" Oh, she's so conflicted. We've become very good friends, but she is under Gray's employ.

"Which car would you choose if you were pissed off at Ryan and wanted to do something to really stick it to him? I'm not big on cars, so I don't know which one is his 'baby.'" I do the air quotations.

"Do you know how to drive a stick?" She arches a brow.

"Yeah, like fifteen years ago, and I wasn't very good at it." Ugh, that will probably decrease my choices significantly. I look out into the garage again. *Which one of you owns Grayson's heart?* I look around. I'm miffed . . . no idea . . . damn it! If I were Grayson, I'd be able to figure it out. He knows me so well—better than I know myself sometimes.

Well, he didn't know that I'm fluent in five languages. *Suck it, Gray!* There's no record for him to learn about it, either, since we paid cash. Two years ago, Claudia and I bought some programs to learn other languages for the business—and our enjoyment. We often have conversations to make sure we stay fluent, and I never told him.

I go back to the key cupboard and grab the ones to the BMW X5. I've liked that SUV since Prue drove it on *Charmed*. "You coming?" I ask Melissa.

"Yes, of course." She follows me. If you can't beat them, join them! We slip in. It smells brand new. I start up the engine.

"Holy shit—this literally has two miles on it!" I'm wide-eyed. I put it in gear and hit the garage opener. "Can you plug Grayson's work address into the GPS?" I ask Melissa. She's on it. My cell plays "Chim Chim Cher-ee"—Grayson's ringtone.

"Good morning!" I answer sarcastically.

"I am *so* going to make you pray in French tonight, sweetheart." I can hear the lust in his voice.

"Aucune priere ne dit ce soir! C'est une promesse!"

"Oh, really? You sure about that?" Damn it—he speaks French.

"Yes, I am pretty sure I will not be saying any prayers," I snap.

"How do you like your engagement present?" He ignores my comment.

"What engagement present?" My ring?

"The vehicle you are driving. It's yours. Do you like it?" *Okay, maybe a little prayer.*

"This is mine?" *Goddamn it!* How does he know me so well? I went into a garage with ten cars, and chose the *one* he got for me? What the hell? *Way to stick it to him, Becca!* Point—Grayson James.

"Yes, sweetheart, it's yours. Do you like it?" He sounds unsure.

"It's too much and not necessary." I feel uncomfortable, actually.

"Becca, you needed a car, and I want you to have your heart's desire. If I got it wrong, I'll get you a different car." He seems disappointed.

"Clearly I needed a car. The other nine you have weren't sufficient enough!"

"It's a gift, Becca. Besides, I've experienced your driving. Better for you to have your own car and not drive any of my babies," he teases.

"I'll have you know I've never been in a car accident," I defend myself, then suddenly acknowledge I'm going twenty miles over the speed limit. *Oops.*

"Where are you going?" He changes the subject.

"To come see you." I'm irritated. I know he knows where I'm going!

"Don't you mean see me, then come?" He laughs at his own wittiness. I hang up, then look over at Melissa.

"Did you know he bought this car for me?" I ask. Her eyes grow wide.

"Uh . . . no. Wow!" She launches into a laughing fit. We've gotten into a few of these before. I laugh with her, though I don't know exactly what she's laughing about. Tears pour from her eyes. I find it pretty funny that she cries every time she laughs. "You spent so much time looking at the cars, and managed to pick the one he *bought you*! Way to stick it to him, Becca!" She laughs at me. My sentiments exactly!

"I know. I can't even stand it! It's creepy. I've never even mentioned this car to him."

"Well, I should have Ryan take lessons from him." She throws her hair back into a tie, and I nudge her with my elbow.

"How are things going with you two?"

"Pretty good. He's a great guy. I love being with him. I wish he was a bit more aggressive, though." She plays with her fingers.

"Do you mean in general, or in bed?" It's amazing how comfortable and confident I feel in a mentoring situation.

"Eh . . . both." She blushes.

"Well, let me ask you this. Do you feel that he cares enough not to judge you?" I glance over again, but focus on changing lanes so I can get off at the exit.

"Um, I don't know. We've only been sleeping together for a week, so it's all new." She tries to brush it off.

"Listen, you've been here since practically the beginning of my relationship. It didn't matter to Grayson whether it was our first or fiftieth time. He waves his freak flag proudly. It kind of forced me to let go and do the same. Maybe that's what you need to do."

"I think he's . . . well, we're both intimidated by your and Grayson's sex life. Sorry." She winces, but I don't care anymore. Practically the whole world has heard us going at it!

"Why? Why are we intimidating?"

"Because you guys sound so hot. All of us women feel like we need an extra pair of panties, and the guys, a sock and lotion."

I practically choke on my laughter. Melissa laughs too, but apologizes again.

"Oh, please, I know you all hear us. I can't be bothered to be embarrassed by it anymore. So we sound hot? That's an ego booster!" I pull into the parking garage and pick a space.

"Um, Becca . . . can you give me some pointers? I don't really have much experience." She plays with her fingers again.

"Sure."

She turns to me quickly. "Well, what kinds of things do you do that, um . . . drive Grayson wild?" I feel as if she is going to whip out a notebook and pen.

"Grayson, as you know, likes to spank me. But what really turns him on is when I beg him to. When he does, I beg for more. It drives him wild. You can do that with anything you like. It doesn't have to be spanking. The biggest thing, really, is communication. You have to let him know when you like something and when you don't. You also need to tell him what you would like him to do, or what you would like to try." God, I give great advice. I should have a booth like Lucy from *Peanuts*. "Remember, neither of you is going to know if you don't communicate it. Unless, of course, you're Grayson!" We both laugh. "Well, that's not entirely true. I do have to tell him things, too."

"I'm going to try to put your advice to work and I'll let you know. We've been talking for half an hour now. Do you want to head in?" She looks at the clock. I pick up my phone and realize I have a few text messages.

November 12, 2012   10:20 a.m.
Gray: I have a meeting now. Just wait.
Gray: Are you coming up?

Gray: Becca, goddamn it! Stop ignoring me!

Gray: I'm feeling a little Grey . . . if you know what I mean!

Gray: What are you doing?!

Me: Driving you crazy!

Just as I hit "send," a knock on the window makes me jump. It's Grayson—a very irritated Grayson. He looks down at his phone, then walks to Melissa's side and motions for her to come out. She does, and stands with Derek. Grayson slides in. He looks as if he just walked out of an ad for men's suits. He has to be the most beautiful man on the planet. Oh, wait—he is, according to the magazines.

"You look very handsome. Sorry, I hit my sound button before." I hold my phone and wave it in front of him for emphasis. He says nothing. He just sits, calmly awaiting the storm he must know is coming his way: Hurricane Becca, I believe they're calling her.

"Becca, can we get this over with?" His eyelids quicken their pace. *God, I want him.* What is wrong with me?

"C'mere." I pull on his jacket.

"Why? So it's easier to slap me?"

"No, baby, you're the one who does the slapping around here. C'mere ..." I bite my lip to hold back something . . . I don't know . . . my smile . . . my thoughts . . . my indescribable urge to jump him. He leans forward, very unsure. "Thank you for the car, baby." I lick my lips before catching his.

"Do you like it, darling?" He pulls back and gives me an excited look.

"Of course I do. You always know what I like. Well, for the most part."

"What do you mean? What have I missed?" I think he's actually going over everything in his mind.

"You've missed how important my business is to me, and how much I enjoy it." I let go of his jacket when he jerks back, his face lined with aggravation.

"Oh, you have to be fucking kidding me!" he yells. "I have done nothing but try to help you make your business better, because I know how much it means to you!"

"Yeah, you've done everything except let me run it! Why is everyone coming to you for approval? Why don't I know what's going on there at all?" I yell back.

"Becca, I am trying to help. I'm a pretty good businessman. I just want to see it reach its highest potential." He takes a deep breath. I can see him trying to calm down.

"Grayson, need I remind you that I've been very successful ever since I opened? I'm not an idiot!" I yell.

"Really? Really, Becca? Only an idiot would piss all of that extra money away by giving it to the goddamn mortgage company instead of her daughter's college fund, or investing it back into the business! No, sweetheart, your ship is sailing much smoother without your hands on the wheel." He quiets down when he sees a few people passing by. I'm silent too, but it's just because I'm trying to swallow the fact that he thinks I'm an idiot. I can't even bring myself to confront him about the other issues. Grayson runs his hands through his hair. "Becca, I can't be bothered with this rubbish at work. Just go home." He gets out of the car and waves for Melissa to come back.

"I think that's just what I'm going to do, Grayson. Go home," I say calmly.

"Good, sweetheart, I'll see you there." He glances over at me when I don't reply. "Wait. Becca, what do you mean?" He holds Melissa back and leans into the car.

"Well, Grayson, since you're not an idiot like me, I'm sure you can figure it out." I keep my voice calm and my focus in front of me.

"No, Becca, you can't—it's not safe! Please, I won't let you!"

"Goodbye, Grayson. Please let Melissa in now." I don't look at him. I can't. I'll lose it if I do. He gets out of the car, leaving the door open for Melissa, and walks over to my side.

"Becca, you are not leaving! *Am I making myself clear?*" I ignore him and lock my door. "Melissa, unlock her door." Melissa looks from me to him. "Unlock the bloody fucking door, or you're fired!" he yells at her. She jumps in and closes the door before he can get back around to her side. Her phone pings. She looks at it.

"I'm fired," she says as I pull quickly out of the space and speed through the garage.

"That's okay . . . so is he," I say as my dam breaks and the tears fall.

"Becca, what happened?" That's why I like Melissa—she's a great friend. She just got fired, and she's concerned about me.

"I just broke up with him, I think." I start crying. My phone rings. It's Grayson's signature tune. She hits "ignore" for me. It pings, and she reads it to me:

November 12, 2012   11:12 a.m.
Gray: Please, Becca! I love you! I'm the idiot!

"Melissa, better make hotel reservations for yourself. I'll pay for it," I tell her. "Can you look up flights for me to Boston, or Manchester if possible?" She starts tapping the keys on my cell. Once she gets into the website and puts in the info, my cell phone rings. She hits "ignore." It rings again. This happens about ten more times.

"Uh, Becca, if I didn't know any better, I'd say he's trying to make it so that you can't stay on the website to order the tickets."

"That's exactly what he's doing. Try your phone."

"I have no access . . . nothing . . . not even for calls. It's a company phone." We both sit back. He won this round. My heart is beating a mile a minute. I just need to get Morgan and leave. I'll get tickets at the airport if I have to.

We pull up to the house. I run inside, yelling for Morgan. Susanna comes out of the kitchen.

"Becca, Tanya took her out for lunch," she says.

"When?" I try to mask my frustration.

"Five minutes before you pulled in." She answers the house phone before it reaches its third ring, and says a lot of *uh-huh*s and *oh, I see*s before hanging up. "Becca, Grayson will be home soon. He wanted me to first tell you that he loves you and everything he does is because of that. He then said he's sorry, he cannot let you leave, but if you would like your own room, the staff will move your things. He also wanted to reiterate that he's deeply in love with you and truly sorry for what he said." She has tears in her eyes.

"He only said what he thinks of me. Please have the staff move my things."

"Becca, I don't know what he said to you, but I can assure you— you are everything to him. *Everything!* Please don't do this. Don't break his heart," she says through tears.

"I'm sorry, Susanna. I can't keep letting him break mine." I wipe my own tears away.

"It will all work out, Becca. It will." She pulls me in for a hug.

Chapter Eighteen

GRAYSON

"Sam, please go faster!" *Oh God, I can't believe this is happening!* I've really done it this time! Sam barely gets to a complete stop before I throw open the door. I run into the house and call out to Becca. I head to our room and stop short. My heart smashes into a million pieces. They are moving everything of hers out. God, I didn't think she would actually do it. I just . . . I thought if I offered, she would see I wasn't really trying imprison her. I just want to keep her safe.

"Susanna, where is she?" I ask as my stomach turns.

"She's in the study. Grayson, honey, you don't look so . . . oh dear."

I run into the bathroom to boot everything, including, I think, a sandwich I ate last week. *I hate vomit.* I head back to our room to brush my teeth. Christ, even her toothbrush is gone. This is absurd. Because I said one stupid thing that I didn't mean in the first place? No . . . no, I'm not letting her get away with this. She is going to hear me out, damn it!

With renewed confidence in my step, I open the study door and slam it behind me. Becca jumps. As she should—I am pissed!

"You are acting like a fucking child! You have no idea of the lengths I'm going to, just to protect you and Morgan and everyone else in your lives! How fucking *dare* you treat me like this? All because I said something stupid out of anger, that I didn't even mean? I have done nothing but help you, love you, and be by your side through everything since I've met you! Grow the fuck up, Becca!" There, I've said it all.

Becca looks down, continuing to read her book. I feel like I'm just about ready to step off the edge here. I lock the door to the study and head over to her. She glances up at me. She's nervous—I can see it on her face. Good! I grab her book and throw it.

"Let's see if you can ignore me now, sweetheart!" I grab her from the chair and practically throw her onto the couch.

"Grayson, don't . . . please . . . stop!" She fights me, but I pin her down so she can't move. I yank at her shorts. She stops fighting. "Grayson . . . Gray . . . look at me." I do so. "This isn't you. What are you doing? You don't want to do this to me. You're not George. Please, please stop." I actually feel my chin quivering. She's right. This isn't me. What am I doing?

"How could you try to just walk out on me? We had a silly fight, sweetheart. People say stupid things when they're fighting. I've called you worse, I think. I find you to be a very intelligent woman. I had no idea you were fluent in French. Every day, you amaze me in some way or another. Every day, I learn something new and interesting about you. I don't think you're an idiot. *I'm* the bloody idiot! I'm always doing or saying something that hurts you. I work so hard to keep you close, and I ruin it all with one weak, ignorant moment I have."

She's not saying anything. She just looks up at me, listening. I'm afraid to let her go. Afraid she will run.

"Becca, if I get up, do you promise to sit and talk with me? And not run?" My fingers trace her lips. God, I want to kiss her so bad. She nods. "Thank you," I say quickly before I go ahead and plant one on her. It really couldn't be helped. And just because I'm selfish, I kiss her again and again.

"Talk . . . not kiss." *Ah, she speaks.* I get up and she fixes her shorts. "Where are Charlie and Hazel? Why didn't you tell me that Stacey is MIA? And what's with all the extra security?" she asks all in one breath.

"Uh, wow . . . well, Aunt Hazel and Charlie are safe. We're looking for Stacey. And the extra security is because we may have uncovered something very interesting, but we haven't been able to pinpoint it yet. That's all you need to know. It's not safe for you and Morgan to return. For your own safety, that's all I can tell you." Ugh Christ, I know that won't go over well.

"Let me tell *you* something, Grayson. I know you think you are protecting me by keeping me out of the loop, but knowledge is power. Your way of protection may be the one thing that makes me vulnerable enough to get hurt. I want you to think about that." She gets up and heads to the door. "Oh, and I want Melissa back on the team. With that and you taking your control issues down a notch, I'll think about moving back into your room. Until then, remember to set your shower on cold, baby." And with that she's out the door . . . but just the door. Not my life.

Okay, I'll give her space and Melissa, but as far as her safety, my control issues are going to go through the roof! I know I have to double my efforts on finding Stacey. I have a terrible feeling. I don't know why she refused security. Something's just not sitting well with me. I sit back and notice Becca's book on the ground. I get up to grab it, and a picture falls out.

I don't know why, but I feel nervous. Why does she have a photo in her book? I pick it up and turn it over. Oh, it's a picture of me sleeping. When did she take this? God, I was such an arsehole today. She really does love me. I don't know why I still need validation, or why this picture seems to give it to me, but it does.

I leave the study and, by process of elimination, figure out which bedroom they've moved her to. Yes, I am quite the Sherlock Holmes! I knock on the door and wait for Becca's permission before I enter.

"Uh, you left this." It's very unsettling to know that she won't be in my bed tonight. What will the Hulk and I do? You can't choke or spank a Hulk. He is meant to do incredible things!

"What are you pondering over there? Oh, is it a theme song?"

Just as she asks, music from the beginning of *The Incredible Hulk* TV show plays in my mind.

"The opening to that TV show, *The Incredible Hulk*—it's a sad tune, isn't it, love?" Hmm, is that a smile I see her trying to fight off?

"Can I have the book, please?" She holds out her hand. I give it to her.

"Incidentally, it's very obsessive and stalker-like behavior, to be taking pictures of people when they are sleeping."

"Really? I love this picture. I may use it as a focal point with my new B.O.B." She sighs nonchalantly.

"Um, new B.O.B.?"

"Yes. Just because I'm cutting you off doesn't mean I have to cut myself off. I'm buying him right now . . . see?" She turns her laptop to show me.

"Becca, get off that website!" *Shit!* "Becca!"

"Don't worry. It's a secured site and they mail it to you discreetly." She hits the payment screen.

I'm ready to lose it! My technical staff is seeing this right now. She'd be mortified! Wait a minute . . . she's got a smirk on her lips. She bloody well knows they are looking at it!

"Oh, Becca, Becca . . . see, you are far from an idiot." I grin and shake my head.

"Actually, I think you're a little too close." Oh, that smart mouth of hers!

I sit on the bed and push a tendril of hair that's come free of her ponytail behind her ear. She takes in a sharp breath.

"Sweetheart, what do you need with a B.O.B. when you have a Hulk just down the hall?" I speak softly near her ear and sound as British as I possibly can. Her attempts at controlling her breath don't seem to be going very well.

"Well, B.O.B. doesn't wear purple pants. B.O.B. does not react irrationally."

"Pot, kettle, sweetheart." I trace her jawline with my fingers.

"Grayson, please leave." She's looking me straight in the eyes. I search for a sign, but she's not giving it to me. I lean in and she pulls away. "Leave . . . please." I palm her face and caress her lips with mine. "You are walking on very thin ice, Grayson! Stop it and get out. Go back to work!" She's getting angry . . . but so is the Hulk. I can't help but chuckle to myself. I've never referenced my guy down there as anything until Becca did, and now I can't bloody stop! I'm like a teenaged boy. "Stop laughing and get off of me."

"I'm not laughing at you, sweetheart. I love you. Thank you for staying." I kiss her again. She pushes me away.

"I didn't really have a choice, now did I?" She turns her head and exits the website. "Go. Please."

"Okay, sweetheart." I kiss her head and slowly get up to leave, just in case she changes her mind. She doesn't. I head back to work.

My cell rings. I answer. "Chris, you have something?"

"Yes. He's using a different cell."

"Have you been able to pinpoint the location?" I sit forward.

"No, but Sub Two is moving."

"What do you mean?"

"He's on the move, sir."

"Where to?" That motherfucker!

"Well, sir, he took a flight to Arizona. We lost his trail for a few days, but then he used his debit card. We think he may have used cash to purchase a car, sir."

"Why, Chris?"

He hesitates before responding. "He's already in California."
Jesus H. Christ!

"Chris, I want you to research any connection he may have out here! Get back to me—bye!" I hang up and call Derek.

"Derek, we need to increase security on the ranch and the girls!"

"Yes, sir, already on it." I end the call and do a silent prayer. I hope we're wrong. This is one time in my life I really want to be wrong.

I need to be careful with Becca. One wrong move on my part, and she could put herself in danger. I try my hardest to focus on work. I think—and hope—that things may be calming down a bit. I received word that the SEC will be dropping all charges by the end of this week and making a full public apology. Once that happens, I will take Becca and Morgan away. See if that son of a bitch can keep up with us!

Work takes forever, but I am able to leave at five o'clock. That's the earliest I've left since I've been back, with the exception of Friday. I call home only to find out that Becca has been in her room all day. No phone calls, emails, or texts.

As soon as we arrive home, I immediately head to her room. I open the door to find her asleep. I know I'll get hell for it later, but I strip down to my underwear and climb in with her. *Jesus—she's only wearing a T-shirt and panties.* I snuggle up to her and she rolls into my arms. I hold her close. My hands caress her bum like they always do. She lets out a soft moan and kisses my neck like she always does. I need to control myself, otherwise she's going to wake up and be pissed. I stop and close my eyes. Sleep comes over me.

BECCA

My head is pounding. It's because I haven't eaten since this morning. I look over at the clock. It's seven. I turn back into Grayson. I have no damn willpower! I want him so bad. I tried the whole "I'm sleeping, take advantage of me" routine when he climbed in, but I think he got nervous.

Ugh—he smells so good. *No, Becca! Stand your ground—back away!* I turn away from him, only to feel him snuggle up behind me. I feel his hand slide under my shirt and up to my breast, and he circles his fingers around my nipple. He often does this in his sleep, and then my hips usually do what they are doing right now— grinding my bottom into him. *Damn it!* This usually wakes him up enough to inform me of his intentions. *Oh, God, I want him.* I really have no willpower. Why did he have to come in here? I can't control my breathing. *Fight or flight? Fight or flight?* Grayson's hand slides slowly down from my breast to my belly. He softly caresses me there as his lips work at my neck.

Horny Sybecca is on deck, moving seductively around her pole and gyrating her pelvis toward it complete. I was so focused on watching her I didn't even realize my own hips' betrayal. Somehow, unbeknownst to me, my hips shifted themselves back enough to allow Grayson's fingers easy access. He slides them deep inside me, commanding the moans that now escape my throat. His palm starts at my clitoris as well. It's all so very slow and so intense—the rise drives me wild. I feel like I can't breathe. I want to cry. It's a sweet misery. I want him to quicken the pace, but he won't. He opens my lips with his, allowing his tongue to find mine and help me work through my sweet, agonizing quakes. I finish and try to catch my breath against his mouth. I don't know how he does it, but he manages to get us both out of our underwear. Before I can tell him to stop, he's inside of me and . . . *God, he feels so good.*

I hold on to the small of his back and his lovely ass, helping him push into me. I wrap my legs around the back of his and suddenly we're making love as if the world was ending tomorrow. We bathe in each other and finally come undone together. No prayers are said . . . maybe silent ones. We muffle the beauty of this moment with our mouths, keeping it private— between us only. Grayson crashes, breathless, onto my chest. As we lie there in our sweaty afterglow, it seems like forever and not long enough. Grayson finally climbs off of me. He grabs my hand in his and plays with it. I close my eyes and feel his lips kissing each one of my fingertips, my palm, my wrist. He turns a little on his side to face me and props himself up on his elbow. His other hand softly caresses my stomach again.

"Hungry, sweetheart?" His voice is almost a whisper.

"Yes." *But I don't want to leave the room.* He grabs his phone and begins to text. Who the fuck is he texting? He gets a ping, then puts the phone down and scoots back over to me. I feel the attentiveness in the kisses he trails along my shoulder. His fingers are doing a pattern of swirls on my stomach. He's always been an affectionate man, but tonight seems very different. I can sense he is treading lightly. His lips find their way to my neck, my jawline, and finally reconnect with mine. He's being so soft and gentle. No hint of his usual aggression in the bedroom.

"I'm so in love with you, Becca," he breathes, and kisses me again and again. My heart is aching; I love him so much. After several minutes of mutual petting and savoring, there is a knock on the door. "Excuse me, sweetheart." He pecks my nose before he gets up. I hear him slip his pants on. I pull myself up and turn the bedside lamp on. It takes me a moment to focus, but he turns back from the door with covered plates in his hands. I have no idea what I even feel like eating. My rush of adrenaline is over and my headache is back. I reach down to my purse to get some Motrin for it.

"Headache, sweetheart?" He climbs back on the bed with our food.

"Yeah. I haven't eaten since this morning." I run my hair behind my ears.

"Let's fix that." He takes the lids off the plates. I'm greeted by gooey grilled cheese and tomato sandwiches with cream of tomato soup.

"What made you choose this?" I glance at him sideways.

"Why? You don't like this? I'll have Susanna fix you something else." He starts to cover it. I stop him and give him a look.

"I love this. I'm just used to you picking out more complicated things for me. So, why this meal?" *Mmm . . . she put cheese in the soup.* So good.

"Um . . . I guess our lovemaking was different tonight. Let me finish," he says before I even open my mouth. I guess I'd usually cut him off with some sort of witty remark. Not tonight, though—I agree. It was different. "There was . . . it was, at least for me, very calming and comforting. Soothing, really. I wanted to eat something that makes me feel the same way. Make sense?" His eyelids are running at a steady, passionate pace.

"Complete sense, Gray." Although I don't think I'll ever tell anyone he compared our lovemaking to grilled cheese. I just don't think they'd understand. "Incidentally, I have a trivia question for you." I smile and kiss his shoulder.

"About?"

"Me."

"Oh, my favorite type of trivia question. Go on." He wipes his mouth, then the corner of mine, with his napkin before he kisses me.

"So, obviously, I love grilled cheese with tomatoes." I wave my sandwich and say "tomato" with an accent. "What else do I like on them?" I bite into mine.

"Bacon, because you've been eyeing mine." He smiles and switches half of his with mine. "Um, ham?" he adds.

"How do you know what I want all the time?" I switch our sandwiches back when I see him eyeing his.

"I make it a point to know what you want and need. You are

my favorite subject." He leans in for a kiss. "I had a theme song while we were making love," he says, and grabs his phone. He messes around with the screen and types the song in. He presses "play" and "The Promise" by When in Rome comes on. It tugs right at my heart strings. I move our tray of empty plates and hit "repeat" on his phone. I straddle him and take his face in my hands, then caress his lips gently with mine. I'm so in love. It's raw, powerful, confusing, freeing, and imprisoning all at once. I get lost in his smell and our lovemaking again.

"Becca," he says breathlessly.

"Yes?"

"Can I have the staff move your stuff back into our room?" He sounds calm and patient. I want to agree for obvious reasons, but I want to hold out because I feel like an idiot. I didn't even last twelve hours. Some stand I made. Grayson kisses my cheek and climbs out of bed. He starts to get dressed.

"What are you doing?" This is so not like him. First of all, he normally wouldn't ask. My stuff would've been moved whether I wanted it to or not.

"Sweetheart, you didn't have an answer for me straight away. That tells me you're not sure. I don't want to pressure you. I almost lost you today. I'm going to try to not do anything to push you away again. I'll be patient. I'll wait. You're here, that's what's important. So, I'll see you in the morning, love?" He leans in for a kiss.

"Are you going to sleep?" I'm curious, because I'm wide awake. I should be. I slept all day. What the staff must think of me. I left Morgan in their care without even asking.

"Um, no, I was just going to do some work in my office. Why?" He sits on the bed.

"Well it's only nine o'clock. I've slept most of the day, so I'm not tired. Do you want to go out and do something? A date? We haven't done that in a while." I wince a little, anticipating a reason why we can't go.

"Hmm. What would you like to do?"

"We can catch the last showing of something at the movies. It's Monday, so there won't be a lot of people." I grab my laptop and lay on my belly to look up the movie times. Grayson's hand caresses my bare bottom. I know he wants to, and I want him to, too. "Go ahead, baby." I turn my neck to look back at him. He takes in a sharp breath, looks at my bum, then shakes his head.

"I did a number on you last night, sweetheart. I'll wait." I can see the longing in his eyes.

"I want you to, baby. Please." I pull my shirt up higher. His eyelids start going crazy. I look back at the laptop and wait anxiously for the sweet sting of his slap.

GRAYSON

Look at her. She's waiting for it. She can't concentrate on the movie times. But if I slap her now, I'm going to want to take her there.

"Becca, I can't," I say regretfully and pull her shirt down, not that it covers her. I kiss the welts from last night softly. That was a result of having the same strong desire and knowing I couldn't do anything about it.

"Why?" There's a sense of panic in her question.

"Sweetheart, if I do, I'm going to want to do something else to your bum as well. My desire for that has been very strong." I feel uncomfortable telling her this.

"Oh," is all she says. She gets up, grabs her clothes, and heads into the bathroom. *Damn it!* I shouldn't have said anything. I resume her movie search. Ugh, the latest chick flick and an action film. I have no idea what she'd prefer. Pretty obvious what I'd prefer.

I glance over to her when I hear the door open. "Hey, sweetheart, new *Avengers* movie or *Pearl's Wish?*"

"Whatever you want. Actually, no. I want to see the new *Avengers* movie. The guy who plays Thor . . . yum!" I just stare at her, trying to control my tendency to be jealous. "And you're in the movie." She giggles. *Huh?* Oh, the Hulk. I shake my head and get up. "I'm sorry."

"For?" I look around the room.

"That you can't do that with me." She glances away.

"Hey." I chuck her chin. "Don't. It's okay. I'm sorry I mentioned it. I'm sorry about last night."

"You were so aggressive. You really hurt me. I thought I did something wrong." She's playing with the buttons on my shirt instead of looking at me.

"It wasn't you, sweetheart. I don't know what came over me. It won't happen again." I kiss her hair and hold her to me. "Shall we go, then?"

Sam brings us to the movies. Monday is a great night to go; I didn't have to rent the whole place out. Becca teases me during the movie—fanning herself and licking her lips every time Chris Hemsworth comes on the screen.

"Hey, could you introduce me?" she leans over and asks. I give her a look and drop her hand. She giggles.

"Just shut up, Becca, and watch the movie!" *Damn it!* Why does she make me feel like this? She keeps glancing over at me. I don't even know what the hell's going on on-screen. "Let's go. You are the most irritating person to go to a movie with!" I stand up and hold my hand out.

"Sit down, Grayson."

I comply, but ignore her. I pull out my phone and start emailing Carol about tomorrow's agenda. I text Chris to see if he's got any more info. Becca grabs her bag and moves two aisles down. Good.

Go ahead, then. I'm never taking her to another damn movie! I don't know why I'm even sitting here; I haven't a clue about what's happening. I get up and leave the theater. As I reach the car, my phone pings.

November 12, 2012   10:30 p.m.
Becca: Lucky u got laid b4 this date because u r not getting it after!
Me: Text me when u r ready 4 me to walk u out.
Becca: Fuck off!
Me: Don't u mean fuck auff? Incidentally, my theme song has changed to "Jersey Girl" by the Boss.

She doesn't text me back. Half an hour passes, and I'm feeling a bit nervous. I shouldn't have left her there alone. Well, Melissa and Ryan are in the theater, but they're having quite the snogging session, so I've basically left her alone.

"Sam, I'm heading back in," I grumble. I walk into the movie theater only to have Becca walk right past me. I turn and grab her hand, my way of letting her know to not even think about trying anything. As soon as we arrive at the car, she yanks her hand away and gets in. *Oh, fuck—here we go again!*

"What was the point of asking me to take you out on a date if you were going to do nothing but irritate me the entire time? I mean, really, sweetheart! What a waste of bloody fucking time!" She opens her mouth as if she's going to say something, but closes it and looks out the window instead. "Yes. Why don't you finish your childlike behavior today with a good dose of the silent treatment—that ought to get me thinking!" I can't help my sarcasm. I've never sugarcoated my feelings before—I'm certainly not going to start now, danger or no danger. I look down at my phone and check my email, glancing up at every once in a while. She's visibly upset—her chin quivers, and she shakes her leg to a point of annoyance (annoying me, that is). I feel myself soften toward her a bit, though I don't know why. She wanted to leave me today. Maybe that's it. Does she want to leave me now? I look down at her ringed finger. I slide my hand under hers and gently grip the ring as if I'm taking it off. She breathes sharply as she looks down at the ring and up at me. *No, she doesn't want to leave me.*

"Just straightening it out, sweetheart," I lie, but turn it a bit to be convincing. She relaxes and looks out the window again. Sam pulls up to our gate and punches the code in. Becca tightens her grip on her purse as we head up the driveway and around the fountain. Becca is out of the car as soon as we stop, as if someone shot the gun at a race. I, being the bloody idiot of the day, charge after her and grab her arm just as she's about to reach her room. I swing her around to me.

"Good night, sweetheart," I say before I crash my lips onto hers. She pulls her face away from me and turns to avoid any more advances. "Goddamn it, Becca!" I open the door for her and turn on my heel to walk away. I wave for her detail to get into position outside of her door. And because she's been acting like a bloody child today, I have detail outside her window as well. Christ! This is going to be a long damn night!

BECCA

I open my eyes to the sound of the gardener running some sort of equipment outside my window. I glance over at the clock. Eight in the morning—great! I got a little over four hours of sleep. I throw the covers back and muster the energy to swing my legs around and let my feet touch the floor. I take in a deep breath and take note of my feelings. I'd like to say that I am calm now, but I would be lying to myself. Nope, I'm still thoroughly pissed. It may be irrational, but I can't seem to shake it. A shower may help my disposition—or at least my appearance. God, I look dreadful! I stare at myself in the mirror. It's like a truck has hit me. My color is nonexistent and I have circles under my puffy eyes. Well, I *was* up until after three. That's what I get! I turn the shower on and proceed to get undressed as it warms up.

I step in and let the water pelt away my problems. I still can't believe he left me in the theater by myself. I don't "do" movie theaters by myself. I hate it. So much for my safety; he left me in there with Melissa and Ryan, who were too busy doing what new couples do. Well, young ones, I guess. Somebody could've been in and out of there with me before they even came up for air. What was he thinking? Christ, I was just teasing him. Something's definitely wrong for him to get so damn bent out of shape like that. Calling me a child? Me? He is the most petulant, irascible, impervious, bombastic (oh, the list could go on and on) man I have ever met. He exercises no prudence in how he behaves! *Ow! Damn it!*

Note to self: Never shave your legs while pulling every describable word out of the dictionary to toss imaginatively at the man you are pissed at! Crap, I hope that doesn't leave a scar. I watch as my blood swirls at the drain before going down. It looks as if I'm on the set of *Psycho*. I may very well be.

I step out of the shower and dry off as best as I can while trying to stop the ever-flowing river of blood down my right leg. Ugh. Not an itty-bitty cut—no! It has to go right up the outside of my entire calf. Might as well have a blaring neon sign that says, "Look at me! Look at me!" Ah, the toilet paper should do. Apparently, there's no room in the budget to garnish each bathroom in this house with some gauze and tape in its medicine cabinet.

Toilet paper intact, I throw my wet, wavy hair up into a tie and brush a little makeup onto my face. In the bedroom, I waltz over to the closet and pull out a simple, olive-green T-shirt dress that cinches at the waist to throw on with black flip-flops. One last look in the mirror before I head out with my new disposition . . . forced to be present against its will. Eh, I'll do!

The kitchen smells lovely, as usual. Susanna's a wonderful cook. We've been comparing a lot of notes and exchanging recipes. I walk past Grayson, who is sitting at the table. He's already worked through half of his breakfast. I grab a mug from the cupboard and fill it with coffee.

"Oh, Becca, cream and sugar's on the table already, honey." Susanna smiles as she comes in from the pantry and rubs my back a little. "Sit down. I'll bring you your breakfast."

"Thanks." I blow on my coffee as I sit at the table. I feel the heat of Grayson's intense stare as I dress my coffee to my liking.

"Here you are." Susanna places a bacon, ham, tomato, and cheese omelet in front of me and begins to walk away. I notice a slight smirk at the corner of Grayson's mouth.

"Susanna, I'm sorry. It looks lovely. I just don't feel like an omelet this morning."

"Oh. Um, what would you prefer?" She looks to Grayson, then to me. I glance over at Grayson. His smirk is now a frown, and he scans his newspaper frantically as if it's the pages' fault he ordered the wrong thing for me. I actually feel bad that I just lied, seeing how much it bothers him to be wrong. That never happens. I am being a bit silly.

"Cinnamon-raisin toast will be fine." I smile and sip my coffee.

"I'm sorry I left you in the theater last night. I shouldn't have done that. It was childish of me to do so," Grayson finally says. He puts his paper down on the other side of the table to look at me. Wow. I wasn't expecting that. I pull my omelet to me and add ketchup. *I'm really not the wasteful type.* "I'm also sorry to see that you've apparently lost the battle with your razor, sweetheart." He leans back in his chair and looks down at my legs. "Here," he pulls his chair back and pats his lap, "let us see what you've done to that gorgeous leg of yours." I offer a slight eye roll. Not very affective, though, when there's a slight smile along with it. I take a bite of my omelet before propping my right leg up on his lap. He pulls my flip-flop off and gives my foot a quick rub before he sets out to pull the long strips of toilet paper off my leg. "Susanna!" he calls out

"Yes?" She walks in with a new loaf of cinnamon-raisin bread.

"Can you fetch me some peroxide and bandages? And never mind about the toast." He arches a brow at me, causing a small giggle to escape my throat. *Damn it.* "Christ, Becca," he says under his breath as he assesses the damage. I wince as well.

"Becca! What have you done to yourself?" Susanna chimes in as she places the peroxide and bandages down. "You're going to need antibacterial cream." She sighs and leaves the room once more.

"Will I live, Dr. James?" I ask with mirth as I pop another forkful of omelet into my mouth.

"Oh, this is funny to you, aye? Bloody hell, Becca! Walking around with toilet paper in a deep gash like this, as if it were nothing! You could've gotten a terrible infection!" He's terse. I can't help but laugh. His accent is so thick I envisioned a question mark after he said "toilet paper." I stifle my laugh at his hardened expression.

"Well, thank you, doctor, for saving my leg from amputation." I attempt seriousness. I mean, this *is* a very serious situation. I could've lost my leg! "It's all my fiancé's fault. You should send him the bill."

"Really, now?" He looks up from lightly patting the peroxide-drenched bandage over said wound. "Please, enlighten me."

"Well, you see, I was very busy mentally pulling words out of the dictionary that would be most descriptive of said fiancé. It was quite distracting, as there are many, many words to describe such a man. It caused quite a terrible slip of the wrist, and now I fear I may be scarred for life." I take another bite as he uses a cotton swab to gently apply the antibacterial cream.

"Yes. I understand. Words like *handsome, masculine, sensual, appealing,* and *irresistible* can be quite distracting." He bites his lower lip a bit as he places the bandage over my wound.

"Hmm . . . yes, you're right. That could be. But I was thinking more along the lines of *petulant*, *irascible*, *impervious*, and, oh, *bombastic*," I say thoughtfully.

"Bombastic?" he asks, unable to hold back his smile.

"Yes. Bombastic." I widen my eyes. Grayson grabs my face and attacks my mouth with his. After the initial shock, I give in to his advances.

"Please tell me you didn't sleep well last night either." He's breathless, resting his forehead against mine.

"I didn't fall asleep until after three," I offer.

"Well, there we have it! Susanna, please have the staff move Becca's stuff back."

"Grayson, I didn't say—" I start, but he puts his hand up.

"This is ridiculous, Becca. No—you are coming back in," he snaps, and pushes his finger over the tape outlining my bandage one more time for good measure. He puts my flip-flop back on and I pull my leg from his lap. I say nothing else about the matter. What's the point? He tried to be patient and less controlling. He lasted longer than the stand I made. Point—Grayson James.

He pushes his plate back and puts his head in his hands. He finally runs his hands through his hair.

"We can't keep doing this, Becca. It's not normal to be arguing this much. I don't want to feel like I have to walk on eggshells constantly. It's bloody fucking annoying!"

I get up and sit on his lap. "You do realize that you are trying to argue with me about arguing?" I attempt to restrain my giggle, but I'm not successful. "Yes, it can be annoying, but Gray, this is our normal. We bait each other. Then we relate to each other." I laugh at my little rhyme.

"Becca, I'm being serious." He seems disappointed.

"Well, I am, too. Gray, you are controlling. You have to expect the results you get sometimes." I sigh.

"Ha! You'll do well to admit to yourself that you like to be controlled by me."

"I do not!"

"You do too, Becca—fucking think about it!" I can feel his heart pounding through his shirt. I take in a deep breath and think about it. Okay he's right, to a point. *Only* to a point!

"You like it when I fight you on a lot of things you're trying to control."

"Oh, I beg to differ, sweetheart!"

"You don't think so, huh?"

"No, I don't."

"Hmm. Okay, we'll see." I kiss his mark.

"What does that mean?" He grabs my chin gently.

"That means, be careful what you wish for, baby." I tap his nose with my finger.

"So you're going to teach me a lesson?" His lips trail down my neck as his hands go up underneath the skirt of my dress.

"Yes I am, starting now. When you've realized I'm right, just say 'old Becca, please.'"

"So 'new' Becca won't be fighting me on anything?" His eyes widen.

"Nope."

"Good. Let's go to our room then! I'm dying for one of your fantastic blow jobs, sweetheart!" He places me on my feet and drags me to our room. *Wow . . . that's romantic.*

GRAYSON

I am one happy bloke! I've had ten whole days of a non-argumentative Becca. No walking on eggshells. I say whatever I want, whenever I want. She doesn't argue with me when I tell her not to ask any more about certain things, like Ray and Stacey.

I've had to heighten security again because he's gotten closer.

She's not allowed to leave the house at all. I can see she's irritated by this, but . . . her lovely, lovely mouth stays shut.

"Becca, sweetheart, you really made Thanksgiving lovely. I've missed your cooking. It was delicious. Everyone enjoyed it." I sit behind her on the bed and put my arms around her waist.

"Thank you, baby." She pats my hand as if to dismiss me. *Well, that's irritating!*

"Becca, what are you doing?"

"You wouldn't let me do my Black Friday shopping, so I have to redo my list for Cyber Monday." She pats my hand again. Is she for real?

"Are you for real, Becca? You don't need to go chasing sales and bargains. I think we can afford to do our shopping without this nonsense."

"It's not a matter of what you can afford. It's the chase in finding the bargain!" Oh, she's irritated. So fucking hot!

"Well, it's silly, really, to chase something you may not end up with in the end. I just get what I want and call it a day." I kiss at her neck.

"Yeah, I'm well aware of that, Grayson." She's flippant with me.

"Good. Then close the goddamn laptop and turn this Black Friday into a Good Friday for me."

"Oh yes, sir. Anything for you, baby." She turns to me. "How does sir wish to be pleased today?" She pulls off her shirt and closes her eyes. She's probably talking Ghetto Sybecca down. Oh, God, I miss her. Maybe she was right. No! Nope, I'm having a moment of temporary weakness. "What do you want, baby? How do you want me? On top like this?" She climbs on me. "In the shower? My mouth? What do you need, baby?" She's speaking so seductively.

"I just need you, Becca. Whatever you want." I pull her bra off and grasp her lips with mine.

November 23, 2012   10:17 a.m.

Me: We have to go to NH in 2 weeks 4 your divorce hearing.

Becca: okay

Me: Do you still want to marry me?

Becca: Why do you ask?

Me: You know why, Becca

Becca: No sir . . . I don't.

Me: I know you're unhappy.

Becca: Only because I am away from you ☹

Me: Becca, stop!

Becca: Would sir like me to come to his place of business to be near him. So I can be ☺?

Me: Shut up!

Becca: Yes sir, but I'm not talking, I'm texting. ☺

Me: Becca, I swear to God! I'm going to paddle your ass!

Becca: Oh sir, as with everything u do 2 me, that will feel so good and be so well deserved!

Jesus H. Christ! I dial her number. "Becca!" I yell when she answers but says nothing.

"Yes, sir."

"You win, sweetheart. You were right. I want my old Becca back, if it's not too late."

"It's about fucking time, you asshole! Oh, I hope you enjoyed yourself and got your fill, because you are not getting any for a while!" I can't even control the smile on my face.

"Really, Becca? You think you can last twelve hours this time without my dick in you?"

"Oh, you arrogant bastard! I'm going to last a lot longer than twelve hours!" She's on fire.

"Really? Well, I'm coming home to test that theory out." I close out my computer after emailing Carol to cancel anything I have this afternoon.

"Do us both a favor and keep your ass at work! Stay the fuck away from me, Grayson!" She hangs up.

November 23, 2012   10:35 a.m.
Me: No can do, sweetheart . . . I'm addicted to you
Becca: I'm leaving ...
Me: LIKE HELL YOU ARE!
Becca: I'm already gone!
Me: What?

I call her again, but it goes to voicemail. I feel my world crashing down as I try again with the same result. Susanna was right. She told me to stop treating Becca like this. She told me how sad and withdrawn she's been. How the hell did she leave? It can't be possible. She complains that she can barely pee by herself!

I call the head of security for the Calabasas location. "Jack! Where are Becca and Morgan?" I loosen the tie around my neck and unbutton my collar.

"Sir, Morgan's right here with her teacher. I'll locate Becca for you." I get into the car and wait anxiously. "Sir . . . uh, I can't seem to find her," he says nervously.

"How the fuck did you lose her?" I yell and hang up. I hit my tech's number, "Chris, track Becca's cell. Where is she?"

"At the house, sir." No, her cell is. *Shit!* I call the house and ask to speak to Morgan.

"Did Mummy say where she was going?"

"No, Daddy." I hang up and slide out of the car. Sam got me here in record time.

"Where's Melissa?" I ask Jack as I walk in.

"Gone too, sir."

"Text her and tell her she's fucking fired! I don't care if Becca keeps my dick in her mouth for a week! She's not getting her goddamn job back! Text everything I've just said!"

"Grayson!" Susanna yells, heading straight for me. "How dare you speak of Becca that way, and in front of strangers, no less?" She smacks my arm.

"You'll do well to remember that you are my employee, Susanna!"

"And you're behaving like a spoiled brat! Now go to your room, take a shower, and calm the hell down." She's out of her fucking mind, this one! "Git!" she yells, turns me around, and slaps my ass as if I'm five years old. Am I in the middle of *The Twilight Zone*? I can't believe she just did that! And yet, here I am, turning the fucking shower on like a good boy! I must be losing my mind.

I lean my hands against the wall and let the water pelt me. "Where is she, damn it?" I say out loud.

"Right here, baby." I hear Becca and feel her touch at my back. I turn sharply to her and grab her face harshly, bringing her to me. I back her up to the wall and search her eyes. "Nice text, by the way." No *I'm sorry I scared the shit out of you*. Typical Becca!

"Where the fuck were you?" I yell.

"Not where you looked. Oh wait, that's right, you didn't look, did you?" *A game?* At a time like this, with all I have on my plate, she wants to play a game?

I let go of her face. "Becca, it's over." I feel my heart breaking as I say it.

"What's over? The lawsuit? Oh, Grayson—that's fantastic, baby!" She throws her arms around my neck and kisses my face.

"No, Becca." I pull her off. "We're over. You're going back to New Hampshire as soon as I get the plane ready." I walk out of the shower and hand her a towel.

"You're kidding, right?" She wraps herself in it and follows me.

"No, I'm not. I can't do this anymore. Your life is in danger. You make a joke out of your safety and out of my concern for you. I have so much on my plate already—I'm done with this sort of behavior. If you don't care, why should I?"

"Grayson, I was baiting you. You've been a real bastard for the past two weeks. Everyone has seen it! You wanted so bad to be right that you set out to humiliate me." She touches my arm, because Becca cannot talk without touching . . . it's so fucking distracting!

"Hu-mil-li-a-shon?" Wow, I just sounded extra British to myself. "You want to talk to me about humiliation? How about the woman I pay to keep your arse safe, who defies my every order? I'm her bloody fucking boss! All because you had to become BFFs with her! How about Susanna, who's been in my employ for fucking *years*, slapping me and calling me a spoiled fucking brat in front of my other employees? You've won them all over, and now their fucking loyalty is to you? I sign their goddamn checks! They all look at me as if I'm some kind of fucking arsehole!" I am wild. I can't control myself one bit.

"That's because you've been acting like a fucking asshole!" She raises her hands in the air and follows me into the bedroom.

I pick up my cell. "Yeah, Smitty. New Hampshire. Okay. Good. Two hours then. No. Becca, Morgan, and possibly Melissa. Okay. Great. Thanks." I hang up. I go to my dresser and grab jeans, a T-shirt, and some underwear. "Dress and get packed. Your flight is in two hours. I want my ring." I hold out my hand.

"Baby, we're just having a fight." Her chin quivers and tears spill down her face.

"Yes, we are, sweetheart—our last one. Now give me the ring so I can say goodbye to Morgan." I take her hand and pull it off. I turn to walk away. Becca moves quickly to block me.

"Please, Grayson. Don't do this. I have forgiven you for far worse behavior. This isn't fair! Please, I'm so in love with you. I'll do anything. What do I have to do?" She's hysterical. I just want her to leave me alone so I can go somewhere in the house and get completely shitfaced. I'm throwing the love of my life out on her arse. I need to go somewhere and be destructive. "Please, Grayson, we love each other. This is not going to work. We'll be miserable without each other. Tell me, what do you want me to do?"

I don't want her to leave. What the fuck am I doing? Ugh, Christ, she drives me fucking mad! My phone rings. I look down at it. It's Gregory Thomas.

"Yes, Greg?" I answer. I listen and feel my heart sink as Greg informs me that Stacey's been found. I slip the ring back on Becca's finger, chuck her chin, and place a gentle kiss on her lips before I head to the bed to sit down. She's barely alive. Raped, sodomized, and beaten to a pulp. She's on life support . . . her prognosis doesn't look good. They're not sure she'll make it through the night. I mouth to Becca to get dressed.

"Greg, did you call Jack and let him know? Okay, good. We're leaving in two hours, which will bring us to you by ..." I look at my watch. "Ten-thirty tonight, give or take. Yes, we'll bring our team from here. Great, thanks." I hang up.

"Where did they find her? Is she alive?" Becca sits beside me. It's creepy how she does this sometimes.

"Barely, sweetheart. Guess we're going to New Hampshire any-way. We'll leave Morgan here, where it's safer." For the second time in twenty minutes, Becca is hysterical. I pull her into my arms.

"Grayson, I'm sorry for not taking things seriously enough. I don't know, when he kidnapped me, it was all about the money. The only time he hit me was when I mouthed off to him. Do you think he didn't do this to me because he thought he would get money from you?" She looks up at me.

"Probably," I say to her. *No,* is what I'm thinking. I think he was already being paid to hold her and not harm her. The plan back-fired, though, and we've been trying to track him and predict his next move. I have a few ideas about who this silent partner is, but it's all circumstantial. We need something more to present to the police . . . and Becca.

"You know what I don't get?" she asks.

"What's that?

"Why he assumed Ray was rich. I mean, Ray is not poor, and his business has survived the economy so far, but he's certainly not rich. Then again, George isn't the brightest bulb in the package." She throws her hair up in a tie.

"Becca, you never said he thought Ray was rich." *Hmm.*

"Yeah, he referred to you both as my 'rich boyfriends.' Come to think of it . . . Grayson, how would he know that you have money? I mean, he's been gone for seven years, and when he kidnapped me, we hadn't been together very long. Grayson, somebody has to be feeding him information. He must have a partner. Who, though? Who would want to partner with him and why?" Oh, she *is* the trifecta!

"Is there anything else you can think of that I can pass along to the team?" I move a tendril of fallen hair behind her ear.

"Nope. Nothing else."

"Okay, sweetheart, let's go tell Morgy we have to go back east for a lawyer's meeting or something." I slap her leg and stand up.

"Gray, how is she?" Her chin starts quivering again.

"Not good, Becca. She's on life support." Becca falls into my arms, sobbing. I hold her tightly and curse myself for almost throwing her out to the same wolves. I need anger-management classes, I think. I was never like this. Ever since this little one here, I have been out of my mind with all kinds of emotion. "C'mon sweetheart, we have a long day ahead of us." I pat her bottom. She looks up and me and searches my face. I palm hers and dip my head down slowly to kiss her.

Acknowledgements

I have so many people to thank. Without them, this wouldn't have been possible.

First, my three beautiful children, who, by the grace of God, still think I'm awesome even though I've been a bit preoccupied following my dreams. You are the biggest blessing in my world and the best dream come true. I love you!

Phil, thank you for your constant love, support, and friendship over the years, and for always believing in me.

Jennifer Bedet, my first beta reader and one of my oldest and dearest best friends. I'd be lost without you. You are the Stacey to my Becca, the Ethel to my Lucy. I thank you thirty-eight times for book one! LOL!

Rebecca Carnahan, your friendship has been a blessing in my life. Thank you for reading, editing, laughing in all the right places, and cheering me on through the whole process!

Amanda LaVita, twenty years ago we began writing fan fiction together, sending them back and forth in the mail for our entertainment only. Who would've known what would come of it? I cherish our friendship, and our dirty minds!

Karen Munday, you tell it like it is, and because of that, my friend—you rock!

To all of my oldest, closest, and dearest friends: you know who you are, and I thank you for your love and support through every aspect of my life.

To my parents, who always praised my way with words, thank you for believing in my dreams as much, if not more, than I do.

My aunts and uncle, who cheered me on as I wrote, impatiently waiting to see the final product—thank you!

A big thank you to Kathryn Powers, who not only guided me back to me, but offered her expertise in the behavioral patterns of my characters. I am truly grateful for you.

To my editor, Jess Huckins—thanks for taking my crazy ass on! I can already tell we're going to be a great team!

My cover designer, Robin: you have the patience of a saint! You are the digital da Vinci and I'm a huge fan of yours, lady!

To the many authors and bloggers who have encouraged me and shared their love of books with me: you guys are amazing and so very much appreciated!

To the fab five brothers from the Beantown land—there are no words to describe what you have brought to my life. I love and cherish you always!

Finally, to all of my readers: THANK YOU! Without you, I am but a voice that would've never been heard. My goal is to bring you many hours of escape over the years!

I'd love to hear from you! You can follow my crazy ass at several social hangouts. (All the cool kids are doing it. ;-P)

Twitter: @jacquelynayres

Facebook: https://www.facebook.com/JacquelynAyresAuthor?ref=br_tf

Pinterest: pinterest.com/jacquelynayres/boards/

http://www.authorjacquelynayres.com/

About the Author

I am a domestic engineer (born and raised in New Jersey) whose sole responsibility is guiding three young, impressionable kids into becoming phenomenal adults. This challenging yet rewarding work requires a lot of love (coffee), patience (wine), and determination (periodic exorcisms). I work all of this magic from the beautiful state of New Hampshire.

Before becoming a domestic goddess (not really), I spent over a decade working in the medical field, where I wore more hats than the queen.

I have loved the written word and the great escape it provides since I was a little girl. When I wasn't reading about people and the places they lived, I created my own characters and adventures. Finally, I started putting a pen to paper and allowing my characters to come to life. When I don't have a pen in hand, you can often find me laughing at the conversations my characters are having in my head.

www.ingramcontent.com/pod-product-compliance
Lightning Source LLC
Chambersburg PA
CBHW051541250626
47157CB00001B/131